Jai Volsc

About the Author

Mark Robson was born in Wanstead, Essex, in 1966, and was raised, for the most part, near Carmarthen in West Wales. In 1982, he gained a scholarship to join the Royal Air Force as a pilot and he is currently serving at RAF Brize Norton, Oxfordshire. His first book *'The Forging of the Sword'* was largely written during tours of duty in the Falkland Islands. The long quiet hours maintaining the constant vigil of the Quick Reaction Alert Force proved to be an ideal breeding ground for flights of fantasy, mainly because the wet and windy weather of the Falkland Islands prevented flights of anything else! Subsequent books have been inspired by the wave of encouragement by readers. Mark now lives in the Midlands and is married with two children.

D1642615

By this author:

The Darkweaver Legacy

Book 1:	The Forging of the Sword	*ISBN 0953819000*
Book 2:	Trail of the Huntress	*ISBN 0953819019*
Book 3:	First Sword	*ISBN 0953819027*
Book 4:	The Chosen One	*ISBN 0953819035*

Forthcoming Titles

| Imperial Spy | *ISBN 141690185X* |
| Imperial Assassin | *ISBN 1416901868* |

Imperial Spy - April 2006

Femke, a gifted and resourceful young spy, is entrusted with a vital foreign mission by the Emperor. It appears a simple task, but nothing is straightforward when your enemies are one step ahead of you. Framed for two murders while visiting the neighbouring King's court, Femke finds herself isolated in an alien country. As the authorities hunt her down for the murders, her arch-enemy, Shalidar, is closing in for his revenge...

For up to date information on future releases see:

www.swordpublishing.co.uk

TRAIL OF THE HUNTRESS

Mark Robson

SWORD PUBLISHING

TRAIL OF THE HUNTRESS
ISBN: 0-9538190-1-9

First published in the United Kingdom by Sword Publishing

First Edition published 2001
Reprinted 2002
Revised and reprinted 2003
Reprinted 2005

Published by Sword Publishing,
9 Wheat Close, Daventry, Northants, NN11 0FX.
www.swordpublishing.co.uk
info@swordpublishing.co.uk

Printed and bound in Great Britain by Technographic, Kiln Farm,
East End Green, Brightlingsea, Colchester, Essex, CO7 0SX.

For my daughter, Rachel,
   who loves books already, although as yet, the stories are
irrelevant as long as the pictures are interesting,

and for my godsons, Anthony and Adam,
   to whom I offer these few words of wisdom: always have
a goal in life – no matter how small. Even better, keep
more than one dream alive, so you will always have
something to look forward to when you achieve an
ambition.

Acknowledgements:

   To Arnie, who said: 'For goodness sake do something
useful... go write a book or something!'
   To Jane, for her constant encouragement and
enthusiasm, and her infinite patience with my awful
punctuation!
   To Nigel and Georgina, without whose professional
knowledge and expertise, I would be totally lost.

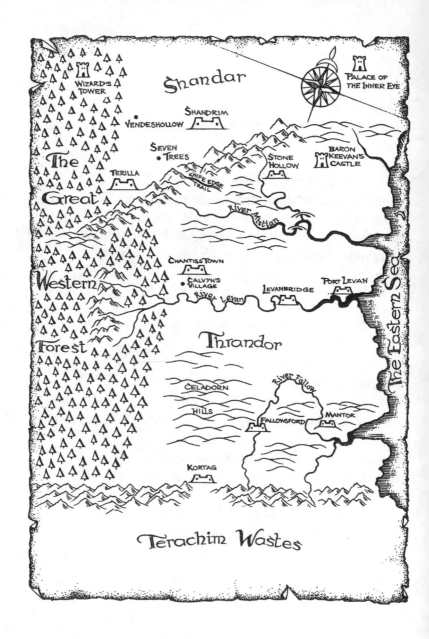

PROLOGUE

'Blast those Tarmin damned recruits! What are they up to now?'

Sergeant Dren slammed his quill down on the table so hard that the rolled parchments littering the tabletop jumped, causing several to fall to the floor. Leaping up, he pushed his chair forcefully away from his desk and strode angrily across the stone tiled floor of the workroom to the window. Outside, recruits were running in every direction across the weapons training area, all discipline seemingly abandoned. A great commotion of confused shouts enhanced the chaos, and the anger that consumed Dren's thoughts swelled to a new level.

Ever since Baron Keevan had gone south to Mantor with the majority of his private army, Sergeant Dren, together with the somewhat ineffective Captain Risslan, had been struggling to maintain discipline levels amongst the fresh intake of recruits. The major problem was the fact that with virtually all of the Baron's trained soldiers away, the recruits were being used to fill duties for which they were not yet ready. All of the Corporals most experienced in training new recruits had also gone south, leaving the Sergeant with an unseasoned training staff who seemed to add to his problems rather than solve them. However, even given the limitations of his training staff's abilities, the mayhem that reigned within the castle at this moment in time was unforgivable, he thought to himself as he wrenched the door open.

'STAND STILL!' he bellowed, the anger boiling in his gut adding even more decibels than normal to his phenomenally powerful voice.

For the most part, the recruits around the eastern side of the castle froze at that huge shout, but two recruits ignored the order and continued running towards the armoury.

'ARE YOU DEAF? I SAID STAND STILL,' Dren yelled at the two recruits who had seen fit to disobey his first command.

'But, Sergeant...' protested the nearer of the two young men, his steps stuttering to an indecisive halt.

'Don't, "But, Sergeant" me!' Dren growled, his voice low and dangerous. 'When I say "stand still," I mean STAND STILL. Is that understood?'

'Yes, Sergeant, but we're under attack...' the recruit blurted so fast that Dren was unable to chastise him further for answering back before the fact sunk in.

'Under attack?'

'Yes, Sergeant. There's a huge Shandese raiding party approaching the eastern wall.'

'Then why has the alarm not been sounded, recruit?'

'Reldan tried to blow the horn, Sergeant, but he couldn't get a sound out of it. So he ran as fast as he could to tell Captain Risslan...'

'All right. The rest can wait,' Dren interrupted, immediately recognising from where the chaos had originated. 'You five,' he ordered, pointing at his designated choices, 'get swords from the armoury. You, you and you... collect as many bows as you can from the bowmaker's store. You four – go into every room in the castle and ensure that everyone – and I mean everyone – is out on the walls. The rest of you get up on the walls now, and be prepared to start dislodging enemy ladders and grappling hooks. Move, people. You haven't got all day.'

Dren was angrier than ever by now, but he gave his orders in a clear, unhurried manner, conveying a calming confidence to the panic-stricken recruits. As a result, with clear directions to follow, the recruits began moving with a sense of purpose that had been lacking only moments before. The Sergeant had no need to ask where the Captain was. He could guess.

The quietly fuming Sergeant walked purposefully across the weapons training area and bounded up the steps to the eastern wall. Each powerful stride carried him up two steps at a time, and on reaching the top Dren's square jaw clenched in annoyance as he sighted Captain Risslan near the guard tower. Pursing his lips in a hard line, Sergeant Dren moved swiftly to intercept the Captain who was transmitting panic through the new recruits. As Dren strode along the wall, he noted that the enemy would be in a position to begin an assault within the next couple of minutes. He had to act quickly.

'Captain Risslan,' he boomed, unable to totally conceal the anger in his voice.

The flustered Captain was oblivious to the undertone, being totally consumed by panic and stressed to breaking point.

'Sergeant, we're under attack. We are not prepared for this. We haven't any trained troops to hold the lines...'

'Sir, forgive me for interrupting,' Dren interjected quickly, unable to waste any more than a few seconds on the panic-stricken Captain. 'I think that it might be wise if you went and prepared your horse for battle.'

'My horse?'

'Yes, sir. It wouldn't be fitting for a Captain to go into battle unprepared. Besides, who would take command if you were killed up here on the walls? You're our only Captain at present, and we'd be leaderless if we lost you.'

'Great Tarmin! I hadn't thought of that!'

'Well, sir, that's just what you have Senior NCOs for. I'll look after things up here, sir. I suggest that you direct the fight from the relative safety of the Weapons Training Area. That way we don't lose our leader, and you'll get a good view of what's going on by being on horseback.'

It was a ridiculous proposal, but it was the best that the Sergeant could think of on the spur of the moment. However, the Captain was not thinking rationally and to his panic-filled mind, what the Sergeant was suggesting made perfect sense.

'Very well, Sergeant. I will go at once and prepare my

mount. I shall endeavour to be in position as fast as I can.'

'Thank you, sir.'

Sergeant Dren breathed a quiet sigh of relief as Captain Risslan virtually sprinted away along the wall towards the nearest steps that led down into the castle interior.

'Tarmin forbid that you ever have to direct the men in anger,' muttered Dren through gritted teeth at the rapidly disappearing officer.

It had not been a surprise to Dren that the Baron had left the young Captain behind when the army had marched south to Mantor. However, what had amazed the Sergeant was that the Baron would entrust his entire castle to someone as obviously incompetent as Risslan without leaving at least one other Captain to moderate his decisions. Captains, though, were in short supply, particularly the good ones. Appointing Captains because of their family background rather than for their ability as leaders was undoubtedly the main reason for the shortfall in able commanders. Only a handful had ever been promoted up through the ranks and those had never held more than junior Captain positions. It had never failed to amaze Dren that someone as obviously intelligent, and in many areas as progressive as the Baron, would not break with tradition to improve the efficiency of his army.

With no time to reflect further on the Baron's reasons for appointing Captains, Dren focused his attention on organising the troops on the wall, and bottled up his anger and frustration as best he could, saving it all for the enemy. With his gruff voice he growled short sharp words of direction and encouragement to each group of soldiers. The recruits that he had sent to collect weapons arrived with arms full of bows and bundles of arrows, which were rapidly distributed along the wall. Dren grabbed a sword from the pile of weapons that had been brought up from the armoury. As he did so, a great clamour of war cries from the enemy announced the commencement of the assault.

'Bowmen, ready!' Dren yelled. 'And... FIRE.'

A wave of arrows sheeted into the enemy ranks. Some found their marks, but the horde continued their charge undaunted.

'Ready. FIRE.'

Another flight of arrows plunged into the Shandese warriors. However, this time the enemy replied and the thrum of Shandese crossbow bolts resulted in a clatter as most of the bolts smashed harmlessly against the battlements. A single cry from amongst the defenders rang out signalling their first casualty, as one of the recruits fell back clutching at the crossbow bolt deeply embedded in his shoulder.

The seething mass of Shandese raiders reached the base of the castle walls and there was another clatter as dozens of scaling ladders were thrust against the battlements. Many of the young defenders were eager to push the ladders away quickly and thus exposed themselves to more crossbow fire.

'Easy, lads,' Dren yelled at the top of his voice. 'Archers fire at will. The rest of you pick off the men as they reach the top of the ladders. Every now and again push some away at random. It's impossible to fight and climb a ladder, so use that advantage to reduce the odds.'

Dren's voice was such that despite the ululating cries of the enemy, his booming tones carried to the furthest of his troops and they responded without question to his orders. Dren himself moved to the nearest of the scaling ladders and hacked at the first of the Shandese warriors to appear at the top of the wall. The swarthy-faced fighter fell backwards off the ladder with a cry of pain, but the view from the eastern wall as Sergeant Dren dispatched his first opponent caused the breath to freeze in his chest. A great dark cloud of unnaturally black smoke was billowing across the field from just behind the attacking force. It only took a split second for Dren to assimilate the facts that firstly, the smoke was appearing from apparently clear air; secondly, it was growing phenomenally fast and finally, it was moving against the wind. It would undoubtedly engulf the wall within the next few seconds and there was nothing that he could do to stop it.

'Great Tarmin!' he cursed. 'They've got one of their damned Magicians with them!'

CHAPTER 1

'Take him into the city. I cannot think clearly in the midst of all this,' King Malo ordered, gesturing around at the hillside littered with bodies.

The distant cries of the retreating Terachite army could still be heard, as the combined armies of Thrandor harried the nomadic tribesmen who were attempting to fall back across the River Fallow. Despite being hugely outnumbered, the allied Thrandorian armies had won an historic victory this day. The fragile discipline of the tribesmen from the Terachim Wastes had rapidly disintegrated in the aftermath of a duel between their leader Demarr, whom they had called 'The Chosen One' and Calvyn, son of Joran, a Private in the army of Baron Keevan. The physical fight between the two men had proved a closely fought battle. However, it had been the titanic conflict of supernatural powers unleashed from Calvyn's magic sword and Demarr's silver talisman which had raged so fiercely that it had captivated the attention of both armies and brought virtually all else to a stand still.

At the defeat of Demarr the tide of the battle had turned almost instantaneously and now the captured enemy leader was on his knees before the King of Thrandor.

'Hand him over to the Captain of the Palace Guards. I am sure that the Captain will be more than happy to re-acquaint Demarr with his old cell.'

'Yes, your Majesty,' Calvyn replied, bowing respectfully to the weary Monarch.

'And... what is your name, soldier?' the King asked, his brow slightly furrowed as he tried to remember if he should already know the answer.

'Private Calvyn, your Majesty. I fight for Baron Keevan,' Calvyn replied.

'Very well, Private Calvyn. Please advise the Baron that I wish to speak with him tomorrow morning at my court and that I wish you to accompany him. I would like to know more of this Shandese Magician Selkor, and the threat that you say he poses to my kingdom. You have my thanks for your actions here today and I would reward you for your bravery and skill.'

'Yes, your Majesty. Thank you, your Majesty.'

Calvyn and Jenna bowed as the King, Baron Anton and their squires remounted their horses and rode off toward the Fallow Bridge. Demarr remained slumped on his knees between them, listless and disconsolate. The defeated leader's eyes stared hollowly into space and his face had a haunted look about it that Calvyn found deeply disturbing.

'Come on, Calvyn. You heard the king. We had better get him into the city. It's going to take some time and then we'll be faced with the problem of finding our squad, not to mention Baron Keevan. That could be very tricky with all that's still going on.'

Calvyn smiled mischievously at Jenna. 'I guess that I'd better brace myself for battle again if we're to go into the city,' he said with a chuckle.

Jenna laughed, remembering the morning only a few days ago when she had half convinced him that he would be so irresistible to the women of Mantor that he would have to fight them off. It seemed incredible to her now that the joke had been so recent. It felt like ages ago and worlds distant from this battlefield, she reflected ruefully. Calvyn was not the young man that she had jested with that day. That Calvyn had been naïve and still almost boyish. The man that was standing before her now used magic, a skill that was almost unheard of to Jenna, as the use of magic was considered a most heinous crime and the punishments for practising the forbidden arts were severe. It was hardly conceivable that the two could be one and the same, but she could not help liking Calvyn and did not want to shut him out despite the secret that he had hidden from her so cleverly for the last ten months.

'I would set fire to that sword again if I were you,' she replied after a short pause, unable to resist giving him a slightly reproachful look for not having told her of his abilities before he had so spectacularly revealed them to everyone today in battle. 'But don't worry too much,' she added, allowing her expression to turn into a coy smile. 'I'll be there to protect you if you find yourself struggling with too many doe-eyed beauties. Let's try and get rid of our prisoner before we make any more conquests, shall we?'

'Whatever you say, Jenna,' Calvyn replied with a cheeky wink and then turned to face his prisoner. 'On your feet, Demarr. It's time to move out.'

Demarr did not respond, but continued staring into space, oblivious to all around him.

'Come on, Demarr. Time to go,' Calvyn repeated, shaking the erstwhile Earl by the shoulder to gain his attention.

Demarr's head looked around slowly until his haunted eyes locked with Calvyn's. An involuntary shudder ran down Calvyn's spine as he felt the anguish in the gaze of his vanquished enemy.

'I... I... what have I done?' Demarr stammered, a tear welling in his right eye and running slowly down his cheek. He made no move to wipe it away. 'I never wanted this... and yet... I did want it. My heart sought vengeance and power, whilst at the same time my soul cried out for me to stop. I have betrayed the very love that forced me to act the first time: the love for Thrandor, which has driven my path from childhood. What, for the love of Tarmin, came over me?'

'This is not the time for questions, Demarr. You will win no allies here with words of remorse. Come. We must carry out the King's command and take you to the palace. This we will do with your co-operation or without it. Which will it be?'

Demarr nodded slowly and struggled to his feet.

'Have you got anything to bind his hands with?' asked Jenna, eyeing the sorry-looking figure in his once pristine white garment, which now hung torn, singed and dusty from his slumped shoulders. Blood still seeped from several minor wounds on Demarr's arms and body, staining the one-piece thobe further.

'No, but I suspect that he will offer no resistance. Will you, Demarr?'

'No. I will add nothing further to the accounting,' Demarr replied, his voice quiet and sorrowful. Slowly he raised his right hand to his chin and ran the pads of his fingers through the hairs of his trim goatee beard. 'I give you my word, for what it is worth. Once it could be trusted and respected. Now...'

'It is enough,' Calvyn stated, not really caring whether he was telling the truth or not. After all, Jenna and he between them would easily be able to prevent any escape attempt that he might make. Taking up position on Demarr's left, with Jenna to the prisoner's right, the three began to pick their way down to the base of the valley.

Bodies lay strewn around them, for the most part nomads peppered with arrows, the result of the ill-advised cavalry charge earlier in the morning. Demarr flinched visibly from each dead face, as corpse after corpse challenged his senses with their accusing stare of death. By the time the three had reached the base of the valley, tears streaked his face as he stumbled along in his private nightmare world of pain and regret.

On the climb up to the gates lay many more bodies. Again most of them were nomad warriors, but here and there lay Thrandorian casualties from the last ditch charge which had been mounted to aid the failing armies of the North. Already the carrion circled overhead, drawn by the blood and death, their raucous cries clamouring for the feast.

'Tarmin forgive me,' choked Demarr.

'I would be more concerned with the King forgiving you if I were in your place,' Jenna muttered.

Calvyn looked across at her and gave an almost imperceptible shake of his head, together with a subtle hand signal for quiet. Jenna pursed her lips and looked ready to argue, but seeing the look on Calvyn's face she refrained from further comment.

The guard commander at the city entrance was reluctant to open the gates for just the three of them. However, when Calvyn pointed out that he was responding to a direct order from the King, and that his prisoner was no less than the leader of the Terachite army, all reluctance dissolved instantly. Loud clangs of heavy steel bars being withdrawn reverberated through the huge metal gates, and with a slight squeaking moan the right hand gate opened outwards just enough for Calvyn, Demarr and Jenna to file in one by one.

Calvyn had never been inside a major city before, and the experience was somewhat awe-inspiring. Thrandor only boasted three large cities: Mantor the capital, and Port Levan and Port Fallow on the coast. The outer walls of Mantor had been impressive, but to see row upon row of houses, mercantile stores of all shapes and sizes, taverns, barracks and other buildings whose purpose he could not even begin to conceive stretching away up the hillside, left him feeling very small and insignificant.

The main thoroughfare appeared to run behind the wall around the perimeter of the city, and was crowded with people - mainly women. All were busy: tending the wounded at makeshift casualty sites, replenishing weapons stockpiles, distributing food from temporary open air kitchens or any one of a hundred other tasks to support those soldiers still patrolling the city walls.

A kind of nervous fear twisted Calvyn's stomach as he grappled with unsettling feelings of insecurity. The seemingly endless mass of people and the size of the city made him suddenly feel lost and out of his depth as if drowning in a sea of people and buildings.

Jenna sensed his momentary anxiety and came to his rescue.

'Could you remind me of the way to the palace please, sir?' she asked the guard commander in a loud voice. 'It's been some years since I was last in Mantor and nothing looks familiar.'

'Just follow any road to the top of the hill,' the Captain replied. 'The palace is at the summit, so just keep climbing and you won't go far wrong. If you follow that street over there it will take you directly upwards more than half the way.'

The Captain pointed to a wide street some two hundred paces to their left. Jenna thanked him, and half dragging Demarr forward, she and Calvyn threaded their way through the bustling crowds to the start of the road that the Captain had indicated.

To all intents and purposes the two soldiers and their prisoner were ignored as they moved towards the desired street. The people of Mantor were far too involved in their designated tasks to take any notice of them, and once away from the outer perimeter road the street leading up the hill was virtually deserted. The only encounter that Calvyn, Jenna and Demarr had with anyone who acknowledged their presence was with a patrol of ten soldiers on a sweep of the inner city streets. As soon as Calvyn informed the squad leader of the King's orders they were waved on their way.

Despite the clear streets and the straightforward route, it still took more than an hour to climb from the city gates to the entrance to the Royal Palace. A high wall made of large blocks of a yellow coloured stone surrounded the grounds of the Royal residence. Guards in black uniforms emblazoned with the gold crest of the Royal household maintained a constant vigilance at numerous set posts around the perimeter and mounted random patrols inbetween. It was one of these guards who had directed the weary soldiers and their captive in the right direction, and now at last they were standing at the impressive entranceway.

'I need to speak to the Captain of the Royal Guard,' Calvyn stated in a clear voice to the tall sentry standing at attention in front of the huge, ornate, gold coloured metal gates.

'Indeed? And who shall I say requires the presence of the Captain?' asked the sentry, eyeing the three dirty, bloodstained characters with an expression that broadcast his suspicion as loudly as if he had yelled it at the top of his voice.

'I am Private Calvyn of the army of Baron Keevan from Northern Thrandor. This is Private Jenna. We have been tasked to bring this prisoner to the Captain of the Guard,' Calvyn replied, somewhat affronted by the guard's tone and disdainful look.

'And why should this sorry looking character be of interest to the Captain of the Guard? There are plenty of holding cells in lower parts of the city, Private. I suggest that you take your grubby looking *prisoner* and secure him in one of those.'

That did it. Calvyn decided that he had taken enough hassles for one day and he was not going to allow this sentry to make life one iota more difficult than it needed to be.

'Very well,' he responded, keeping his voice deliberately mild. 'Your name and rank please?'

'What business is that of yours, *Private* Calvyn? I am of the Royal Guard. That is all you need to know.'

'Ordinarily I might agree,' Calvyn replied with a tight smile. 'However, I will undoubtedly need a name to give to the King tomorrow, when I attend court and explain to him why I did not carry out his express instructions to hand this man over to the Captain of *his* Royal Guard. I suggest that you take a closer look at the prisoner. He is no stranger to your cells.'

Demarr's head had been hanging forward throughout the brief discussion, but at a sharp dig in the ribs from Calvyn he looked up. The guard took a sharp intake of breath.

'Great Tarmin! It's...'

'The former Earl Demarr,' finished Calvyn in a tired voice.

'My apologies! I just didn't think...'

'No, you didn't think,' interrupted Jenna in a cold, hostile voice, her hand going to the hilt of her sword. 'So best you scuttle off and find your Captain pretty damned fast, or you are going to have some serious explaining to do yourself. Also, you might like to consider the fact that whilst you have been up here guarding your cosy little palace, some of us have been fighting to save your prettily-dressed, Royal Guard butt from getting seriously kicked by a rather large army of marauding Terachite Nomads. I, for one, am very tired, thirsty, hungry and *very* irritated by your attitude. What do you think, Calvyn? Do you think if I kill one more irritating man today that it will make any difference?'

The guard did not wait for Calvyn's reply but hurried off to a small building just down the street, which Calvyn presumed was the Captain's office.

Jenna looked across at Calvyn with a grin. 'He looked a little wild around the eyes,' she said, her eyes dancing with merriment. 'Do you think that I overdid it a bit?'

'No. It was absolutely perfect,' Calvyn chuckled. 'I was itching to say something along those lines but it was so much better coming from you.'

'Why, thank you.'

'You're welcome.'

Demarr looked from one to the other, but his face betrayed no emotion. His expression remained blank and neither Calvyn nor Jenna could tell if the look was one of appreciation for the joke, or sheer incomprehension of what was going on around him. The former Earl had looked on the verge of collapse all the way up the hill to the palace, and Calvyn was privately amazed that Demarr was on his feet at all. Only a few hours had elapsed since Demarr had absorbed the full force of the magical explosion, which had both rendered him unconscious and effectively ended the battle with the Terachite Nomads. 'It was a miracle that Demarr still lived,' Calvyn reflected, though in all probability the King was likely to rule that he would be executed. For a brief moment Calvyn felt a surge of pity for the broken character standing alongside him. However, his heart was hardened once more by memories of his village and the scattered, hacked bodies of his parents and friends murdered in this man's name. If ever a man deserved execution it was Demarr, he told himself firmly.

The Captain was more than happy to relieve Calvyn and Jenna of their charge, and personally ensured that they were given refreshments before they left to find Baron Keevan and returned to their squad. Whilst they ate and drank, the Captain questioned them on the battle and it quickly became apparent that the Captain had not won his exalted status by guarding a palace gate. He nodded thoughtfully as Calvyn and Jenna related the events of the last two days, the tactics employed and the near disastrous climax. When Jenna described the duel between Calvyn and Demarr, the Captain regarded Calvyn with a look that held a lot of respect.

'I've seen Demarr fight,' he said, his eyes distant. 'You must be good with that sword if you defeated him.'

'To be fair, Captain, Demarr had me well and truly beaten when fate decided to intervene. However, I am still here and Demarr is now safely in your hands. The results are what count in the long run and today the field was ours. Let us pray that the Terachite tribesmen continue to retreat all the way to Terachim Wastes, or you may yet get your chance to cross blades with them.'

'Yes indeed, Calvyn. Well, I shouldn't keep you from your duties any longer. Is there anything else I can do before you go?'

'No, sir. Thank you. We should really be on our way. We must find Baron Keevan before nightfall and it is already mid-afternoon.'

'You are bound by the King to seek out the Baron, are you not?'

'Yes, sir.'

'Then I insist that you take horses. Your errand should not be delayed. We have several fast horses in our stables for use by the King's messengers and from what you have just told me, your task fits that description. You do ride, don't you?'

Calvyn and Jenna both nodded enthusiastically, their faces alight with excitement at the prospect of getting mounts from the King's own stables.

The Captain laughed at their expressions. 'Well we'd best get you on your way then. You can return the horses tomorrow when you attend court, Calvyn.'

A few minutes later, mounted on sleek black horses, Calvyn and Jenna trotted away from the palace gates and down into the maze of streets towards the north gate of the city. Heads turned wherever they went, the people gazing in wonder at the two soldiers wearing the colours of some northern Lord of whom most had never heard, riding horses which were tacked with gear from the King's own stables. It undoubtedly made an unusual sight, Calvyn reflected, but then this had been a truly unique day.

When they finally found Baron Keevan, he was in conference with his Captains. The Thrandorian army was holding a defensive formation and allowing the Terachites to continue their withdrawal unhindered across the Fallow Bridge. Captain Tegrani was quick to brief the Baron as Calvyn and Jenna rode up, dismounted and saluted smartly.

'Privates Calvyn and Jenna, my lord,' he informed Baron Keevan swiftly. 'Both were recently promoted from the Recruit Company.'

'Ah yes, Tegrani. I remember Calvyn. He was the one who fought that fine match with Bek, the eventual winner of the First Sword title, was he not?'

'That's correct, my lord. He was also the one involved in the duel with Demarr today. When I left these two earlier, I gave them orders to guard Demarr until my return. It seems that they have some explaining to do.'

'Yes, indeed.'

Captain Strexis ordered a Private out of the lines to assist Calvyn and Jenna with their horses. Having handed the reins to the soldier, the two then marched smartly across to the Baron, where they halted and saluted in unison.

This was the closest that either of them had been to the Baron, excepting their graduation parade, and then they had been so intent on staring straight ahead that neither of them had actually dared to focus on him as he had inspected the lines of newly graduated Privates. The Baron was shorter than Calvyn remembered, and his dark brown hair, streaked with grey, was obviously not normally tied back into a warrior's tail, as it showed signs of waves where it had been styled in the past. The silver clasp of his cape was the characteristic crown and crossed swords that designated him a Baron, rather than a Lord or a Marquis, and whilst he wore the uniform of his troops, the cloth that it was fashioned from was of infinitely higher quality.

When the Baron spoke, his voice was a rich rolling baritone that conveyed warmth and friendship as well as authority.

'At ease, Privates. I sense a tale in the making here, but we do not have time for lengthy discussion, so please keep it brief. Now tell me, where is Demarr and how did you come by those horses? If I am not much mistaken those saddles bear the markings of the Royal Household.'

Calvyn quickly outlined the series of events that had led to the Captain of the Palace Guards lending them the horses, and included the King's request for the Baron to attend court in the morning. Slightly embarrassed, he added that the King had also specifically requested Calvyn's presence to answer questions about the Shandese Magician, Selkor, who now possessed the magical talisman that had enabled Demarr to raise the massive invading Terachite army.

'I too would like to know more of this matter,' the Baron said thoughtfully. 'However, I shall save you the trouble of telling it twice. My questions can keep until tomorrow. For the time being I have other things to attend to. Well done, Privates. I would like you both to meet me at the ninth hour tomorrow morning. The King's court is normally convened at the tenth hour. I appreciate, Private Jenna, that you were not specifically invited, but I would like you to accompany Captain Strexis, Calvyn and myself so that you can return your borrowed horse to the Palace stables. Make sure that you each have a spare mount to ride back on and do your best to present yourselves in clean uniform.'

'Yes, my lord,' Calvyn replied respectfully and then turned to Captain Tegrani. 'Could you please direct us back to our unit, sir? If we are complete with our tasks, we should report to Corp... Sergeant Derra for new orders.'

After looking to the Baron for confirmation, Captain Tegrani dismissed them with instructions to rejoin the remainder of their squad in the Thrandorian battle lines.

When they arrived, Sergeant Derra raised one sharply angled eyebrow in a quizzical expression but refrained from comment at their beautiful black horses. Instead she assigned them positions in the defensive line and gave them what Calvyn deemed an unnecessary reminder to maintain the discipline of silence whilst monitoring the retreat of the enemy. On reflection, he realised that the warning was as much for the benefit of those around him as it was for himself. Undoubtedly his compatriots would have numerous questions about the events of the day, just as he had for them. As he had been taught during training, however, discipline in the ranks was essential for effective warfare. If you were talking to someone, your mind was not on the job at hand and that could prove a very effective way of getting yourself killed. The only person to talk should be the person giving the orders. That way the orders were the only words that everyone heard and mistakes were minimised.

The lack of speech did not prevent Calvyn from surreptitiously glancing along the lines to locate those of his old squad who had survived the fierce battle earlier in the day. Tondi was not far away and she flashed him a grin as he caught her eye. He was fairly certain that he could see Bek further along the line too but there was no sign of Tyrrak or any of the others. With time, Calvyn gradually picked out some of those he had trained with, but as the light began to fail he gave up looking and concentrated instead on watching the enemy's withdrawal across the river.

That evening was a solemn time. The captains had them pitch camp where they were in a long line across the valley, posting a heavy guard to continue the watch throughout the night. Calvyn and Jenna met up with Bek who had not been aware that Matim had been killed in the fighting up on the hillside. Bek in turn had news of Tyrrak, who had apparently been seriously wounded and would not be fit for duty for several weeks and maybe months. It seemed that the surgeons were not yet sure if the wound to Tyrrak's leg would heal well enough for him to walk without a limp, but were confident that they would not have to amputate.

Bek had suffered several minor cuts and bruises, but remarkably few considering that he had spent virtually the entire battle in the thickest of the action. Several times during the battle it had been Bek's quick thinking, formidable sword skills and almost suicidal disregard for his own skin that had prevented the Thrandorian lines from being penetrated.

Bek had changed, Calvyn noted, as he listened to his friend's candid account of his part in the battle. Indeed, all of the survivors had changed in one way or another, but Bek in particular, Calvyn thought to himself. His self-assurance had grown without becoming arrogant and his bearing had altered subtly too. There was something about him that Calvyn could not quite put his finger on, but whatever it was, the change was for good.

One thing that was most notable was that both Bek and Calvyn now commanded the respect of all their fellow soldiers. Even the older veterans treated them both with a deference that Calvyn found almost embarrassing. However, their new-found status did afford them some privacy in their mourning for Matim, and Calvyn managed to fend off most of the questions about his duel with Demarr by mentioning that he had to give an account to the King and the Baron in the morning. Everyone deferred to those names without further question.

'Demarr has a lot to answer for,' muttered Bek as the three of them sat in a huddle near one of the watch fires. 'The King will have no choice but to publicly execute him now.'

Jenna murmured an agreement but Calvyn just sat quietly, lost in the past, as he recalled those who had died. Matim had been a good friend through their training: steadfast and supportive. Sergeant Brett, the man who had co-ordinated the six months of hell that had trained him for this conflict, had been a hard taskmaster but fair in all his dealings with the recruits. And of course he remembered his parents and friends from his home village who had been killed by the group who had called themselves 'Demarr's Rebels'. If anyone deserved personal retribution from Demarr it was he, and yet... the old rage that had boiled at the mere mention of the former Earl's name no longer bubbled its hatred through his belly. Instead, pity welled inside him as he alone of the thousands of angry Thrandorian people had the insight and knowledge of the forces that had been at work in his arch-enemy's heart and mind. The talisman, which harboured the evil magic of

Derrigan Darkweaver, had caused this disaster. Demarr was just the wrong person, in the wrong place, at the wrong time.

A tendril of cold fear wrapped itself once more around his heart as he thought again of the man who now possessed that deadly power. Selkor. He was already a powerful Magician in his own right. What would he do with the dread talisman? Or maybe, more terrifyingly, what would it do to him?

These questions haunted his dreams that night, and despite being left off the watch rota to get a full night's rest before appearing at the King's court in the morning, his sleep was fitful, leaving him tense and weary as he mounted up beside the Baron. Jenna and Captain Strexis accompanied them into the city. Captain Tegrani, to his chagrin, was left behind to command the Baron's army in his absence.

'Are you all right?' Jenna asked Calvyn quietly, her muttered question projecting her concern.

'I'll be fine, thanks,' Calvyn replied, affording her a weak smile. 'A bad night's sleep, that's all.'

The four of them rode up to the city gates in line abreast, with the two spare horses trailing behind Calvyn and Jenna's horses on lead reins. Once inside the city though, Baron Keevan and Captain Strexis led the way with Calvyn and Jenna following closely behind. The outer streets were still a hive of activity despite the enemy withdrawal across the river. A continual buzz filled the air with the sound of the people's determination, quiet anger and purpose. The citizens of Mantor had been pulled together by conflict and now worked with a singleness of mind that was almost tangible. Merchants and street beggars worked in unison, whilst richly dressed women of noble bearing toiled alongside harlots and washerwomen with no regard for each other's upbringing or social status.

It would be interesting to see how long this harmony would last once the immediate danger had passed, Calvyn mused to himself as they followed the Baron and the Captain through the throng and up into the quieter streets of the upper city.

This time on reaching the palace gates an entire squad of the Royal Guard was standing smartly at attention, with their Captain at the front and the enormous golden gates wide open. At their approach, the Captain of the Guard ordered men forward to take their horses and another to escort them into the palace. Before Calvyn and Jenna had managed to look around after dismounting, the horses were being led away and the two soldiers were being ushered forward through the gates after the Baron and Captain who were already striding ahead.

Calvyn's breath caught briefly in his throat as he looked up at the palace frontage ahead of him. It was one thing to see it through the metal barred gates, but an entirely different experience to be walking up the broad steps to the huge ornate building that had housed the Kings of Thrandor for centuries.

'Wow!' he mouthed to Jenna, whose eyes danced with excited anticipation as she acknowledged his sentiment with a quick grin and a nod.

At the top of the long shallow stepped approach they passed between the two central pillars and up to the main entranceway. Two more palace guards were standing rigidly to attention, one either side of the large doors. Awaiting their approach at the threshold to the main doors was a butler. He was an elderly man, slight of build with a smartly cropped head of silver grey hair. Dressed immaculately in a dark blue doublet with large gold buttons in a double line from top to bottom and further buttons at the cuffs, he looked every inch his part as the Head of the Royal House Staff.

'Baron Keevan. Welcome,' the butler stated, performing a most impressive bow and a grandiose gesture for them to enter.

'Thank you, Krider. It's been a long time,' the Baron replied.

'Indeed, milord. Too long. Please, come this way.'

The butler turned and led them into the entrance hall. Calvyn and Jenna alike found their heads and eyes drawn up and around the enormous room with its vaulted ceilings and huge statues. The hall was constructed on such a grand scale that they were both overawed by the sheer size of everything.

Tapestries, which each would have more than covered the entire floor of their dormitory back at Baron Keevan's castle, hung regularly spaced along the walls. Each was a work of art that would have taken years of effort to complete, and depicted many scenes from Thrandorian legend and history. Indeed, Calvyn noted with interest that there was a tapestry whose scene portrayed what could only be the defeat of Derrigan Darkweaver. The fantastical scene of that magical battle seemed to pull at him as he walked past, compelling him to study its detail. Steadfastly he resisted, and concentrated instead at looking straight ahead at the Baron's back.

'Now is not the time,' he told himself firmly. 'Maybe later – if we are given the opportunity.'

Running straight down the centre of the hall was a plush line of rich, royal purple-coloured carpet. Krider led them swiftly along this carpeted road, wide enough for six men to walk abreast, and the only covering on the otherwise plain stone flagged floor.

On leaving the hall the four were taken along a series of passageways until they reached their destination, a large open doorway from which could be heard a low buzz of whispered conversation between many people. Krider quietly asked the names of the Captain and the two soldiers before stepping through the door.

'Baron Keevan and Captain Strexis,' he boomed in a loud voice, and the two walked briskly inside.

More people were arriving behind them, but before Calvyn could get any idea of who or how many, they too were announced.

'Privates Calvyn, son of Joran, and Jenna, daughter of Nathan.'

Calvyn and Jenna marched forward into a large square room, which had a strangely circular feel about it. Ahead of them sat the King on a throne that was situated on a raised dais. All around the room was tiered seating that had been cleverly curved around the corners to give an almost amphitheatre effect to the central space in front of the throne.

Pausing briefly to bow to the King, the two soldiers were then led to seats adjacent to their Baron on the very front row of seats. Once seated, Calvyn gazed around at the rows of people who already occupied most of the available seating.

'The Lord Valdeer and Captain Lobaire,' the announcer called, causing Calvyn to glance across to the entranceway, where he saw the familiar figure of the Lord from northern Thrandor striding into the room.

More names were called in fairly quick succession, and each new arrival was led to the rapidly dwindling number of empty places. Then with a slight squeak of protesting metal the doors were swung shut with a loud emphatic thud and silence descended like a blanket as all eyes turned to the King.

A pregnant pause thickened the air of expectancy as the silver haired monarch collected his thoughts. The King looked decidedly tired, Calvyn thought to himself as he, along with many others, realised that they were holding their breath in the quiet stillness of the courtroom. Bags sagged under the King's eyes, highlighted by dark lines of sleeplessness, and the whole drained set of his posture as he sat in the throne betrayed a weariness of body and soul.

The King drew a deep breath. 'Fellow citizens of Thrandor – we, the leaders of our people, are gathered in this courtroom to take council on the grave events of the past two weeks. Much has happened and there is much yet to be done to restore peace and order to our land. A great victory was won yesterday, but at the cost of many good lives. The long peace between Thrandor and the nomadic tribes of the Terachim has been shattered and as yet we remain none the wiser as to why these hostilities have occurred. However, there is one who knows the answers for which we crave and he must answer for the many thousands that he has led into this conflict. Guards... bring in the prisoner.'

Again, the squeal of the metal hinges split the silence as

the door was swung open and the slumped figure of Demarr was virtually hauled into the room by two royal guards.

A sharp intake of breath seemed to hiss around the Council Chamber, and it was obvious to Calvyn that many of those present had been unaware of who the enemy leader was until that moment.

'You bloody traitor…'

'Hold, Count Dreban!' the King said firmly, quelling the momentary buzz that had welled up and quieting the incensed noble who had leapt to his feet.

'Demarr will be held to account today and you will all be given a chance to present charges and questions in due course. However, this ultimately is *my* responsibility and I will not have it said that my court holds biased trials, even in cases as extreme and seemingly clear cut as this one. Justice will be done, have no doubt. Now take your seat and we will proceed.'

Reluctantly the fuming Count sat back down, his face glowing red with suppressed rage.

Demarr, still dressed in his battle stained thobe, was dragged forward and thrown to his knees before the King. He truly looked a pathetic and dishevelled shadow of his former self, a man of broken spirit.

'Well, Demarr. For the second time you kneel before me accused of treason. Tell me, for I am more than a little curious, how you came to lead the united tribes of the Terachim in a mere three years since you were banished from Thrandor. And why, with supreme command over those numerous peoples, did you choose to invade the land of your birth?'

The King paused, waiting for an answer. The court was breathlessly silent. Demarr, however, remained still, head slumped and unmoving.

'Come, Demarr. Tell us the tale,' the King insisted, more firmly this time.

A guard prodded Demarr gently with the toe of a highly polished boot and he stirred slightly, his head rising up slowly to regard the King, who was still seated on his throne. Demarr's glazed eyes seemed to focus briefly on King Malo.

'The talisman,' he croaked, throat obviously closed from a lack of water. Then, as if the effort of saying those two words was too much for him, his head slumped forward once more.

'Get him some water,' the King ordered, not taking his eyes from Demarr for as much as a second. Krider, the palace butler, disappeared swiftly out through the door.

'What about the talisman, Demarr? Surely you cannot hope to blame this entire invasion on an inanimate object? Come, tell us the story.'

Demarr did not move. Even when Krider returned with a jug of water and Demarr was forced to drink some, he remained silent, either refusing or simply unable to answer the King's repeated questions. Eventually, in sheer frustration the King delivered an ultimatum. 'Demarr. Either you will answer my questions or I will be forced to pronounce you guilty of the crime of treason and have you summarily executed.'

The statement hung in the air, an even deeper and closer silence than ever seemed to suspend time as everyone awaited the former Earl's response.

Nothing was forthcoming.

'Very well...' the King sighed.

'Hold, your Majesty. I will speak for him.'

CHAPTER 2

From the moment Demarr had entered the King's courtroom, a feeling had been building within Calvyn that he was unable either to define or control. It wasn't completely pity for the broken character slumped and defeated before them, though pity had its influence. Nor was it a feeling of responsibility for what was happening here, although this too was mingled within his response. No, something different entirely had welled up inside him, building to a crescendo at which he could no longer fail to act in response to the King's ultimatum.

'I will speak for the former Earl,' Calvyn repeated firmly, now standing at his place.

'Sit down, Private. Now,' growled Captain Strexis in a low voice.

'Be at peace, Captain,' the King ordered, holding out a calming hand. 'I would hear what the soldier has to say. Besides, had it not been for him, yesterday could have ended far differently, and we would probably not be here today with Demarr as our prisoner. Speak, Private Calvyn. How and why do you intend to defend this man who has brought such bloodshed and chaos to our kingdom?'

Calvyn's heart pounded hard in his chest and a lump settled uncomfortably in his throat as he struggled to find words to convey the thoughts and emotions racing through his mind and body.

'Your Majesty,' he stammered nervously, 'I probably have more personal reasons to see this man suffer than anyone in this room. It was in his name that my parents, friends and indeed many of the inhabitants of my village were brutally murdered less than three years ago. Since that time I have suffered recurring nightmares of the days that I, together with a total stranger and the few survivors of the massacre spent burying the bodies as best we could. Yesterday I lost yet more friends and colleagues in a battle, which again appears to be of this man's making. I have longed for this day of vengeance with a passion that few here could understand...'

Calvyn's voice cracked with emotion. Glancing briefly down at his feet, he cleared his throat and then looked the King pointedly in the eye as he continued. 'Yet despite my hatred of what this man has done I find myself as the only one with the true knowledge of what has driven him to this, and thus must defend him. Your Majesty, much as I know that this will be hard to accept, I truly believe that Demarr did not lead this army here of his own free will, nor did he even raise the army which invaded your kingdom.

An angry buzz of muttered comments erupted from all sides of the courtroom, but the King held out a hand for quiet, and order was gradually restored. One thing was certain, Calvyn had everyone's attention. Even Demarr was looking at him now with an expression that was completely unreadable.

Calvyn stepped out into the centre of the room not far from Demarr and every eye followed him.

'With whom then would you lay the responsibility if not with Demarr?' the King asked, his voice remaining mild but his slightly tightening lips conveying a hardening of attitude.

'Not whom, so much your Majesty, as what!' Calvyn replied, his resolve strengthening. 'For two hundred years a ban has been imposed on any kind of magic within this land and yesterday it was nearly our undoing. Demarr cannot be held responsible for his actions because a magical silver talisman was controlling his mind and body. It was a talisman crafted and worn many years ago by a magician so corrupted by evil that his name has become a legend... Derrigan Darkweaver.'

'What utter rubbish!' exclaimed a rather overweight nobleman with a sneer.

'Here, here!' agreed another in a pompous voice.

'My lords, might I ask if you were on the battlefield yesterday?' Calvyn asked politely but pointedly.

There were a couple of quiet sniggers from the back of the room. The two noblemen in question gave no answer.

'Because if you had been on the field you would have seen this,' and with a flourish he drew his sword, which at the muttered command *'Ardeva,'* promptly burst into flame.

The courtroom as one took a sharp intake of breath. Calvyn remained defiantly standing with his feet planted shoulder width apart and his sword held aloft for all to see, the blue flames flickering brightly up and down its full length.

'I think that's enough, young man,' the King stated firmly, raising his voice above the wave of muttering and whispering that raced around the courtroom. 'You have made your point and gained everyone's attention, but blatantly breaking a law that has been held in place for two centuries in the King's very courtroom will not win you many friends. Tread carefully, Private Calvyn. You may have won my gratitude yesterday, but do not seek to flaunt it, for it can be quickly withdrawn.'

'My apologies, your Majesty,' Calvyn said, extinguishing and sheathing his sword. 'However, I sensed that had I continued without some form of demonstration, the more sceptical members of your court might have dismissed me as some sort of a lunatic. My point is that outlawing all forms of magic has weakened our kingdom, and made it all the more susceptible to magic's more evil manifestations. I admit, your Majesty, to deliberately breaking that law, but Demarr can make no such admission, because the evil of the talisman had completely ensnared him. I was at hand to see his response as he recovered from its influence, and I truly believe that he will be punished more by the memories of his acts whilst wearing Darkweaver's handicraft than he could possibly be by an execution.'

'Where is this talisman now, Private? I see no magical item controlling Demarr. Where is the physical proof?' asked someone from high up in the tiered seating to Calvyn's left.

'Unfortunately, the talisman was taken from the field by a Shandese Magician named Selkor. He is a man of considerable learning and power against whom my little knowledge of magic would be useless. That alone should worry everyone here far more than Demarr does. This man before you knew nothing of magic before obtaining that artefact, but Selkor is a different prospect entirely. You have been witnesses to what the talisman can achieve through a man who is ignorant of the ways of the arcane arts. Imagine what might now happen if it exerts its influence over one already more powerful than any I have met.'

'Private Calvyn, please bear with me as I am old and all this seems too fantastical for belief... and yet none who saw your duel yesterday or your sword just now could deny the reality of magic. However, if this talisman is as powerful as you say, then how did it come about that you had the power to defeat it and yet claim that you were powerless to prevent this Selkor from taking it away?'

'Defeating the talisman was pure luck, your Majesty. As I outlined to you yesterday, my tutor in magic was an old healer who taught me how to channel the earth's magical energy into cures for common ailments. If he ever knew any spells of battle and power over others then he did not share them with me. He was a good man, who used his skills with magic to help others for minimal personal gain. It was the Magician Selkor who caused us to part company.'

Calvyn proceeded to tell the assembly of the confrontation between Perdimonn and Selkor in the small town market place in northern Thrandor, and the subsequent chase across the countryside. With a pang of regret he recounted their parting and went on to explain how he had then joined Baron Keevan's Training Company and had not seen the old man again, nor Selkor until the previous day. The court sat silent and unmoving, as all who listened were held rapt in fascination by the tale.

'So you see, your Majesty, that if my tutor could not stand before Selkor's power, I would not have a hope of doing so. As I said before, I defeated the talisman's power by luck alone. Selkor confirmed as much when I spoke with him. He examined my sword in the belief that he had found two powerful artefacts to claim for himself, but he dismissed the sword as a child's toy. I truly believe that whether he manages to control the talisman, or whether it controls him, we would do well to fear and prepare for the worst.'

Even as he was finishing his account, Calvyn and others around the room became aware of a commotion breaking out just outside the closed door of the courtroom. Heads turned towards the door as the voice of the butler, Krider, could be heard trying to calm the situation. Thumps were then heard as bodies jostled against the outside of the door, and the brass handle rattled several times as there was an obvious struggle by someone to enter the room.

Calvyn, along with several others, drew their swords and prepared to defend the King.

Suddenly the door was flung open and a soldier whom Calvyn did not recognise, but who was dressed in the livery of Baron Keevan, forced his way past Krider and several others to enter the courtroom.

'What is the meaning of this?' the King demanded, still standing in front of his throne. 'Baron Keevan, do your men all break laws as they wish? Have they no discipline?'

'I'm sorry, your Majesty. I'm as much in the dark as you are,' Keevan apologised, and then turned to his soldier, who had managed to shake himself free of the grasp of Krider and the others, and was now standing at attention, still panting from his exertions. 'This had better be good, Private. In fact this will have to be a lot better than good.'

'Your Majesty... my Lord. Captain Tegrani sent me to inform you that we've received word from the north that the Shandese have pushed across the border in force. They've not stopped at raiding villages and caravans this time, my Lord. They're attacking everything and everyone.'

'Great Tarmin! First the Terachites and now the Shandese! We cannot hope to fight wars on two fronts. What have I done to provoke the Shandese?' exclaimed the King, flopping down onto the throne and his shoulders sagging in defeat.

'You've done nothing in particular, your Majesty. But as we from the north of Thrandor have been saying for years now, the Shandese have been systematically raiding and probing, just waiting for the opening to hit us hard. Now that we are weak they're making the most of that opportunity,' said Baron Keevan in an even voice.

'We may yet not have to fight on both fronts, your Majesty' said the calm, thoughtful voice of Baron Anton. 'The Terachites are in full retreat and our scouts have reported several skirmishes between the clans as they go. I think that a fairly token force could be sent to shadow them back to the Terachim. It seems that without their leader to hold them together, the old inter-tribal hatreds are rapidly resurfacing and should keep them busy enough to keep them from realising that we're not pursuing them with our entire army.'

'That's awfully risky, Anton. What if they decide to turn and fight again?'

'Then we'll just have to fall back. If necessary, we'll retreat all the way back to Mantor. To be frank, your Majesty, if we don't use this tactic we'll be totally unable to help those in the north, without whose aid we would even now be fighting for our lives.'

Murmured noises of agreement rumbled around the room.

'Unfortunately, your Majesty, there's more bad news,' interrupted the soldier who was still standing close to the doorway.

'More?' the King asked, almost incredulously.

The soldier hesitated.

'Well... spit it out man.'

'The report says that the Shandese are using some form of magical powers during most of their attacks, your Majesty. I cannot vouch for this...'

'Selkor?' the King asked, looking at Calvyn questioningly.

'I doubt that, your Majesty. He is powerful but he is also human. He was only here yesterday and he can't be in two places at once... at least, I don't think that he can.'

'It seems that perhaps I should have taken more heed of your warnings after all, Demarr,' the King said, looking back to the prisoner who now looked more long-faced than ever. 'If I had listened, then maybe we would not be facing this mess, but that does not in any way condone your treasonous actions of three years ago, for which you have already been justly tried and banished. Also, despite Private Calvyn's brave words on your behalf, I find myself unable to totally forgive you for leading the Terachites to invade this kingdom. I admit that it's more than a little tempting to order the guard to take you out and execute you here and now. I think that few here would mourn that decision, but I've never been one for the easy option, so I am going to give you one last chance. Banishment did not work, and as both of us have made poor choices in recent years I will not make an irreversible decision in haste because of the feeling of the moment. Therefore, you shall live and serve the north, which you loved enough to risk everything for.'

The King turned to Baron Keevan. 'Keevan, I place Demarr into your hands. He is to serve as a Private in your army with no prospect of promotion for the rest of his days. If he gives you any trouble, kill him with my blessing, but I believe that we'll need all the sword-bearing men we can find over the coming months.'

The Baron grimaced slightly. 'Very well, your Majesty,' he replied tightly.

'The court is dismissed. Anton, Keevan and the military leaders from northern Thrandor, please remain here for a council of war,' the King stated firmly. 'Private Calvyn, I said that I would reward you for your actions yesterday and I will. You'll be given one hundred pieces of gold and an open offer of a place in the Royal Guard for as long as I am King. However, whilst I agree that the ban on magic needs reviewing, I am also unwilling to make a hasty decision on this either. Therefore, the law stands for the time being. Is that clear?'

'Yes, your Majesty. Thank you, your Majesty,' Calvyn said, his heart once more in his mouth as his mind raced over what he could do with a hundred pieces of gold.

'I will send the monies with the Baron, but for now please see to it that Demarr is taken to his new unit would you?'

'At once, your Majesty.'

Calvyn bowed deeply and then beckoned Jenna across to join him. Together they led Demarr out of the door, with Baron Keevan's other soldier falling into step behind them as they left. Retracing their way back through the corridors and into the huge entrance hall they quickly reached the main exit from the palace where they were halted by the guards.

'Where are you taking the prisoner, Private?' asked the Corporal at the right hand side of the door.

'He is no longer a prisoner, Corporal. The King has released him. He is to join Baron Keevan's army and march north with us,' Calvyn replied, seeing instantly that he was going to have similar problems all the way back to the Baron's campsite.

'I'll have to confirm that. I'd heard that he was to be executed.'

'Of course, Corporal, but when you have done so, could you please detail one of the Royal Guard to escort us back to our camp. If not, I foresee us being stopped at every checkpoint along the way.'

The Corporal nodded and marched quickly away down the hallway.

'I'll be back in a minute,' Calvyn muttered to Jenna. 'I just want to take a closer look at that tapestry down there whilst we've got a moment or two's grace.'

Jenna raised one eyebrow quizzically at him, but didn't reply as he strode diagonally back across the hallway, his echoing footfalls in counterpoint to those of the Corporal who was still moving towards the inner end of the great chamber.

What impacted on Calvyn's conscious mind first as he stared up at the great picture depicting the fall of Darkweaver, was the incredible detail that the craftsmen had incorporated into the work. The depth of the colours was such that he almost felt as if he were being sucked into the momentous scene. The mountainous background, the barren rocky surrounds all picked out with every shadow in place, and the Magicians, nine in all, surrounding the doomed Derrigan Darkweaver in various dramatic poses of spell casting. Strangely, there were four other characters standing to one side of the scene who appeared to be just observing the magical struggle. Who they were supposed to represent, Calvyn couldn't begin to guess. Three of them were men and one was a woman, and despite the small size of the figures on the tapestry Calvyn couldn't shake off the feeling that one of the three men looked somehow like his old mentor, Perdimonn. Maybe it was just because the figure was bald on top like Perdimonn, or maybe it was the character's stance. He could not quite put his finger on what it was. The resemblance raised hairs on the back of his neck.

Then he took a closer look at the image of Darkweaver himself, surrounded, outmatched and yet defiant to the last.

Suddenly, Calvyn's breath caught in his throat. 'Great Tarmin!' he exclaimed, his voice echoing around the hall.

'What is it Calvyn? Is something wrong?' called Jenna, running across to his side.

'You could say that,' he replied, his eyes still locked on the image of the evil Magician before him and his stomach feeling like he had swallowed a large lump of lead. 'I may be paranoid... but that picture is supposed to be of Derrigan Darkweaver and yet it looks exactly like Selkor!'

'What? Are you serious?'

'Yes, but too many things don't add up. It can't be...'

'Calvyn, Darkweaver was killed two hundred years ago. You can't seriously think that Selkor is Darkweaver?'

'Defeated, Jenna. Not killed. In no tale that I ever heard was it specifically stated that Darkweaver was killed. However, you're right. Selkor is not Darkweaver. His reaction to getting the talisman would have been different if he was... but if this is a true depiction of Derrigan in this picture, the resemblance between Selkor and the evil Magician is unnerving. I don't know what it means but this whole situation gives me the creeps.'

'You and me both. Come on, the Corporal is coming back.'

The Corporal returned with another guard, who obtained extra horses from the stables, and accompanied them back down through the city and out across the valley to where Baron Keevan's troops were camped. The whole site was a hive of activity. Captain Tegrani demanded a briefing on what they had heard in the King's Court, and once satisfied that they would shortly be marching back north, he initiated more preparations for the journey.

The Captain's reaction to gaining Demarr as a Private was predictably cool.

'Well, Calvyn, you recruited him so you look after him. I've spoken to Sergeant Derra and she wants you as one of the new Corporals. Your rank is to be acting only for the time being, but if you're up to the job your rank will be made substantive in a few weeks. Report to Sergeant Derra and she'll explain your new duties.'

'Yes, sir. Thank you, sir,' Calvyn stuttered, unable to believe his fortune of the previous two days.

'As for you, Demarr… if you cause any trouble among my troops I will carry out the King's orders myself. Is that understood?' the Captain stated firmly.

'Yes, sir,' Demarr replied, the words sounding wooden and unnatural from the man who had been used to command and respect all his life.

'Very well. Dismissed.'

Calvyn and Jenna led Demarr over to where the recently promoted Sergeant Derra was briefing a squad for a weapons recovery sweep of the battlefield. The Sergeant's hard angular features, accentuated by her stubble-short dark hair and sharply angled eyebrows, were set in particularly fierce lines.

'…and when you return, if any of you are found in possession of anything other than weapons, you'll wish you'd been the ones to die on the field yesterday. Am I making myself clear, people?'

'Yes, Sergeant.'

'Good, because unlike some of these sick scum around here, we didn't march all this way to rob the dead. Concentrate particularly on recovering as many usable arrows as you can. If we don't find enough shafts to furnish our archers with, you can bank on spending every evening of the next week making new ones.'

The squad groaned at the prospect of the tedious chore.

'OK, people, get to it.'

Derra turned, and with her cat-like grace she covered the short distance to where Calvyn, Jenna and Demarr awaited her attention. The Sergeant's large brown eyes automatically scanned each one of them, lingering slightly on Demarr before returning to Calvyn.

'Report.'

'I've just come from Captain Tegrani, Sergeant. Demarr here will be joining us, and the Captain informed me of my new status. Thank you for putting me forward.'

'I wouldn't thank me too fast if I were you, Corporal,' Derra replied, the corners of her mouth twitching up into the slightest hint of a smile. 'With the amount of work to be done around here you'll probably be cursing me within a few days. Anything else that I should know?'

'You've heard about what's happening back up north?' Calvyn asked.

Derra nodded.

'The Baron and the other military leaders are all now locked in a council of war. I would think that one way or another we will be moving out from here in a hurry within the next day or two.'

'Good. In the meantime, Jenna, get Demarr fitted out with uniform and show him where to bunk down tonight. He can have Calvyn's old position.'

The Sergeant turned and faced Demarr.

'I suppose that you've already been threatened with various dire consequences for stepping out of line?' Derra asked, her expression flat and her tone nondescript.

Demarr nodded, his eyes wary.

'Good. Then I shouldn't need to add any further warnings. I've heard a lot about you, Demarr... you will be pleased to know that not all of it was bad. You must know that you are in for a tough time for the next few weeks, because many of the troops will not understand the King's decision to spare your life, let alone his decision to send you to us. To be honest, I'm not sure that I do either. However, I will not tolerate lapses of discipline of any kind amongst my soldiers, so if they start anything that you can't handle, bring it straight to your Corporal's attention. If he's not available, come to me. Understood?'

'Yes, Sergeant... and thanks.'

Jenna and Demarr moved off towards the supply wagons and Calvyn found himself assaulted by a mixture of feelings. Excitement blended with apprehension at the prospect of his new rank and responsibility, and a touch of jealousy and regret that Demarr was to spend more time with Jenna than he from now on.

Derra noted Calvyn's expression as he watched Jenna and Demarr depart and allowed herself an inward smile. Derra had known that Calvyn and Jenna were close and was mildly surprised that no overt attachment had developed. It would not be long now, she decided.

*　　*　　*　　*　　*

'Do Corporals never sleep?' asked Bek with a yawn as he met Calvyn by the field kitchen, a cup of hot liquid steaming in his hands.

'I'm beginning to think not. I got all of about three hours of shut-eye last night,' replied Calvyn, yawning in sympathy.

Calvyn had been delighted to find that his friend Bek had also earned a field promotion to Corporal after the battle with the Terachite Nomads. There was no doubt about it, Bek was a formidable swordsman and he had shown considerable leadership and courage during the fighting. He had changed considerably from the insecure recruit who had started his training with Calvyn less than a year before. Few would argue with his early promotion, for he had more than earned it.

'So who did you get in your squad, Bek? Anyone I know?' Calvyn asked, recovering a cup of the steaming brew from the cauldron and giving a nod of thanks to the Private on cooking duty.

'Well there's Kaan...' started Bek slyly, with a grin that spoke volumes of his amusement and pleasure at that inclusion.

'Oh, I'll bet that pleased him no end,' Calvyn replied with a laugh.

'You're not kidding. I understand that he went straight to Derra to request a transfer. She told him to grow up.'

Calvyn choked slightly on his drink, sputtering and coughing whilst his eyes, sparkling with amusement, filled with tears as he tried desperately to clear the inhaled liquid from his throat.

'Oh yes and I got Tondi, Geldarian and a couple of others that I recognise by face from Squad One. All the others are Privates who joined before us. How about you?'

'I got Jenna, Tyrrak when he's healed, Garret and Tamar. There are a couple of others who I recognise from our training days too, but the rest are older like yours.'

'Jenna and Tamar! That could make for a few sparks flying in weapons practice!' Bek exclaimed, a glint of humour still lighting his eyes.

'Maybe, but I doubt it. The two are competitive I'll grant you, but I don't think that either of them will let that get out of hand. I'm more concerned about Demarr.'

Bek's grin faded. 'So you should be. You should have killed him when you had the chance. He'll be trouble you know.'

'Well, to be honest, I thought that I had killed him at first, but when I discovered that he was still alive I could hardly just run him through in cold blood, could I?' Calvyn asked, peering at his friend over the rim of his cup as he sipped his drink again. 'A fight's a fight, but that would have been straight murder.'

'I suppose you're right,' sighed Bek with a shrug of his shoulders. 'But rumour has it that you then defended him in the King's court. Tell me that's not true at least.'

'I'm afraid that it is, Bek. Please don't ask me why, because I am still finding it hard to reconcile to myself,' Calvyn replied, looking Bek straight in the eye.

Bek returned the look for a moment and then gave another shrug and a wry lopsided grin.

'Well, I never did totally understand you, Calvyn, but I have always trusted your judgement. I just hope that he doesn't bring you more trouble than he's worth. If you need a hand at all, give me a shout.'

'Thanks, Bek. I appreciate that,' said Calvyn, clapping a friendly hand on his shoulder. 'And if you have any trouble with Kaan...' he continued with a chuckle.

'Then I'll give him another good beating on the practice ground,' laughed Bek.

The two friends fell to discussing their new duties and swapping ideas and banter over how they should be preparing for the imminent march north. As they chatted the dawn broke, the morning sun rapidly withering the low-lying ghost-like tendrils of mist from the valley floor into nothingness. With a parting slap on the shoulder and an admonition to pass on his regards to Jenna, Tyrrak and the others, Bek left to rouse his squad and get started on the day's tasks. Calvyn took a last swig from his cooling mug of dahl and flung the dregs into the long grass. With a little water from his hip flask he rinsed the mug before stowing it neatly into his pack.

The chill of early morning seemed to suck warmth from every part of Calvyn's body. Gritting his teeth against the self-induced pain he stamped his feet to warm them and fire up his circulation as he too now moved swiftly to wake his squad. The customary groans and peevish banter greeted him, but did not detract seriously from the orderly way in which his troops organised and prepared themselves to break camp and start the long march home.

It was with a certain sense of pride that Calvyn presented his Squad for their morning inspection by Sergeant Derra an hour after sunrise. He stood before the three precisely formed ranks standing in open order formation with weapons gleaming as if they had never been used, and only the larger nicks in blades that had not been easily blended out with whetstones gave any hint that these paraphernalia of war had seen recent action.

Derra surveyed the soldiers with her critical gaze.

'Stand at... ease,' she ordered, her face giving no hint of approval or otherwise. 'Word from the Captains is that we start marching north at noon. Corporal, ensure that your Squad is completely ready to move out by mid-morning and then have them all report to the wagonmaster to help with loading all the weapons that were collected yesterday.'

'Yes, Sergeant,' Calvyn replied.

'Look sharp, people. Let's get our act together and get moving, or we may not have homes to go to,' she finished, and then moved on to where the next squad was standing, awaiting her inspection and orders.

The morning passed swiftly in a flurry of activity as Baron Keevan's troops, together with all of the survivors from the other northern armies, got ready to move. Calvyn's squad met the deadlines that Derra had laid down and his troops were all standing ready, awaiting the order to move out as the sun reached its zenith.

Calvyn had taken particular interest in Demarr's activities that morning. As Calvyn had expected, many of the other squad members either needled him with 'accidental' knocks and snide remarks, or gave him the 'stone-wall' treatment, completely and blatantly ignoring his presence. Interestingly, though, Demarr had not risen to the bait at all. He had taken all that the other squad members had given him with an uncaring silence of his own.

The only person who had shown him any kindness at all was Jenna, who had stepped in to help him gather up a bundle of arrows that had been 'accidentally' bumped from his grasp. However, the look of gratitude that Demarr had flashed her rang warning bells in Calvyn's mind, as a pang of jealousy had struck deep within his heart.

As long as the actions of his squad members did not get out of hand he would not interfere, he decided. He would let them give Demarr a hard time for a while... Tarmin only knew he deserved it. But he also realised that he would have to speak with Jenna, or she could find herself ostracised too.

Calvyn found that his chat to Jenna had to wait that afternoon, and indeed that evening too, for it transpired that the King had taken Baron Anton's plan to heart and was sending everyone who could be spared to intercept the Shandese invaders. Moreover, he was determined to lead the small force that was to pursue the Terachite army back

45

towards the Kortag gap. In turn, Baron Anton insisted on being a part of that force too, as it had been his idea and if it went wrong he wanted to be on hand to try and sort out the mess.

King Malo had designated Lord Valdeer as overall commander of the main force that was to go north. Baron Keevan was named as second in command and virtually every man capable of wielding a sword was drafted to join that force. Even the majority of the Palace Guards were to see action, for they were to accompany the King on the southern expedition.

There were mumblings among some of the veterans about the untrained conscripts and how they would be more of a liability than a help, but overall the mood of the combined armies that were to march north was buoyant.

Calvyn took the opportunity of talking to Jenna during her early watch shift the next morning and warned her of his observations about her friendly attitude towards Demarr.

'Thank you, *Corporal* Calvyn. I'm well aware of the possibility that the rest of the squad might turn on me for showing kindness to Demarr,' Jenna retorted haughtily after he had aired his concerns. 'But I thought that you, of all people, would have understood. They're not giving him a chance.'

'He's used up all his chances,' Calvyn replied coldly.

'No he hasn't. You gave him this chance yourself by saving his life back in Mantor... twice if I recall correctly. Was that all just a sham so that you could exact your own sort of justice out of sight of the King?'

'As I said in the King's Court, Jenna, not a day will go by when he isn't going to be haunted by what he's done. The squad isn't physically hurting him...'

'Yet,' Jenna interrupted hotly. 'But it won't be long before they do unless you put a stop to this nonsense now before it all gets out of control.'

Calvyn thought carefully about that for a moment.

'Demarr can look after himself...' he started stubbornly.

'Against a whole squad?! I've always regarded you as a good leader, Calvyn. Believe me, I cheered louder than anyone when I heard that you'd been promoted so quickly, but you're beginning to make me wonder whether I was wrong about you all along. Open your eyes, Corporal. If this were my squad, I wouldn't want it torn by petty division or guilty of bullying. Every time I think that I've got to know you there's some new surprise that you spring on me.'

Much as it galled him to admit it, Calvyn knew that she was right. He could not afford to indulge in revenge. Demarr had been served his sentence by the King himself and it was neither his, nor anyone else's place to add to that punishment. Calvyn's eyes remained distant and he stayed silent for some time as he thought things through. When he made his decision and re-focused on Jenna he was mildly surprised that she was still standing with exactly the same posture and regarding him with an expression that almost dared him to disagree with her.

A wry smile twisted Calvyn's face.

'You're right, Jenna. I haven't been myself lately. It must be the frustration of being dragged away from Mantor before having a chance to fend off the hordes of beautiful women.'

Jenna's expression softened at his reference to her joke again. So much had happened since then, and the close friendship that Calvyn and she had enjoyed before the battle at Mantor had been distanced by one thing after another. First had come the discovery that Calvyn secretly practised magic, and now their sudden difference in rank added a different dimension to their relationship. The almost constant banter that had been a major part of their interaction now seemed inappropriate since Calvyn's promotion to Corporal and it had driven yet another little wedge between them.

'I'll talk to the Squad before we move out today and do my best to put an end to the Demarr situation. Just promise me one thing, Jenna.'

'What's that?'

'If I start to lose my perspective again, make sure that you poke me in the chest real hard, would you? I really appreciate your friendship and honesty and I would hate to lose that over something like this.'

Jenna immediately stepped back a pace and adopted a dueller's pose, with her left hand on her hip and her right arm extended as if her index finger were a sword. With a completely straight face she carried out a couple of practice lunges in Calvyn's direction.

'Sure,' she said, her face breaking into a grin again. 'I'll get into training right away.'

CHAPTER 3

Calvyn roused his squad slightly early for their inspection after his chat with Jenna. When they were all lined up on parade he made sure that they were in no doubt that the stone-walling and 'accidents' around Demarr were to stop immediately.

'Remember your training,' he admonished them sternly. 'A squad eats together, sleeps together and fights *together*. If you don't make each and every member of the squad a sword brother, then how can you expect the whole squad to be there for you when you are in need? Now whether you like Private Demarr or not is no longer an issue. What he has done in the past is history. What matters now is that there's more fighting to be done against a foe that is more organised than the Terachite Tribes could ever be. This man is a good fighter and I for one would rather have good fighters swinging their swords with me than against me. Think about that.'

Some of the squad were quite obviously not convinced by Calvyn's speech, but he made a mental note of those who looked sceptical and made a conscious decision to work on them later.

'Sword drill will recommence when we've halted for the night. We'll be doing some line practice and a bit of solo work every evening from now on.'

A wave of low groans flowed through the squad at that announcement, but the sounds were immediately silenced as Calvyn called the squad to attention. Sergeant Derra arrived shortly thereafter and carried out her inspection, then the march recommenced.

That evening a half-hour of weapons practice was held before the squad was allowed to set up camp for the night. Deliberately, Calvyn singled out those whom he thought had been least convinced about accepting Demarr into the squad, and made them fight solo against the man that they had been so blatantly victimising. As Calvyn had expected, Demarr proved to be superior in skill in every case. Some of those that he trained with went away with thoughtful faces. Only two seemed to become less receptive by the experience, and Calvyn again made a mental note to keep an eye on them and to try to win them round by other methods.

Somehow the march northward seemed to drag interminably. During the march south to Mantor the excitement and almost unreal anticipation of a battle, the like of which had not been seen in Thrandor for several decades, had carried the troops along on a relative high. However, having seen the reality of the blood and death, and having faced one army of superior numbers, the prospect of facing another so quickly caused a melancholy mood to spread amongst the soldiers. The growing number of reports being received of Shandese Magicians using their arts during the fighting added further tension, and the days and miles crawled past at a snail's pace.

By the time that the combined forces of Thrandor were within a day's march of Baron Keevan's castle, signs of skirmishes were being encountered. There was nothing major, but there were signs that some of the smaller hamlets and villages had been attacked by what were probably fairly small parties of Shandese warriors. It was deemed from the trails and signs that these were likely to have been large scouting parties who had seen the opportunity of a soft target, rather than deliberate calculated attacks.

During the morning of the day that was to bring the Baron and the remnants of his men back to Keevan Castle, the first major encounter with the Shandese occurred. By chance it was the Baron's troops who were taking their turn at the head of the main column when the scouts reported back that there was a large caravan of merchants under attack less than a mile distant. The Baron and his Captains

wasted no time. Having got a quick estimate of the numbers
of the enemy and the location of the fight, they called Lord
Valdeer forward, and after a quick consultation dispatched a
substantial force to race to the merchants' aid.

All of Baron Keevan's troops were to be involved, along
with many of Lord Valdeer's cavalry. The cavalry rode on
ahead, and after a rapid march for just over ten minutes the
sound of the fighting became clearly audible to Calvyn.

The road at that point wound its way around the edge of
an expanse of woodland, which blanketed a large area of the
hills to the left of the road. Captain Tegrani ordered all of
the Baron's troops off the road to approach the fighting from
the trees and so maintain the element of surprise for as long
as possible. Trying as best they could to move quietly,
Calvyn led his squad through the woods, working hard all
the time to keep them parallel to the road. As they neared
the beleaguered caravan of wagons, the sounds of heavy
fighting gradually got louder.

As soon as the scene of the fight came into view, Calvyn
spotted the major flaw in sending the cavalry on ahead. The
wagons of the merchants had all but blocked the narrow
road and the horsemen were struggling to manoeuvre their
mounts freely. Consequently all the advantages of being on
horseback had turned into a liability and Lord Valdeer's men
were suffering heavy losses.

'Bows ready, people. Pick your targets carefully. Let's try
to thin out the enemy a bit before we go hand-to-hand,'
Calvyn ordered his squad. 'Come on. Let's go.'

Other squads were preparing similarly as they rapidly
approached the enemy, and all attempts at stealth were
abandoned.

Jenna nocked an arrow even as she ran forward. Using
her long legs to good advantage she sped ahead of the others
and cleared the tree line first. On reaching the edge of the
trees she immediately sighted a merchant valiantly holding
off three Shandese swordsmen at the rear of his wagon. As
quick as lightning Jenna stopped, aimed, released and re-
loaded her bow. The second arrow followed so fast that the
first had not struck home before the second was buzzing

through the air after it, and the third followed in similar fashion.

Even as the third arrow left her bow, Jenna realised that she had snatched the shot, so she automatically re-loaded and drew the bow a fourth time with the same fluid speed as before.

The merchant was more than a little amazed, as in the space of a few heartbeats his three opponents all fell dead at his feet. The first two had arrows protruding from the centre of their backs, whilst the third had a shaft through his neck. The merchant looked up to see Jenna, tall and slim, her fourth arrow nocked and aimed at where the third assailant had fallen.

Suddenly lots more soldiers wearing Baron Keevan's livery burst forth from the trees and joined the fray. Jenna nodded at the merchant to acknowledge his stunned wave of thanks and moved on to find new targets. There were plenty of easy targets initially, but they rapidly became increasingly difficult to sight clearly as more and more friendly fighters became embroiled in the hand-to-hand fighting.

After a couple of minutes Jenna ran out of arrows and so put her bow aside and drew her sword. With a piercing cry she leapt forward to where Calvyn and Demarr, together with several others from her squad, were battling against a larger number of Shandese swordsmen. Seemingly from nowhere, Bek and a couple of his squad crashed headlong into the rear of the enemy group at the same time. The speed and ferocity of the attack overwhelmed the Shandese fighters and rapidly reduced them to a pile of bloodstained corpses, then with this minor victory complete, the Thrandorian soldiers moved on.

There was nothing really organised about the fighting. There were no battle lines, nor formations of fighters. It was all just one confused melee of fighters and horses, screaming and clashing amongst the wagons. The cacophony of sound reduced all thought to basics... kill the enemy... stay alive.

The Shandese fighters quickly realised that there could be no retreat from this encounter and they fought all the more ferociously for being faced with no other option.

Demarr was like a man possessed. Some men went berserk in the midst of such fighting but Demarr was not one of them. He was quite obviously in full command of his senses but deliberately fought with no thought for his own safety. There was nothing defensive about anything that he did. At one point Calvyn could hardly believe his eyes as Demarr charged headlong into a group of five Shandese soldiers who had just killed one of Lord Valdeer's horsemen. Such was the swiftness and power of his virtually suicidal charge that two of his opponents went down almost instantly. However, if Calvyn and Jenna had not raced to Demarr's aid so quickly, he would have struggled to stay alive for more than a few moments as he was faced with three skilled opponents who were quick to counterattack.

As at Mantor, Bek moved around the wagons like a whirlwind. Death followed his footsteps like a shadow as one opponent after another fell to his formidable speed and skill. No one who crossed blades with him lived to witness the superlative fluidity of his strokes for more than a few seconds. Calmly and purposefully he swept all aside with ease.

When the last of the Shandese had been downed, Captain Tegrani called the Baron's troops to order and the sergeants supervised getting all the squads into marching order. There were very few of the caravan guards left alive and even less of the merchants. However, the survivors were all effusive in their thanks to Lord Valdeer and Baron Keevan.

Jenna was being attended by a medic who was one of several who were moving through the ranks treating minor injuries where they could. Those who were more seriously injured had already been carried to the tail end of the column of troops on stretchers, which were to be loaded onto wagons when the main body of the army caught up.

Jenna held her tunic up to expose her stomach, wincing as the medic stitched the cut on her side with rapid dipping movements of his needle.

'Hey! Take it easy,' she gasped through gritted teeth.

'Do you want this to stop bleeding or not?' the medic grunted without pausing. 'Hold still, dammit!'

'OK, OK!' Jenna breathed. 'Just remember that I'm not a blanket, all right?'

The medic did not reply, his concentration totally fixed on the task at hand.

Jenna was so busy craning her neck to watch the medic that she did not hear Sergeant Derra and the merchant approach.

'Private Jenna,' Derra said, making Jenna jump slightly.

'Ow!'

'Well stay still then,' the medic said, unrepentant.

Jenna ignored him and answered the Sergeant instead.

'Yes, Sergeant?'

'This gentleman would like to have a private word with you.'

'Of course, Sergeant Derra, though I'm a little tied up right now,' she said, grinning at the pun.

Jenna immediately recognised the merchant as the man she had saved when she had first reached the fight. However, there was something about him that seemed vaguely familiar, as if she had met him somewhere before. Her eyes narrowed slightly as she wracked her brain to pinpoint exactly from where she might know him.

'All finished here,' the medic said, tying off his last stitch and cutting the gut cord with a razor sharp knife.

'Very well then,' Derra said as Jenna twisted to see what the medic's handiwork looked like. 'Don't be too long. We will be moving out in about half an hour.'

'I won't keep Private Jenna for long, Sergeant,' the merchant promised. 'Please follow me, Private.'

Jenna pulled her tunic back down over the top of her trousers and tested the wound through her clothing with her hand. It hurt, but fortunately the cut was not too deep and should heal cleanly. With a slight shrug of her shoulders at Calvyn's questioning look, she followed the merchant who was already moving off towards the caravan.

Striding out, she caught up with him quickly.

'I am Senior Merchant Garfeddon,' he said, smiling at her as they walked.

'Jenna, Nathan's daughter,' she replied carefully. 'What

can I do for you, sir?'

'Oh, you have done more than enough for me for one day. You saved my life and I would like to repay you a little for that.'

'Oh no, sir! That's not necessary. I was only doing my job and I don't think that Sergeant Derra would approve of my accepting gifts for that,' Jenna said quickly. 'No offence meant of course but it wouldn't be right.'

'Actually, Sergeant Derra has already approved this, so please just accept my gift before my profit sense returns and I change my mind. After all, it is something that I know you would dearly like, and I now know that it will be in hands that will not only look after it, but use it to good effect too.'

Even more confused now, and more than a little intrigued, Jenna looked across at the merchant with a frown. He laughed.

'It's obvious that you don't remember me,' he chortled, 'but I remember you. Look, here's my wagon. Give me a moment and I'll fetch the gift for you, then your memory will no doubt put you out of your misery.'

Jenna watched Garfeddon as he jumped up onto the tailboard of his wagon and began unlacing the ties that held the canvas flaps closed. The more Jenna looked at him, the more she felt that she should remember this merchant from somewhere, but as hard as she tried, Jenna could not place where she had met him before. Then he emerged from the back of his wagon carrying a beautiful black longbow and the memories flooded back.

'You!' Jenna gasped in amazement. 'The weapons stall at the market place... it all makes sense now. But I couldn't possibly...'

'You could and you will take this gift, Private Jenna. I insist,' the merchant stated firmly, jumping off the back of the wagon to land next to her. 'Here... it's yours with my heartfelt thanks.'

'But... but this is worth a small fortune!' Jenna exclaimed.

'It would have been worth nothing to me if I'd been killed earlier,' Garfeddon replied with a smile. 'I'm sure that the revered Vandar would be pleased to know that at least one of his bows is in the possession of someone who knows how to use it.'

Jenna took the proffered weapon almost reverently, marvelling again at the silky smooth finish of the jet-black akar wood. The last time she had seen this bow was at a local market town whilst out on her first town patrol. Calvyn had been with her when she had asked the merchant its price. The merchant Garfeddon had quoted twenty-five gold pieces and she had not been in the least bit surprised at this. Akar wood was very rare and the fact that this wonderful weapon had been crafted by none other than Vandar, the premier bowmaker in the north of Thrandor, added greatly to its value.

'Tell me, Private Jenna, when you shot those three Shandese warriors, was the third shot aimed at his neck? If so, it was an audacious shot from what must have been at least sixty paces.'

Jenna gave a little embarrassed cough, hiding her mouth with her hand.

'Actually I thought the shot was going to miss altogether,' she admitted, removing her hand to reveal a rueful smile. 'It was a snatched release that pulled the trajectory a bit higher than the others. That's why I readied another arrow.'

Garfeddon laughed. 'Well, it was a pretty good result for what you name a poor shot. Use the bow well, Private Jenna. May Ishara guide your arrows to their targets.'

'Sir, I can never thank you enough for this gift. I shall do my best to ensure that its maker is not dishonoured by its use.'

Garfeddon bowed.

'Go,' he said. 'You must not be late on my account.'

Jenna saluted in return and almost ran back to where the rest of the troops were getting ready to march.

When she reached her squad, Calvyn noted the long bow and raised his eyebrows in surprise. 'So that's who he was,' he said. 'I thought that I recognised him.'

Jenna nodded, gently caressing the silky smooth surface of the precious bow, her mind obviously elsewhere.

'Permission to fall in, Corporal?' she asked.

'Permission granted... and Jenna,' Calvyn's voice dropped to a mere whisper, 'Tamar is going to turn green with envy when he gets a close look at that!'

Jenna's smile broadened as she considered that. 'Won't he just!' she murmured.

There were no further encounters with the Shandese that day, and the march to Baron Keevan's castle passed easily. As the landmarks became progressively more familiar, Calvyn used the opportunity to move amongst his squad as they marched, to get to know them better and to make sure that none of them were harbouring injuries that had not been treated.

When Calvyn spoke to Demarr he was very forthright in his speech.

'What was all that about today, Demarr?' he asked regarding the former Earl with a hard stare.

'All what, Corporal?' Demarr answered innocently.

'Don't mess with me, Demarr. Have you got a death wish or something? Because if you have, then I want to know about it. I've put my neck on the line for you firstly with the King and then with the squad. I didn't do that to have you throw yourself on some Shandese soldier's sword,' Calvyn stated, his voice icy.

'No, Corporal, I don't have a death wish, but I did lose my mind for a while during the fight today. I can't say that I particularly fear death any more... after all, I've stared it in the face on several occasions recently. That gave me an advantage today over those who still place value on their continued existence. For me, though, I no longer particularly care whether I live or die, so I can fight unfettered by those cares. All I want to do now is to fight as hard as I can for the land that I love.'

'That's all very well Demarr, but like it or not you have responsibilities as a Private in this squad. Those responsibilities do not include getting killed unnecessarily. You're a good fighter, and if you fight with the discipline that I know you can, then you will quickly regain the respect of the rest of the squad. Sure they don't like you much right now. Tarmin knows I have little time for you either.

However, I do respect your abilities and experience. Just because you can't be promoted does not preclude you from regaining the trust and respect of those around you. Think about it. I don't want to see any more suicidal charges, OK?'

Demarr fixed Calvyn with a baleful stare for a few seconds and then nodded. Calvyn could almost see him thinking that he did not need this sort of a speech from a junior Corporal, and was not sure whether he had really got through to Demarr or not. However, Calvyn was glad that he had tried.

When the Baron's castle finally came into sight, Calvyn was quite surprised to experience the feeling that he had come home. The grey-stone sprawling structure with its low outer walls and tall central keep held many memories for him and he was more than a little glad to be back. Things would be different now though, and not just because he had been promoted.

Now that everyone knew of his ability to work magic, he would be watched much more closely. Regardless of what he had done at Mantor, the King had more overlooked than endorsed Calvyn's use of magic to overcome the power of Darkweaver's amulet. Magic would still be an illegal practice and he was sure that if he were to be caught using it around the castle, he would be punished. Still, that was a bridge that he would cross when he came to it, he decided.

As they approached the castle, the gates opened and Captain Risslan emerged to meet the Baron and the other Captains. Calvyn could not hear what Risslan was saying but he appeared to be very het up about something, and he was speaking very fast. After about a minute or so the Baron barked an order at the Captain and he turned very red in the face.

Baron Keevan dismounted, pushed past the crimson-faced Captain and strode in through the castle gates, leaving Captain Risslan to bring the Baron's horse along behind.

'Something's up,' Calvyn muttered to no one in particular.

Jenna, who was standing close by had also reached the same conclusion. 'Risslan was certainly upset about something,' she commented quietly.

It did not take them long to find out what that something was. When they entered the castle the first thing that everyone could not but fail to notice was the number of people manning the walls who sported bandages. Everywhere they looked people were limping or had arms in slings and there were far fewer manning the walls that there should be during the day. That there had been fierce fighting was without doubt. It remained to be seen just how high the casualty rate had been, but Calvyn surmised quite correctly that it had been higher even than the armies of the north had suffered against the Terachite Nomads at the battle of Mantor.

All available beds in the castle were put to use that night. Two of the barrack rooms were used as a makeshift hospital for the wounded that had returned from Mantor on wagons and those badly wounded in the battle at the castle.

The Mess Hall was packed at dinner that evening. The cooks worked without rest, preparing food for those accommodated both within the castle walls and many of those who were camped in the mass of tents outside. A constant stream of soldiers filed into the Mess Hall to sit, eat, or to collect trays of food to take out to their campsites. Not surprisingly the story of the battle for Keevan's Castle spread quickly.

The scuttlebutt was wild and difficult to believe, but Calvyn was fortunate enough to get an accurate account from Sergeant Dren who called a meeting for all of the NCOs later that evening.

The Sergeant's account was brief and to the point. The Shandese had attacked with a large force. The soldiers holding the castle had mainly been raw recruits barely into their basic weapons training, and they had been outnumbered at least three to one. When Dren started to talk about the Magician, and the dark cloud of magical smoke that had blinded the castle's defence force, Calvyn sat bolt upright. He had heard rumours that magic had been involved, but to hear Sergeant Dren confirm it gave real credence to the fact that the Shandese had Magicians who were making it their business to support this offensive.

As he listened to the Sergeant's account of how the cloud had bloomed out of nowhere and engulfed the castle walls, Calvyn realised that something did not quite add up.

'Excuse me, Sergeant?'

'Yes, Corporal Calvyn. What is it?'

'I don't understand what the Shandese Magician hoped to achieve by the cloud. Surely by blinding both sides with the smoke, the balance of the battle would not be changed? If anything, the cloud would hamper the attackers more. It doesn't make any sense.'

'Well it wouldn't have made any sense except that the attackers did not appear to be affected at all by the cloud. I got the distinct impression that they didn't even see it,' Dren answered. 'As a result they swarmed all over us in a matter of seconds. If it hadn't been for the message rider from Ravenshome village we would have been done for. By chance, the message rider was on his way to the castle to get help because Ravenshome was also under attack. The rider saw the Magician standing alone some distance from the wall and managed to get close enough to him without being seen to put an arrow in the Shandese magic-worker's back.'

Dren's eyes went distant as he relived the moment.

'It was incredible. One second everything was darkness and we couldn't see the enemy two feet away, the next it was clear as a mountain stream. The Shandese were all over us, but fortunately they never managed to establish a strong enough foothold on the wall that we would have no hope. When they realised that we could see them again and their Magician had been eliminated, it hit them hard and they crumbled. I think they were expecting an easy victory, but they suddenly found themselves with a serious fight on their hands and they didn't have the nerve to press home their advantage. They paid. It cost us dearly but they paid. All things considered, the recruits did well, but I'm sure that if the Shandese had realised just how green our fighters were they would have hammered home their attack regardless of their Magician. As it was, we managed to beat them back... just.'

Calvyn's mind wandered a bit as he thought about the

spell that the Shandese Magician had cast. Something about it did not fit with what he knew of magic. He could see how the creation of an illusory cloud could be achieved, but to direct it specifically just at those defending the castle, especially once the Shandese had climbed the wall and were among the defenders, baffled him. The complexity of the spell would have to be immense to aim the effects at so many specific individuals.

Combinations of runes and ideas tumbled through Calvyn's mind as he tried to make sense of the conundrum and consequently he didn't hear Sergeant Dren's request the first time.

'Corporal Calvyn?' Dren asked, his voice accentuating the name with a touch of sarcasm. 'Hello! Are you with us?'

'S...sorry Sergeant. I was just thinking through what you were saying about the battle. I guess I got a bit carried away.'

'I hear you got a bit carried away at Mantor too. I've heard the bones of the story from others, but I'd like to hear your version,' the Sergeant said. 'It would have sounded very far-fetched if we hadn't seen magic for ourselves so recently. Are you really a Magician?'

'Well Sergeant, I'm not quite sure what a Magician is any more, but yes, I can work some limited magic.'

Sergeant Dren gave a low whistle of surprise at that admission. 'Go on then, lad. Out with the story.'

By now Calvyn had the story well rehearsed, as he had been asked to tell it many times. His charge through the ranks to meet Demarr, the protective shield of energy and the conflict between the evil magic of the silver talisman that Demarr was wearing and Calvyn's flaming sword all rolled off his tongue with ease. The appearance of the Shandese Magician Selkor and his taking the talisman, which he had revealed to be the long lost amulet of Derrigan Darkweaver, came next. Finally, the trial of Demarr and the King's judgement rounded off the tale.

Dren's face was a sight to behold as it changed from interest, to amazement and finally to wonder as Calvyn's story concluded.

'So Demarr is now a common soldier! Which squad is he in?'

'Mine, Sergeant,' Calvyn replied.

'Humph! Poetic justice I suppose,' Dren grunted with satisfaction. 'Make sure that you watch him well. He could be trouble. Well, we could've done with your magic skills, banned or not, to help us with that Shandese Magician. May I see this magical sword of yours?'

Calvyn nodded and drew his precious weapon. He handed it over to Sergeant Dren who inspected the blade carefully and turned it in his hand.

'Weird, isn't it?' Derra chuckled from the other side of the room.

'Ye gods! It feels completely unbalanced. How can you fight with this thing? The sword looks pretty enough but it feels awful in the hand.'

'It's because the blade is keyed to my hand alone, Sergeant. To me it feels perfectly balanced and lighter than any normal blade of that size,' Calvyn explained. 'The flames were more for dramatic effect than for any practical use.'

'Ah yes, the flames. So how do they work?'

'May I?' Calvyn asked, reaching to take his sword back.

Dren nodded, intrigued.

Calvyn held the blade upright in front of his body. '*Ardeva,*' he mouthed quietly.

Instantly, blue flames burst from the blade, licking hungrily up and down its length. Dren inhaled sharply with surprise, as did several others around the room.

'The flames don't really do anything,' Calvyn said with a grin. 'But if you're going to have a magic sword, it might as well look impressive, don't you think?'

Dren barked a short laugh of amusement. 'Well it does that, young Calvyn. If nothing else it's very distracting. OK, you can stop it now.'

Calvyn extinguished the flames with the word of power, and placing his sword back in its scabbard he returned to his seat.

'Well, let's return to the business at hand, people. The intelligence that we have indicates that the Shandese have pressed home attacks right the way from the coast to the start of the Vortaff Mountains. There doesn't seem to be any main army as such, just lots of small forces each made up of hundreds rather than thousands of men. Each force by itself could be easily defeated if it weren't for the fact that virtually all of the larger groups are accompanied by at least one Shandese Magician, and some have several. There have been tales of all sorts of unnatural attacks – armies of invisible soldiers, hordes of hideous beasts that turn back into men when killed, defending villagers suddenly just going berserk and attacking their own people, not to mention the cloud that we witnessed here. It is difficult to know what we can do against such magical powers.'

Many of those present turned to look at Calvyn and he suddenly felt very uncomfortable. He glanced around at the expectant faces and swallowed hard.

'I cannot even begin to imagine how the Shandese Magicians can do any of these things,' Calvyn stammered nervously. 'I certainly couldn't do any of them myself and I've no idea how to counter them. I will think on it, but what little magic I know doesn't include anything like these things. If anyone had asked me if they were possible I would have said no, as the spells required to produce the effect you have described would be complex beyond belief. However, they're happening and I'm at a total loss as to how to explain them.'

More important in Calvyn's mind was the question of why Magicians were involved at all, never mind *what* they were doing or were capable of. Perdimonn had always stressed that Magicians kept themselves to themselves and didn't generally get involved in the affairs of normal folk unless it suited their purposes. So what were their motives? Why were all these Magicians suddenly aiding the Shandese military in this strange campaign?

The whole situation made no sense at all. The Shandese were attacking but not holding the villages that they conquered. This was not a strike towards a specific target, or a methodical invasion of territory. It just seemed to be a haphazard series of uncoordinated attacks at random villages and strongholds right along the accessible border between the two kingdoms. It was a conundrum right enough, but the more that Calvyn thought about it the less sense it made and he was left with the feeling that he must be missing some vital piece of information.

Sergeant Dren concluded the meeting shortly afterwards. His parting comment was that Lord Valdeer and the Baron were in conference and would be disseminating orders in the morning. Calvyn walked back to his old barrack room with his mind spinning through all that he had heard.

'Corporal Calvyn,' Derra's gravelly voice called, bringing him to an abrupt halt.

'Yes, Sergeant?'

'I suggest that you and Corporal Bek here move your belongings to the NCOs' quarters whilst you have a chance. Your bunk in the barracks will certainly have been re-allocated by now. Corporal Beren will show you both to your new accommodation. I will direct him to wait for you at the entrance to the Corporal's block in about ten minutes.'

'Right, Sergeant. I'm on my way.'

Calvyn had thought long and hard about his new status during the long march north from Mantor, but because his was initially to be a temporary promotion, he had not been sure that he would ever get to move into the Corporal's quarters. Maybe this meant that Bek and he were to have their new rank made substantive, he thought speculatively. At any rate this was certainly a positive step.

Jenna's large brown eyes were sad as Calvyn removed the few personal belongings that he had stored in his locker. Things had not worked out quite the way Calvyn had expected and he found that he had to fight hard to control the urge to run over to Jenna and hug her. He could see that tears were hovering in her eyes and he desperately wanted to say something, anything, to make her feel better. However, he could not bring himself to initiate a conversation and had Jenna not broken the silence he would have left quietly, with his heart beating loud in his chest and his conscience berating him for his cowardice.

'I'm going to miss you, Calvyn,' she said softly as he

prepared to leave.

'I'm not going far,' he replied with a gentle smile. 'I'll still see you every day.'

'I know. It just won't be the same, that's all.'

A tear broke free from Jenna's right eye and trickled slowly down her cheek. With an irritated gesture she dashed it away and, looking down, tried to blink away any more before they had a chance to escape.

'Everything changes with time, Jenna. This promotion won't end our friendship though. I promise,' Calvyn vowed. 'I obviously can't treat you any differently from anyone else in the squad, but we can still do things together when we're off duty, can't we?'

'Yes, of course we can,' Jenna said quickly, still looking down and blinking hard.

'Good. I look forward to being just Calvyn again soon.'

Briefly, Calvyn placed an empathic hand on Jenna's shoulder before turning and walking smartly down the length of the barrack room to the exit at the far end. Demarr, who had watched the whole scene with interest, began to place his spare items of uniform into the empty locker and almost imperceptibly shook his head.

'He still doesn't understand,' he said, his back to Jenna as he neatly stacked his immaculately folded clothes in the locker.

Jenna looked up in surprise and glanced around to see if Demarr was addressing her or someone else. There were only two or three others in the room, all of whom were busy cleaning boots or polishing weapons, leather belts, and scabbards. He could only have been talking to her, she decided.

'Understand what?' she asked eventually.

'That you love him, of course,' Demarr said, turning to fix her with an amused smile.

Jenna flushed bright red.

'It looks like you're going to have to be much more direct if you want to get through to him. He's obviously somewhat naïve when it comes to women.'

'And you, of course, understand women perfectly?' Jenna

snapped, her cheeks still glowing.

'Oh no!' Demarr laughed. 'Hardly! But I know enough to understand what I just saw. If you want things to progress then you'll have to make the moves. The good Corporal there doesn't know what to do. Trust me.'

'Trust *you*! That's rich!' Jenna said, sarcasm barbing her tone.

'Only trying to help,' Demarr said, extending his hands in a calming gesture.

'Well mind your own business in future, Demarr. I didn't ask for your help and I don't want it. Clear?'

'Crystal,' Demarr said calmly, and closing his locker he too walked away down the barrack room without a backward glance.

Despite her harsh words it was a very thoughtful Jenna who watched Demarr exit through the door to the Drill Square.

CHAPTER 4

The next morning, Sergeants Derra and Dren organised the squads on the Drill Square and inspected everyone. When the inspection was complete, Captain Strexis appeared from between the Quartermaster's Stores and the Keep. After the customary brief dialogue of orders between the senior Sergeant, the Captain and the parade was completed, everyone was ordered to 'stand at ease' while the Captain addressed the troops.

'What I'm going to do today breaks with all tradition, but the present situation requires drastic measures. The Baron has decided that due to the losses that we have suffered over the last month, the current recruits are to be divided amongst the squads to boost the numbers that we can field in battle. I fully appreciate that this is unfair to both you and to them. It is unfair to you that we're asking you to take untrained soldiers into battle as your sword brothers, and unfair to them that they're to go into battle ill-prepared. However, I expect all of you to make the best of this bad situation. Soldiers, do your best to help the recruits with their weapon skills as and when you can. There will be no trouble with this or heads will roll. Take note, people. You are professional fighters, not bullies or brawlers. Anyone discovered giving the recruits a hard time unnecessarily will be dealt with severely. The Sergeants have the orders for the squads and will give you the details shortly. That is all. Carry on, Sergeant Dren.'

Sergeant Dren exchanged salutes with the Captain who then departed towards the Captains' quarters. The parade was dismissed in short order, after which the Corporals were called forward and Sergeant Dren designated which recruits were to supplement their respective squads. Calvyn's squad was to get six of the trainees, five men and one woman.

'And what a woman!' thought Calvyn to himself as he was introduced to his new charges by the Sergeant.

'Recruits Sten... Marco... Kedreeve... Verne... Fesha... and Eloise,' Dren stated, indicating each in turn.

Eloise deserved more than a cursory glance, Calvyn decided, whilst trying very hard not to stare at the raven-haired beauty. There weren't many women who could make 'recruit greens' look stylish, but this was one girl who would have to work exceptionally hard not to look good whatever she wore. With the swift inspection that he made of her, Calvyn instantly absorbed the curving lines of her perfect figure, the jet black hair, the greeny-brown eyes, the full curving lips, the delicate slightly upturned nose and the classic cheek bones.

'What made a woman like that want to become a professional fighter?' Calvyn wondered as he silently walked around the six, inspecting their uniform and general bearing.

'Are they to get full uniform, Sergeant? Or are they to fight in greens?' Calvyn asked, having completed his circuit of the recruits and trying to imagine how Eloise would look if dressed in the smart stylish blue and black colours worn by the Baron's regular troops.

'Full uniform, Corporal Calvyn. Get them to the Quartermaster's stores as soon as possible. The Quartermaster is expecting them,' Dren replied, grimacing slightly at the smiles of delight that appeared on the recruits' faces. 'Just remember that the uniform doesn't make the fighter,' he added, directing his admonition to the trainees.

'Yes, Sergeant,' they chorused, obviously trying to control their elation at being issued with the smart uniform of the Baron's fully qualified troops.

'Carry on, Corporal.'

Calvyn acknowledged the Sergeant's order, then as Dren moved on to introduce the next batch of recruits to their Corporal, Calvyn walked back down the line and made eye contact with each recruit in turn.

Sten was tall and broadly built, with fair hair and huge hands. He would undoubtedly wield a sword powerfully with that sort of a frame. Marco and Kedreeve were both of average height and build, but whilst Marco had brown eyes that seemed warm and friendly, Kedreeve had eyes of ice blue that conveyed a barely controlled viciousness. Meeting that cold gaze, Calvyn's eyes inadvertently narrowed slightly in response to the challenge that he found there. Verne looked like he could afford to shed a few pounds in weight. He was not fat as such, just blocky in stature, whilst Fesha was wiry and had a look about him that Calvyn could only categorise as 'mischievous'.

Finally Calvyn brought himself to look into the green-brown eyes of Eloise and his mouth went instantly dry. All Calvyn could think was that having a beauty like this in the squad was going to cause no end of trouble.

The corners of Eloise's mouth twitched upward slightly in silent amusement as she held Calvyn with her hypnotic gaze. There was not an ounce of self-consciousness in her expression as she returned the compliment of a rapid visual inspection.

'Is something amusing you, Recruit?' Calvyn barked, making her jump slightly with his sudden burst of volume. 'If so then speak up and we can all have a laugh.'

'No, Corporal. Nothing at all,' she replied, her mouth resuming a pursed straight line but her eyes continuing to sparkle slightly with some hidden source of mirth.

'Shame. I haven't found anything good for a laugh for some time now. A good joke would have been quite refreshing. Listen up, people, because I don't like having to repeat myself. If you're thinking that I look young to be a Corporal then you're right – I'm probably the youngest Corporal around. However, if you think that I'm wet behind the ears – think again. All the recruit dodges are still well and truly fresh in my mind and they won't work with me. You'll no doubt hear the stories of how I came to be promoted so quickly. All I will say on that subject is that you shouldn't believe everything that you hear. I'm already aware of several wildly inaccurate versions of the events that occurred at Mantor. If you want an accurate account then ask Private Jenna or Private Jez... or if you're feeling particularly brave, you might try asking Private Demarr.'

Calvyn paused for a moment to let the name sink in. News and rumours always travelled fast around the Baron's Castle, but he was not sure how much would have filtered down to recruit level. The six remained unmoved, giving nothing away.

'Why will you not tell us, Corporal?' asked Sten, his voice deep and full, in keeping with his stature.

'Maybe I will, if you ask me again at a more suitable time. For now though, our time would be better spent preparing you as best we can for battle, as you can be sure that we have little enough time left for that. Get yourselves to the Quartermaster's store, fetch your uniforms and then go to the second dormitory from the northern end of the Private's quarters. Skill at arms training will begin as soon as you have dropped off your new uniforms, so don't be all day about it. I'll be waiting. Any questions?'

'No, Corporal.'

'Very well... recruits atten... shun. Turn to the left... left... turn. In single file, to the Quartermaster's store, quick... march.'

Half an hour later the recruits appeared around the side of the Quartermaster's store to cross the Drill Square, each laden with a large bundle of clothing. The six were doing their best to maintain a marching column despite their burdens. Calvyn directed them to their newly designated bunks but allowed them no time to get settled. Quickly, they formed back into marching order and with Calvyn barking out the orders they marched smartly around to the Weapons Training Area just as the sun disappeared behind a large grey shower cloud. With the sudden loss of sunshine, the temperature dropped noticeably as the recruits halted in an open area of the Weapons Training Area.

The rest of Calvyn's squad was already involved in practice on the sandy square, as were several other squads. Jenna and Tamar were busy coaching half a dozen others at the short-range archery targets whilst two of the older Privates, Trask and Cymon, were leading sword drills.

Jenna was frustrated. The joy of releasing arrows deep into the centre of her chosen targets from her beautiful new bow was overshadowed by the incompetence of her students. Here, Tamar was most definitely her superior. His ice-cold demeanour refused to be flustered by the poor technique and relatively wild arrows of the soldiers he was training. Calmly he would re-demonstrate again and again the correct posture, breathing technique and smooth release of an expert bowman. With no hint of frustration he would reposition his students' elbows and adjust their head position, virtually hypnotising them with his low, murmuring voice.

To Jenna, the repetitive mistakes of the other would-be archers were irritating her so much that she was finding it difficult to find the calm required to make the perfect demonstration shots. Only the smooth feel of the Akar wood bow and the even power of the release of her marvellous new weapon kept her from ranting and raving in despair at the inept efforts of her students.

When she spied Calvyn leading the new additions to their squad onto the Weapons Training Area she was glad of the momentary distraction – glad that was, until she noted Eloise.

Jenna had never really experienced jealousy before, but the longer the morning wore on, the more the sickening wave threatened to drown her. Calvyn had never shown any real signs of being attracted to any of the other women in Baron Keevan's army, and he had joined in the same recruit intake as Jenna. Also, it was true to say that Calvyn and she had always shared an especially close friendship, which she had kept thinking was going to develop further. Somehow, though, something always managed to get in the way and the romantic attachment for which she had silently craved had not yet developed.

Now it seemed that every time Jenna glanced across to where Calvyn was drilling the recruits, he was either looking at the dark-haired woman, helping her with her sword strokes, or even worse – the long-legged beauty was gazing at him with her devastating greeny-brown eyes. Grinding her teeth silently with annoyance at this unforeseen competition, Jenna growled in sheer gut-wrenching frustration as the obviously snatched twang of a poorly released arrow sounded from the bow of the recruit that she had just been coaching.

'Do you have a brain in that thick-headed skull of yours?' she snapped at the rueful trainee, who was looking at the most recently released arrow protruding at a strange angle from the top edge of his target with a resigned expression on his face.

'Sorry, Jenna.'

'Sorry!' she exclaimed loudly, her voice cracking slightly. 'Sorry! You certainly would be sorry if you were trying to stay alive by the skills of your bowmanship. Not for long though – you'd be dead before you had a chance to be really sorry. How many times must I say it? The release must be smooth. If you rush and don't draw fully before releasing, the shot will fall at your enemy's feet. If you snatch the shot, it will go high and most likely fly right over his head. If you are making these mistakes in the practice ground where there is no pressure, what do you think will happen on the battlefield?'

Jenna suddenly noticed that just about everyone on her side of the Weapons Training Area had stopped what they were doing and all were watching her angry outburst of emotion at the hapless archer. All of a sudden she felt incredibly exposed and foolish. Glancing around quickly, she happened to briefly lock eyes with Demarr. To her intense annoyance and embarrassment, he wore a knowing little smile on his face that spoke volumes. He knew, she thought to herself guiltily. He knew what she was really feeling.

At that moment, the bugler blew the signal for the midday meal. Jenna did not think twice. She whirled and stormed off towards the dining hall without a backward glance, hoping with all her heart that Demarr would not share his insight with anyone else.

Pausing at the weapons rack outside the Mess Hall, Jenna briefly considered leaving her bow on the rack and going straight in to eat. Although she was sure that no one from Baron Keevan's army would steal it, with so many soldiers from other forces using the eating facilities in the castle, Jenna decided that it would be prudent to lock it out of temptation's way. Momentarily she considered taking it to the armoury, but then quickly dismissed the idea, as others from the training ground would undoubtedly be there right now and she needed some space to calm her thoughts. Her personal locker in the dormitory was the only other option. Striding out along the edge of the Drill Square, Jenna quickly made it to the solitude of the empty dormitory, and with the door safely shut behind her, she ran down to her bunk and flung herself onto it.

Tears flowed unchecked down Jenna's cheeks and her chest heaved with uncontrolled sobs as she berated herself for being so foolish. Indeed, she was so enwrapped in her misery that she failed to hear the dormitory door open and close softly, nor did she hear the quiet footfalls approaching from behind where she lay weeping.

'What's wrong, Jenna?' Calvyn asked gently.

Jenna jumped at the unexpected sound of Calvyn's voice so close. Guiltily she dashed the tears from her cheeks and tried hard to blink any further drops from her eyes before reluctantly turning to face him. Of all the people she could imagine seeing her in this state, Calvyn was the person that she felt least prepared to face. 'Why did he have to be here now?' she thought to herself frantically.

'It was difficult to miss your uncharacteristic outburst on the Weapons Training Area. When you weren't at the Mess Hall it wasn't hard to figure out that you'd be here. Are you all right? Is there anything I can do?'

'Of course there is!' her heart screamed in frustration. 'You could hold me close to you and comfort me in your arms.' But her mind would not let her voice echo that cry and she merely shook her head instead.

'I'm fine,' she croaked finally, her voice broken and

unsteady.

'Like heck you are!' Calvyn replied and placed a hand gently on her shoulder in an empathic gesture.

Jenna flinched from his touch, a reaction which both surprised Calvyn and hurt him deeply.

'I'm sorry,' he said, his voice unable to keep from betraying his feelings. 'I only wanted to help. I've never seen you this way before and I just wanted to offer you support in whatever it is that you're going through. Jenna, you're the best friend I've had since I arrived here at Baron Keevan's castle, and you have always offered me support when I've been in trouble. I had hoped that I'd be able to be there for you. If you don't want me here though, just say and I'll leave...'

'Go, I'm sure that the dark-haired recruit you've been attending to so closely all day long will be waiting for you, ready to hang on your every word. Dammit, but life around here is frustrating,' she said, gritting her teeth at the fact that he had all but acknowledged that their friendship was just that – friendship. Nothing more.

'What, you're frustrated with the teaching?' Calvyn asked, misunderstanding the source of her discontent. 'And incidentally, I have spent the morning teaching *all* the new recruits basic swordplay. I don't believe that I was giving Eloise any more or less attention than the rest.'

Jenna's heart sank. The girl even had a pretty name. Unable to believe that she had blurted out the accusation that Calvyn was infatuated with Eloise, she grabbed at the first question like a lifeline.

'Yes, I find teaching idiots incredibly frustrating! I'm obviously not cut out for it. They just don't seem to learn anything from me. Tamar has the patience of a cleric, but it just roils me up inside that they keep on making the same mistakes again and again, and nothing that I say or do seems to make any difference.'

Calvyn thought about that for a moment before replying. 'You're wrong, you know,' he said carefully. 'They are learning. I've noticed quite a significant improvement in all of the students, both Tamar's and yours. But if the teaching is making you so unhappy, then I'll get someone else to do it. After all, I'm going to need the First Bow on good form when we face the Shandese again soon.'

Jenna winced at Calvyn's use of the title that she had won in the final inter-squad tournament of their training days.

'And what's all this nonsense about Eloise? Has she upset you in some way?' Calvyn continued.

'Oh it's nothing, right now the First Bow needs some space to rethink her life,' she said reaching into her locker for a square of cloth to blow her nose into. Then, after clearing her nose and wiping her cheeks and eyes clear of tears, Jenna turned a hard face to Calvyn.

'Thank you for coming to look for me, Corporal. I appreciate the sentiment if not the timing. Please just leave me alone.'

'I don't know what's got into you, Jenna, but I want you to know that if you change your mind and you want to talk about it, I'll always make time to listen. I could offer no less to a friend like you.'

Jenna was more than a little glad at Calvyn's unconscious embarrassed glance down at his feet during his final statement, for he did not see her wince at the repeated use of the word 'friend'. By the time he looked up again, she had schooled her expression back to a stony expressionless gaze.

'I'm going,' Calvyn said sadly. 'I'm going for some lunch before the wolves pick the bones clean.'

Jenna nodded and turned her back on him, then with her heart in her throat she listened to the slowly retreating footsteps. As the door closed, she glanced back down the dormitory to be sure that he had really gone and then burst into tears again as a wave of guilt broke over her, convicting her of the awful way that she had just treated the man she loved. 'Why did I not have the courage to just explain how I feel about him?' she groaned, wracked with remorse at the totally unjustifiable way that she had just treated him. 'Because I can't stand the idea that he might reject me,' she answered herself.

The more she thought about it through the day, the worse the situation seemed. As a result, Jenna spent a virtually sleepless night running over and over again through the words that she should have said, and still longed to say to him. Worse still, she dreamt of all his possible responses.

The next day weapons practice resumed again for those not involved in the extensive scouting parties that the Baron and Lord Valdeer had organised. Jenna was to join the recruits at their sword drill, having been relieved of her teaching role for a couple of days under the pretext of allowing her to brush up on her blade work. Jenna was given a reprieve from facing Calvyn, as Bek was directing the drill whilst Calvyn was out leading one of the scouting patrols. Ironically, Bek decided to pair Jenna with Eloise for one-on-one practice.

It did not take Jenna long to realise that aside from being stunningly attractive, Eloise had already become more than a little proficient with a blade. Consequently, the two women were remarkably well matched as training partners. To begin with Jenna was determined to teach Eloise a lesson or two the hard way, but the recruit moved with a fluid grace and intuition that belied her lack of training and experience. No matter what Jenna did to try to throw her sparring partner off balance, Eloise countered with moves of her own which Jenna was sorely stretched to block.

By the end of the session, Jenna was glad to have ended it with at least some semblance of her pride and credibility intact. Bek had not exactly helped, as he had made so many encouraging comments to Eloise on her style and technique that Jenna was ready to vomit over the way that he, along with lots of the other men, appeared to be fawning over the newcomer.

'Good session, Jenna. Thanks,' Eloise said, her obviously genuine gratitude irritating Jenna more than ever.

'You're welcome, Eloise. Anytime,' she replied, trying very hard not to put an edge on her voice.

She failed.

'Have I done something to upset you, Jenna? If I have then I can assure you that it hasn't been intentional.'

Jenna gritted her teeth as they walked side-by-side towards the Mess Hall for lunch. 'It isn't fair,' she thought to herself. 'The competition isn't supposed to be so genuine.'

Steeling herself against any unwanted outpouring of emotion, Jenna did her best to keep her voice level as she answered. 'No, Eloise, you've done nothing to upset me, but tell me – what do you think of Corporal Calvyn?'

'Oh, he's a really nice guy. So genuine and... now just you hold on a minute!'

Eloise stopped in her tracks and Jenna with her.

'You don't think that I'm making a move for the Corporal, do you?' Eloise asked indignantly.

Jenna blushed, realising that she may have just made yet another monumental mistake, so she raised her hand in apology.

'Sorry if I'm wrong, Eloise. It just looked that way to me the other day. If you're not interested in Calvyn, then please forgive my over-active imagination.'

'Very well,' Eloise replied curtly. 'Accepted, but I must admit that I didn't realise that you and he were...'

'We're not,' Jenna stated, now even more embarrassed than ever, her head swinging round to see if anyone else was within earshot. No one was. 'Let's just say that I'd like to move my relationship with Calvyn to a more intimate level, but he hasn't quite latched on to my feelings yet.'

Eloise laughed, suddenly seeing the funny side of the situation. 'He's a little on the innocent side for me. Don't worry, Jenna, I'm in no hurry to make moves on any man here. Calvyn is safe from my attentions for now, though I won't promise that this will always be the case, for who can say what the future will hold for any of us? Besides, there are more than enough attractive men around to keep me amused should I wish intimate male company,' she said with a little sideways nod of her head towards where Bek was deep in conversation with a couple of his friends. 'On the other hand, though, Calvyn is quite cute...' she added with a mischievous smile.

Jenna gave a mock growl, but acknowledged the joke for what it was with a gentle slap on Eloise's shoulder and the two women resumed their walk to the Mess Hall.

'You know, Eloise, sometimes life just isn't fair.'

'Oh really? How's that?'

'Well I've been friends with Calvyn for over a year now and he's never looked at me in the way he was looking at you yesterday. He's not walked out with any other girl since he's been here, and we've always been close, but I just can't seem to get him to see me in a romantic way at all.'

Eloise placed a casual hand on Jenna's shoulder and turned on her devastating smile. Her greeny-brown eyes sparkled again with mischief as she answered. 'The gods certainly dealt me a good hand when it came to attracting men's attention,' she said, fluttering her long lashes and raising one eyebrow slightly in an inviting, inquisitive sort of gesture.

Jenna could not help but smile.

'However, those attentions are more often than not a nuisance rather than a blessing. I came here to become a fighter, not a lover – I already know how to tangle in bed. I only hope that I can keep my instructors interested in trying to teach me the things that I want to learn, rather than what they think that they want to teach me!'

Covering her mouth with her hand, Jenna stifled a spontaneous giggle by turning it into a cough. Eyes sparkling with amusement at the dark haired beauty's frank observations, Jenna realised that despite her being a potential rival for Calvyn's attention she could not help but like Eloise.

'If you want my advice, Jenna,' Eloise said boldly, 'just tell him how you feel. If you don't, it will just eat you up inside.'

Jenna nodded. 'I'd just about reached that decision already after a virtually sleepless night last night,' she admitted. 'Thanks anyway though.'

'You're welcome.'

'Men aside, you certainly seem to have learned how to handle a sword pretty quickly,' Jenna offered encouragingly, switching the subject to something that she felt infinitely more comfortable with. 'Of course I'm not in the same league as Bek or Calvyn, but you were pressing me hard in those drills this morning. You're certainly much more natural and fluid in your movement than I'll ever be.'

'Do you really think so? I thought that Calvyn and Bek were just saying that. That's the problem, you see. I can never tell whether there are ulterior motives behind what men are telling me.'

With a flash of insight, Jenna suddenly gained a measure of understanding of what life must be like for such a beautiful woman trying to make her way in a male dominated occupation.

'No. They weren't just saying it, Eloise. You obviously have potential, but if you want to excel then you will need to develop the speed to go with your grace. Have you ever seen Sergeant Derra fight?'

Eloise shook her head.

'Take time out when you can to watch her drill. Derra is the only person that I've seen best Bek with a blade. I'm not sure that she could do it now as Bek has gained in speed, stamina and experience since that bout. Nevertheless, she is a formidable fighter and employs a grace to her swordplay not unlike your own – just faster and with more grit.'

'I'll do that. Thanks,' Eloise said thoughtfully. 'And I hear that you are the person to learn archery from...'

'No, not really. Tamar is the better teacher.'

'That's not what I've heard. Anyway, I may be half decent with a sword but I hardly know which way up to hold a bow, let alone how to shoot straight with one!'

'Make sure that the pointy end of the arrow goes away from you,' Jenna replied, with her best deadpan face.

Eloise just looked at Jenna for a moment, before bursting out laughing. 'I'll try to remember that,' she chuckled.

The two young women chatted and bantered their way through lunch and then made their way out to continue their weapons practice in the afternoon. Jenna resumed her role as archery instructor as if nothing had happened the previous day. Tamar raised one eyebrow in as much of a gesture of surprise as he ever showed, but he said nothing.

With a renewed sense of patience, Jenna took Eloise, Marco and Fesha through the basics of archery, whilst Tamar instructed Sten, Kedreeve and Verne. Though it made her feel as guilty as sin, to Jenna's secret delight

Eloise was almost as bad with a bow as she had admitted. Fesha was even worse. However, Marco was a complete natural. His arm was steady, his eye for the target good and his breathing was controlled at the correct pace and depth.

Jenna quickly warmed to both Marco and the irrepressible Fesha, who seemed to take his incompetence with a bow as light-heartedly as he bantered his fellow recruits over everything else. At one point he brought everyone to laughter as he put down his bow and threw an arrow like a spear at the target. Even Tamar's face cracked into what could almost have been described as a slight smile, as the hand thrown arrow struck the target closer to the centre than Fesha had managed to hit in the conventional manner, though not with enough force to stick in.

'Not bad, Fesha,' Jenna congratulated, 'though you'll have to work on a way to put a bit more force behind it if you want to stop anything bigger than a rat!'

'Hmmm... it's definitely not as effective as this,' Fesha replied, and with a blur of motion he whipped a knife from his boot and hurled it after the arrow. With a resounding thud the knife impaled itself squarely into the centre of the target.

'Who needs a bow anyway?'

'Impressive,' Jenna agreed. 'But how many throwing knives do you carry around with you?'

'Three.'

'Well, unless you're going to increase your arsenal to at least twenty then I suggest that you keep practising. Believe me, you'll run out of knives very quickly if we meet the Shandese in battle.'

Fesha grimaced and dutifully picked up his bow again. With a big sigh he pulled another arrow from his quiver and nocked it.

'It's at times like these that I wish I'd listened to what my mother told me,' he said, drawing the bow and taking aim.

Jenna watched him settle his breathing and release the arrow, which struck the target high and to the right.

'Why? What did she tell you?' Jenna asked, intrigued.

Fesha glanced across at her with a wicked grin and

shrugged his shoulders. 'I don't know, I never listened,' he said, drawing another arrow with a chuckle.

Jenna could do nothing but laugh with the others, as Fesha blithely continued to set up his aim, but she did wonder privately to herself if he would ever take anything seriously. It was already a source of amazement to her that these recruits had survived what by all accounts had been a fiercely fought encounter with the Shandese, and what was more astonishing was that these six had come out virtually unscathed. Many of their compatriot recruits had not been so lucky, and Jenna did wonder how she would have fared in the same situation, given the small amount of training that they had undergone at that stage. 'Certainly each of them had something to offer, even if it was just luck,' she mused.

It was some time later in the afternoon when the commotion broke out at the gate. Everyone knew that something unusual was happening when the watchman on the northwest tower started signalling to the guards on the Main Gate Tower. Although Jenna and the others could see nothing of what was going on at the castle entrance, it quickly became obvious that it was nothing good as they espied a runner entering Sergeant Dren's office across the Weapons Training Area. Very shortly thereafter, the Sergeant emerged, grim-faced, and strode off towards the gate.

Jenna did her best to keep her students focused on their practice, but she rapidly found that with all the shouts and people running around in the background, she was struggling hard to concentrate on the teaching. It was little wonder that the recruits were not able to keep their minds on the archery with all the distractions.

The situation became still worse when it was noticed that wounded soldiers were being helped into the medic's rooms, which were just visible from the short archery range, as the treatment rooms were situated at the South East corner of the Drill Square.

'Looks like at least one of the patrols was hit pretty badly,' Marco noted to no one in particular. 'I wonder which one it was.'

No one spoke for a few moments as all watched the injured being carried or supported towards the waiting medics.

'We'll find out soon enough,' Jenna said finally. 'Come on, people. This just highlights how important this practice is. Let's get back to it before we run out of time. I'm sure that we'll be briefed on developments in short order.'

In her heart, though, the last thing Jenna wanted to do right now was weapons practice. It took every ounce of her self-control to prevent her legs from breaking into a run to go and find out if Calvyn was all right. The guilt of her unjustified harsh words to him the previous day settled back over her like a dark thundercloud, and once more she found her mind and heart at odds with each other over what she ought to do.

What if Calvyn had been injured because he wasn't concentrating on what he should have been due to the cruel way in which she had treated him? Or worse, what if he had been... no! Jenna could not bring herself to even think about the possibility that Calvyn may have been killed. Surely the gods were not that unkind, she reasoned.

'It probably wasn't even his patrol. I'll go and find him as soon as this training session comes to an end and I'll confess everything,' she promised herself firmly. 'Even if he rejects me totally, I will surely feel better than this.'

As is always the case when waiting specifically for a period of time to come to an end, the last part of the afternoon training session dragged interminably. The passage of time slowed to a veritable crawl for Jenna, and her patience was tried to the very limit as she awaited the bugle call that announced the evening meal.

At long last the call came, and dismissing her students to the armoury to return their weapons, Jenna strode off between the keep and the south wall towards the quarters where the medics were treating the wounded.

A Corporal at the door refused to admit her. Jenna did not recognise him and he was certainly not forthcoming with any information about any of those being treated within.

'Details will be disseminated through your own NCOs,' he

stated curtly, and he would not be drawn further.

Frustrated, worried and angry, Jenna went back to the dormitory and stowed her bow in her locker before making her way to the Mess Hall to get something to eat. Someone would know something at dinner. Someone always did. Rumours and inside information were a part of army life and nothing remained a secret for long.

When she arrived at the Mess Hall, however, Jenna found that although the place was buzzing with speculation and conjecture, no one seemed to know anything factual. There was no sign of Calvyn though, and indeed no sign of Dren, Derra, Bek or any of the other Sergeants and Corporals with whom Jenna was familiar.

'Invisible warriors I heard,' one Private was saying across the table to one of his friends.

'Invisible! What rubbish!' scoffed another a few seats down.

'The patrol were probably half asleep and walked into a trap more like,' said a third.

'But what about these Shandese Magicians then?' asked the first. 'Are you saying that they don't exist?'

'Pah! Magicians! The Shandese probably take it in turns to dress up in a fancy black robe to frighten gullible mugs like you,' retorted the sceptic.

Jenna ate her meal in silence, not wishing to be drawn into debates on magic. Other conversations around the dining hall impinged on her consciousness, as her ears seemed to be attuned to lifting out references to magic and Magicians. There was a lot to listen to. Whatever had actually happened today, there was one thing that Jenna was sure about – magic was involved somehow.

Having finished her meal in short order, Jenna stacked her plate and eating irons at the serving hatch and left the dining area in search of Calvyn once more. By chance as she was going out of the Mess Hall into the Drill Square, Jenna noticed Private Jez, his short-cropped, bright ginger hair virtually glowing like a beacon as he left the medics' domain with his arm in a sling.

Jenna angled across the square to intercept him.

'Jez,' she called, attracting his attention. 'Wait a moment.'

Jez stopped, his face paling slightly as Jenna approached.

'Hi, Jez. I don't need to ask what you've been up to. How bad is the arm?' Jenna started, almost afraid of asking the question she most wanted to ask.

'Oh, not too bad, Jenna. The medics are making something out of nothing if you ask me. It was little more than a scratch,' he replied.

'Good, I'm glad to hear it,' she said, and then took a deep breath. 'Were you out on patrol with Calvyn this morning?' she asked, the words tumbling from her mouth in a rush.

Jez nodded warily.

'It's just that I haven't seen him this afternoon and I need to talk to him about something really important...'

Jenna's voice petered out as she noted the look on Jez's face. 'He isn't... dead is he?' she asked, dreading the answer.

'No... at least... we don't think so,' Jez replied, and then looked around quickly to see if anyone else was in earshot. 'I probably shouldn't be telling you this, as we were told to keep everything under wraps for now, but when we were ambushed this morning, those of us who survived were scattered to the four winds. We rendezvoused back at the pre-arranged point but Calvyn didn't show up. At first we thought he was dead, but when those of us who were still fit to fight went back later to scout the ambush site a second time, we found all the bodies of those who had not made the rendezvous except Calvyn's. The only sign of him that we found was his sword. It looks like he's been captured by the enemy.'

CHAPTER 5

Dusk always seemed to sneak up and settle early when Edovare was working on an intricate project. One minute he would be carefully grinding away at a brooch or a pendant with one of his tiny craftsman's files, or delicately picking out a shape in a cuttlefish cast, and the next minute he seemed to find himself squinting in poor light as the day faded into night.

Gone were the days when Edovare could work into the late hours by the light of oil lamps and still produce faultless work. Years of straining his eyes on infinitesimally detailed silverwork had weakened his sight such that over recent years he had resigned himself to working only when the light was at its best. Even gloomy days when the sun refused to show her face through the fog, or rain clouds darkened the skies, reduced him to preparing, casting and working only on simpler forms.

With a sigh Edovare put down the oval silver serving dish, around the edge of which he had been painstakingly engraving a series of dragons and firedrakes. It was a brilliant piece of work, worthy of his status as a Master Silversmith. Indeed, he would be sad when he had to hand it over to the Emperor's Emissary, but Edovare would value the money from this commission more than the dish, as it would bring him closer to retiring his tired eyes from their long hours of labour. His only hope was that the Emperor appreciated how cleverly the creatures had been depicted, chasing each other in an endless circle of frustrated battle lust.

There would not be many more works of such detail and

vision from this smithy, he reflected sadly. None of his many apprentices over the last twenty years or so had shown the potential of true Master status and that still irked him. Had he been such a poor teacher? Or was it that he had failed to recognise a spark of talent because he had been too tied up in his own labour to appreciate that of his juniors? Whatever the reason, it was too late to worry about it now.

Outside, the street lamp fire boys were out with their ladders, their buckets of oil and their tapers. Already, several of the street lamps flickered their yellow glow into the shadowy half-light of the end of the day.

Rubbing his tired eyes, Edovare looked out of his wide front window and appreciated once more the outline of the almost silhouetted rolling landscape that filled the skyline. Having the smithy towards the top of the village where the main village street turned a corner to contour the hillside had always been a blessing to him. Apart from the fantastic view down the street and of the surrounding countryside, Edovare, or more often one of his less focused apprentices, would frequently notice any expected customers coming up the hill. This gave Edovare a chance to find and present customers finished commissions in the best possible way when they entered the smithy.

With the practice of many years, the smith gathered his scattered gravers from around the worktable and slid each of them home into an open pocket in a rectangular leather roll. When all were stowed, he rolled up the leather and secured it with a tie before placing it into a nearby drawer.

Metal shavings and dust layered the table, the floor and virtually every other horizontal surface in the smithy.

'Humpf! I really must get the apprentices to clean this place up one of these days,' he muttered to himself as he took the silver plate over to his lock-up.

Opening the cunningly constructed cabinet, he took his customary few moments of pleasure in handling and studying his latest work, before carefully placing it in its pre-prepared space. Several other pieces lay inside the one haven of cleanliness in the otherwise filthy smithy, their total value enough to make any man sleep lightly for fear of burglars.

Not Edovare.

The cabinet had been without doubt the best investment of his long career, though it had cost him dearly, for it was protected against those who might wish to steal its contents by a magical spell. No axe could shatter the wood with which it was made and no pick could open the lock on its door. The only key that would open the cabinet was in Edovare's possession, and the key would only open the lock if activated by speaking the rune of power to which it was tuned. The Magician who had traded the cabinet to Edovare had demanded a vast price, as much for the rune of power as for the cabinet itself, he felt. But the resulting security of his work had been worth every copper penny.

Edovare did not like magic, and for the most part he had refused to work on any magical items. There had been a couple of notable exceptions, but they had been a long time ago and Edovare preferred to try to forget about them.

Having locked the plate away, the Master Smith rolled his shoulders gently, trying to work the stiffness from his muscles. On an impulse he walked back for one last glance out of the front window before retiring up the stairs to his small quarters on the first floor. He grimaced slightly as muscle and bone popped and cracked in his joints as he stretched out after another day of cramped concentration. Tomorrow would see the plate completed with still more than a week to go before the Emperor's Emissary was due. 'Maybe I ought to use the time to get the place straight. Then I could welcome the Emissary into the smithy without any embarrassment at the dirt and grime of the place,' he thought, picking out a small, curly metal shaving that had lodged itself unnoticed until now under one of his finger nails.

'Foolishness!' he muttered, and then silently berated himself for his train of thought. The Emissary would undoubtedly have eyes only for the plate, he realised. He would probably stop no longer than the time it took to inspect the work thoroughly and to pay the commission. It was highly unlikely that he would accept any form of offered hospitality in a smithy like his, no matter how clean it was.

Looking out of his front window again, Edovare stared almost vacantly out at the evening vista for a few moments, as the final embers of the day faded into night. He was about to draw the shutters closed when a movement some way down the street caught his eye.

The street lights were all lit now and the dark figure of a traveller on a horse making his way slowly up the hill was visible even to Edovare's weakened eyes. The sight of any traveller in Eastern Shandar these days was unusual, for the Emperor's troops who were stationed in every town had orders to 'strongly discourage' any unnecessary roving, and they took their orders most seriously. No one travelled without good reason these days.

Some sixth sense told Edovare that this traveller was here to see him, and the hairs on the back of his neck prickled with the premonition. It could not be the Emperor's Emissary this early. Besides, the Emissary would not come alone, but would have at least a token military escort. A customer then? If so, then he would have to be someone of importance to be able to travel the country freely. But if he had status, then why did he not have an escort?

Edovare's mind tumbled over the alternatives, as the rider on his weary horse plodded slowly up the cobbled street towards him. He could hear the hoof falls of the great dark animal now as it slowly approached the smithy, its huge hooves clopping loudly against the smooth cobblestones.

The rider halted the horse outside the main door to the silversmith's building, and wearily sweeping his long black cloak to one side he dismounted, landing heavily on his high-booted feet. Despite not being able to see the man clearly in the quarter light of late dusk, Edovare sensed that he should recognise this dark rider. With a feeling of trepidation that he could not quite justify in his mind, the old silversmith made his way to the front door just as the stranger knocked on it with three, slow, heavy thumps.

'Who is it? The smithy is closed,' Edovare called, unwilling to open the door.

'Come now, Eddy. You should know better than that. Your doors are never closed to me, remember?'

'Malek's Anvil!' Edovare muttered aghast. 'One moment,' he called back, and took a deep breath.

Hands shaking slightly, Edovare drew the bolts and lifted the bar that held the double doors firmly in place. There, standing in the doorway, was a figure that he had not thought to see again.

'Hello, Selkor. What brings you to this part of the world?'

'What, no, "Nice to see you again"? No, "How have you been?"' Selkor asked smoothly, his voice silk-like and his perfect white teeth showing through his tight-lipped smile. 'I'm hurt, Eddy,' he continued, sounding anything but hurt. 'Aren't you going to invite me in?'

Edovare stepped back and silently gestured for Selkor to enter. There was no point in unnecessarily aggravating a Magician as powerful as Selkor, but Edovare's heart sank within his chest as he contemplated what could possibly have brought this most unwelcome visitor to his door.

Selkor strode into the smithy, his prowling steps showing little sign of the fatigue that had been apparent only moments before, as he had dismounted from his great black steed. The man was an enigma, Edovare thought to himself. Just when you thought that you had figured him out, he would do something utterly unexpected – so the old smith was not about to anticipate anything. The Magician would make his purpose here known when it suited him.

As if aware of Edovare's thoughts, Selkor went straight to the Master Smith's workbench and once more managed to surprise Edovare by being uncharacteristically frank and to the point.

'I'll not waste your time, Eddy, and I hope that you'll not waste mine. I have a repair job that I need doing on a silver amulet. It's not that difficult a job, but I need it done properly. The chain that holds the amulet has been broken and it will need a link re-forging.'

'Very well, Selkor. Just leave the amulet and chain on the desk and I'll do it first thing in the morning,' Edovare said quickly, relief evident in his voice.

'I'm afraid not, Eddy. I'm not letting this amulet out of my sight. Not even with you, old man,' Selkor replied with a wry smile.

'Is it that valuable then?' Edovare asked, intrigued.

'More than you could ever imagine...' Selkor said softly, his eyes suddenly distant. 'But it is not its value that worries me,' he continued abruptly, his eyes snapping back into focus and drilling into the old man as if he were a deadly enemy.

Edovare sucked in a sharp intake of breath at that look, and with a silent gulp he faced up to what he knew must be the catch to this 'simple' repair.

'Magical I suppose?' he asked, trying to sound as casual as he could about it.

Selkor nodded, the sardonic grin returning to the Magician's face, and the single oil lamp making his thick black eyebrows shadow the dark brown eyes beneath into wells of blackness.

'That's why I've come to you, my old friend. I remember the fine job that you made of my ring all those years ago and I immediately thought of you when I acquired this latest trinket.'

Edovare walked slowly across to the workbench, his shoulders slumping somewhat as if in resignation at the direction in which this encounter was progressing.

'I am old, Selkor, and not as strong as I was. Working on magical objects is not easy work. Why not use young Filawn over in Jemaille's Crossing? He's looking to build a reputation as a Master Smith and a piece of work like this might...'

'No,' Selkor interrupted, his voice stern and carrying a resolve that Edovare immediately recognised as unswerving. 'It has to be you, Eddy. I will not let some untried whelp loose with a hammer around this piece.'

'Filawn is hardly an "untried whelp". However, if you insist on my hand for this repair, then bring me the piece in the morning and I will make an assessment for you.'

Selkor's eyes glittered, hard as diamonds, as they drilled at Edovare from under their heavy brows.

'No, Eddy. Not tomorrow. Now. Tonight,' he said firmly.

'But the forge is all but cold and I may need at least one of the juniors to aid me with the work...'

'Listen to me, Edovare son of Mandon. There will be no juniors involved in this work. It is to be done by you, and you alone. No one else is to hear anything of it. No one. I will have your oath on this before you begin. Furthermore, you will do it tonight, old man. If you need a second pair of hands, then mine will have to suffice. Understand this – I am not going to accept "no" for an answer.'

Edovare was more than convinced that if he wanted to live to see his imminent retirement, he was going to have to follow Selkor's instructions to the letter. The Magician was not to be trifled with at any time, but this was the most adamant that Edovare had ever seen him. Fear gripped Edovare's heart as he thought of the stress that he would have to bear in order to re-shape silver imbued with magical energy. If this amulet was even half as potent a magical item as he suspected, then he may not survive the forces that would flow through him as he worked.

'Damned if I do, and damned if I don't,' he thought to himself sourly. 'Whatever possessed me to do work on magical objects in the first place?'

Deep down though, the answer to his question was easy enough to find. He had once been much like young Filawn was now – keen to prove his mastery of any work of silver, and ambitious enough to try what many had died attempting before him in order to make his name. Now the foolishness of his rash quest for renown as a youthful Master was coming back to haunt him. Yes, he was receiving commissions from the Emperor for an excellent return, but was the renown and money worth the risk that he would now be forced to take? Unlikely, he reflected bitterly, but he could not change his past, so he would have to face up to this new challenge as best that he could.

'Very well, Selkor, as you give me no choice, let me see this amulet that you wish me to repair,' Edovare said gruffly, holding his hand out and bracing himself for the touch of that which he feared.

91

Selkor's right hand went to a large leather pouch hanging from the belt around his waist. He paused slightly as his hand found that which he sought inside the pouch, and his mouth twisted into a strange smile that sent shivers down Edovare's spine as Selkor drew out the silver amulet.

At the touch of the amulet against his skin, Edovare leapt backward in surprise, coughing and spitting, trying hard to clear the acerbic taste that formed in his mouth at the foul touch of that metal.

'Blood silver!' he spluttered, spitting again though little moisture remained in his mouth. 'Are you mad? I don't need to touch that amulet again to know who made it. No good will come of restoring it, Selkor. Even you must recognise this evil for what it is.'

'Even I?' Selkor hissed venomously, replacing the amulet in his hip pouch. 'Beware, old man. You tread dangerous ground with your words. You'll be paid handsomely for your work this night and your name and renown, when word eventually gets out about this, will never be forgotten. Now shall we begin, or do I have to lose my temper first?'

'I'll not feed my blood to that monstrosity, Selkor. If you want to bind your soul to it, then by all means damn yourself to the hell it holds, but I want no part in it.'

Selkor's dark eyes glittered dangerously in the light of the single oil lamp that lit the now gloomy forge. He took a breath as if to make another angry retort, but to Edovare's surprise the Magician held his temper in check and released the breath slowly, calming himself.

Silence held reign for a few moments as Selkor regrouped his thoughts. Edovare folded his arms loosely across his chest in a subconsciously defensive gesture, his tongue feeling slightly swollen in his dry mouth.

'All right, Edovare. You have me at a disadvantage,' Selkor admitted finally. 'I'm not quite sure what you're talking about now, but I can see that some degree of caution is required here. Blood silver is not a term that I've come across before and I'm certainly not about to bind my soul to anything resembling hell. Tell me what you know about this amulet and I'll reconsider my desire to see it re-forged.'

Edovare was surprised once more by Selkor. This apparent sudden change of heart was not what the Smith had expected, and a wave of relief that he might yet be spared the ordeal of working on the magical amulet flooded over him. If he could only convince Selkor of the acute dangers involved in working the dread metal, then the Magician might back down and go away, leaving Edovare to look forward to the visit of the Emperor's Emissary in a week or so.

'Where to start?' mused Edovare, pulling his chair from under the worktable and sagging into it.

'The beginning will do,' Selkor cut in sarcastically.

'The beginning?' Edovare laughed slightly in spite of himself. 'Oh I don't think so, Selkor, for that is a long time ago indeed. Blood silver long predates Darkweaver. I assume this is his amulet?'

'I believe so,' Selkor nodded, his interest piqued.

'It would certainly make sense,' the old silversmith affirmed. 'The style of the runes is consistent with those of two centuries ago, and I know no tales of such items having been forged since that time. There are few with both the skill and the willingness to risk themselves in such a foolhardy venture. In the days of the ancient Magicians, before the wars of the gods, it is said that there were many Magicians who worked blood silver. The oldest remaining annals of the Silversmiths record that those who worked the metal were more often than not Magicians in their own right. How many in total, and what works were wrought, is not recorded. However, what was recorded was that every last one of those who worked with blood silver allied themselves to the gods of evil during the subsequent wars. It is one of the first things that silversmiths are taught in their apprenticeships. Blood silver corrupts like a rapid cancer, eating away at the soul until all that is left is rotten to the core.'

Selkor's mouth had twisted slowly into a one-sided grin as the old man spoke.

'Old wives' tales,' he mocked. 'You should know better than to try to scare me off with old wives' tales, Eddy. What proof do you have of this? Are there names that I will have heard of, or deeds that are renowned in history? I can but wonder that silversmiths have kept records of things that the renowned loremasters of the Magicians know nothing of. Don't you think it strange that there is no mention of this in any of our books of lore?'

Edovare sighed heavily, his heart sinking again as he could see now that Selkor was not to be moved from the dark destiny laid before him. With a sad resignation the Silversmith shook his head slowly.

'I have no solid proof for you, Selkor. I can only plead that you consider this – many old wives' tales hide a grain of truth. This amulet is made of blood silver; of that I have no doubt. I can feel in every fibre of my body that it harbours an evil power and I marvel that you can carry it around without feeling anything. Could it be that the loremasters of the Magicians wanted to forget this part of their past so badly that they destroyed all records of it in an attempt to prevent Magicians from being tempted by its evil power? In truth I don't know if any of these things are true, but I implore you, don't rush into this. Go and do some research first, and see for yourself if what I'm saying has any substance. If you are still of the same mind, then you know full well that I can't deny you what you ask of me. If you still want the amulet re-forged then I will have no choice but to help you.'

For a brief moment, Edovare thought once again that he might have got through to the Magician. Then, as marks in the sand are removed by the incoming tide, so the slight doubts that Edovare had sown seemed to be washed from Selkor's face, leaving his features set in lines of strong resolve.

'No, Edovare, I don't have time to go trekking across the country searching through mouldy old records. Time marches on and events are occurring that require me to act now, before it's too late,' he stated firmly. 'There is no recourse. It will be tonight. Start preparing what you need. I will help where necessary.'

Edovare nodded, and pursing his lips into a tight line, he

set to work loading fresh fuel into the forge.

It took some time to get the forge hot enough to meet the Silversmith's satisfaction. Selkor had roiled with frustration at the delay as he felt that the old man was stalling for time again, but when he confronted the Mastersmith with his suspicions, the old man just smiled in amusement.

'Blood silver is no ordinary metal,' he laughed. 'It's not soft like normal silver. You could strike that amulet with the heaviest hammer in my workshop, using all the strength you could muster, and it would make no dint in it. Try it if you like...'

'If you think to trick me into damaging it further, Edovare, think again. And if you try anything...'

He left the threat hanging.

'Pah,' the old man spat in derision, and continued to work the bellows with a strength that belied his age. 'You could do naught to damage it in your own strength, Selkor. So I could hardly do anything with my old bones, now could I? Even if you were to heat this forge until it glowed white hot with the most intense flame you could raise and you were to throw the amulet into the heart of that fire, the heat wouldn't touch it.'

'Then why the forge at all, if it will do nothing to the metal?' Selkor asked angrily.

'The heat will soften the metal, but only if the metal is first treated with a very specific flux.'

Selkor looked at Edovare expectantly, but the old Silversmith continued on with his preparations, oblivious to the Magician's stare. After a few moments, Selkor could not hold his curiosity in check any longer.

'Which is?' he asked eventually.

'Pardon?'

'The flux? You have some I presume?'

Edovare laughed again, for he no longer feared the Magician's response. Selkor needed his help, so he knew that he was safe at least until the amulet was re-forged, and after that... well Edovare could not focus that far ahead at this time. He would do well to survive the next few hours.

'Of course I do! Everyone does. Haven't you been listening

to anything that I've said? The metal will require blood in order to make it malleable. Blood and intense heat are the only things that will change the nature of blood silver. I can only wonder that it has been damaged in the first place. That link was broken recently or I'm no Mastersmith, but I marvel that someone had the knowledge and the strength of will to break a blood silver artefact.'

Selkor grunted in response, as he knew that it had been luck that had caused the chain to be broken. There was no way that the young apprentice of Perdimonn's could have anticipated the need for heat and blood when he had ordered that sword of his to be forged. Aside from that, the blade would not have been particularly hot if it hadn't absorbed so much magical energy from the amulet in the first place. There would undoubtedly have been blood on the blade from all the fighting, so the whole incident had to have been pure chance.

Thinking about that magical sword made him question again why he had not kept the blade instead of handing it back to the boy. It was easy enough to justify the action as a show of strength, and it was true to say that the blade had felt awkward and poorly balanced in his hands. Deep down inside though, Selkor knew that these were excuses that he made for his own benefit. All his life Selkor had gathered items of power to himself. Then, for no apparent reason, he had held a magical item in his hands, and instead of claiming it for his own, he had handed it back to the apprentice of one of his greatest adversaries. At the time, the action had felt right. Now, with hindsight, he could not imagine what had got into him.

'Still,' he murmured to himself, 'at least I can go and get it at any time.'

'Eh? What was that?' Edovare asked, pausing in his pumping of the bellows to listen.

'Nothing, Eddy, I was merely thinking aloud. Don't stop. It has nothing to do with you.'

'Humph!' the old man grunted, sweat making streaks on his dusty face as it ran down in rivulets from his hairline.

With a heave he began pumping again, the forge roaring

once more in response to the rush of air.

'After all,' Selkor thought, a slight smile alighting upon his face as he watched the old man work. 'A sword like that might just come in useful some day.'

Having resolved in his mind to retrieve the sword at the next convenient opportunity, Selkor turned his mind back to the task at hand and ground his teeth in frustration as the old Silversmith continued to heat the forge hotter and hotter.

'For Tarmin's sake, man, isn't it hot enough yet?' he asked eventually.

'The truth?' the old man panted with a grin. 'I have absolutely no idea!'

Stepping back from the bellows, Edovare wiped yet more sweat from his brow with the sleeve of his tunic.

'No one has worked blood silver for two hundred years to my knowledge, so I don't have much experience to draw on. However, I know the principles. Here... take over the bellows for me whilst I get a few more tools to hand. Just try to keep the forge as hot as you can get it.'

With that, Edovare moved swiftly around the workshop gathering the basic tools that he required: tongs, hammers, pliers and files, a graver, a fine brush and a tiny ceramic cup. Having satisfied himself that he was as ready as he could be, Edovare signalled Selkor to stop pumping.

'I am ready to begin, with one exception.'

'No more delays, Eddy. What do you need?' Selkor demanded, his eyes flashing dangerously.

'Give me some of your blood in this cup and we can begin. Do you need a knife? You can use my belt knife if you wish,' Edovare said quickly, reaching for his small holstered blade.

'Why mine?' Selkor asked warily. 'I'm sure that yours is just as red as mine is.'

'As I said before, Selkor, I have no desire to bind myself to the amulet. You clearly wish to use its power. If I were to re-forge the amulet with my own blood, then it would be bound to me and the power imbued in it would be my power to wield. I don't think that's what you are here to achieve. Anyone not bound to the amulet would never have complete access to its power. Indeed, without that binding, it is more likely that the amulet would use anyone who possessed it to its own ends.'

'How can an inanimate object have ends?' Selkor scoffed in disbelief. 'You're being ridiculous.'

'On the contrary,' Edovare replied. 'The blood gives it a life-force of its own. In some ways, blood silver is very like any living creature, but in most it is truly alien. Here, I even have a clean bandage that you can use to bind the cut with afterwards.'

Pulling open a drawer in one of the wall cabinets, Edovare fished out a tightly rolled, clean linen bandage, which was pinned to prevent it unravelling.

'How do you know all this, old man?' Selkor asked, his voice tinged with suspicion.

'Old wives' tales!' Edovare replied with a grin. 'It's your choice, Selkor. Give me a little blood or kill me now, for I will not feed it my soul.'

Selkor hesitated for an instant, and then took the proffered linen bandage and the little ceramic cup.

'I'll use my own knife thanks,' he stated coldly. 'How much will you need?'

'Not much. A dozen or so drops should do it.'

'Very well.'

Placing the ceramic cup on top of the nearby anvil, Selkor drew his belt knife, and wincing slightly he made a careful incision in the palm of his left hand. A line of blood immediately welled, and turning his hand sideways whilst cupping the hand slightly, he allowed the blood to fall drip by drip into the waiting container.

When the Silversmith gave him a nod to indicate that there was enough blood in the cup, Selkor pulled the pin from the bandage roll with his teeth and quickly bound the wound. Spitting the pin into the forge, he tore the end of the bandage with hand and teeth and roughly tied off the binding in similar fashion.

'The amulet, please?' Edovare asked, his face blank as he focused himself on preparing for the sensation of the touch of the dread amulet again. Then, with a moment's thought, he added, 'Place it on the anvil.'

Selkor reached into his waist pouch and once again drew out Darkweaver's amulet. Carefully, he placed it on the anvil with the chain laid out to its full extent.

Taking meticulous care not to touch the metal unnecessarily, Edovare leant over and inspected the amulet and the chain carefully. The creator of this piece of work had been very clever, he decided as he admired the finish of the piece for the craftsmanship that it displayed. The amulet itself had been attached to the chain with a circular ring that looped through one of the links in the chain. The chain links, though, were not circular. Nor were they oval. Each link in the chain was almost oval but had been twisted slightly in the lateral plane and cinched slightly at each end to lock the adjoining link into a kind of groove. It was this clever design that had prevented the broken, twisted link from becoming detached from the rest of the chain and possibly lost.

Although the broken link had come loose from the groove in one adjoining link, thus breaking the chain, it was still held in the groove of the other. Edovare considered the repair minutely and decided that overall he was lucky. The broken link was big enough that he should be able to do the entire repair without actually having to physically touch any part of the amulet with his bare skin. It could all be done with tongs and pliers if all went well.

His course of action decided, Edovare wasted no time, as he was aware that the Magician's blood would be drying out quickly. With an appropriate sized pair of tongs in his heavily gloved left hand, he picked up the amulet close to the broken link and thrust it into the fiercest heat of the forge. Directing Selkor to pump at the bellows once more, Edovare held the chain in the heat with his left hand and dipped one of his gravers into the blood in the small cup with his right.

In one swift motion, the silversmith withdrew the amulet from the flames and smeared the bloody-ended graver across the broken link. Despite having been drawn from the blazing hot furnace the metal displayed no signs of heat, and the blood ran over the silver as if it were stone cold.

Edovare swiftly put down the graver, instantly reached for

the fine brush and carefully painted the blood as evenly as he could over the surface of the metal. Then with a pair of fine long-nosed pliers he hooked the good link through the broken link and adjusted his grip with the tongs to hold it in place. Having secured it to his satisfaction, he thrust the chain back into the fire and held it there for about another ten seconds.

On withdrawing the chain from the fire this time, the broken link was sparkling with an energy that was far from natural. Ignoring the phenomenon, Edovare immediately held the chain to the anvil, and squinting in the poor light he started to delicately tap the link back into shape.

Twice more Edovare smeared the link in blood and returned it to the fire. Selkor could but marvel at the old man's skill, as after each heating the Silversmith managed to craft a virtually miraculous change with the little time he had to work with. After the third time, the link looked virtually identical to the others but for the fine line of a crack where the link had been broken.

'Quickly,' Edovare gasped at Selkor, his throat gagging at the acerbic taste in his mouth. Despite all his preparations and the lack of physical contact, the old Silversmith was still finding that the foul magic of the amulet was affecting him intensely. 'Pour the last of the blood over the crack.'

Selkor let go of the bellows and picked up the little ceramic cup with the remaining dribble of blood in it. Edovare was holding the amulet by its chain over the top of the flames of the furnace when Selkor, gritting his teeth to brace against the blistering heat, thrust his hand forward and emptied the remaining blood in the cup over the reshaped chain link.

The result was as shocking as it was instantaneous.

There was a blinding flash and a deafening explosion, which shook the floor and rattled the doors and window shutters.

Selkor flinched from the flash, closing his eyes against its intensity. When he looked back an instant later with yellow flash spots dancing before his eyes, and his ears ringing with the aftershock of the explosion, he was momentarily confused as Edovare was no longer standing where he had been but a second before.

A quick glance around the room revealed that the old man had been hurled across the smithy by the explosion, yet it had not so much as ruffled the Magician's hair. Edovare was half sitting in a crumpled heap against the wall cabinets some four paces back from where he had been standing. But whether he was alive or dead became suddenly immaterial as Selkor's searching eyes located the precious amulet on the floor not far from his feet.

Scooping it up he gasped as the power of the restored amulet surged through his body. A flood of energy and magic infused him as he involuntarily looped the chain over his head and cradled the talisman on his chest. Throwing his head back in exultation, Selkor began to laugh, and the chilling sound of that laughter emanating from the smithy all but froze the hearts of the folk gathering outside, folk who had been drawn from their homes by the explosion, curious to find the source of the thundering crack which had rocked the small country village.

Without a backward glance at the motionless body of the old Silversmith, Selkor strode out of the doors of the smithy, mounted his horse and rode off into the night.

Afterwards, the townsfolk could recall little of the figure dressed in black, other than the fact that they had suddenly been rooted to the spot as he had emerged from the smithy door. Those who had been closest to the door swore to a man that the stranger had not only worn a silver pendant, but also that his eyes had flashed with the same colour.

Back in the smithy the old Silversmith, half sitting, half lying against the cabinets, suddenly drew in a short, stuttering breath. There was a long pause. Then he drew another.

CHAPTER 6

Jenna could not sleep.

Three nights had passed since Calvyn had disappeared during the ambush on his patrol and there was still no word of his whereabouts. The first night, Jenna had been tormented by memories of her harsh and unjustified words to him when they had last spoken. Every breath she took as she re-lived the conversation again and again seemed to bring a pang of pain to her chest, as the muscles around her torso tensed so much that they constricted her ability to inhale.

'If only I'd told him how I truly felt about him,' she had told herself over and over again. 'If only, if only, if only...'

The words had mocked her as she had tossed and turned, wondering time and again where he was and what he was going through. However, from the moment that Jez had told her of Calvyn's disappearance, Jenna had felt a deep-seated conviction that Calvyn was not dead yet – in deadly danger maybe, but not dead. How she knew it she could not tell, but the belief kept her from being totally consumed in grief.

Her first thought had been to ask Sergeant Derra if they would be mounting a rescue mission to get Calvyn back. The Sergeant had looked her directly in the eyes with the most compassion that Jenna had ever seen in Derra's normally harsh and often forbidding features.

'Where would we send a rescue party?' Derra had asked. 'How many fighters should we commit to trying to recover Corporal Calvyn? Not knowing where, or even if the enemy has taken him, makes it a cause that no commander worth his salt would ever commit his forces to undertake. I'm sorry, Jenna. There's nothing we can do.'

It was not what Jenna had wanted to hear, but even to her aching heart it made undeniable sense. There could be no rescue at this time, unless by some chance they learned more of what had happened to Calvyn after the ambush. Even if they did get word of him, it was unlikely that the Baron or his Captains would risk more men in some foolhardy adventure to liberate him from his captors.

All of the guilt and feelings of remorse were perfectly understandable to Jenna. Though she was wracked with personal guilt and desperately worried about Calvyn, her mind accepted that this was a necessary process. As she loved Calvyn, it was both logical and right in her mind's eye that she should suffer these feelings under the circumstances. What Jenna could not begin to comprehend, though, were the dreams that had kept her from sleeping after that first awful night.

Dreams of Calvyn like those of the night after his disappearance would be a welcome relief from this repetitive and seemingly unrelated nightly vision, she decided groggily, as she closed her eyes and tried to relax into sleep once more. However, there was to be no such surcease.

It seemed as if the moment Jenna's mind began to relax, the voice started calling to her. It was particularly confusing as it was not a voice that she recognised, but the call was inflected in a way that suggested the caller knew her. It was a man's voice – an older man, she mused, even as the dream gripped her again... yes, definitely older by the timbre of the speech.

'Jenna. Come to me, Jenna, I need your help,' the disembodied voice called insistently.

As before, the voice repeated the same phrase again and again, and once more she felt as if her spirit rose from her body and soared up into the cool air of the night. High, high above Keevan Castle she climbed, before turning and flying across the dark landscape at an ever-increasing speed.

The dark woods and hills raced by beneath Jenna, as her dream eyes perceived details that no physical eye could see by the dim light of the half-moon: cows standing still in the fields, their mouths chewing gently on the cud; a caravan of merchants parked just off a country road, the sentries playing a quiet gambling game with bone dice in the flickering light of the watch fire; a fox stalking round a chicken hutch, intent on finding a way in to its oblivious prey within. Each time she made this same eerily silent flight, different details caught her eye: a barn owl gliding on silent wings as it swooped on an unsuspecting vole; a horse in a field prancing suddenly away from the hedge, startled by the sudden movement of a weasel as it raced along the edge of the field.

Then, as with each time before, her flight turned from westerly to northerly, her nightly body climbing even higher as it flew up into the Vortaff Mountains.

'Jenna. Come to me, Jenna. I need your help.'

The insistent voice pulled her up along the line of a mountain pass, the track through the mountains clearly visible to her enhanced vision. The point at which she left the line of the pass was now familiar and the last soaring climb up to the unusual mountaintop no longer unexpected.

'Jenna. Come to me, Jenna. I need your help.'

There on the strange, bowl-shaped summit was the huge stone monolith, solitary and imposing.

'Jenna. Come to me, Jenna. I need your help.'

Gently floating down to alight upon the mountaintop, Jenna slowly approached the great rock, which was standing proud like some great monument to a forgotten age. The voice seemed closer now, and yet still somehow far away. Cautiously she searched around for the source of the voice, but with no success.

'Where are you? What do you want with me?' she called.

'Jenna. Come to me, Jenna. I need your help.'

No matter where she went on that mountaintop, Jenna could not seem to fix on the source of the voice. It was so terribly frustrating and yet the person calling her had to be here somewhere, as she was brought to this same place with every recurring dream. At least she knew how to end the dream now. Placing her hands against the great stone had caused her to wake up on every occasion, but she was reluctant to do this, as she desperately wanted to discover who this man was that kept calling out to her so insistently.

'Please,' she called out, 'show yourself. How can I help you if I don't know where you are?'

As with each of the previous times, the voice did not acknowledge her presence but merely kept repeating the same call over and over again. It was so terribly frustrating. The voice was not frightened, nor was it frightening. There was no malevolence in it and yet neither was there any sense of great benevolence or kindness. It was merely insistent and patient... and maybe there was just a hint of desperation in the undertone of the call that had not been there the previous night.

Eventually, not knowing what else she could do, Jenna moved to stand facing the great rock. With one last look around the shallow bowl she called out to the voice again.

'Look, I don't know who you are and I don't know what it is that you want me to do to help you. If you won't tell me then please just leave me alone.'

With that she placed her hands, palms forward, against the rock and woke up with a start back in her bunk in thc barrack room.

Three times last night and now twice tonight Jenna had gone through the same dream journey. Each time the route had been the same and the dream had ended with her touching the great standing stone. However, it was the subtle differences that troubled her, together of course with the fact that the whole experience seemed so totally unrelated to her troubles in the waking world. Jenna could not even begin to imagine what had sparked this sudden unusual repetitive dream.

With a slight shudder, Jenna pulled herself up into a sitting position and looked down the dormitory at the other members of her squad all sound asleep. Unwilling to close her eyes again for fear of starting the whole process again, Jenna settled herself to try and stay awake.

Twice more during the night Jenna nodded off... each time with the same result. By the time reveille was sounded, Jenna was totally exhausted.

'Tarmin's teeth, Jenna! You look awful,' Demarr said sympathetically as he climbed out of his bunk. 'I don't need to ask you how you slept last night. You ought to go see the medics and see if they'll give you some sleeping draft. Without it, you're going to be in no fit state to do anything soon.'

Jenna nodded, her weary eyes bloodshot red and her complexion pallid as she fumbled her way into her uniform. It would be pointless to try and explain that it was not Calvyn's disappearance that was keeping her from sleep, for Demarr would not believe that for one minute, she mused. So with the mechanical precision derived from months of repetitious practice, she stripped her bed, folded the sheets and blankets into an immaculate bedpack, and then brushed her hair back and tied it into a tight ponytail.

Corporal Alana arrived shortly thereafter to conduct the morning inspection and assign duties for the day. Demarr looked almost as surprised as the rest of the squad when he was assigned to teach the recruits at sword drill. Jenna was not specifically tasked to a duty, but Alana did encourage all those not assigned duties to work on their weapons skills and to help the recruit training in any way that they could.

Jenna was quite impressed with the blonde Corporal so far. There were not that many female NCOs around and it was certainly unusual to have both a female Corporal and Sergeant in the immediate chain of command above her. Jenna was not sure that many of the men in her squad appreciated the unusual circumstances much and she was certain that they would have preferred to have Calvyn back if they could... if only to preserve a bit of male solidarity.

Corporal Alana had not been a familiar face to most of the squad, as she had not been based at Baron Keevan's castle for the last couple of years. Jenna had seen her around the campsites during the long march south to Mantor and again at times on the way back home, but had never really got to know her. From what Jenna had seen and heard over the last three days, though, Alana had struck a good rapport with the squad during a difficult time.

It would have been easy for the Corporal to have waded in

and changed everything to the way that she liked to have things done from day one. However, Alana had not done this. Instead, she had continued as best she could to let the squad run as it had under Calvyn's command, and used the time to make her own assessments of the various characters' strengths and weaknesses.

Making Demarr teach swordplay was Alana's first truly independent act as the squad's leader. It would be a bit controversial amongst the rest of the squad, Jenna thought to herself with a slow smile, but it was a fair reflection of his skill with a blade. Few would be able to dispute that.

As Jenna made her way out of the dormitory, Corporal Alana was waiting outside and pulled her to one side.

'Jenna, you look wrecked. I want you to report to the medics before this evening and get them to issue you with something to help you sleep,' Alana said quietly.

Jenna found herself wanting to explain, but instead she merely nodded in acquiescence to the order. 'Yes, Corporal,' she acknowledged meekly.

Alana, who was a good three to four inches shorter than Jenna, narrowed her eyes a little and made a slight grimace as she studied Jenna's face.

'You're bottling far too much up, Jenna. You're going to have to let it go sometime. If you need someone to talk to, then I'll be happy to listen. In the meantime – sleep when you can, or you'll be of no use in any sort of a fight when the time comes.'

Jenna held the eye contact for a short while, mildly annoyed that both people who had spoken to her this morning had noted her fatigue. However, she could not muster any intensity to the look that she gave the wiry blonde Corporal.

'I'll bear that in mind, Corporal. Thanks,' she replied after the short pause, and then turned and joined the rest of the squad who were formed up and ready to march to breakfast.

That morning, Jenna had worked with Eloise again at sword drill and despite her weariness Jenna had enjoyed chatting with her and the other recruits over the lunch period. During the afternoon, though, her sleepless nights interfered with her archery practice in a most unexpected fashion.

Tired as she was, Jenna still consistently managed to place arrow after arrow in the centre of her target, her deep sense of pride in her skill concentrating her mind on the job at hand. However, as she focused and relaxed her muscles, slowing her breathing to the optimum rate and detaching her mind from everything else around her, she began to hear that persistent calling voice once more.

Although she did everything she could to ignore it, every time she relaxed into a shot, the voice was back calling to her again. In some ways, Jenna realised that she should have anticipated what happened next, for even as she reached her most relaxed state and released another devastatingly accurate arrow, she felt her spirit leave her body. It was strange to be looking down at the chaotic scene as people rushed to tend to her collapsed body, but she had little time to contemplate it, for once again her spirit flashed across the countryside on its all too familiar route.

Although it was broad daylight, the pattern did not change. New details impressed themselves impossibly upon her spirit senses. Her path through the sky was identical to all the previous trips with one small exception. There was no mistaking the change of tone of the old man's voice now.

'Jenna. Come to me, Jenna. I need your help.'

Desperation and a hint of panic were clearly inflected in that call now. Whoever was calling to her was getting seriously worried about something.

Then it came. The change in the dream cycle came just as Jenna was soaring up towards the summit of that lonely mountaintop. The simple change in that desperate call was as sudden as it was unexpected... as it was devastating.

'Jenna. Come to me, Jenna. I need your help. Calvyn is in danger.'

Something inside Jenna snapped. What it was, she did not know but as she alighted on the mountaintop once more, she cried out with all her heart to that disembodied voice.

'I'm here. What do you want me to do? I'm here, I'm here.'

Virtually sobbing out the last repeated words she ran to the great stone and then stopped stock still in her tracks as the image of an old man's face seemed to appear briefly in the textured side of the grey monolith.

'Ah! There you are. Come to me, Jenna – in person, for there is no other way now. Together we may be able to save Calvyn for he's in grave danger.'

'Who are you?' Jenna gasped, incredulous.

'There's no time for that now. This calling has taken great amounts of my energy and I have no more to spare. You know what to do. Will you do it?'

'I will do anything to help Calvyn. Tell me what I must do,' she asked frantically, for the old man's image was fading fast.

It was too late. The face was gone and all Jenna seemed to hear was an echo of his voice calling 'Come to me, Jenna,' in the distance.

'No!' she cried. 'Come back!'

There was to be no answer. The bleak mountaintop with its forbidding views was deafening in its silence. The breeze made no whisper and the clouds no sound as they sailed by oblivious to her lonely soul. The sun glanced around the edge of one of the larger passing clouds, but even the warmth of her smile was not enough to lift the depression that had descended on Jenna's spirit.

'How am I ever going to be able to come here?' she asked herself numbly. 'There is no way that I could leave Baron Keevan's army now. The Thrandorians are in the middle of a war that no one understands and appear to be outnumbered at every turn. How can I approach my seniors and ask to set off into the mountains in search of a place that possibly doesn't exist outside of my dreams?' It was madness. But one thing was sure – she would try anything, however mad it seemed, if it would save Calvyn.

Her mind made up, Jenna decided that she was solving nothing here like this. With a determined heart she walked up to the stone and addressed it one last time.

'OK, old man, I'll try to come here. I'll try my damnedest, do you hear?'

With that, Jenna placed her palms on the stone where the old man's face had been only moments before, and with a gasp she woke up on the weapons training area floor with lots of concerned faces looking down at her.

'Are you all right?'

'What happened?'

'Can you hear us?'

A welter of voices clamoured for her attention as she looked uncomprehendingly around at the blurred sea of faces. It took a moment or two for her to realise that people were acting as if only a few seconds of time had passed since her spirit had left her body to embark on its dream-like flight. Before she had a chance to gather her thoughts to respond to anyone, another voice intruded on her consciousness.

'OK, everyone. Stand back. Give the girl some air.'

The gravelly voice of Sergeant Derra cut through the clamour. Respectfully, everyone drew back and then the familiar angular features of the Sergeant, with her stubble-short haircut, dominated Jenna's vision. Derra's thick, angled eyebrows were drawn together in a frown as she gently touched Jenna's forehead with the back of her fingers.

'Well you're not fevered but you look a little wild around the eyes. Calm down, Jenna. We'll get you in to see the medics shortly.'

'I don't think that I'll need the medics, Sergeant,' Jenna replied, as calmly as she could. 'But I am going to need to talk with you privately, as soon as possible.'

'Nonsense, Private. You're as white as a sheet. Now, are you hurt in any way? Should I get a stretcher brought out, or can you walk?'

'I can walk, Sergeant.'

Jenna gripped Derra's proffered helping hand and hauled herself to her feet. Once upright, she instinctively started brushing the sand and dust from the front and sides of her uniform, and retrieved her bow from Fesha, who had picked it up to prevent anyone from accidentally treading on it.

'OK, everyone. Back to work, the drama's over,' Derra ordered firmly.

No one deeded telling twice.

The small crowd dispersed quickly back to their respective practice areas and resumed their training, whilst Derra led Jenna purposefully towards the medics' quarters. It was a measure of Derra's presence that all hands and eyes immediately bent to the task at hand. Tempting as it was to look at the cause of the excitement, no one was foolish enough to contravene the Sergeant's orders by so much as a sly glance.

'Sergeant Derra, I...'

'Not now, Jenna. It can wait until later. Let the medics do their work first. We can talk later. When you are released from medical quarters, report to me straight away, but I am not going to discuss anything with you while your head is still fuddled. Is that clear?'

'Crystal, Sergeant.'

The medic on duty was not exactly helpful. It would have been pointless trying to explain her recurring dream flights to him, Jenna reflected later as she made her way to find Sergeant Derra. The first thing that he had asked was if she had been taking banewort regularly with her meals. More than a little annoyed that this medic employed by the Baron seemed predisposed to linking any illness or medical complaint by a female fighter to pregnancy and contraception, Jenna had immediately let loose with a fully fledged verbal barrage in response. As this herb, which was proven to prevent women falling pregnant, was made available at all meals by the Baron's cooks, then not taking this basic precaution would be considered irresponsible. The medic's opening question had therefore been a clear implication that he thought her sense of duty and responsibility was in question. Having received an earful for his first question, he had then been foolish enough to ask her whether it was 'that time of the month'.

Jenna had managed to leave with a bottle of sleeping draught and the satisfaction of having given vent to a lot of pent up emotion, so she had not considered the visit to be a complete waste of time. However, if, as she expected was the case, this afternoon's encounter on the mountaintop had not been just a dream, then she was unlikely to have any further problems sleeping anyway. The biggest problem facing Jenna now was to convince Sergeant Derra to release her to go and find that lonely place in the mountains. The red-faced medic was history.

Derra was still out on the weapons training area when Jenna left the medic's treatment room. In some ways, Jenna wished that the Sergeant had stayed long enough to hear her eloquent verbal assault on the medic for his tactless assertions. She had been pretty tough on him though, and while the Sergeant was an expert at maintaining discipline, Jenna was not sure that Derra would have approved of her haranguing him so harshly.

On seeing Jenna striding purposefully towards her, Sergeant Derra made eye contact and signalled Jenna to follow her. Without looking back, the Sergeant went straight to the office that had formerly been used by Sergeant Brett, before his death during the battle at Mantor. Jenna had not realised that Derra had become the official Training Sergeant, but there was no doubt in her mind that Derra would be excellent in the role.

When Jenna reached the door to Sergeant Derra's new office, Derra was holding the door open for her. Jenna stopped and saluted smartly before going into the echoingly bare office. A large, solid-looking wooden desk was angled slightly across the back left corner of the room, behind which sat a high-backed wooden chair. Aside from this there was a solitary long wooden bench along the right wall, but no decoration or personal belongings adorned the walls, or marked the office as Derra's in any way.

'Take a seat on the bench, Jenna,' Derra said, notably dropping the prefix of her rank as she closed the door behind them.

The clashing racket of the sword drills suddenly reduced to a much more ear-pleasing background song of steel.

'There. That's much better. At least we won't have to shout at one another now,' Derra continued with a tight grin, which Jenna found almost as forbidding as one of her grimaces or frowns.

112

To Jenna's surprise, instead of going and sitting behind the desk, Derra came over and sat on the bench beside her. The Sergeant did not sit close enough to crowd her, but as Jenna had not been expecting the Sergeant to put on such a friendly demeanour, it was disconcerting nonetheless.

Jenna crossed and then uncrossed her legs, put her hands together on her lap and then put them on her knees. Derra affected not to notice the obviously nervous body language and quickly settled herself on the bench.

'I see the medic sorted you out with something suitable,' Derra noted blandly. 'So does your trip to the medics this afternoon relate to what you wanted to talk to me about?'

'No, Sergeant... well, yes... sort of,' Jenna stumbled, not sure quite where to start.

In the end she told the whole tale, including an outline of her parting words to Calvyn and how she actually felt about him. The Sergeant listened at first patiently, then interestedly, and by the time Jenna had recounted the final flight and encounter on the mountaintop, Derra was leaning forward, her dark eyes intent. When Jenna finished the tale, Derra arched her eyebrows upward briefly and then let out a long slow whistle as she sat back.

'Well, you have either been keeping a minstrel's imagination and storytelling talent well hidden this last year, or you have truly had a remarkable experience these last few days,' Derra said thoughtfully. 'When you first said that you needed to speak to me, and even when you started telling your tale, I thought you were on a put up job.'

'A what, Sergeant?'

'A put up job, a spoof, a practical joke,' Derra said, running her fingers back through her stubble short hair. 'You could still be, but something in my gut says that you really believe in this incredible tale of yours. After all that happened at Mantor I suppose that where Calvyn is concerned I should not be surprised at magical or supernatural happenings.'

'Excuse me, Sergeant Derra, but why would you think that I would have the temerity to try to pull a practical joke on you?' Jenna asked, genuinely surprised.

'Oh, I never for one moment would have suspected that you would have originated it, Jenna. No, it's just that I've been waiting for the other Sergeants and Corporals to try to catch me out with a spoof ever since I was promoted to Sergeant back at Mantor. It's a bit of a tradition that they have, but I entrust you to secrecy on that. No word goes out of this door, do you understand?'

'Of course, Sergeant.'

'But this isn't it, is it?' Derra asked, her dark eyes dangerous.

No one with any sense of self-preservation would have dared to lie under the intensity of that dark gaze and Derra obviously knew its capability well. For when Jenna gently shook her head, Derra gave a curt nod and the subject was dropped.

'So can I...' Jenna started.

'Out of the question,' Derra stated flatly, not even allowing Jenna to finish.

'But I...'

'Jenna, you are not going to be released to go off on a hair-brained journey to a place that may not even exist, when your skill and expertise are required here. Need I remind you that you are still indentured to the Baron's service for another year before you have the option of leaving?'

Jenna shook her head forlornly.

'Then much as I sympathise with your loss, I have to point out that even this last dream of yours was very vague in its message. It could all be a ruse to lure you away from here at a time when you are needed. The most effective weapons against the Shandese so far have been our archers, and it should come as no surprise to you that you are one of the best, if not *the* best that we have. There is no way that the Baron or any of his Captains, or I for that matter, could sanction your release from service at this time.'

Jenna's heart sank. It was not that this was an unexpected turn of events, but that it confirmed her fears. Getting away would not be easy.

'If you're thinking about running away, forget it,' Derra stated flatly, as if reading her thoughts. 'The Baron would have you branded a deserter and you wouldn't want to live your life as an outlaw. If you were ever caught in this part of the world having deserted the Baron's army, then your life would be worth nothing.'

Jenna sighed mournfully. Events seemed to have been spinning out of control for months now and she seemed to have little or no say in her destiny any more. Everything had been so simple before the brief conflict with the Terachite Nomads had shifted Thrandor's military and political balance of power. Now it seemed that the ripples set in motion by Demarr when he had seized power in the Terachim Wastes were continually expanding in her life, and there appeared little that she could do to counter them.

Then a thought struck Jenna. Indeed it was more of a memory than a thought. What was it that the old fortune-teller had said to her in that market place so long ago? Aside from calling her 'The Huntress' the old crone had said that she would go on a long journey... that was it.

'Sergeant, do you remember when you took Calvyn and I to have our fortunes told? In seems ages ago now, but her predictions for you and in a strange way for Calvyn have both come true,' Jenna started hesitantly.

Derra's dark eyes narrowed slightly with suppressed anger as she recalled the incident. That had not been a happy day for Derra, as the crazy old woman had nearly killed Calvyn with a concealed dagger. The wizened crone, with her twisted smile and uncanny ability to predict the future, had given fore-tellings for all three of them. The prediction for Derra had been simple – promotion – promotion and war. Both had already come to pass. Calvyn's had been about encountering 'The Chosen One'. Again, this had already occurred at Mantor, when the duel that Calvyn had fought with the Terachites' 'Chosen One' had turned the tide of the battle. But Jenna's?

'She told me that I would go on a long journey...'

'And you have - to Mantor and back,' Derra interrupted.

'Agreed, Sergeant. That was a long way, but why didn't she mention it in all of our fortunes if that was what she meant? We all went to Mantor after all.'

'She was a crazy old woman, Jenna. I made a mistake taking you and Calvyn there that day. Who knows why she said what she did? I don't, and I no longer care. You are not going to turn her demented predictions to suit your desires, and that is the end of the matter. Put the dream flights out of your mind and get on with what's happening in the real world. How are the recruits in your squad doing? Do you think they will hold together in a fight?'

Jenna held the Sergeant's gaze briefly in a vain attempt to stare her out, but Derra's expression was set and immovable. It would have taken an extremely strong-willed person to gainsay that look, Jenna told herself. It would need one stronger than she felt right now, anyway. So instead, Jenna ran through her initial impressions of the group of recruits that she had been teaching.

Before Derra dismissed Jenna from the interview, the Sergeant gave her one final warning.

'None of this dream flight story is to leave this office, Jenna. I don't want the castle buzzing with more rumours of magic and the supernatural. There is far too much of that nature going around already. You haven't been sleeping well recently and you had a fainting spell through exhaustion is the story. No variations, and definitely no mysterious mental calls and remote mountaintops. Clear?' Derra growled menacingly.

Jenna could hardly argue now.

Meekly she nodded her head in acceptance, though in her chest her heart pounded the rebellious desire surging through her veins to yell 'Go to hell!' at the top of her voice. It would have been satisfying, but pointless. All it would have achieved was more trouble and probably a spell in the dungeons that she could ill afford right now. After saluting and withdrawing from the office into the late afternoon sunlight where the clashing and crashing of practice combat made the very air seem alive with sound, she decided that she had been wise to not follow her heart.

That evening at dinner and again later in the dormitory, Jenna was swamped with questions. Dutifully she fended them all off with the Sergeant's simple fabrication, flourishing the sleeping draft as corroboration to the lie. However, once into bed that night, and despite the drowsiness induced by the dose of sleeping potion that she had taken at lights out, Jenna's mind turned the encounter over and over in her mind. Her final thought before succumbing to the relief of sleep was that if this journey were really a way of helping Calvyn, then she would find a way to go – regardless of the consequences.

CHAPTER 7

As Calvyn's mind struggled up towards a fully conscious state, his first thoughts were filled with panic. It took every ounce of self-control that he possessed to remain still as he analysed his situation and calmed his racing pulse.

Laying motionless, Calvyn quickly realised that he was bound at wrists and ankles, and there was a soft bag of some sort over his head, which was making the air that he was breathing taste stale. It was that staleness that had caused his initial surge of panic, as the fear of suffocating had been foremost in his mind. Having identified the reason for the taste of the air, he concluded that what he was breathing must be good enough to keep him alive, or he would have been long since dead already.

Sounds burbled a meaningless background babble in his ears, and pressures on various parts of his body changed at random short intervals. Gradually forcing his mind to focus, Calvyn started to work his senses around his body to surreptitiously assess the extent and severity of any wounds that he may have suffered, and to collate any information he could on his surroundings.

The fact that his skull was pounding with a splitting headache made the first injury easy to locate. Someone or something had hit him hard on the back of the head. When or why, he could not remember yet. However, aside from the bag over his head, someone had also tied a blindfold over his eyes and had left the cruelly tight knot pressing hard on the exact source of the pain. The pulses of agony from that wound intensified as he thought about them and threatened to block out all else with their mind-blinding severity.

With sheer force of will, Calvyn drew his focus away from the head wound, and with a discipline of mind born from months of mental exercise, he set a block in place to shut out the torturous throbbing, allowing himself to think more clearly. The effort involved was immense, and despite not moving so much as a hair's breadth he felt a trickle of sweat run across his forehead.

With the pain block in place, Calvyn then worked systematically around his body, gently tensing and relaxing each muscle group in turn, being careful to not move limbs or digits for fear of someone watching him. Everything seemed to still be working, and apart from sensing what felt like some caked blood on his right upper arm, he seemed to be in reasonable condition. Even the caked blood told him something, if it was blood and not mud. For if the blood had caked, then he had been unconscious for some time. Also, the wound that had released the blood had either been treated, was superficial, or the blood was not his own. Whatever its history, it was nothing to worry about now.

Jolts of pressure again assaulted his senses. A wagon, that was it - he was on the floor of a wagon and the sounds now becoming recognisable were those of hoof falls and the rattle and clatter of wheels on a stony road.

Voices too.

He could hear murmuring voices outside the wagon. Then two more, closer this time, and strangely elevated. 'Must be on the driver's bench,' Calvyn thought to himself and then bent his concentration towards their conversation.

It was hard to make out anything at first, for their accents were strange and their voices were low. After a few minutes, though, Calvyn began to make out some words and gradually he started to pick up the gist of the conversation.

One voice was easier to hear than the other. It was not that the voice was louder or higher pitched so that it could cut through the air more clearly. No, there was a strange resonance to the voice, and once Calvyn had attuned his ears to it, the man's words seemed to echo into his mind somehow. In comparison the other voice seemed thin and empty, hardly worthy of his attention. But without listening

119

to both voices the effort would not yield anywhere near as much information and so Calvyn channelled as much concentration as he could muster into listening to the thin voice as well.

The voices had been talking generally about the raids and the success of the tactics employed – at least, as far as Calvyn could tell from the few snatches that he had caught up until now. Then, with all his energy fixated on listening, it was as if he reached out with his mind to hear what his ears could not.

'...Ah!' exclaimed the resonant voice mid-sentence. 'So our young captive is awake at last.'

'What? How can you tell? He hasn't moved,' said the thin voice. 'He's not moved since we threw him there.'

'You ask what you could not possibly understand. Trust me. He is awake. I can sense his mind listening to us.'

'You mean he has abilities like yours, Sire? How can that be?'

'No, not like mine. They are similar in some respects, though, which is why we are taking him to Shellia. The Lords of the Inner Eye will decide what to do with him. At the very least, they should be aware that not all of the pathetic inhabitants of Thrandor are powerless.'

'The Lords of the Inner Eye!' the thin voice said, fear and awe colouring his voice. 'He's that powerful?'

'No, you fool! He's not powerful. Think about it though, if Thrandor starts fielding Magicians or Sorcerers against our raids, it will change everything.'

The thin voice started to reply again but the rich, resonant voice interrupted him.

'Say no more for a moment. Let us not feed the open ears with too much information.'

Calvyn's mind was racing. He remembered now. It was all flooding back. The patrol – the ambush – how his men were being cut down by seemingly invisible opponents. He had drawn his sword and it was glowing, clearly indicating an evil presence or force at work.

'*Ardeva!*' He had yelled the rune of power, igniting his sword into blazing flames through which he could see shadowy figures attacking his soldiers. Leaping forward, he had lunged at one, his sword striking home with deadly force. Then he had been battling for his life as he could make out vague outlines of his enemies surging all around him. It was as if they were shimmering mirages, insubstantial and ghost-like. The bloody devastation of their attack, though, had been all too real.

Even as he had yelled out the order to retreat, Calvyn had spotted the figure in the dark, hooded cloak pointing straight at him. For an instant he had thought that it was Selkor, but only for an instant. The figure had been too short and his bearing was all wrong. Then there had been a blinding pain on the back of his head and he was falling... falling into a deep dark sea of pain, which swallowed him in a gulf of blackness.

Whatever had hit him had been physical rather than magical, Calvyn reasoned, as the lump that was poundingly uncomfortable under the knot of the blindfold was all too real.

'Let me just take care of our inquisitive young friend,' the resonant voice was saying, the words now echoing louder in Calvyn's mind.

Instinctively Calvyn tensed his body and gritted his teeth against what he thought was an inevitable further blow to the head. The impact never came. Instead, Calvyn just heard the resonant voice, this time within his mind.

'*Time to sleep,*' the voice intoned, and a deep chuckle resounded through Calvyn's head, though his ears registered nothing but the rumbling clatter of the wagon's wheels.

Then an image began to appear in Calvyn's mind. It was as if he were standing on a sandy shore looking out to sea. The waves were rolling in to the beach in majestic procession, white trails of foaming spume following the dark greeny-grey crests as they thumped their steady pounding, roaring beat against the sand. Then in the distance there rose a great towering wall of water, many times larger than the other waves. As the huge tidal wave reared its great might above the otherwise relatively calm sea, Calvyn's chest tightened in a rising sense of panic. Every fibre of his body was telling him to turn and run away from the water as fast as he could, but his legs would not move and he could do nothing but watch in horrified fascination as the wave accelerated towards him with deadly speed.

A great hissing rush sounded as the incoming wave sucked water across the sand to pile it up into the mountainous wall. As if reluctant to break, the wave appeared to slow slightly as it curled in inexorable fashion over the beach. The last thing that Calvyn was conscious of, whilst holding his breath and awaiting oblivion to strike, was that faceless resonating chuckle mocking him with its amusement.

*   *   *   *   *

'Dammit, Anton! We were so close to getting these blasted nomads back to where they belong. I can't back down and just give them Kortag. It may be a flea infested dust trap but it's politically unacceptable to just let them have the place. It's part of Thrandor, whether we really want the place or not. We just don't have the forces available to storm the town and yet we can't wash our hands of it and walk away. What can we do? Is there any news from the north? Do you think that we could get them to send forces back down to help us?'

Baron Anton looked past his King at the sandstone walls of the fortified town behind him. He felt the frustration of his old friend all too keenly but he knew that there was little that could be done in the short term. Events had conspired against them, and even if they recalled the entire northern force, it was not certain that the combined forces of Thrandor would be enough to dislodge the tribes from their newly acquired city.

'I know no more than you about events in the north, your Majesty. From all that we have heard it appears unlikely that moving forces back southward would be wise. The situation here is simple, but we are not in a position to solve it. The situation in the north on the other hand is perplexing, and who knows what would solve it? I don't understand why the Shandese are employing such pointless cat and mouse tactics. They have effectively achieved nothing other than to draw our attention and the majority of our troops to their doorstep. As I can see no possible advantage to them for doing this, the whole situation is a bit of a mystery.'

The King grimaced and nodded. Then, after licking his dry lips, he hawked and spat to one side.

'Blasted dust!' he muttered with irritation as he looked around at the orderly campsites of his army. 'Well, I'm open to suggestions Anton. With no help from the northern Lords we can hardly storm the place, but we can't just sit here either.'

'On the contrary, your Majesty. Sitting here is one thing that we can do... and if we do it effectively enough, we may just force the Terachite Nomads to go back to their desert without a fight.'

The King raised his eyebrows in surprise. 'Surely you're not suggesting that we lay siege to Kortag with these few men, Anton?' he asked.

'Not exactly a siege, your Majesty. However, we could probably disrupt supplies to the city sufficiently enough to lessen its attractiveness. We will need to arrange our own supply lines carefully of course, and we will need to split the force up a little to ensure that we cause maximum disruption. Overall, though, we should prove to be a significant annoyance. I'm just glad that it was only a couple of tribes that decided on keeping the town. If they had managed to maintain any greater unity and more tribes had joined them, I honestly don't think that we'd have ever shifted them.'

The King turned back to face the fortified walls of Kortag and scratched his cheek thoughtfully. It galled him that the best he could hope for was to be a 'significant annoyance' to a couple of nomad tribes totalling only a few thousand men, but that was the hand he held. He could only be thankful that he had managed to win the first contest from a position of weakness. That had taken a minor miracle in the form of Calvyn, the young soldier who had broken the long-standing taboo on the use of magic, and in doing so had turned the tide of the battle. Here it seemed that they needed another miracle, but King Malo could not even picture a solution, let alone believe in one.

'It's such a shame that they did so little damage to the outer defences when they took Kortag on their way north to Mantor,' the King observed wryly. 'At least if they had destroyed sections of the wall they would have had potential weak spots to exploit.'

'Absolutely, your Majesty. Unfortunately, they battered down the gates and overwhelmed the small force within easily. I believe that a large part of the city was gutted by fire, but there is obviously enough of it left for them to want to keep it.'

'Tell me, Anton, what if we annoy them enough that they decide to attack us?'

'Then we run away, your Majesty. Pride or foolish heroics have no place here. We just need to make enough of a nuisance of ourselves that Kortag becomes no longer worth the effort of keeping. It won't happen overnight of course. The process will take time. It will be weeks at the least and probably months. With care and a bit of luck, we should be able to slowly augment our numbers whilst we play the role of a thorn in their side. In time we should be able to force them out if it comes to that.'

'Let's pray that they have a low pain threshold then, Anton.'

Anton smiled. 'I think that I could say 'Amen' to that.'

*   *   *   *   *

'Come on. On your feet.'

A hand grabbed Calvyn by the back of his tunic and hauled him upright. Though he did his best to stand, Calvyn's legs were stiff from inactivity and weak from a lack of food. Muttering and cursing in virtually unintelligible dialect of the common language, the guard all but carried Calvyn across the room to what Calvyn could only assume was the doorway.

Ever since his capture, Calvyn had been kept constantly blindfolded and hooded with his hands securely bound behind him. All concept of time since the initial blow to his head had rendered him unconscious, had long since blurred into one endless night. The incident in the wagon when the man with the strange resonant voice had once again rendered him unconscious, this time with some form of magic, had confused his mental clock even further. As far as Calvyn could tell, he could have been held captive anywhere from a couple of days to a couple of weeks. He had no way of gauging it other than the hunger in his belly and the stiffness of his limbs, and neither was a very reliable guide.

Another set of hands grabbed him as he staggered through the doorway and the door groaned slightly before thudding closed behind him. There was a clank and the guard cursed loudly. From the little that he could decipher from the following stream of heavily accented cursing, Calvyn ascertained that many of the cell door bolts were stiff and inadvertent removing of skin from one's knuckles was a common occurrence among the guards.

The second guard gave the first a bit of banter about being clumsy. However, both fell silent shortly afterwards, concentrating instead on guiding their blindfolded and hooded prisoner along a series of corridors and up several flights of stairs.

To where Calvyn was being led, or to what end, he had no idea, but when the guards took him through the final doorway he instantly knew that he was no longer in a corridor. Even hooded as he was, Calvyn could sense the change in the size of the space around him. Stopping suddenly, Calvyn was already off balance when the guards forced him to his knees.

'Take off his blindfold and let's see what you have brought us,' ordered a voice, rich with tone and depth.

'At once, Lord,' the guards responded gruffly.

Rough hands pulled off the hood and fumbled at the tight knot of the blindfold.

'Just cut it!' the imperious tone of the one that the guards had named 'Lord' demanded impatiently.

Kneeling impassively, Calvyn felt someone saw at the cloth with a blade, and then it was gone. Initially, Calvyn felt more blinded than when he had enjoyed no vision at all. Having not been subjected to daylight for days on end, Calvyn's eyes were completely dazzled and it took several moments of frantic blinking and severe squinting before he could make out anything at all.

Gradually the chamber came into focus.

Apart from the earlier speaker, whom Calvyn assumed to be the figure seated in the huge, central wooden throne, there were eleven other figures seated in high-backed, ornately carved wooden chairs that were arranged in a large semicircle in front of him. Calvyn was kneeling in the centre of the semicircle, and he was acutely aware of the scrutiny of these mysterious people who could only be 'The Lords of the Inner Eye' mentioned by the man on the wagon.

Each member of this strange group was robed in black, with a deep hood shadowing the person's face and making it impossible for Calvyn to gain a sense of emotion or body language from any of them. None of them moved as he looked at each in turn, using his peripheral vision to take in what he could of his surroundings.

The chamber was large and spartan, the twelve chairs being the only furnishings. Several arch-shaped windows admitted light to the room, but no pictures adorned the walls and no rugs softened the hard flagstones that made up the floor. This was not a place of comfort.

Calvyn finished his scan of the room and its occupants and turned his attention back to the figure seated on the central throne. He said nothing, for he was sure that these mysterious looking people would start talking to him soon.

He was wrong.

'Yes. He is the one. I am certain of it,' the figure on the central throne said with conviction.

'Are you sure, my Lord? He is hardly more than a boy!' questioned someone to Calvyn's left.

'Do you question my vision, Torvados? The vision is true. This is the one I've been waiting for. We will discuss how to proceed once our young friend here is out of earshot. You may replace his hood and return him to his cell now,' the High Lord directed the guards.

'Wait!' Calvyn exclaimed in surprise. 'What are you going to do with me? Why are you holding me hooded and bound like this?'

The hood went over his head, and he was dragged back onto his feet. There was no point in struggling, but Calvyn could not resist giving one defiant twist against the guards. A punch to the kidneys took away his breath, together with any thoughts of further resistance.

'And, guards – tell your Captain that he can cease the raids. They have achieved their purpose,' the figure on the throne continued. 'No... wait. I think that one more raid would be useful – a specific one. I want a handful of prisoners from the same force as this one. I might have need of them in time.'

'Very well, my Lord. At once,' replied the senior of the two guards.

The Lords of the Inner Eye impassively followed the departure of Calvyn from their chamber, and once the doors had closed, the leader drew back his hood. At that signal the rest of the Lords also bared their heads and heated comments began to fly almost immediately.

'High Lord Vallaine, you cannot seriously believe that this *boy* is going to have the power to lead our armies to victory? Particularly against his own people,' said one.

'Did you touch his mind? He is steadfastly loyal to his country, and it will be immensely difficult to sway him to our cause,' interjected another.

'He won't lead our forces against his own to save a few hostages. Why should he? He'd be condemning more than he'd be saving.'

Others too added their voices. All were negative, or at the least questioning. The wizened old figure on the central throne sat silently, his deep-set eyes almost buried in wrinkles, flicking from one speaker to the next with a sparkle of amusement that seemed to light them from within. After a few moments, the voices stilled under his gaze, and a corner of his thin-lipped mouth curled upward in a wry, twisted grin.

'Again I ask you – do you question my vision? Has it ever

failed in the past? We have gained our power by judicious use of my prescience and I am now telling you once again what I have seen of the future. That young man will lead our armies into Thrandor and the armies will be victorious. In every vision that I have had, I see him leading our armies to victory. You may believe it or not, but that young soldier is going to cause the fall of Mantor. It will not be easy though. The King of Thrandor and his main southern force may be trying to dislodge the Terachite tribes from Kortag, but the people of Mantor will man their walls with enough men to make a fight of it. The vision is clear, that youngster will lead our forces to victory, and Mantor will be ours.'

The old man paused, looking around at the sceptical faces of the other Lords.

'Come now,' Vallaine continued. 'Did none of you notice the clarity of his mind. The boy may know something of magic, but his mind is made for sorcery. With training, he could in time be more powerful than any one of us in this room. He has already developed a respectable level of mental discipline, with no discernible training at all. Who of you could say that you achieved that before you were inducted into the ways of the Sorcerer?'

No one answered.

'I thought not. Now, as to winning him around to support us, the vision was not totally clear, but with the few clues that I did have, I believe that I now know how to proceed. You were right, Cillverne, it will not be easy. Indeed it will be neither easy to do, nor to swallow.'

'My Lord?' asked Cillverne, voicing the confusion felt by all, 'What do you mean it will not be easy to swallow?'

'I mean that we cannot hope to win him around to our cause using sorcery. The powers of illusion that we wield and the power that we can hold over another person's mind are all limited, and require constant effort and focus. Against a determined mind that already held some limited understanding of what we were doing, it would take all of our attention, all of the time, to quell that mind to our will. Therefore, I have decided that we are going to get Barrathos to do our dirty work for us.'

'The old Wizard? Isn't he dead yet?'

'Not yet, Torvados.'

'But my Lord Vallaine, I fail to see how wizardry could help us. What good would the summoning of a demon or a spirit do? Are you thinking to frighten the boy into doing our will? I don't think he'll be won around so easily.'

'Ah yes, you are right... if that were my plan, then it would certainly be flawed. But I am not going to get Barrathos to summon just any demon. I am going to get him to summon a gorvath.'

'A soul-eater!' someone breathed in frightened awe.

'Old Barrathos could never control a gorvath...'

'Alone,' interrupted Vallaine quickly. 'Alone, you are correct. Only the greatest of Wizards could hope to control a gorvath on his own, and while Barrathos was powerful in his day, I would hesitate to suggest that he was ever capable of such a feat. However, with our help it could be done.'

'Our help?' Cillverne asked in surprise. 'I know little to nothing about wizardry, and I suspect that the others here know little more than I. What difference would we make?'

'We would lend him our power, our strength of purpose, and our focus. From all that I know of wizardry, it seems to be very much about strength of mind. So if we strengthen Barrathos and sustain him, he should prove worthy of the task.'

'What would happen if we summoned the demon but failed to control it?' someone asked tentatively.

'Lets just say that the outcome would not be pleasant,' Vallaine answered grimly. 'But we will not fail. Without a soul to trouble him, the boy will be completely malleable to our will. Then it will only be a matter of time before Thrandor falls.'

'Or in other words, if we fail – Shand protect us, because nothing on this earth could!' Torvados muttered under his breath.

*   *   *   *   *

Talking to Derra had not been a good idea, Jenna concluded dolefully. It had been nearly a week since her conversation with the Sergeant and she had been under virtually constant supervision ever since. Any ideas of slipping away quietly from the castle had long since gone, and it seemed that wherever Jenna went, the watchful eyes of Corporals Alana, Bek, Sergeant Derra, or one of the other NCOs went with her. The word was out to keep her from leaving, of that Jenna was certain.

There was nothing to do but wait. Jenna would have to carry on as if all was normal, biding her time for a chance to present itself, and preparing as best she could for the journey that she knew was awaiting her footsteps.

Discreetly, Jenna began subtly altering the contents of her patrol haversack and belt pouches. At every opportunity she acquired more of the condensed biscuits that were given to the soldiers as marching rations and squirreled them away into her backpack. A length of climbing rope, albeit not a long one, also went in along with a pair of fleece-lined mitts that she liberated from her personal belongings in the Quartermaster's Store. A small hatchet, fishing gut and hooks, together with some snare cord, were all surreptitiously added to her packs and pouches.

If any of Jenna's watchers noticed her quiet preparations, then they said nothing of it to her. However, it was noticeable that whenever she was rostered for patrol duty, Jenna was always placed close to the patrol leader in the troop marching order.

Patrol groups had doubled in size since the ambush on Calvyn's patrol nearly a fortnight before. There had been one or two minor skirmishes in that time, but overall the Shandese had remained remarkably elusive. Considering the size and frequency of their raids before this, all agreed that the sudden lull was most strange.

Why had the Shandese not pressed home their obvious advantage? Why had they not simply invaded in the first place? The perfect opportunity had been there with the majority of Thrandor's fighting forces having been pulled south by the invading Terachite Nomads, and yet the Shandese had secured no footholds. They had merely mounted bigger, more destructive raids and employed magic to aid them in their seemingly pointless hostilities. When their raid was complete, the Shandese forces simply withdrew with no tangible gain for their effort. It was baffling. How could you plan a strategy against an enemy who fought with no apparent goal?

These and many more questions like them had become standard mealtime discussion in the Mess Hall. It seemed that no one had any answers. The Baron met frequently with the other Lords and noblemen to collate information and plan strategy, but if they knew any more than the common soldiers, then it was not apparent to Jenna.

One thing was certain – the Captains were using the respite in the raids to good advantage. Constant preparation was the order of the day. When the soldiers were not out on patrol or involved in weapons training, they were busy fortifying local strongholds and improving defences around the castle. Ranging markers were placed at various distances out from the walls to enable the archers to gauge their effective range more accurately. Great stocks of arrows were being produced and stacked in bundles around the walls, and Gerran's forge was in constant use producing swords, arrowheads, pike blades and all other manner of the paraphernalia of war.

Lastly, the old defensive ditch around the castle was being freshly dug out and the earth piled outward to make yet another barrier for the enemy to overcome. The men grumbled at this last measure, as it was backbreaking work for little gain as they saw it. The ditch would stop no one, on that point all agreed. It was pointed out however, that the ditch and mound would slow the enemy just as they reached the defenders' ideal range for making best use of their archers. Unless the attackers were supremely well organised, they would pay an expensive toll in crossing that ditch.

Today's rota designated Jenna to weapons training in the morning and out on patrol in the afternoon. She would have enjoyed the training had the burning desire to embark on her quest not been so strong. Eloise was fast becoming a good friend, and Fesha, Marcos and the other new recruits were good company, bringing fresh humour and seemingly unstoppable enthusiasm.

Sword drill with Eloise had become a fairly regular part of her practice now, and there was no doubt that training with the lithe, raven-haired beauty was improving Jenna's blade work markedly. It was a shame that the captains were not yet allowing the recruits out on patrol with the regular troops, Jenna mused, as she re-adjusted the position of her heavy pack again. Their excitement and enthusiasm for 'action', as they saw it, would have made this gruelling slog through the hills less tiresome if the patrol party had been injected with a little zeal. Instead, everyone trudged along the roads and paths in the resigned knowledge that in their four to five hours of patrolling they were likely to see nothing more exciting than a few stray sheep or cows.

No one had spotted any sign of the Shandese in over a week, and levels of alertness were gradually dropping despite the exhortations of the Corporals and Sergeants.

It was about half way around the patrol that Jenna, together with many others, wished she had paid the pleas more heed.

The enemy marauders were on top of the patrol even as the first warning call of 'ambush' was raised. They came in a rush from the higher ground to the right of the road, giving the patrol virtually no time to form any sort of defensive formation, and their charge made the sort of image that nightmares are made of.

Werebeasts, goblins and evil-looking lizard men ran alongside trolls and twisted ape-like creatures that loped with ground-eating bounds towards them. All were armed with a variety of spiked, barbed and hooked weapons. The larger creatures favoured great curved scimitars and mighty looking clubs, whilst still others carried whips and throwing nets designed to incapacitate rather than maim or kill.

Corporal Alana was quick to react to the situation, but not nearly fast enough. The enemy had a fair, but not huge advantage of numbers. However, the element of surprise had been used to devastating effect and the majority of the patrol was overrun in seconds.

Two knots of fighters formed defensive stands, one around

Alana, and one that Demarr had pulled together. Jenna found herself separated from both and fighting all the harder for it. For a few moments she battled her way towards the Corporal's nearby group, only to be forced back. There had been no time to release any more than a couple of arrows and then Jenna suddenly found herself glad of all her recent sword drill. There was no space for archery here, and despite her newfound confidence with a sword these gruesome opponents were pressing her hard.

The decision that Jenna made to run from the battle could easily have been attributed to fear, or to her desire to escape the Baron's army and pursue her destiny elsewhere. In the end though, it was a practical decision, made to make the best use of her skills.

Ducking under a sweeping swing of the great studded club being wielded by the evil-looking troll who faced her, Jenna lunged, driving her blade into the creature's stomach. Even as it cried out, she whirled on her heels and sprinted off the side of the road. Bounding down the open hillside, Jenna made for the wooded area at the base of the hill. Instantly she knew that she was being pursued, but by what, or how many, she dared not look to see.

Weaving as she ran, Jenna dodged between rocks and raced through bracken at breakneck pace. Stretching her legs and concentrating solely on where she was going, she put all her skill and speed as a runner to good use. Running with a pack and belt pouches was hard enough, but holding her bow in one hand and sword in the other proved too precarious. Not having the luxury to stop and sheathe her sword, nor the skill to sheathe it while running, Jenna elected to cast it aside and keep her bow.

Now less encumbered and absolutely flying down the hillside with her legs only just keeping pace with her forward momentum, Jenna had no time at all to compensate when her ankle turned slightly in an unseen hole. As her upper body overtook her legs, she twisted her long bow horizontally across in front of her and flattened herself into a forward dive. To the amazement of her pursuers, and with the agility of a gymnast, Jenna tucked into a forward roll as she hit the floor, rolling straight up onto her feet and running on with no perceptible loss of forward speed.

By the time she reached the tree line at the base of the hill, Jenna sensed that she had built a small lead over the enemy and decided to assess the odds. Grabbing at a young tree as she reached it, she used the relatively narrow trunk to help spin at speed around to face the enemy. There were three of them – all closing fast.

Chest heaving, Jenna whipped out an arrow, nocked it, drew and released in one easy motion. To its credit, her intended target saw the arrow coming, and despite its uncontrollable forward momentum, the charging lizard-man managed to twist such that the arrow merely sliced its arm. However, the manoeuvre cost the beast its balance and it fell awkwardly, rolling and bouncing down the last few yards of the slope.

The second arrow, released within seconds of the first, found its mark squarely in the middle of a hideous looking goblin's chest. The thudding impact punched the creature from its feet and it did not move from where it fell.

There was no time for a third arrow as the final pursuer was already upon her. The beast looked like a form of werewolf with its elongated snout, sharp canine teeth and fur-covered face and hands. Tall as Jenna was, the werebeast was slightly taller, and it sprang at her with all the speed it had gathered in its charging pursuit, swinging a broad curving scimitar even as it leapt.

Instinct and training gave Jenna the clarity of thought to survive the beast's assault. Even as the werewolf leapt, Jenna cast her bow from her left hand, drew her dagger with her right and, ducking under the deadly scimitar, drove her short blade home up through the beast's solar plexus and deep into its vital organs. Unfortunately, the weight and speed of the mortally wounded beast wrenched the dagger's handle from her hand, and she suddenly found herself unarmed with the lizard-man that she had wounded first now regaining its feet.

There was no time for a plan. It was kill or be killed. Shrugging her pack from her shoulders, Jenna ran forward and launched a stinging drop kick, which landed squarely on the creature's scale covered face. The beast's head snapped to one side with the impact and it roared with pain... but it did not go down.

The lizard-man too was unarmed, having lost its weapon during its tumbling fall. Now it sprang forward again with surprising speed to stamp at Jenna's midriff as she had not had a chance to recover to her feet after the drop kick had left her flat on the ground.

Twisting and rolling to gain a low fighting crouch, Jenna narrowly avoided being stamped on only to take a chopping blow to the shoulder. Before the lizard-man could follow up on the blow, Jenna responded with a stinging uppercut, which again landed on the creature's chin. Then with equal speed she jumped back out of its reach again.

'Fassst... very fassst! Thissss ssshould be an interesssting contessst,' the lizard-man hissed, its reptilian tongue vibrating outside its scaled lip-less mouth.

Jenna did not bother replying, but launched again into an all-out attack, her hands and feet a blur of rapidly delivered blows. Some connected, but the majority were blocked and she quickly found herself defending as much as attacking. Her opponent counter-attacked with similar speed and skill to her own, only with more weight and power behind the kicks and punches. Taking a blow to the left side of the body, Jenna felt the burning pain as one or more of her ribs cracked, and a second blow to the side of her face forced her to make an evasive diving roll to gain some distance from her opponent.

Gritting her teeth against the pain, she crouched poised for the follow-up attack. It was not long coming and another rapid exchange of blows ended with the lizard-man landing another stunning blow that spun her off her feet and left her laying dazed on her uninjured side.

With a strange hiss that Jenna interpreted as some sort of a laugh, the lizard-man strolled in for the kill. Jenna had other ideas. With a last ditch surge of adrenaline she rolled towards the creature and drove her foot upward with every ounce of force she could muster, the toe of her boot pointed straight into the creature's groin. The impact was satisfyingly solid and accurate. A low groaning hiss emitted from the lizard-man's throat as he doubled over in pain, and with a strength that Jenna had not realised she possessed, she followed up with a vicious, driving punch into the creature's throat.

The punch proved the killing blow as it crushed the beast's windpipe, leaving it unable to breathe. However, Jenna was in no mood to celebrate her victory. Her broken ribs made drawing breath difficult, and she could already feel her face swelling as well as various other tender areas where she had taken hard blows. Her knuckles were bloodied and swollen. It would be some days before she would have pain-free use of her fingers, she realised, grimacing as she extended and folded them experimentally.

The main fight up on the road was still continuing to rage furiously and Jenna could just distinguish groups of her fellow soldiers valiantly battling against the odds. With a pang of guilt and regret, she realised that there was no way that she could rejoin her compatriots now. Even if she slogged her way back up the hill, Jenna was in no fit state to fight again, so the time of choice was upon her. Should she go back to the pre-arranged rendezvous point to try and meet up with the rest of the patrol members who survived the ambush? Or should she take this opportunity to set out on the journey that her heart yearned to make?

Jenna had thought that this would be an easy decision, one that she would make without hesitation. In the event, she agonised for some time and then continued to question her choice for weeks afterwards.

Jenna recovered her belongings even while debating if her duty to the Baron and the rest of her squad should outweigh the chance of helping Calvyn to escape his captivity. On picking up her backpack, she could have sworn that it had doubled in weight as she gingerly hoisted the straps over her shoulders, and she doubted that her bruised fingers could draw the great akar wood bow that she had recovered from the long grass where it had landed. Lastly, she wrenched her bloody dagger from the werebeast's chest and wiped it as clean as she could on some nearby fern leaves. Then, with her mind made up, Jenna walked determinedly into the woods.

'Hang on, Calvyn. I'm on my way,' she muttered. Then, slightly louder, and with a ring of challenge she continued. 'You'd better exist, old man. You'd better exist.'

CHAPTER 8

Jenna awoke with a yell and began to scrabble from her blankets, her heart pounding in fear... and the horse that had nuzzled her with its nose whilst she slept, shied away and whinnied at Jenna's shout. Collapsing back to the floor in relief, and laughing as she realised that her momentary terror had been caused by nothing more than an inquisitive old cart horse, Jenna grimaced up at the animal, her previously forgotten cracked ribs now causing her considerable pain again.

'You gave me quite a turn there, old girl,' Jenna said in a gentle, soothing voice, whilst carefully easing her body into a more comfortable position.

The horse regarded her suspiciously and blew a long shuddering snort.

'Yes, well I'm sorry I yelled like that, but what do you expect if you go frightening people from their sleep?' Jenna continued, seeing the funny side of the situation.

With slow deliberation the huge dappled grey horse raised one of its front legs and then stamped its massive hoof down hard.

'Are you trying to tell me I overslept?' Jenna laughed, and then chuckled even more as the horse whinnied again and nodded its head. 'Oh, don't make me laugh... it hurts too much.'

Groaning and putting her hands to rub at her lower back, Jenna dragged herself upright. Kneading the muscles just below her kidney area with her fingers and rolling her head around in slow circles to stretch the stiffness from her neck, she then gently probed at her ribs with her fingers and winced at the pain she invoked.

The cold night had held the promise of an early winter, which was not a pleasant thought to Jenna with the prospect of a journey into the Vortaff Mountains ahead of her. Even with all the extras that she had managed to harbour in her pack and pouches, Jenna knew all too well that she did not have enough equipment to survive in that hostile environment.

'It's a shame that I can't take you along really,' Jenna said, wistfully addressing the horse again as she stripped the canvas poncho from where it had been sheltering her packs from the morning dew. 'I could do with a horse, but I am not going to steal you away from your owner.'

The horse ignored her, chewing instead at the lush green grass in a leisurely fashion.

A little while later, after a meagre breakfast of oat cake and a cup of dahl that she had heated in her quickly rekindled fire, Jenna very carefully eased her backpack straps over her shoulders and secured all of her belt pouches in place. The solid-looking grey horse had watched her preparations disinterestedly as she had repacked her bags and scattered the remains of her fire before covering the small fire-pit with moist earth.

'Cheerio, old girl,' Jenna said to the horse, patting its neck affectionately as she made her move from the campsite.

Jenna walked gingerly away from the small copse of trees that had been her shelter overnight. Gradually, little by little, she lengthened her stride as she managed to settle the pack more comfortably on her back. However, the old horse, it seemed, was not going to be left behind so easily. Jenna had not taken more than a hundred paces or so before she realised that the animal was following her. With a sigh, she stopped, turned and addressed the horse once more.

'Stop where you are, horse. I'm in enough trouble as it is without adding "horse thief" to my list of crimes. Go home.'

Jenna knew it was ridiculous talking to a horse as if it were human, but she had not spoken to a soul since making the decision not to attempt to rejoin her comrades. Although that had only been the previous day, her need to talk was strong, even if it was only to an animal. 'Besides, horses are quite intelligent creatures really,' she rationalised. 'It may understand some vocal commands, particularly those relating to the functions of its work.'

With this in mind, Jenna tried some commands as she backed slowly away from the horse.

'Stop! Whoa, there. Halt. Stay,' she said firmly, altering her tone and pitch to try to convey her authority over the animal.

The horse stopped... and as soon as Jenna turned her back on the animal it began to follow again. Several times more, Jenna tried to dissuade the horse from following without success. Eventually, with a slight shrug of defeat she just concentrated on walking and tried to ignore the great grey animal trailing along behind her.

After half a day or so of walking across the open countryside the horse was still there, nonchalantly wandering at her heels like a faithful old dog. Unwilling as she was to invite more trouble, Jenna's cracked ribs were hurting so much by this stage that she no longer cared about the outcome.

'OK, old girl. You win. Come over here.'

Jenna had been thinking for hours about what she would do if she did keep the horse. It was not saddled. Nor was it wearing a bridle or reins. Mounting and dismounting even with stirrups would have been difficult enough in her present injured state, but with the horse bareback and Jenna carrying packs it would be nigh on impossible. Impossible, that is, unless she could somehow virtually step onto the horse's back.

For the previous hour or so now, Jenna had been looking for just such a place, and here it was. A tree had been felled from a hedgerow leaving an elevated stump. It had been a bit of a scramble, but Jenna had managed to climb up the bank of the hedgerow and then step up onto the stump. Now if she could just get the horse to stand in the right place.

'Here, girl. Come on... over here. That's it. Steady now. Steady!'

140

Grabbing a handful of the horse's mane, Jenna swung her right leg over its broad back and plopped down with a jarring thump to sit astride the great horse. The horse did not move so much as an inch as Jenna laid back to rest her backpack against its rump. Quickly she worked at lengthening her shoulder straps so that the weight of the pack would sit on the horse's back instead of Jenna's shoulders. With the straps lengthened to maximum extension, Jenna sat back up and adjusted the backpack until it was comfortable.

'Good girl,' she said thankfully and patted the horse's neck. 'Come on then. Let's get going. We've got a long walk ahead.

*   *   *   *   *

Corporal Alana was not looking forward to delivering her report to the Captains upon her imminent return to the castle. The bedraggled ragtag bunch of soldiers that remained of what had been a forty-strong patrol, were in a sorry state. Not one was uninjured, and Alana had begun to rue her decision to keep the survivors out overnight. With hindsight, searching the battle site for survivors would have been better left to a fresh patrol. However, the job was done, and Alana would at least be able to present a complete report, no matter how galling the content.

The castle gates opened long before Alana and the others reached them, and the medics' team of helpers came sprinting out with several stretchers. What made the whole situation even more difficult to stomach was that the large camp of troops from other Lords' forces were all witnessing her ignominious return.

Stopping the patrol briefly to allow the worst of the wounded to be loaded onto the stretchers, Alana then formed the remainder back into three ranks and marched them on towards the gates. The stretcher-bearers, with their patients strapped safely into their stretchers, quickly overtook Alana and her patrol, running at a steady jog to transport their injured passengers to the medics as fast as they could.

Alana could see Sergeants Derra, Dren and Capello waiting at the gates. Captain Tegrani was with them and, not surprisingly, his face was grim.

Alana saluted the Captain as she approached the gate. Tegrani returned the compliment.

'Are you wounded, Corporal?' the Captain asked, noting the various tears in her uniform.

'Just a few shallow cuts, sir. Nothing serious,' she replied, not wishing to delay the inevitable.

'Very well. Dismiss the patrol and have those who need to see the medics report to them at once. I'd say that would be just about all of them by the look of it,' he said, as he surveyed the soldiers with a slight wince. 'Then we'll debrief in Sergeant Dren's office, as that's closest.'

'Yes, sir,' Alana acknowledged, saluting smartly again.

With a display of energy that she did not feel, Alana whirled in an immaculately precise about turn.

'Patrol, dis… miss,' she yelled.

The eighteen remaining soldiers performed a forty five degree right turn and then broke formation to hobble, limp and walk gingerly across to the medics' treatment room. Alana followed the Captain and the three Sergeants with some trepidation around the corner to Dren's office. Captain Tegrani took the seat behind Dren's desk and Sergeant Derra closed the door behind Alana as she entered.

The Captain got straight to the point. 'Report, Corporal,' he stated in a neutral voice.

'Well, sir, as you have probably already deduced we were ambushed during yesterday's patrol. The enemy hit us from above, on the hillside where the Ravenshome Road curves around the side of Rowantop Peak…'

'From the open ground?' the Captain asked, with a touch of surprise in his voice.

Alana nodded. 'Yes, sir. They were either very well camouflaged, or some form of magic cloaked them. Whichever it was they were on top of us before we had a chance to react and they looked like something out of a child's nightmare.'

The Captain raised one eyebrow quizzically and Dren glanced across at Derra with a look that told Alana that this was not totally unexpected news, but no one interrupted.

'They looked like trolls and werewolves, goblins and lizard-men... all sorts of weird creatures from someone's twisted imagination. I estimate that there were about sixty to seventy of them. They weren't real of course, but I'm getting ahead of myself. The ambush was so well timed that we had no chance to get into any sort of defensive formation. I managed to gather about a dozen or so around me and Demarr got about fifteen into another group. The rest were scattered or killed. It was strange really, because the attackers appeared intent on taking captives rather than killing. I saw several being dragged off in nets.'

'That *is* strange,' Tegrani said thoughtfully and glanced across at the Sergeants, who all looked as nonplussed as he did. 'In the past the raiders have merely killed and moved on. The only other possible captive that we know of was Corporal Calvyn, and that was never confirmed. How many did they take?' he asked.

'Well, sir, we think that they got eight. Certainly we have eight unaccounted for. We were really tightly engaged when the opportunity arose for me to break my group out of the fight. I managed to signal my intent to Demarr and his group broke free at the same time. We managed to scatter quickly enough to throw the enemy into confusion and they didn't bother to pursue us. Those of us who got clear made our way to the last nominated rendezvous point. Twenty-three of us made it there. Some were in quite a bad way. With hindsight we should have come straight back to the castle, but I wasn't willing to leave possible survivors without any hope of help for a full day.'

'You could have at least sent a runner back with news, Corporal. Other patrols may have benefited from that information.'

'I thought about that, sir. My reasoning at the time was that by none of us returning it sent the direst message of all by default. I really felt that I needed all the able-bodied that I had left to complete my task.'

The Captain scratched at his chin thoughtfully for a moment. 'Well,' he said carefully, 'the point can be argued at length later. Continue your report.'

'Those that were too badly wounded to reconnoitre the battle site, I left to get some rest and set up a temporary camp. The remainder came with me to scout Rowantop Hill as covertly as we could.'

Alana's eyes were distant as she relived that trek.

'We climbed Rowantop from the far side and remained hidden among the trees at the summit until dusk, watching for any movement. Nothing stirred at all, so as the sun was setting we descended to the road and searched through the bodies for any survivors. Unfortunately, there were none. Nine of the bodies were members of my patrol, the rest were those of Shandese men wearing a strange livery. They certainly weren't members of the regular Shandese army... unless they've changed their uniform of course. What's more, they definitely looked nothing like the hideous beasts that had attacked us only a few hours before. The whole goblin army thing was all some sort of elaborate illusion. But I'll say one thing for it, it was *very* convincing at the time.'

The Sergeants had all remained quiet until now, so Dren's gruff voice made Alana start slightly when he interrupted her with some questions.

'Did you see a Magician at all during the fighting, Alana? A figure dressed in black? Maybe hooded with a long cloak?'

Alana shook her head. 'No. Nothing like that, Sergeant, but to be honest I was concentrating pretty hard on just staying alive. We were pretty badly outnumbered and taken by surprise, despite the knowledge that the Shandese routinely use magic.'

'So who were the dead, and who is missing?' Sergeant Derra asked, her voice sounding harsh, even compared with the gruff voice of Sergeant Dren.

Alana recited the names of the dead and explained that there were too many to carry back to the castle, so they had buried them by the roadside.

'The missing soldiers are Demarr, Rand, Jenna, Garath, Soffi, Tarkon, Bakra and Fex. It is possible that we could have missed the odd one or two in the half-light, but I really don't think that we did. We searched the whole area thoroughly and there was no sign of any of them.'

Derra's eyes had narrowed slightly at the mention of Jenna's name as one of the missing, but she said nothing in front of the others. The drilling stare that Alana was getting from the hard-faced Sergeant was enough to tell her that there would be more questions later. Her instincts were not wrong.

Alana rounded off the report, explaining that by the time they had buried their dead and returned to the campsite set up by the rest of the patrol, even the fittest of the patrol were exhausted. Therefore, the survivors had rested there overnight and had risen shortly after dawn to get back to the castle as early as possible.

'How many enemy dead did you count, Corporal?' the Captain asked, having noticed that she had omitted this fact.

'We found twenty-six, sir,' Alana said without emotion.

'Twenty-six! And you lost only nine – impressive,' the Captain stated, clearly pleased.

'Well, seventeen really, sir. If you count the missing, that is,' Alana replied.

'Yes, of course,' Tegrani said quickly. 'But you can't be held totally to blame for that. Taking captives is not a tactic that the Shandese have been routinely employing up to now, and we have no clues yet as to why they want these people, unless you have learned any more?'

'No, sir. I'm afraid not.'

'What did you do with the enemy dead?'

'There were too many for us to bury and there was not enough wood up by the road to make a pyre. None of us were in a fit state to collect wood from the woods in the valley or from the hilltop, so in the end we had to just drag them into piles a little way off the road. I'm afraid that it was the best we could do.'

'Understandable,' the Captain agreed. 'I'll send a patrol out to deal with it. I don't want to leave bodies decaying around the countryside, as that is just the sort of thing that starts disease. We have enough to handle right now without inviting a plague to hit us as well.'

The Captain paused for a moment to ponder all that he had heard and then pushed himself positively to his feet. 'Have you anything to add to your report, Corporal?' the Captain asked suddenly.

'No, sir, at least not that I can think of right now,' Alana replied.

'Very well then, I won't pretend that I'm totally happy with your decision to remain out overnight, but I understand it. In future, Corporal, if you have so few people left after a fight that you can't even spare a runner to report, then you're not to consider any action other than getting back somewhere to reinforce your squad. Have I made myself clear on that?'

'Yes, sir.'

'Good. Now go and see the medics and get cleaned up. I need to talk to the Baron but I may call for you again later if I think of further questions.'

Captain Tegrani was out of the door almost before Alana had managed to throw her hand up into a salute. As soon as the door closed behind the Captain, she let out a sigh of relief that the mild reprimand was all that he had seen fit to give her. Sergeants Dren and Capello left the room hard on the heels of the Captain, but Derra stayed.

'Tell me one thing, Alana,' Derra growled dangerously when she was sure the others were out of earshot. 'Did you see Jenna taken? Or do you think that she's gone off on this damned dream quest of hers? The truth please.'

Alana looked Derra squarely in the eyes.

'The truth... I don't know for sure. Jenna got cut off from the two main groups early in the fight. I saw her run from the fight being followed by at least three of the enemy. It was a good decision from where she was, as several others who didn't run paid with their freedom or their lives. When we scouted the lower hillside in the direction that she ran in, we did find three bodies – all male. One man at least was definitely killed by Jenna, as one of her arrows was through his heart. I'd recognise the fletching on her arrows anywhere. The second died of a stab wound to the chest and the third appeared to have asphyxiated. His larynx was crushed. Jenna could have killed all three and escaped only to be captured or killed by another band that the rest of us didn't see. I would be speculating heavily if I were to suggest that this was what happened, but she didn't show up at the rendezvous point, so I really don't know.'

Derra's eyes narrowed slightly as she assimilated the facts. Then with a slight chuckle she shrugged her shoulders and shook her head slowly.

'Well, whatever happened, she has given herself a good alibi for a while. Let's hope that Jenna finds what she seeks, and if she returns that she can spin a good enough yarn to prevent the Baron from branding her as a deserter. Come on, Alana. You look dead on your feet. I'll walk with you to the medics and you can fill in a bit more of the detail of this fight.

*   *   *   *   *

Calvyn had the ominous feeling that something very bad was about to happen.

He had been led from the cell where he had been held hooded and blindfolded again for what seemed like an age after his encounter with the Lords of the Inner Eye. This time, though, the guards did not lead Calvyn to the hall where the Lords had gathered before, but down many flights of steps to a place that he surmised to be deep underground.

When he had finally arrived in what proved to be a deep subterranean cavern, the guards had once again removed his blindfold and hood to reveal the black-cloaked figures awaiting him. However, the Lords were not alone. Standing to one side of the familiar figures in black was a huge mountain of a man. A full three hands taller than Calvyn, the veritable giant was barrel-chested and more than just a little overweight. A bulbous nose protruded from his rounded face and his mass of greying black hair was unkempt and wild. For some reason he was red-faced and sweating profusely, though he did not appear out of breath from physical exertion.

'Strange,' Calvyn thought. 'He can't be hot. The temperature down here is cool enough to store unsalted meat for days.'

Torches set in metal holders in the solid rock walls of the

cavern cast their flickering orange light around the chamber, causing shadows to leap and dance with a life of their own. The constantly moving shadows pulled at Calvyn's peripheral vision with an almost magnetic attraction, but determinedly he focused his attention on the people standing in front of him.

Goosebumps rose on Calvyn's arms and he shuddered slightly. He did not feel particularly cold, but his apprehension was growing fast. He thought about turning and making a run for it, but even as the thought occurred, the large wooden door to the cavern thudded closed with an echoing finality behind the departing guards. They had not stayed a second longer than needed to complete their task, a fact that did not go unnoticed by Calvyn as he watched the large, sweating man rub his podgy hands down the sides of his vast tunic.

'Very well, Barrathos. Let us begin,' the High Lord announced.

Barrathos wrung his hands together and wiped them against his tunic again, looking around at the waiting Lords nervously.

'You are sure that I cannot persuade you to change your mind, High Lord Vallaine? This is a desperately dangerous summoning and I cannot guarantee your safety,' Barrathos said, wiping a sleeve across his forehead in a vain effort to staunch the flow of sweat.

'Do not fear for our safety, Barrathos. We will look after ourselves. Just tell us what you need us to do and then begin the summoning,' replied Vallaine, his voice emanating his self-assurance and confidence.

Barrathos looked around at the other Lords of the Inner Eye, but whether he could see anything of them under their deep hoods, Calvyn could not tell. Then the large man glanced at Calvyn for a bare instant before reaching into his belt pouch and withdrawing a soft cloth bag. It might have been his imagination, but Calvyn could have sworn that there was a hint of apology in that glance.

'High Lord Vallaine, exalted Lords, please listen very carefully. There is little that you can do to assist me in this summoning – that is the easy part. It is the controlling and the dispelling that will demand the combined focus of all our wills. All, that is, except you, Torvados. Your job is to ensure the young man there does not move. If he or anyone else here breaks the circle that I'm about to draw during the time the demon is present, then you had better hope that whatever deity you worship has a personal interest in you. Believe me, there isn't much short of a god that could stop a gorvath otherwise.'

'Consider it done, Barrathos,' Torvados said curtly.

For Calvyn it was as if someone had nailed his feet to the floor and tied his hands by his sides. He was fully conscious, but he no longer had any control over his limbs. Try as he might, he could not move a muscle, and could only watch in growing horror as Barrathos cut a tiny hole in the bottom of the cloth bag and carefully paced around Calvyn in a wide circle. As Barrathos walked around, a tiny trickle of sparkling powder fell from the bag, eventually forming an unbroken line of the strangely luminescent dust on the floor.

'The circle is complete,' Barrathos boomed, his voice now stronger, more powerful in the knowledge that he must now control this situation or die. 'Providing no one breaks the circle, the demon will be contained within it. Note that I say contained, not controlled. You want the demon to devour this young man's soul without harming his body and that will take great control. A gorvath will not bend to man's will easily. Be strong – be of one mind. To send it back before its appetite has been sated will be yet more difficult. It would take many souls to satiate this creature, so to offer it a tasty morsel and then attempt to deny it a feast will be the greatest test. If you can provide a unified resolve, I will be able to give it the final shove through the gate. Fail and at least some of us will die – probably all.'

Calvyn's heart was threatening to run up his throat, it was hammering so hard. 'Demon... devour his soul.' The words were like swords cutting at him and yet no matter how hard he tried, Calvyn just could not move so much as a whisker in any direction. Panic robbed his mind of clarity. He desperately needed to think of a spell, any spell, to get him out of this situation... and fast.

'One final word of warning,' Barrathos was saying, the booming voice demanding attention from all. 'Beware of the eyes.'

The old Wizard paused for effect.

'Never look a demon in the eyes, for therein lies its power. If it makes eye contact with you... you are held in its power and only a mind of indomitable strength could ever hope to break that hold. My suggestion is that you close your eyes or look at the floor, your feet, the roof of the cavern, anywhere but at the gorvath throughout the summoning. Aside from the obvious danger of being caught in its power, there is little point in looking at it anyway. The gorvath is a shape-shifter. It is highly unlikely to appear in its true form, so you will miss out on nothing.'

Barrathos wiped the sweat from his forehead again and cleared his throat noisily.

'Is everyone ready?' the Wizard asked.

Calvyn wanted to cry out for them to stop, to ask why they were doing this to him, to do anything to prevent the whole bizarre situation from progressing any further, but he was held completely powerless.

'We are ready,' Vallaine confirmed.

Closing his eyes in concentration, Barrathos held his arms out wide in front of him, his fingers splayed. Then, in a deep guttural language that Calvyn had never heard before, the huge man began to chant.

At first nothing happened, and Calvyn found that he was almost hypnotised by the strange recitation. The chant sounded repetitious, but in fact no two stanzas were exactly the same. Each was subtly different from the last, with one, or sometimes two altered syllables teasing the listener's mind with their changes.

Gradually, Calvyn became aware that something was happening. A shimmering, not unlike a heat haze but localised, was starting to distort the air no more than three or four paces in front of him.

Panic escalated in Calvyn's mind as he frantically grasped for ideas. Then it finally occurred to him to create the magical barrier that he had used in the battle at Mantor. Grabbing hold of this positive idea, Calvyn realised that he had not got much time left with which to make it work. With iron determination he forced his mind to calm down enough to mentally pronounce and picture the runes, and it did not take long before the spell began to take effect. A glowing green bubble of magical energy formed around him, and he reinforced it with rune after rune, drawing energy from everything around him.

The barrier was in place not a second too soon, for where the shimmering haze had been only moments before, a grey amorphous 'something' was forming. Shifting and changing like a great grey piece of dough being moulded by huge unseen hands, the sinister blob grew rapidly until it dwarfed Calvyn with its immensity.

To ignore the grey heaving mass totally was impossible, but now that Calvyn had decided on his defence, he committed every last ounce of his strength and energy to making it as impregnable as possible. The barrier fizzed and popped with magical energy as he poured more and more into it.

Then, with a startling suddenness, the grey mass coalesced into the shape of a great bear. However, it was like no bear that Calvyn had ever seen, or even heard of before. For a start the creature had heavy overlapping scales instead of fur, and its great curving claws and inwardly curving teeth were like none that naturally occurred in this world.

The creature roared in fury and it seemed to Calvyn that even the depths of the cavern could not possibly contain that mighty sound. Inadvertently, Calvyn glanced up at the demon's face. He had not meant to do it, but the sound of the creature's unrestrained fury had been so intense that his eyes had moved unconsciously to the source of that ear-splitting bellow.

Eyes held him.

Eyes that were burning red with an inner glow of evil - evil and a driving, savage hunger which boiled and raged with an intensity that was incomprehensible to the human mind.

Calvyn tried to rip his gaze from the demon's hypnotic red eyes, but it was too late. They were like holes into another world – a burning, savage world of fire and lust, evil and pain.

He was trapped, held still by the mental power of Torvados and now engaged in a battle of wills with a powerful demon. He had no idea how to fight either of them. It was a battle that he could never hope to win.

The creature moved closer. One step... then another. It roared again in frustration as the combined wills of the Wizard and the Sorcerer Lords controlled its progress. However, even in the midst of its fury at being held in check, the demon never allowed its gaze to wander from its young victim.

Closing on its prey, the demon appeared either unaware or unconcerned at the hissing, spitting barrier of glowing magical energy that still surrounded its intended quarry. With a realisation of indescribable terror, Calvyn discovered why. The demon reached its great claws towards him and to his horror they passed through his magical barrier as if it had never existed.

Calvyn felt Torvados release his mental grip, but it no longer mattered. As the great claws gently touched him he was lost. Spinning and tumbling, falling and flying, Calvyn's memories flashed and spun before him, seemingly sucked into the great grey creature's open maw. Then... there was nothing.

Vallaine allowed himself a small twitch of a smile as he felt the first phase of his plan come to fruition. The old Wizard had been right. Holding this creature would have been virtually impossible for a single man, but with eleven of them doing the holding and Barrathos to steer their combined strength, the task was not proving to be as difficult as he had imagined. With a surge of power the Sorcerers forced the creature away from Calvyn, denying it the final kill, and it roared and snarled its frustration once more.

Barrathos began again to chant the guttural syllables to bind the creature, as the group prepared to hurl it back to its own world.

Then disaster struck.

Torvados, now effectively redundant, having released Calvyn to the power of the demon, sought to aid his fellow Sorcerers by adding his will to theirs. Unfortunately, the unexpected thrust of his mental power unbalanced the others and for an instant their grip slipped. It was only for a fraction of a second, but it was enough.

The creature's head snapped around just as one of the Lords glanced up, having felt his mental hold slip. The two locked eyes.

'Reth! No!' Vallaine gasped, feeling the man's horror through their link.

Before anyone else could react, Reth had stepped forward, called by the demon. There was a flash as he broke the line of the circle and Barrathos' chant stuttered to a spluttering halt.

Another roar split the air, this time a great bellow of triumph as the combined wills of the Lords of the Inner Eye crumbled and the demon leapt forward, free of their smothering power. A second later and Reth was dead, the great curving claws tearing through his body like a hot knife through butter.

Fear swept the room. Fear and panic.

Only Vallaine kept his head, and even as his fellow Lords scattered before the great beast, he rallied them with a shout that was both mental and verbal.

'Hold it, you fools! Hold the beast with your minds or we're all lost.'

Torvados died next, the curving claws gouging great tears through his upper torso. The creature was not feeding, merely venting its frustration in a spree of killing.

'Join with me, everyone. Now,' Vallaine ordered, a desperate edge in his voice.

One by one, minds joined with him in directing the combined power of their wills to attempt to control the gorvath once more. The Sorcerers were strong of mind and the demon sensed the growing force gathering against it. Defiant and hungry for revenge as it was, the gorvath was also intelligent. It quickly realised that if these men all combined their wills, then once again it would find itself held in their power.

With a last roar of its great voice, the gorvath charged at the heavy wooden doors that were the only exit from the cavern. With hardly a pause, the demon smashed through the doors with unstoppable momentum and made its escape up the stairs at a pace that belied its great bulk.

Lord Vallaine heaved a sigh of relief and looked around to find the remaining members of the Inner Eye slowly walking back out from the corners to which they had run. Barrathos was on his knees, not having moved from where he had been conducting the summoning. He was sobbing quietly, great tears mingled with the sweat already streaking his face.

Calvyn had also not moved. The magical barrier that Calvyn had created was still crackling with an energy that Vallaine found fascinating, but the young man was completely still and staring vacantly into space.

Curious, High Lord Vallaine walked slowly around until he was facing Calvyn from just outside the glowing field of force surrounding him. At first, Calvyn showed no sign of being aware of Vallaine's presence. Then, slowly, his eyes focused in on the wizened old figure in the dark robe.

'Who am I?' Calvyn asked slowly. 'What am I doing here?'

Vallaine's mouth twitched into a smile under the deep cowl and he could scarcely keep his pleasure from his voice as he answered.

'You are Lord Shanier, a member of the Inner Eye, and you have had quite a day.'

CHAPTER 9

Jenna shivered as another icy gust of wind sliced through her clothing. It had been a difficult two weeks of travelling. Her ribs still stabbed her with sharp pain if she bent or twisted in certain ways, which had made the daily challenge of mounting and dismounting her 'acquired' horse particularly difficult. The other bruising and swelling around Jenna's face, hands and various other parts of her body that she had gained during the fight had all but healed. However, even the cracked ribs troubled her less than the threat of injury from the cold up here in the Vortaff Mountains.

Cold was a subtle killer.

Jenna only knew a little of the theory about how cold could inflict damage on the human body, but she knew enough to be on her guard against the obvious symptoms of hypothermia and frostbite. Some of her knowledge had been gained during her recruit training. The rest had been gleaned from a conversation in a tavern that Jenna had stopped at the night before starting up the Knife Edge Pass.

The conversation had not been of Jenna's instigation. A man by the name of Reeve had approached her at the table where she had been quietly enjoying a bowl of the thick, chunky stew recommended by the Innkeeper. The warming meal and the mug of mead that Jenna had been supping slowly had relaxed her to the point that her head had started to nod in weariness. The flickering flames of the fire in the hearth had crackled their whispering lullaby into her ears as they licked across the large oak logs, and the low mumble of conversations around the large taproom had only served to increase her drowsiness.

'Hello there. May I join you?' the stranger had asked boldly, making Jenna start, as she had not heard him approach.

'I suppose so,' Jenna had replied warily, eyeing the lean, weather-beaten stranger suspiciously.

'Thanks,' he said with a slight smile, and turning a chair around so that the back of it was in front of him, he had sat astride the chair with his arms folded across the top of the back. 'The name's Reeve.'

'Jenna,' she replied, and then wondered if she would have been better giving a false name.

It was too late to take it back.

'You heading up into the mountains?' Reeve had asked, not looking at Jenna for a response but seemingly focused on watching the fire.

'What's it to you if I am?'

'I just thought that you might need a guide. I'm the best there is. You don't need to take my word for it – ask anyone. If you want a guide in this part of the Vortaffs, I'm your man.'

'I don't need a guide, thanks. I know precisely where I'm going. Besides, I couldn't afford to hire a guide even if I wanted one, so I'm afraid you're wasting your time with a sales pitch.'

The man had glanced at her and shrugged slightly.

'Well you can't blame me for trying. There's not many as travel into the mountains with winter drawing in. Only the foolish and the extremely hardy travel in the Vortaffs at this time of year, so guides are not in great demand.'

Reeve paused slightly.

'Which are you I wonder?' he added softly.

'Pardon?'

'Oh, I'm sorry. I didn't mean any offence. I didn't mean to say that out loud. It just kind of slipped out.'

'None taken,' Jenna said grudgingly, but she was not at all sure that she meant it, nor was she sure that she liked this self-assured mountain guide in the slightest.

'It's just that many of the people that I guide through the

mountains don't have a clue about even the most basic of dangers. Of course they know of avalanches and rockfalls – well they know that they are a danger, but often not how to avoid them, or protect against them. What most are unaware of though are the subtle dangers: hypothermia, frostbite, trench foot, snow-blindness and other cold induced or cold enhanced injuries.'

Jenna had vaguely remembered some of the very basic principles from her recruit days, though she had never even heard of snow-blindness. So with a subtlety of her own, she had drawn the guide to reveal some of his knowledge. Pandering to the man's obvious ego and buying him a couple of drinks had worked wonders. It had even been quite easy to get rid of him when Jenna felt she had learned as much useful information as Reeve was going to share. As a result, she had gained vital knowledge for minimal cost and had become more aware than ever of the dangers that had lain ahead.

'I'll bet you wish you'd never hooked up with me, don't you, old girl?' Jenna said out loud to the big, dappled grey horse that she was leading with the reins she had made from a piece of her climbing rope. Her teeth chattered even as she spoke, and the thought crossed her mind again that she might have been better to find a sheltered spot to leave the horse while she had made the final climb.

For this was her dream mountain. Of that Jenna had no doubts. It had been a constant comfort throughout the long, lonely miles of her journey that everything had been so familiar. True, the perspective of some of the landmarks had been different when seen from ground level, and the recent snow showers had caused a bit more disorientation. However, considering that Jenna had never travelled this part of the world before, everything along her route had possessed a haunting familiarity. Now, with the end of her quest so tantalisingly close, she had decided that being parted from the horse was not an option that was acceptable even if it was sensible.

'C..c..c..come on. N..n..n..nearly there.'

Wrapping her cloak even more tightly around her body,

Jenna determinedly drove her feet onwards and upwards. The path that she took wound ever higher towards the summit, the bitterly biting wind gnashed its teeth at her with increasing fury as she was forced always to take the longer, easier path for the old grey horse's sake.

The climb seemed never-ending. Every time Jenna thought she was approaching the summit there was another rise awaiting her over the apparent top of the mountain, and then another. The cold had gradually eaten its way into every fibre of her body so that she felt as if she would never get warm again. Then, although the wind howled its ferocity with more viciousness than ever, and driving snow added its sting to the deep bite of that icy blast, Jenna began to feel a warm lassitude spread through her.

Alarm bells rang warnings of danger in her mind, but she found that despite the knowledge that her body was suffering all the signs of exposure, she no longer cared and her earlier driving pace slowed to a staggering stroll. Music filled Jenna's mind, sleepy, dreamy music that invited her to rest – to lay down and stop this pointless, crazy climb and to get some long overdue sleep.

Jenna nearly fell as the horse nudged her in the small of her back with its nose.

'You're right, old girl,' she mumbled, her lips barely moving with cold. 'Sleep later. Let's get this over with first.'

It might have been moments later, or it might have been hours, before Jenna finally stumbled over the top of the final rise and saw the great monolith standing proud in the shallow bowl ahead of her. Snow still swirled in the air, though not as thickly as it had earlier. A shallow drift had accumulated in the lee of the great rock, but otherwise the mountaintop had collected very little of the fine icy flakes.

Nothing mattered.

The snow, the wind, the cold, her horse – nothing mattered any more. The rock was everything. It was her dream and if she was to die on this bleak and remote mountaintop, at least she had reached her goal.

Staggering down the slight slope to the rock, Jenna dragged her reluctant feet across the final few yards, and with an inarticulate cry she fell forward against the stone. Her hands hardly broke her forward momentum at all, and her face and body smacked against the rock with considerable force as she ended leaning spread-eagled against the monolith.

Jenna felt no pain.

She was tired... so tired.

It was in a semi-conscious state that Jenna felt hands pushing back against her own and arms catching her as she fell: a dream state that had long since failed to be able to distinguish reality from illusion; fact from fiction. All spun into the warm oblivion of unconsciousness.

When Jenna awoke, it was to the luxurious sensation of warmth. It was not the false warmth that her body had tried to convince her that she had been feeling during the latter stages of her climb, but real warmth. Thus it was a shock to find that the view awaiting her when she finally managed to prise her eyelids open was not much different from her vaguely remembered last few seconds of consciousness.

Jenna was still on the mountaintop, only a few paces from the stone monolith. Snow still swirled and swept its way over the mountaintop, but somehow it was being deflected around the area where she had lain. A kind of transparent bubble of calm, silent air about a dozen paces across maintained a strangely unnatural haven in the insanely blowing snowstorm. Silent, that is, apart from the snuffling breath of the large grey horse and the sound of gentle snoring.

Seeing the figure, wrapped in a grey cloak, sleeping peacefully only a few paces away made Jenna surge up into a sitting position. Even as she lurched up, Jenna belatedly remembered her cracked ribs and automatically braced herself against the pain. To her great surprise, it never came.

Experimentally she poked, gently at first and then harder at the ribs where they had been broken during the fight with the lizard-man. There was no pain.

'I must be dreaming,' she said out loud to herself. 'This is all some bizarre nightmare and I'm going to wake up any second and find myself back in the dorm at Baron Keevan's castle with someone poking me in the ribs because I'm late on parade.'

'No, I'm afraid that you're not,' said a sleepy voice, and the previously sleeping figure pushed himself up slowly so that he was half way into a sitting position, leaning on his elbows.

The man was old. How old Jenna would not like to have guessed. His head was bald on top with iron-grey hair at the back and sides, and his brown, weather-beaten face housed a gentle smile and blue twinkling eyes that seemed to exude friendliness and warmth.

'It's nice to finally meet you, Jenna,' the old man continued, as Jenna was still unsure of what to say to this strange character. 'I owe you a debt of gratitude for coming. It could not have been easy, and I must surmise from the injuries which you carried here that you faced considerable danger along the way.'

Initially, Jenna was dumbfounded. Pinching herself had failed to cause her to wake up and so, as extraordinary as it seemed, she concluded that this was no dream. Where did one start? There were so many questions and yet Jenna could not seem to formulate any, let alone articulate anything coherent.

'You must have many questions,' the old man said, as if reading her mind. 'I'll do my best to answer as much as I can, but first I think that we ought to have a little to eat and something warm to drink, don't you?'

Jenna nodded, and with her mind racing she recovered her pack and dug out some food, some water, some dried dahl to add to the water, and a small can to heat the liquid in. It was only then that she noticed where all the heat was coming from to make her feel so comfortably warm, for there was no fire.

It was most eerie.

Several small rocks piled together in the centre of the calm bubble were literally glowing with a red-hot heat. Jenna's jaw dropped slightly as she noticed them and her eyes widened as it finally sunk in that this was a truly magical haven.

The old man merely smiled at her expression, and beckoned for her to bring her offerings closer.

'I'm sorry that I cannot add to your food or drink stocks at this time,' he said sincerely, 'but the warmth and shelter will have to suffice as my contribution to this meal. Be assured though that I shall endeavour to repay you properly at the earliest opportunity, Jenna. I owe you much already.'

Finally, Jenna found her tongue.

'I can only assume that you somehow healed my ribs?' she asked, already knowing the answer.

The old man nodded.

'And I was almost certain to die of exposure if you had not made this strange shelter and the unusual fire with no flames. Therefore, I would say that I already owe you a large debt of my own. I don't think that I shall worry overly much about a little food and water. It's the least that I can do.'

'Ah, but you wouldn't have been in that dire situation had I not called you to it. That you were willing to come this far into the Vortaff Mountains on my behalf, and that you brought my old friend "Steady" safely along with you places me deeply in your debt, young lady. Whether you understand it fully or not, my debt stands and I shall keep my word,' the old man replied easily.

'So I wasn't dreaming it. You did call. That the horse is yours should come as no surprise I suppose, after everything else that has happened, but who are you and why did you bring me here? When you called, you said that Calvyn was in grave danger. Where is he and what sort of danger is he in?' Jenna asked, her focus suddenly snapping back to the main reason for making this journey in the first place and the questions tumbling off her tongue in quick succession.

The old man's eyes darkened slightly with worry and sorrow.

'I will shortly answer as many of your questions as I can, but one that I can no longer answer is the whereabouts of Calvyn. I can't link with him any more, so he could be anywhere. Come though, Jenna. Let us eat, for you are hungry and you would not believe how long it has been since

I last ate or drank.'

Jenna did not really understand what the old man had meant by a link, but she forced herself to be patient.

Moving surprisingly lightly and easily for someone who looked so old, the man gathered the few travel rations that Jenna had retrieved from her pack and set them down on a naturally flat rock. With a practised hand he measured enough dahl and water into Jenna's can to make a fairly strong brew, and then balanced the can carefully on the glowing rocks, which were radiating heat better than any campfire.

As he was working, the old man talked, and in doing so, he answered many of the questions that were uppermost in Jenna's mind.

'As we have not been formally introduced, please allow me to introduce myself,' he started. 'My name is Perdimonn. I travelled with Calvyn for some time before circumstances forced us to part company about a year or so ago. I'm afraid my sense of time is not that accurate right now, so you'll have to forgive my vagueness. I was being pursued, you see, and I didn't want Calvyn to be dragged into what was an old and very dangerous feud.'

'With Selkor?' Jenna asked.

'Yes. That's right. I take it that Calvyn told you about it then?' Perdimonn asked stopping for a moment to look at Jenna while she answered.

'Not really,' she replied. 'But Selkor appeared at Mantor and Calvyn explained some of the story to the King. I was there. He didn't name you, but the story could hardly have been about anyone else, and what he didn't say fitted in with what you were leading up to.'

'Quick,' Perdimonn said, obviously approving of her deduction. 'You're right of course. What Calvyn didn't completely understand was just how dangerous Selkor could be – even more so now that he has Darkweaver's amulet. Indeed, the world itself is largely ignorant of the significance of that fell combination. Magically, I was no match for Selkor when it came to straight power-play even before he gained the amulet, but with that dread talisman he has gained a source of power that is monstrous in more ways than one. Anyway, I digress. Calvyn and I parted company, Selkor followed me here and let's just say that we had a bit of a quarrel...'

'And he sealed you up in that rock?'

'Actually, no. That was my idea,' Perdimonn said, looking a little embarrassed. 'You see, Selkor wasn't trying to kill me straight away. He merely wanted something that I have. He may have killed me after gaining it. Who knows? But by sealing myself in the rock I put myself beyond his reach. He could have shattered the rock with his magic, but he knew that in doing so, he would have more than likely destroyed the very thing that he was after.'

'Why did he not come into the rock after you?' Jenna asked, intrigued.

'To be honest, I don't know if he could have,' Perdimonn replied with an infectious grin. 'But even if he had the ability, on entering the rock he would have become as trapped as I was. The only way out was to get someone with whom I was soul-linked to touch the rock and give me a physical link back to the outside world.'

'So can you do this soul-linking thing with anyone then? Because if so, then I don't understand why you picked me,' Jenna said, confused. 'Why not pick someone closer, fitter or with a better knowledge of mountain-craft.'

Perdimonn shook his head slightly and paused to hand Jenna a mug of dahl before pouring his own into her spare cup. Both took a sip of the hot liquid and wrapped their hands around the warming sides of their relative cups. Jenna had already eaten half of her waybread cake and now delicately nibbled at the remains as she sat, fascinated by Perdimonn's tale.

'No, Jenna. Soul-linking is not easy... even with someone that you know well. To link with you was nigh on impossible. I am still amazed that I managed to form any sort of a bond with someone that I'd never met. The only reason that it proved possible was that I'd gained such vivid images of you from my previous links with Calvyn, and his feelings for you were strong enough that I felt as if I did know you after a fashion. That young man's mental focus can be quite sharp when he's sufficiently motivated. The reason I called you was that when Calvyn got taken by the Shandese, I suddenly had no one else to try.'

Jenna's heart skipped a beat as Perdimonn told of Calvyn's feelings for her. Could it be that he did love her after all? She couldn't bring herself to ask that, and other equally burning questions pressed hard for answers that were slightly easier to ask... but only slightly.

'Why can't you link with Calvyn any more? He isn't dead is he?' Jenna asked tentatively, fearful that the answer would not be what she desperately wanted to hear.

'No, he's not dead... I hesitate to say it, but in some ways he would be better off if he were.'

Even as her heart leapt again at the news that Calvyn still lived, anger flared just as brightly.

'Why? What has happened to him?' Jenna demanded abruptly. 'Stop skirting around the issue and tell me, Perdimonn. I only came here because you fed me the line that Calvyn was in danger. It worked. I'm here. You're free from your rock. Now tell me what has happened and what I can do to help him.'

Perdimonn looked Jenna directly in the eyes, his face grave. 'A sect of Sorcerers who call themselves "the Lords of the Inner Eye" have fed Calvyn's soul to a demon,' Perdimonn said slowly. 'It is a very powerful demon, and in all honesty I don't know if there's much that anyone can do for him.'

Jenna was stunned. First it was Magicians and magic, now Sorcerers and demons. It was just too unnatural to take in. She opened her mouth to speak but could formulate no questions to ask. The whole situation was becoming more bizarre by the day and the only thing that Jenna knew with any certainty was that she was totally out of her depth.

'There is just one shred of hope,' Perdimonn offered after a considerable pause.

'What's that?' Jenna asked numbly.

'I don't think that the demon has returned to its home

world, because I can still pick up a vague trace of Calvyn's soul in this one. I just can't link with it, as it's no longer with his body,' Perdimonn said thoughtfully. 'The demon must have escaped those that called it before they had a chance to send it back.'

'Why should this bring hope? Did I miss something somewhere?' Jenna asked, her eyes distant.

'Because it may be possible to kill the demon and free Calvyn's soul to return to his body, that's why.' Perdimonn said firmly. With an encouraging sort of smile, he placed his right hand over hers and squeezed it gently. 'This feels to me as if it is your destiny, Jenna. The hand of some higher force is in this somehow. You must go after the demon and kill it before it decides to return to its own realm by choice... for it will do that eventually. If it goes before you can kill it, Calvyn will almost certainly be lost forever.'

Jenna focused in on the old man's kind face. This was the hunt – it had to be. 'The most dangerous prey of all time' the old seeress had said. A powerful demon certainly measured up to the description in Jenna's mind.

'Don't you mean "our destiny", Perdimonn? After all, Calvyn was your apprentice. You're not just going to abandon him now, are you?' Jenna asked in genuine surprise.

Perdimonn shifted uncomfortably and broke eye contact with Jenna, looking around awkwardly.

'Listen, I know that this isn't going to sound good to you, but Calvyn isn't my only concern right now. Selkor has probably had the amulet re-forged by now and Tarmin only knows what he's up to with it, so I am going to have to entrust Calvyn to you, Jenna. My heart wants to go with you, but I feel sure that I, along with many others, would have cause to regret my decision if I were to let my heart rule. This task belongs to you unless I am much mistaken. You are far more of a hunter than I.'

Jenna looked at Perdimonn sharply for his choice of the word 'hunter', but was not to be landed with sole charge of tracking a demon without at least some sort of an argument.

'You're just going to abandon Calvyn to go off and continue

squabbling with a Magician who you have already admitted could probably squish you at a whim, like a noisome fly? What sort of a mentor are you? Surely Calvyn deserves better than this?' she asked angrily.

Perdimonn flushed slightly.

'Yes, he does deserve better, but duty calls. I cannot defeat Selkor on my own, so I'm going to have to canvass some help from somewhere and I am going to have to get it fast, or it won't matter how many allies that I get to support me. If Selkor plumbs the depths of the power locked in that amulet, then the entire world is going to be in trouble before long. Believe me, Jenna, I wish things were different, but I cannot come with you.'

'Well is there some spell you can give me to kill the demon with? Some weapon that I can use to free Calvyn's soul?'

'Well... er... no, I'm afraid not,' Perdimonn said awkwardly.

'Jenna shook her hand free of his, her eyes flashing her anger and disappointment.

'No, you don't understand,' Perdimonn continued quickly. 'The demon that has Calvyn's soul is a gorvath. It is immune to magical spells. Even if I had such aggressive spells at my command, they wouldn't avail you one iota. What I can offer you though is a magical device to help you to find the demon. I will make it for you. You see, the demon has come from a different world, so I can make you a device that should enable you to track that alien presence.'

Jenna's anger did not abate that easily. 'And so assuming that you give me this device and it leads me to the beast, how do I kill it?'

'Honestly, Jenna, I have no idea. My knowledge of demons is sketchy at best. The only warning that I can give you is that whatever else you do, never look into the gorvath's eyes. Demons catch their prey with a form of hypnotism. If you look into a gorvath's eyes, you are lost. Focus on its chest, its arms, anything but its eyes. Oh, yes, and one other thing to be aware of is that the gorvath is a shape-shifter. It can assume any shape that it wishes, but it cannot change very often as the shifting takes a great deal of energy and it will not burn that energy without good reason.'

Jenna sat back, shaking her head slightly as she tried to assimilate this latest twist of events. The old woman in the market place had named Jenna as 'The Huntress', but what else had she said? *'Be sure of your target lest you find yourself as the hunted'.* That was it. The old crone had said something else as well. It was something along the same lines, but as hard as she tried, Jenna could no longer recall what it was. It was not important, she decided. The point was that she had already decided in her heart to attempt to track and kill this gorvath... whatever it was... and yet the whole concept of there even being such a beast in existence seemed preposterous. Still, she mused with an inward grin, if someone had told her that she would one day sit on a lonely mountaintop, eating with a Magician inside a bubble of magical energy, and warming herself at a pile of magically heated rocks... she would probably have thought them crazy too.

Gritting her teeth, Jenna faced up to the task ahead: to track a demon that could choose its own appearance by some unnatural shape-shifting ability, was impervious to other magic and could steal away her soul if she so much as looked into its eyes. It was not a quest to be undertaken lightly. What was more, the creature could have other abilities that she knew nothing about. Perdimonn's knowledge of it was certainly far from comprehensive.

As Jenna saw it, she had no choice but to follow this strange path and pray that Perdimonn was right about some higher force or purpose guiding her. A touch of inspiration from the gods before she had to face this thing would certainly be useful.

'OK, Perdimonn, do your stuff. A magical guide to find this demon is a starting point. I'll take any help I can get right now. I'd prefer to have a magical weapon like Calvyn's sword, but I suppose a weapon without a target would be a little pointless.'

Perdimonn nodded and removed his cloak. 'Do you wear a necklace or a bracelet?' he asked.

'No. I've never been a great one for jewellery,' Jenna replied, curious to see what the old Magician was going to do.

The old man grunted in acknowledgement, and began picking at the neck of his cloak. Within a minute or so, he had pulled loose a leather thong and then, taking one end in each hand, he pulled at it to test its strength.

'Hmm. This should do,' he said, flashing his infectious smile at her. 'Now, do you have anything silver with you? Anything will do.'

'Silver,' Jenna thought to herself. 'Do I look like the sort of person who hauls silver around in my pack?'

Nevertheless, she rummaged through her belongings. One of her hair clips was silver in colour, but when she handed it to Perdimonn he immediately handed it back, shaking his head.

'It's got a bit of silver in it,' he said, 'but it's mainly tin I'm afraid.'

'How can you tell?'

'Silver feels different. Trust me. I know what I'm talking about.'

Jenna found nothing else even vaguely resembling silver in her bag and Perdimonn sighed heavily.

'I'd hoped that this wouldn't be necessary, but I suppose that it can't be helped,' he said sadly, and started working a heavy silver ring from the middle finger of his left hand.

It took a little while for him to work it loose, but when he finally managed to get it over his knuckle he slipped the ring off and sat it on the palm of his hand, studying it minutely.

'Not quite enough,' he muttered quietly, and slipped another, much slimmer ring from the little finger of his other hand.

Placing the smaller ring next to the first, the old man appeared to lose himself in staring at the two silver bands in his palm, or so it seemed to Jenna. It was almost as if the old Magician was lost in reminiscing about the origin of the jewellery, or maybe in some strange way communing with it, Jenna thought as minute after minute passed. All the while, Perdimonn sat unmoving and seemingly enraptured.

Time appeared to slow to a crawl.

'What is he doing?' she asked herself and shifted her

weight uncomfortably. 'Is he going to sit here like a statue all day? After all he's been stuck in a rock for Tarmin knows how long.'

Just when Jenna thought that she was going to have to say something to break the silence, Perdimonn began to speak. The words were strange and foreign, many of them sounding like oddly random syllables which were being uttered for effect rather than for any true meaning. Whatever it was that the old man was doing, Jenna thought better of interrupting.

The strange speech continued for several minutes with Perdimonn still unmoving, staring intently at the rings. Then, slowly and carefully, he leaned forward and placed the rings on the flat top of one of the glowing hot rocks. There was no pause in the strange stream of speech, but having placed the rings precisely on the rock, Perdimonn closed his eyes and his brows wrinkled in concentration.

Unsurprisingly, the silver rings began to melt with the heat of the glowing rock. However, instead of the molten metal simply pooling or running away down the side of the rock, it shifted and moved almost as if it were alive. When the rings had totally melted away, the liquid gave a slight shudder and in the blink of an eye it had formed into the shape of an arrow with a tiny block and a delicate ring attached to the middle of the shaft. The tone of Perdimonn's voice shifted in that instant to one of command, and although Jenna still understood nothing of what he was saying, the underlying sentiment was clear. Never had Jenna heard a tone of command like that which the old Magician delivered. If she could perfect a tone like that, Jenna had no doubt that she would make Corporal in a week.

The rock beneath the little silver arrow stopped glowing and Jenna winced as Perdimonn reached out and picked up the newly shaped little charm. Surely it would still be scorching hot. It had been molten only seconds before... and yet the old man was turning it in his hands as if it were perfectly cool.

Perdimonn fell silent. Then he picked up the thong of

leather and threaded it through the tiny ring. With a nod of satisfaction, he tied the ends of the leather thong together and passed the newly made neck charm to Jenna.

'There,' he said with a smile. 'The perfect necklace for a huntress.'

'Very pretty,' Jenna replied. 'Thank you. I don't quite see how it will help me find the gorvath though.'

'Here, let me show you,' Perdimonn offered, his eyes twinkling with that sparkling blue of amusement that often needed little encouragement.

Holding the arrow-shaped pendant up by the leather thong with one hand, he flicked the tail end of the arrow and Jenna suddenly realised that the tiny block attaching the arrow to the ring was actually a minute swivel. The arrow spun several times before coming to a stop.

'The arrowhead will always come to rest pointing in the direction of the demon. As you get closer, the direction will become more and more precise. Cunning, don't you think?'

'Cunning and more than just a little useful. Thank you, Perdimonn.'

'It was the least that I could do really. Beware, though, for the spell that I cast on the charm was not as specific as I would have liked. It should point you at the gorvath, but I wouldn't go wandering too close to any wizards' towers if you can help it, or you may find yourself tracking more demons than you bargained for.'

'The gorvath is more than I bargained for! I don't want to go wandering around the world battling with demons at random,' Jenna said, horrified at the idea that she may have to face more than one.

'Don't worry yourself unnecessarily,' Perdimonn assured her. 'There isn't likely to be any demonic presence in the world strong enough to overcome the pull on that charm from the gorvath. Wizards are few and far between in this part of the world. This is the first summoning of this magnitude that I have been aware of for many years, but I just wanted you to know that the charm will be affected to some degree by any alien presence.'

'Well, I suppose that's useful to know,' Jenna conceded,

trying to sound convinced of her words. 'Where will you go now, Perdimonn?'

'To Terilla. I need to warn the Council of Magicians about Selkor. Then... well you don't really need to know any more than that. What you don't know about my movements won't hurt you.'

'Terilla? That's on the Shandese side of the Vortaffs, isn't it?' Jenna asked, not quite sure of its whereabouts.

'Yes, that's right. In south-western Shandar.'

'Then it looks like you will be stuck with me for at least a little while longer,' Jenna said, looking at the silver arrow, which was pointing firmly north – deep into the heart of the Vortaff Mountain range towards Shandar.

CHAPTER 10

Lord Shanier was mildly amused.

The rest of the Lords of the Inner Eye had been trying for weeks to pretend that he had been one of their élite number before that strange day when everything had changed. Shanier had known that they were lying from very early on. The only truly competent liar amongst them was Lord Vallaine, but the fact that Vallaine chose to lie about Shanier's past was one of the main reasons that Shanier had chosen to go along with the whole charade.

One did not cross Lord Vallaine lightly. Instinct told him that much.

Memories of Shanier's past had started coming back to him within a day or two of his strange awakening in the eerie underground cavern. There was nothing much coherent to begin with, just isolated images, none of which fitted with his present circumstances.

That something terrible had happened in that cavern was obvious, for there had been dead bodies on the floor. Shanier had gained a glimpse of the corpses before Lord Vallaine had led him away to rest. Great claw marks had been clearly visible, and something had plainly smashed its way out of that chamber through what appeared from the shattered remains to be a very solid door. Yet Vallaine had acted for all the world as if nothing were out of the ordinary, and had shown no concern that there might be a dangerous creature loose somewhere in the palace.

Shanier had been disoriented at the time and the calm, collected voice of Vallaine had been a balm to his confused mind. Subsequently, Shanier had kept his silence on the

172

subject despite his curiosity, as he had quickly deduced that there was much about his whole situation that was not as it appeared.

Indeed, nothing about the entire palace was truly as it appeared, he reflected, running his fingers through his short, fair hair. The whole place was a maze of illusion, created and maintained by the many junior Sorcerers who were busy learning their craft. There were rules of course as to the sort of illusions that were allowed. Certain areas were out of bounds and no illusions were to be dangerous in nature.

Pranks were tolerated to a degree, and hardly a day went by without the fountain pond 'moving' slightly, or changing shape subtly. It was a brave or foolish person who strolled through the gardens without their mind one hundred percent on penetrating the many illusions that abounded there.

Lord Vallaine had begun 're-teaching' Shanier the subtleties of sorcery almost as soon as he had rested, and if it had not been for the fragments of memory that kept resurfacing, it would have been easy to believe that he had previously been exactly what Vallaine claimed, for the illusion element of sorcery came as naturally to Shanier as building webs came to a spider. Imposing his will on others and learning to break into their minds to discover what they were thinking did not come so easily. However, Lord Vallaine had smoothly claimed that Shanier had been selected as a Lord of the Inner Eye for his illusory skills, rather than for pure mind power, so this was to be expected.

It was another lie, but Shanier could see how the cunning old Sorcerer tailored his deceptions so neatly to fit the circumstances that it would be easy to fall for them. If only Shanier could figure out why Vallaine seemed so set on advancing him and giving him the powers that he would need to fulfil the role into which he was being cast... so he began spinning deceptions of his own.

Memories and faces from the past had resurfaced more and more frequently during the past few weeks. His old name, the name of his birth, was also on the tip of his tongue now and it bothered him that he was so close to re-discovering it, yet still it eluded him. Kalten... Callum... it was something like that, but neither was quite right. It was not that he was at all concerned with re-discovering his past life other than the fact that information was power. Lord Vallaine and the others were working hard to maintain the deception that Shanier was one of them for a good reason. Undoubtedly that reason was for their gain rather than his, so he would have to figure out their secret somehow.

It was all quite unusual really. Shanier got the distinct impression from his surfacing memories that he had once enjoyed having many friends and colleagues. Now he felt nothing for anyone. It was not that he had become selfish exactly, but something inside him had changed – something that held him from getting emotionally worked up about anything. Satisfaction had replaced joy, and a cold, calculated malice had driven out the heat of anger and any burning desire for revenge.

As such, Shanier used his calm exterior to lull the other Sorcerers into thinking that he was clay to be moulded into whatever it was that they had originally desired. Patience would reveal their motives. Patience... a little cunning and a lot of ingenuity.

Already Shanier had been forced to use that cunning and ingenuity to prevent Lord Vallaine from discovering how much he already knew, or at least guessed, about what was going on. Fortunately, Vallaine had not made a determined effort to 'look' into Shanier's most private thoughts for a little while after he had begun the training in sorcery. By the time that he did finally probe the depths of Shanier's mind during one of the mind-strengthening exercises, Shanier had set up such a good illusory boundary wall within his own mind that Vallaine did not even push against it. Whether Lord Vallaine had been totally fooled by the wall, thinking that he had plumbed the depths of Shanier's most private thoughts, Shanier did not know. However, whether he did or not was rapidly becoming irrelevant, as Shanier was gaining in mental strength daily. It was quite possible that before Vallaine realised that Shanier had been concealing his most intimate thoughts and the true level of the power that his mind was capable of generating, Lord Vallaine might no longer be able to master his protégé.

Shanier had gleaned from his memories that he had once belonged to some sort of military force and it was plain that he had not held a high rank. Consequently he had no desire to give up his luxurious suite in the Palace of the Inner Eye to return to the lowly dormitory that haunted his memories. He had no attachments to the past and thus no reason to care for it, therefore, he had resolved in his secret innermost thoughts to do everything that he could to secure this position of power such that none could question the legitimacy of his appointment.

A knock sounded at the door to his main living room.

'Ah! The games begin again,' Shanier mused, pulling his deep black hood up to cover his head as he sensed Lord Vallaine and one other outside.

Vallaine was a presence that Shanier felt he would know anywhere after these weeks of training. The other had power as well and it was no novice Sorcerer who accompanied the High Lord of the Inner Eye. Lord Cillverne, he guessed as he opened the door. It was gratifying to find that he was correct. Lords Vallaine and Cillverne were standing patiently outside.

'Are you ready?' Vallaine asked, his voice betraying no emotion.

'Certainly, Lord Vallaine, come in,' Shanier replied, keeping his tone equally as bland. 'Lord Cillverne,' he acknowledged as the second Sorcerer entered the room behind the High Lord.

Cillverne nodded curtly as he passed, but chose not to extend his courtesy any further.

'The task was to conceal an object of some respectable size by illusion alone. What have you chosen to hide?'

'I chose to disguise my staff, Lord Vallaine. It is the one you had made for me with the dragon's head as a handle.'

'A distinctive choice, Shanier. Would you like a fuller description, Cillverne, or are you content to find the staff? It is in this room somewhere I presume?' he asked, turning to

Shanier for confirmation.

Shanier nodded.

'No need, Lord Vallaine, I believe that I will cope,' Cillverne said, a hint of disdain in his voice.

With a glance around the room, Cillverne hardly paused before striding over to the tall, palm-like miniature tree in the corner of the room.

'Not exactly original, Lord Shanier,' Cillverne said, flashing a triumphal little smile at Shanier even as he reached for where he could 'see' the staff beneath the façade of the plant.

The smile disintegrated as his hand grasped the stem of the plant and tried to lift what he thought was the staff from its resting-place in the pot. The plant was real. The image of the staff had been an illusion, but subtly created such that only a mind of some power would have seen it at all.

Lord Vallaine laughed.

'A nice ploy, Shanier. Very clever. The illusion was clever enough to fool the unwary Cillverne, but I know you a little better. Please, Cillverne, do try once more.'

Cillverne was clearly annoyed at having been made to look a fool, and now bent all his concentration to searching the room for the staff. However, despite his best efforts Cillverne could not locate it and eventually was forced to admit defeat.

Lord Vallaine looked smug. 'Very good, Shanier. Very good. Your invisibility illusion is now virtually perfect. Here, Cillverne, it was right in front of you all along.'

Vallaine walked over to an elaborate couch and, seemingly appearing from thin air, Shanier's staff materialised in Lord Vallaine's hand as he picked it up from where it lay angled across the cushions.

'Your progress has been most pleasing, Shanier. Even I had a few problems penetrating that illusion. This afternoon I want you to practise reaching out with your mind. Your task is to discover which junior is providing the décor in the Hall of Statues today and which reprobate is making the lawn fountain appear to stutter every few minutes. Bring me the names by the fourth hour.'

Shanier bowed.

'Yes Lord Vallaine. Thank you,' he stated blandly, no

emotion in his voice and his facial expression schooled.

Cillverne was trying hard to mask his hostility as he and Lord Vallaine left. Vallaine on the other hand had obviously enjoyed himself immensely, and could scarcely contain his mirth as he handed Shanier the staff on his way out.

Shanier remained impassive – impassive, that is, until the door had closed behind the other two Sorcerers, when a tight, satisfied smile crept across his face. For a moment or two he waited, listening hard with ears and mind to the retreating steps. Then, when he was sure that they were truly gone and that no one was eavesdropping, he threw his head back and allowed himself to release a chilling laugh.

The staff that Vallaine had given him dissolved into nothingness and another, which looked identical, appeared on the small decorative table in the centre of the room.

Sensory perception was more than just visual, and Shanier had just proven to himself that he could fool even the most powerful mind into seeing and feeling something that was not really there. Even Vallaine had no idea just how powerful he was becoming, and that in itself added another dimension to his power.

'Whatever Vallaine is hatching by pushing me into this privileged position will have to be good,' Shanier thought to himself, 'or he may find that he's created a force that he can't handle. High Lord of the Inner Eye is a coveted position that should be held by the person best suited to handle the power that it wields. If I work at it, that person could well be me,' Shanier mused with a satisfied smile.

* * * * *

'Think, Eloise, think! Don't allow your emotions to cloud your mind in a fight. Your focus should be on the motion and balance of your opponent or opponents. If you over-extend on your lunge like that through frustration or anger, you will not live long enough to regret it. Stay calm. Focus. Be patient. Your strokes are good, your speed is improving and your balance is normally excellent. Don't be stupid and you will be more than a match for the vast majority of the Shandese soldiers.'

Bek had been tutoring several groups of recruits ever since

he had arrived back with the rest of the army from Mantor. This group, though, was his favourite and the reason was not hard to figure out. No matter how much he told himself that Eloise being a part of the group had nothing to do with his preference, he knew that in reality he was merely trying to fool himself.

To be fair, even putting the stunning beauty of Eloise aside, the rest of the group formed an interesting bunch in their own right. Fesha, with his quick mind, sharp wit and constant banter always lightened the tone of a training session. The wiry joker's blade-work had progressed well over the weeks, though his limited reach meant that he would never be a truly deadly swordsman.

Sten, Kedreeve, Marcos and the others all had likeable qualities as well. Bek just wished that Matim, Calvyn and Jenna were still around to share in the camaraderie. First Matim had been killed at Mantor, then Calvyn had gone missing after the first ambush, and finally Jenna, in the more recent incident, had also disappeared. All of his closest friends had gone in a matter of weeks. It was almost enough to make Bek want to prevent himself from becoming overly attached to anyone else in case he lost them as well.

'OK, Eloise, let's try that again. Remember – patience. Don't try to rush it.'

Eloise looked suitably chastened and prepared again to match blades with the Corporal. Sweat glistened on her arms and forehead, but her breathing was steady and her features composed as she began the drill again. Concentration and determination gleamed in her greeny-brown eyes, and Eloise attacked again with a level of dexterity and skill that was rare in one so fresh to the art of swordplay.

To Bek it was like dancing at a midsummer ball with the girl of his dreams. The song of the steel blades rang out the beat, and the harmonious and complimentary move and counter-move of their bodies effected a motion that was both aggressive and yet intimate. Anticipation and knowledge of his sword partner's moves and counter-moves, together with close observation of balance, posture and muscle-play combining to help both partners make the dance a beautiful thing to behold.

After several minutes, Bek called a halt.

'Good, Eloise. That was much better. Could you feel the difference in your balance on the lunges?'

'Yes, Corporal Bek. Thank you. It's been a very useful session. I can feel the flow of the strokes more now and I feel as if I can read the moves much better.'

'It shows. You're improving every time you come out here. What you need now, is a bit more consolidation against opponents who are faster and stronger than you. Your natural abilities will help you to hold your own... trust me on that. But by constantly being pushed into a defensive position, you will be forced to either find ways to slow your opponent down, or to add speed to your counter-attacks. I'll teach you a couple of useful tricks to keep up your sleeve, but there is nothing like raw speed to throw an opponent, so we'll do our best to develop that.'

Eloise nodded thoughtfully, obviously somewhat daunted by the prospect of being continually outmatched in training for the foreseeable future, but also plainly determined to do her best. After all, the challenge of combat was what had drawn her to become a soldier in the first place. There was no place in her make-up for defeatism.

Not for the first time, Eloise found her eyes drawn to the sword hilt protruding from the scabbard on Bek's right hip. Bek followed the line of her attention and grimaced slightly.

'Is that...?' Eloise began hesitantly.

'Yes, it's Corporal Calvyn's sword,' Bek said calmly, gently patting the hilt with his left palm. 'I'm just looking after it for him for a while.'

'Is it really... magical?'

Bek's forehead furrowed slightly as he pictured Calvyn in his epic duel with Demarr at Mantor and the flames leaping from his shining blade. Then he remembered the other times that Calvyn had surreptitiously used magic during their training days and he shook his head.

'No, I don't think so,' Bek answered eventually. 'At least not in the way that you mean. As far as I know, the magic was Calvyn's. I think that he used the sword as an object through which to channel his magic, and he felt that the perception of him having a magical sword would be more acceptable than that of him being a Magician.'

Even as the words were coming from his mouth, Bek suddenly found that he doubted his own observations fiercely. Ever since he had started wearing the sword on his belt in addition to his own, he had been feeling a strong desire to run off to Shandar to try to find his friend. It was most strange. Although Bek knew that it would be categorically unacceptable for him to go off on some solo expedition in search of his friend, as some suspected Jenna had done, he felt an incredibly strong sensation that the sword should be restored to its rightful owner: preferably sooner rather than later. If that meant Bek going to Shandar to find him, then that was what he should do. However, common sense and military discipline kept Bek from doing anything foolish. He just continued to hope against hope that one day he would be able to hand his friend the blade back. 'Strange though,' he mused, 'first it was Jenna's dreams and now my own strange desire to go off after Calvyn. Something unusual is afoot.'

'So Calvyn really was a Magician?' Eloise asked, a little sceptically.

'Is a Magician,' Bek corrected. 'He always claims that he isn't, but he can certainly work a variety of magical spells. In my book that qualifies him for the title, but what do I know? I'm certainly no expert on the subject.'

'You don't think he's dead then?' Eloise asked, a little surprised at the conviction in Bek's voice with his use of the present tense.

'I'm as sure that he's alive as I am that the sun will come up tomorrow morning. Don't ask me how I've gained this certainty, but I know that he'll make his way back here eventually. Maybe it's just wishful thinking... but somehow I don't think so.'

Bek's eyes had gone distant again as he spoke and Eloise found her interest piqued even further.

'May I?' she asked, extending her hand to receive the

sword.

'Certainly. Why not?' Bek replied and drew the sword.

With a flourish, he presented the blade, hilt first for Eloise to hold. He could not help but smile a little as she reached to grasp the hilt for he had seen the reaction of several others to the feel of that sword. Everything about it felt wrong. The balance, the weight – everything, and it appeared to affect everyone the same way. It was something to do with a spell that Calvyn had put on it to make the sword his own. Apparently it was light and well balanced in Calvyn's hand – at least, that was what he claimed and he had certainly always used it effectively enough.

Eloise gripped the hilt and for a split second, the spidery silver symbols on the blade flashed in the sunlight. Bek almost laughed as her eyes widened.

'Strange, isn't it?' he said with a grin.

'We have got to get this back to Calvyn,' she replied in a strangely awe-struck voice.

'What did you say?' Bek demanded, his grin fading rapidly.

'The sword... it doesn't belong here. We need to get it back to Calvyn as soon as we can. Come on, Corporal. If we get supplies from the Quartermaster's we can start now. I know the way.'

Bek looked in amazement at the enraptured face of Eloise. Her voice was distant and it was echoing the words that had been on his heart for weeks. It was also clear that these thoughts were not her own, which meant that his thoughts had probably been tampered with as well. The hairs on the back of Bek's neck started to rise and a shudder ran down his spine. Magic was at work here and he did not know how to handle it. Something or someone was trying to draw them from the castle. It might be the sword. It might be Calvyn. However, it could be anything or anyone with magical powers and Bek would know no different.

What to do?

'Very well, Eloise,' he said quietly in a calm, placating voice, not wanting to draw attention to the situation. 'For appearances sake, you ought to at least see out the training period. Let's not make it too obvious what we are doing. I'll go and prepare packs and supplies. Here... give me the sword for now and we'll set out as soon as I can get you away from the others without raising suspicions.'

Eloise handed the blade back and her eyes cleared a little. Bek called Marco and Kedreeve across.

'OK guys, this exercise will consist of two on one practice with the limitation that you two must fight as if in a line. Eloise here will be your opponent. I'm sure that you'll all benefit from the exercise. Start the drill slowly and gradually work it up. Any questions?'

'No, Corporal.'

Bek sheathed Calvyn's sword and then his own.

'Good. Get to it and I'll see you shortly. I've just got a couple of things to do.'

With that, Bek turned and left, striding across the weapons training area with a purposeful snap to his walk. However, it was not towards the Quartermaster's Store that his pounding strides carried him, but to Sergeant Derra's office.

Bek knocked once and entered, not waiting for a reply.

'Corporal Bek, have you no manners?' Derra growled, as she glared dangerously at him from behind her desk.

'Yes, Sergeant, but this is not the time to be showing them off. There's magic at work here in the castle and I need your help to prevent whatever is happening from going any further.'

'Don't tell me you've started having dreams now?' Derra warned, her voice still barely controlling her anger at Bek's abrupt entrance.

'No, Sergeant... not exactly. Here – try holding Calvyn's sword for a moment and you might see what I mean.'

'I've held it before, Bek. I know how awful it feels. If this is the reason for your lack of respect...'

Derra left the sentence hanging, but Bek was not daunted.

'You've not held it since he disappeared, I'll wager. Try it and then berate me if you must.'

Derra's eyes narrowed a little, and then she rose and prowled around the desk until she was standing face-to-face with Bek, her hands on her hips. Bek drew the sword again and proffered the hilt to the Sergeant. Derra eyed it suspiciously, and then looked over Bek's shoulder to the windows as if looking for someone else.

'If you're worried about the traditional spoof, Sergeant, forget it. I know all about that and I can assure you that this isn't it.'

Derra's eyes locked with Bek's and stared at him with an almost frightening intensity.

Bek was unmoved.

Calmly, he held out the hilt for the Sergeant and patiently waited for her to take hold of it. Derra broke off her stare and shifted her attention to the hilt of Calvyn's sword. Slowly, almost reluctantly, the Sergeant reached out her right hand and closed her fingers around the cloth bound hilt. This time there was no mistaking the reaction of the blade to that touch, for in the dimmer light of the office, the sudden glow of the runes was unmistakable.

Derra's eyes widened, much as Eloise's had done a few minutes before. Having been pre-warned that something unusual would happen, the Sergeant was not affected as strongly by the pull of the sword to supposedly return to its owner. However, there was no doubting that the magical call was having an impact on Derra. Bek could see it in her face.

'Interesting,' she said thoughtfully. 'How long has the sword been doing this?'

'Certainly ever since I took custody of it, and probably since Calvyn disappeared,' Bek stated. 'At first I thought that it was my own heart calling me. It wasn't until I handed the sword to one of the recruits to look at just now and saw the immediate reaction that I decided to bring it to you.'

'The pull is strong. I'm impressed that you have resisted it all this time. It must have been tempting at times to set off and find him.'

Bek grinned and rubbed his palms together. 'You have no idea,' he chuckled. 'Particularly as I really felt convinced that I would be able to find him.'

'Yes, I'm getting that feeling as well. There is no doubt

that the sword would lead us somewhere, but where and to whom it would lead us is a different matter entirely. Did Calvyn ever mention this phenomenon at all?' Derra asked, handing the sword back to Bek, who immediately sheathed it.

'No, Sergeant. To be honest though, Calvyn said very little about it at all. We all knew about the flames, and I believe that he said something about the blade glowing in the presence of evil. Apart from that, and the balance thing about it only feeling right to him, I don't recall him mentioning anything else about it.'

Derra chewed at her lower lip thoughtfully for a moment and then grimaced slightly as she made the same decision that Bek had made.

'Going after him is out of the question,' the Sergeant stated firmly, though Bek suspected that this was as much to reinforce her own mind as his. 'It would be sheer folly to risk lives in such an uncertain venture. Who was the recruit who touched the sword?'

Bek felt his face redden as he named Eloise, though he maintained his eye contact with the Sergeant. Derra raised one angled eyebrow slightly and a glimmer of a smile brushed her lips.

'Ah, yes, the dark-haired girl. I've been hearing good things about her progress. Are they well founded?'

Bek's face reddened a little more.

'There's no doubt that Eloise has some natural talent and she's learning fast. Her basic blade work is sound, but understandably she still lacks the speed of a truly accomplished swordswoman.'

'I'll make a point of crossing blades with her at the next training session. In the meantime she'll have to be watched. I don't want her disappearing off on a magically induced quest. Out of interest, did Jenna touch the sword at all?'

Bek shook his head immediately.

'No, Sergeant. I'd swear to it that Jenna didn't touch it. The sword has been on my belt ever since Private Jez brought it back from the ambush site. Do you think that Jenna has gone after Calvyn then?'

Derra turned and walked back around her desk to the solid wooden chair. With a sigh, she sat down.

'I don't know, Bek. I suspect that she has followed the call that she received through her dreams, but according to her words that call was not from Calvyn anyway. Who knows where she is now? She could be just about anywhere. The important thing now is that we prevent anyone else from disappearing off on unauthorised, half-cooked missions. I've got a really uneasy feeling about the lack of Shandese movements recently. Something big is brewing, and we are going to need every hand we can find when the storm breaks.'

'I'll make sure that no one else handles the sword, Sergeant.'

'Good. I'd like you to bring Eloise and Private Jez to see me after the morning training session tomorrow and we will try to keep this whole thing under control. In the meantime, keep an eye on Eloise.'

'Well if you insist, Sergeant,' Bek replied with a sly grin. 'Can I take that as a direct order?'

'Get out of here and do some work, Corporal!' Derra growled, her face stern but her eyes twinkling with amusement.

'Right away, Sergeant,' Bek snapped, throwing up a salute and turning for the door.

'Oh... and Bek,' Derra said, just as Bek opened the door.

He stopped and looked around.

'About that spoof...'

'Sorry, Sergeant. Can't stop. Recruits to train, people to see, places to go,' he said quickly and slipped out of the door before Derra had a chance to say any more.

CHAPTER 11

Jenna felt like dancing. At last the long trek through the mountains was over, and in front of them snow-capped craggy peaks no longer dominated the horizon. The ground sloped steeply downwards from where Perdimonn and Jenna had paused briefly to take in the welcome view, but it was not so steep as to be impassable. Indeed, the way ahead looked easy going when compared with some of the paths the weary travellers had been forced to tread over the previous fortnight.

The Knife-Edge Pass had lived up to its fearsome name and reputation. In many places the track through the mountains had been frighteningly narrow, following the line of a ledge around the side of one mountain after another. Often the vertical drop from the track had been many hundreds of feet, with a sheer rock-face on the other side. Several times vertigo had assaulted Jenna's senses, and she had suffered an almost overpowering urge to flatten herself against the rock-face, as far from the edge of the precipice as possible. Only the calmly unperturbed pace of Perdimonn, now leading his old horse carefully along the perilous track, kept her focus sharp enough to keep her from faltering, and helped her to concentrate instead on just putting one foot in front of the other.

Every evening Perdimonn had shielded them within a dome of magical force, and had heated rocks in lieu of a fire. Thus the night and rest periods were relatively comfortable. However, Perdimonn had not been able to shield them from the elements whilst they were moving, a restriction that Jenna did not understand and that she had regretted on more than one occasion.

The weather had proved capricious. Whirling snowstorms, driven by viciously biting winds, had struck hard and often, only to change within moments to glorious sunshine and a benign chill breeze. Visibility had often been poor, as the path through the mountains was frequently drowned within the clouds. However, Perdimonn had never faltered as he led Jenna through all that the elements chose to throw at them.

There had been times when the scenery had been breathtakingly beautiful and Jenna had found that she could understand the attraction which some felt for the high places of the world. However, for the most part the treacherous trail had taken so much of her concentration that she had looked at no more than where she was going to put each foot next.

Water had never been in short supply in the mountains, as whenever they had run out of it in liquid form, ice or snow had been available at virtually every stopping place. Placed in a pot and heated on one of Perdimonn's magically warmed rocks, ice quickly reverted to its liquid form, though Jenna was most surprised at how much snow it took to melt into a useable quantity of water. Also, even if the water was heated to boiling point it never really felt all that hot. Perdimonn had explained the phenomenon and its relationship to the altitude at which they were camped, but Jenna had been far too tired to really understand what he was talking about. Accepting the fact was altogether the easier option.

The one major problem had been food supplies. Jenna had packed as much as she had been able into her pack and pouches before entering the mountains. However, it had not been anywhere near sufficient to sustain the two of them for the entire journey, and sources of food in the mountains were not plentiful.

It was Perdimonn once again who had solved the problem. He seemed to have a sixth sense of some sort, and on several occasions over the course of their trek had stopped and quietly directed Jenna to string her bow. With a mixture of quietly uttered one-word directions and subtle hand signals, he had guided her eyes onto the prey that he had spotted, and once she had acquired her target, Jenna did not disappoint with her aim.

The available game that they saw consisted mostly of a form of snowy-white, rabbit-like creature, and some days Jenna managed to shoot several of them. Obviously there was no game available on those days where the path led them around the mountainside ledges. However, on one occasion, when the surrounding terrain was not so severe, Perdimonn pointed out a mountain goat. To her disgust, Jenna had problems seeing it even with his directions. Finally having spotted the creature, Jenna had unerringly sent an arrow on a deadly trajectory to fell the animal before it had a chance to run. Afterwards Jenna had taken some time to clamber up to where the carcass lay, the body rapidly freezing in the sub-zero temperature. To Jenna's embarrassment she lost sight of her kill during the climb and had to be guided to the body by Perdimonn, who called out directions to her from the track below.

The coat of the goat was a subtle camouflage of stone-grey and white that Jenna failed to distinguish from its surroundings until she was virtually on top of it. Later, Perdimonn had assured her that even many of those who claimed to be experienced in the ways of mountain-craft had problems picking out the animals through their protective colouring. He claimed that it was a knack that he had picked up over many years of travel. For some reason, though, his assurances had not made her feel any better at all. Somehow she had felt that had she not been there, Perdimonn would have survived quite happily without her abilities as an archer to bring down their food.

Every now and then, Jenna had lifted the magical charm from her chest to see if there were any noticeable change in direction to the position of the gorvath. The little arrow pointed consistently northwards, indicating that by crossing the mountains they were getting closer to her goal. At first Jenna had thought it her imagination that the little arrow had been settling a little further west of north each day that she had drawn it out to look at it. Now, standing as they were at the northern edge of the mountain range, it was quite clear. When she lifted the charm to check the direction, it definitely pointed northwest.

The mere fact that the head of the little arrow had definitely changed direction brought Jenna a surge of hope mixed with a tang of fear. Every time the arrow changed direction it presented her with a corner that she could cut and thus gain ground on the beast. Granted, this was assuming that the demon was not travelling much faster than she was, but somehow Jenna did not feel that the demon would be travelling anywhere in a particular hurry. After all, what possible agenda could the demon have? It had been pulled into this world against its will and, other than feeding, Jenna could not imagine that it would be in a rush to do anything else.

The countryside spread below them looked lush and fertile. There was evidence of farming in all directions, though no major settlements or towns were visible to Jenna as her eyes scanned across what she could see of this part of southern Shandar. Some of the planted fields had obviously grown wheat or barley, but the harvest had been and gone. Herds of animals, mainly sheep she judged, grazed in segregated areas of grassed fields, though they were far too distant to distinguish any more detail.

'Well, Jenna, what do you think of your first glimpse of Shandar?' Perdimonn asked, his blue eyes twinkling.

'It's a welcome sight, I'll not deny that,' Jenna said quickly. 'After the last few weeks I won't be unhappy if I never set foot on a mountainside again.'

Jenna paused and her forehead wrinkled slightly as she frowned in thought. Perdimonn chuckled knowingly at her answer.

'I can't help feeling just a little disappointed though,' she added after a moment or two.

'Disappointed? Why's that?' Perdimonn asked.

'I just thought it might look different somehow. I mean, for all I know of our route, we could have turned around in a big semi-circle and be looking at northern Thrandor. I know we haven't because the position of the sun would be different, but it looks so similar to Thrandor that...' Jenna ran out of words and so just repeated, '...well, I just thought it would look different somehow.'

Perdimonn laughed. 'I know what you mean. How convenient it would be if each kingdom and land looked different. Then maybe men would stop squabbling over borders and kings would be content to rule only that which was uniquely theirs. Unfortunately nature doesn't always provide distinct borders to lands that men divide with imaginary lines. The Vortaff Mountains have always provided a natural barrier between Shandar and Thrandor. It's just a shame that they don't run all the way to the sea. Maybe if they did, the two peoples might be more content to just trade goods instead of continually contesting the area between the mountains and the sea.'

Jenna could not agree more, but found herself thinking that if the mountains had stretched all the way to the sea, then she would not like to have been a merchant if it meant travelling backwards and forwards through these mountains.

'As it is, young Jenna, it really won't do to have you walking around Shandar in those clothes,' Perdimonn said, gesturing at her tunic. 'Baron Keevan's colours may suit you, but they'll get you locked up or killed around here, so we had better do something about that sooner rather than later.'

Perdimonn looked around at the land immediately below them, and then settled his gaze on an area of woodland to their left.

'We'll head for the trees over there, and you can hole up and rest while I get you suitable attire for moving around Shandar without drawing too much attention to yourself,' he said after a moment or two of consideration. Then, without waiting for a response from Jenna he flicked at the rope lead rein. 'Come on, Steady, old girl. Let's keep moving, or we'll still be up here come night fall.'

The horse nickered and plodded forward at its usual sure-footed gait. Jenna paused a moment, and marvelled once more at the seemingly indefatigable energy of the old Magician. Perdimonn had walked the legs off her over the last couple of weeks and now once more, it was he who suggested that she rest, whilst he did the hard work. Jenna could not even begin to guess at his age, but even if his face had aged beyond his years she would have placed him in his sixth decade. For a man of even those years he possessed a surfeit of energy, and she suspected that he was older than her conservative estimate.

It took another couple of hours to reach the woods that Perdimonn had identified as their campsite, and a further half an hour to locate a good site to make a shelter. The place they chose was near a spring of beautifully clear water that fizzed and bubbled out of the ground, and trickled and gurgled its way down through the trees in a tiny, rock-strewn stream.

Perdimonn stayed only long enough to take a draft of the water and eat one of the few remaining strips of cooked goat meat whilst allowing Steady to drink from the spring. Then, with a parting admonition not to leave the woods or to do anything that would attract attention to the fact that she was here, the old Magician left Jenna and led Steady away through the trees and down towards the inhabited lands below.

Jenna wasted no time.

Perdimonn had been able to give no assurances that he would be back that night and so her first priority was to construct herself a shelter. There was no shortage of materials with which to work, and within an hour or so Jenna had built a wooden lattice style, single-sided, sloping-roofed shelter. A sturdy branch, tied horizontally about three feet above the ground between two young trees that were standing only six feet apart, supported the structure. Other branches propped at a shallow angle between the horizontal support and the ground, together with other thin branches woven between them to form the lattice, made up the make-shift shelter. The lattice was then covered with layer upon layer of fern leaves collected from a nearby clearing, and more fern leaves were heaped under the roof to form a soft bed. By the time that night fell, Jenna was snugly wrapped up in her blanket within her shelter and warming her hands at the tiny fire, which she had cleverly laid in a hole that she had dug at the shelter's entrance.

Carefully, Jenna only fed the fire with the driest of wood to ensure that no smoke gave her presence away. There had been no time to waste on hunting for food, though Jenna suspected that she would have few problems finding game to shoot come daybreak.

Idly she played with the magical charm that Perdimonn had made for her, spinning the little arrow with her finger in the flickering light of the tiny flames to watch it settle time and time again in the same direction after every spin. For the first time in weeks, different sounds filled the night air. Instead of the howling of wind through rocks, the hushed whisper of falling snow, or the sudden clatter of an occasional falling stone, branches creaked in the treetops above her as the night breeze ran its fingers gently through the boughs. The occasional scurrying sound of mice or voles moving among the carpet of twigs and pine needles that covered the floor of the wood sounded unnaturally loud, and without fail Jenna's eyes would snap around in search of the source of movement. Once, later in the evening, as she was dozing off to sleep, a sudden flutter of wings from some way up-slope of her spoke of something larger moving among the trees that had disturbed the roosting birds. However, despite being startled into a heart-pounding state of alertness for a while, Jenna heard nothing more and eventually drifted off into a blissfully warm and comfortable sleep.

The sun was well up and spearing the ground around her shelter with golden shafts of light when Jenna finally surfaced from her deep slumber. There was no sign of Perdimonn so she busied herself, first with washing in the icy cold spring water, and then with setting a series of snares along some of the more obvious animal runs. The local wildlife was obviously not used to being hunted or trapped, for within an hour Jenna was rewarded with not one, but three rabbits. By lunchtime, when Perdimonn arrived back at the campsite, Jenna had gone out and collected the snares back in for fear of catching more small game than they could usefully keep. It was not in Jenna's nature to kill any creature for fun or convenience. When she killed, it was out of necessity.

Perdimonn was quietly impressed by Jenna's camp-craft skills. He nodded minutely to himself as he noted the location and type of shelter that Jenna had constructed. The campsite was neat and well organised, with what little equipment that she had, stored carefully to prevent loss. Also, the string of rabbits that hung already gutted, skinned and cleaned, spoke volumes of Jenna's return to self-sufficiency.

'Good day to you, Jenna. I come bearing gifts,' Perdimonn said with a weary smile. 'It was a bit of a trek, but it was worth the effort. Here, this should fit you.'

The old man tossed her a bundle, which Jenna caught deftly and placed down beside her shoulder pack.

'Sit down, Perdimonn. You look exhausted. Let me get you a cup of dahl and a bite to eat.'

'I'll not argue with that,' he replied. 'But I just need to get Steady's packs...'

'I'll do that,' Jenna interrupted firmly. 'Sit yourself down and tell me where you've been whilst I take a turn at looking after you for a change.'

Jenna took the lead rein from Perdimonn and gave Steady a gentle pat on the neck. The old man walked wearily across to where a large, flat-topped rock made an inviting seat, and with a small sigh, he sank onto it.

'Ah, that feels good,' he breathed, and gently rubbed at his face with his hands as if to wipe away the tiredness.

Jenna had already loosened the straps of the packs that Perdimonn had secured on Steady's back and was lifting them down when he began to explain where he had been. Jenna did not pause in her work as he talked, but listened intently while she stacked the packs next to hers, gave Steady a quick brush down and then reset her small, covert fire to boil water for the dahl.

'I've passed this way many times over the years,' the old

man started. 'And when you've travelled the Vortaffs as many times as I have, you learn to make provision against bad luck in the mountains. The nearest village to this end of the pass is a small one called "Seven Trees". It's well named, as there's not much there aside from the seven large oaks growing on the central green, but having passed through the place many times I've a few folk living there who I'd name as friends. The blacksmith in particular has proved his worth in the past, and today he demonstrated just how trustworthy he is.'

Perdimonn rubbed at his chin, his eyes alight with his pleasure that his trust had been well founded.

'I left money with him against such a circumstance as this. One can never be too careful when travelling the mountains. A single wrong step or loose rock could easily cost you: your horse, your packs, your money and your livelihood. Against that risk I left money with friends at each ends of the passes that I used most often. I had hoped that I would never need it, but it is well that I made such provision, particularly as I can now say that I chose a man of honour to hold that responsibility, for many entrusted with such money as I left, might easily have been tempted to "borrow" a little during hard times. Whether he was tempted or not is immaterial now, for he proved true when it counted, and you and I now have what we need to continue on our separate quests.'

Jenna had allowed Steady to wander unleashed, as Perdimonn always did. There was never a problem in finding the mare when she was needed and she came at the call of her name, so there was no need to tie her. As the horse wandered off towards the nearby glade, Jenna lit her little fire and placed a small pot of water over the small fire pit, allowing just enough of a hole to let the flames draw.

Perdimonn looked on with curiosity, certain that the fire would go out in seconds with the pot all but smothering it.

'So which way will you head?' Jenna asked, smiling to herself as a low roar began under the pot.

'Southwest along the line of the Vortaffs to Terilla. I must warn the Brotherhood of Magicians about Selkor and Darkweaver's Amulet... and speaking of magic, how in

Tarmin's name is that fire drawing so well?' he asked, intrigued.

'It's a trick that Sergeant Derra taught us in training,' Jenna grinned. 'The fire pit is actually dug as a U shaped hole in the ground with the fire laid at the bottom of one of the vertical shafts. If you dig it cleverly enough, the second opening can be fairly small but will allow the fire to draw well. It's an excellent way of having a fire with no flames visible for when you are trying to stay hidden from prying eyes. Fed with only dry wood and tinder, such a small fire makes virtually no smoke as well, so it's the perfect covert source of heat for cooking – aside from magic of course,' she added with a cheeky wink.

Perdimonn laughed.

'Very impressive,' he chuckled. 'I've never seen that before, but you can be sure that I won't forget it.'

'So, what do you think that they'll do?' Jenna asked.

'Who?'

'The Brotherhood of Magicians. Will they go after Selkor, do you think?'

Perdimonn shook his head and frowned. 'I very much doubt it, Jenna. The Brotherhood is not what it once was. Days were when the Brotherhood was formed of Magicians at the peak of their power and knowledge. Today I fear, it is formed of sour old men who steep themselves in memories of better days, and are so busy looking inwards that they have forgotten how to act.'

He drew a deep breath and let it out in a long sigh that spoke volumes of his frustration.

'Nevertheless,' he continued, 'I must try to rouse them. For despite their stagnant, old school attitudes and cantankerous humour, the Brotherhood do wield considerable power when they act in unison. Providing that they act before Selkor has a chance to tap the power of the amulet too deeply, it is possible that they could stop him from being swept into the abyss. Just possessing the amulet has him teetering on the brink, but if he descends into the darkness, who knows what he will unleash?'

'I don't understand,' Jenna said, her brow furrowed as she

tried to sort out what Perdimonn had said. 'You want to stop Selkor, but you sound as if you also want to save him. Why not just kill him? Surely that is the neatest solution?'

'There speaks the heart of a true soldier,' Perdimonn replied with a gentle smile. 'If only life were that simple. This man is bad – kill him. That man is good – pat him on the back. Black is black, white is white, and everyone is happy...'

Perdimonn paused and sighed again.

'Unfortunately, my young friend, life is seldom that simple. The whole earth is filled with shades of grey, many of which are too subtle for us to distinguish. It is true that Selkor appears to be plummeting into the pit of evil where black is truly black, but who is to say that with encouragement or direction, a small chink of grey might not blossom into something good that we cannot foresee? The last wielder of the amulet was not totally evil, was he?'

'Who? Demarr?' Jenna asked, startled by the question. 'No, I suppose not,' she said after a moment or two of thought. 'He was responsible for a lot of bad things happening, but I would not name him evil.'

Perdimonn smiled, his eyes bright.

'Good – very good. So you can appreciate then that I feel that there is still some hope for Selkor, no matter what harm he may have caused in the past?'

Jenna frowned thoughtfully.

'Surely there has to be a line, a point beyond which there is no way back. There must be some distinction that would enable you to say with certainty that someone is truly evil. Otherwise, how would you know when to stop trying to save him and start trying to kill him?'

'Well put, Jenna, and all too true I fear. But how do you draw such a line? When does someone become truly irredeemable? It is a very, very difficult distinction to make. No doubt many in Thrandor would have said that Demarr had crossed that line and should be killed... and yet you find some good in him. Likewise, there are many Magicians who will feel equally strongly that Selkor has stepped too far and that he should die for his actions. Make no mistake though that death is an unforgiving solution. By killing an enemy, you remove their threat, but also you remove their potential. Who is to say that by killing one who is partially evil you are not just paving the way for one who is truly evil?'

Jenna thought about that for a moment or two before letting out a low groan and shaking her head at Perdimonn's argument.

'You are as bad as our tactics instructor,' she accused him with a grin. 'Take a simple situation and look at it closely enough and you will make it progressively more complicated the longer that you look. I perhaps should point out that the simple solution, to the apparently simple problem, often does not change from being the best solution just because the background to the situation is complex. If I were to go through life worrying about the consequence of my every action then I'd never get anything done.'

'Ah, but if you don't even consider the consequences of your actions, then you are worse than reckless,' Perdimonn said seriously, his index finger raised to emphasise the point. 'Not that I would call you reckless, Jenna. Far from it...'

'Me? Reckless? Perish the thought!' Jenna laughed. 'After all, I only deserted Baron Keevan's army on the strength of a dream and entered a mountain range inadequately equipped to survive. I'm sure that any rational, forward-thinking person would have done just the same under similar circumstances.'

Perdimonn laughed with her.

'When you put it like that, I suppose that I should consider myself fortunate that you are a little impetuous, or I would still be languishing in that rock.'

Jenna poured out a cup of boiling hot dahl from the little pot and handed it to Perdimonn, who sipped at it gratefully. Then, not wishing to waste the heat from the fire, she proceeded to prepare one of the larger rabbits into a tasty meal.

While setting out her snares, Jenna had discovered a few plants that she recognised as having edible tubers and roots. With care not to leave excessively obvious signs of her digging, Jenna had harvested a few of each. The only problem was that her small fire would only allow a single pot to be heated at any one time. Not to be beaten, Jenna elected to make a rabbit and vegetable stew in a single pot. By cutting the roots and tubers into small pieces and stripping the rabbit flesh into small strips of meat, the resulting concoction cooked quickly and smelt divine to the two hungry travellers.

'It's a shame that I didn't think to buy some herbs while I was in the village,' Perdimonn commented, as the wafting scent of the simmering stew reached its peak. 'A little tamarat and ground jate would have complemented your pot nicely.'

'Never mind, Perdimonn. You got me clothes, for which I can only thank you. I'm sure that I can forgive you for not thinking of herbs and spices when you got the things that we really needed.'

'Speaking of which...' Perdimonn said, his voice trailing off as he fished around in his waist pouch. A jingling of coins sounded as he dug his fingers deep into the leather stowage. 'Here, take this.'

Perdimonn pressed a small stack of coins into Jenna's hand, for which she could only murmur yet more embarrassed thanks.

'That should be enough to keep you from having to sleep rough for a few weeks,' he said with a gentle smile.

It took a moment for his words to sink home. Then Jenna looked down at the coins in her hand and gasped. The coins in her hand were not copper, bronze or even silver. A dozen gold coins shone brightly in her palm and left her dumbstruck. Jenna had never seen so much money in her life. That she would not have to sleep rough for a while was a major understatement.

'Perdimonn, I...'

'Don't have to say anything,' Perdimonn interrupted. 'I only wish that I was free to join you on your quest, but I am needed elsewhere as I have explained. The least that I can do is to give you what aid I can to help you on your way. Now it is important that you know a little about prices and the currency in Shandar... unless you are already familiar with such things?'

Jenna shook her head and Perdimonn nodded, giving her a look that acknowledged her welter of emotions.

'Well, these gold pieces are called "Sen", and each Sen is worth fifteen silver "Senna"...'

Perdimonn went on to explain the various coins and their relative values. Prices in Shandar were higher than in Thrandor for food and accommodation, but not outrageously so. Therefore, with a thrifty attitude, Jenna calculated that she would be able to live fairly well for a good few weeks with what Perdimonn had given her.

'Having the money in gold has the advantage of being small and easy to store,' Perdimonn said gravely. 'The disadvantage is that gold attracts thieves like flies, so don't flash it around. Don't keep it all in one place. Spread it about your person so that it becomes less likely that some lucky pickpocket will rob you of everything. Change only a single coin at a time and preferably at a moneychanger's office rather than at an Inn or Tavern. I would hate to think that I had brought more trouble on you by giving you this gift, so please treat it with caution and use it well.'

'I will, Perdimonn. I promise. Also, you can be sure that if I ever have the opportunity, I will repay your kindness and generosity.'

'Be successful in your quest, Jenna, and you will have more than repaid me. Kill the demon and set Calvyn's soul free, and I will count the money as the most worthwhile investment that I ever made.'

Shortly thereafter, the stew had simmered long enough to be ready to eat, and despite there being a fairly large quantity, it was all consumed very quickly. Perdimonn had brought some bread at the village and both he and Jenna enjoyed mopping up the last of the juices with slices of the soft, nutty loaf.

When they had finished eating, Jenna took the pot and the eating utensils to the spring and scrubbed them out thoroughly. Then, feeling better than she had in weeks, Jenna packed what she needed for herself into her pack and unravelled the bundle of clothes that Perdimonn had bought for her.

There was a tunic of green and another of brown in a soft, warm material; hose of complementary colours; a sturdy brown leather belt and a leaf green cloak that would not look out of place with any combination of the other clothes. Holding the brown tunic up in front of her, Jenna decided that Perdimonn was a good judge of size and commented as much.

'I didn't buy you boots though, as boots are very much more difficult to judge by appearance alone,' he replied. 'However, yours won't look drastically out of place for now. Bury your uniform somewhere today. If you are found with a Thrandorian uniform, you will almost certainly be branded a spy and thrown into jail. It is just as well that your Baron does not supply boots with any particularly distinguishing features to them. Even so, I suggest that when you have secured a locally made pair then dispose of your current pair discreetly and thoroughly, as there may be the odd person around who might recognise them as Thrandorian made.'

Jenna was not happy at the thought of discarding her hard-earned uniform, but recognised the necessity for what it was. So with her heart hardened to the loss, she went a short distance into the trees and changed into her new clothes. Then, wrapping her uniform in a bundle, Jenna scraped out a shallow hole and buried the symbols of her training there.

It was not an easy thing for her to do, but there was no apparent alternative.

Jenna looked at the patch of loose earth under which she had buried the smart blue and black clothes that had been her last visible links to Baron Keevan's army, and with a start she realised that it would not be enough.

Her heart sank.

Scattering a few branches, twigs and leaves to disguise where she had been digging, Jenna trudged disconsolately back to where Perdimonn was wearily putting his things together.

'Why the long face, Jenna? The clothes look fine,'

Perdimonn said encouragingly.

'It's not the clothes, it's me,' she replied. 'I'm never going to pass as being Shandese. Why, I don't even know the first word of their language.'

'Don't worry. Neither do many of them,' Perdimonn assured her with a chuckle. 'Particularly down here in the south of Shandar. If you say that you're from the eastern seaboard near the borderlands with Thrandor, then your accent of the common speech is passable. If people ask why you are travelling then tell them a variation of the truth. It is always easier to make a lie convincing if it is close to the truth. Tell people that a beast killed your brother, and that you have sworn an oath to track it and kill it to avenge his death. That is plausible, and as you get closer to the demon, it may draw people into helping you if they have suffered losses as well, as they inevitably will have.'

Jenna thought about the old Magician's suggestion and realised that he was right. It would work. It had to.

With a grateful smile, Jenna hugged the old man and kissed him lightly on the cheek.

'Thank you, Perdimonn. Thank you for everything. I hope the other Magicians listen to you. Take care of yourself. I will miss your wisdom and your company.'

Perdimonn clasped her right hand in his and smiled, his bright blue eyes sparkling.

'A blessing on you and your quest, young Jenna. May the gods of light guide your feet and keep the powers of darkness from hindering you from your goal. And may the Father of Creation himself inspire you to overcome the power of the gorvath and keep you from its clutches. Live well, Jenna. I know you will.'

As if the gods themselves had heard Perdimonn's words, the sun chose that moment to poke its head briefly from behind a cloud. A golden shaft of light speared down through the treetops to shine directly on the old man as he finished his words, and for a moment, Jenna's heart seemed to leap up into her throat.

The moment passed. The sun hid its face again and Jenna found herself smoothing down the hairs on the back of her neck that had prickled with the intensity of the experience.

Shouldering her pack, Jenna lifted the little silver charm from her chest. Once again the little arrow pointed resolutely northwest, and so with a last smile and a wave of farewell to the old Magician, she set off on her own once more.

Even as she left, Perdimonn called out to her one last time. 'Jenna.'

She stopped and turned.

'The eyes, Jenna. Don't forget. You mustn't look at its eyes.'

Unable to think of anything else to say, Jenna waved in acknowledgement and moved on, stepping deeper into Shandar with every step.

CHAPTER 12

For several days, Jenna had walked steadily northwest into Shandar. Changing one of Perdimonn's gold pieces for smaller denominations had proved to be fairly straightforward, as she had found a moneychanger on the second day. The crotchety old man had whined on and on about the lack of trade, and how times seemed to be getting worse and worse for honest businessmen. However, he did give Jenna the correct change and only charged two coppers for the service.

Jenna had not stayed in the village where she had changed the coin, as even one gold piece was enough money to interest anyone with a penchant for robbery. It was not that she distrusted the old moneychanger with the confidentiality of their transaction exactly, it was more that she did not trust him without reservation. Instead, she had walked on well into the evening to get as far away as she could... just in case.

Innkeepers in Shandar seemed no different from those in Thrandor. Most were keen to serve any that had the money to pay their bills, and the majority were friendly of face and welcoming in nature. The fact that Jenna was not local had raised a little interest, but on the whole it had made her no less welcome in the Inns and Taverns where she chose to stop over.

Several times Jenna had been obliged to tell the story of her poor dead brother, killed by some nameless beast, and how she was tracking the creature to kill it and claim her vengeance. Heads nodded in sympathy each time she told the tale, but when she asked if any had heard tell of the beast she was met by consistent negatives.

On a couple of occasions Jenna had been asked if she had reason to believe the beast was in the vicinity of the village at which she was staying. To this question she had kept her answers as vague as possible. All she would say was that rumour had it that the beast had headed in this general direction and so she was following in its wake as best she could.

Then one evening trouble arrived in the form of a drunken villager at a Tavern called 'The Jolly Ploughman'.

The Tavern was much like any other. There was a low, heavy, oak-beamed ceiling with the painted plasterwork tarnished by smoke. The large open fireplace housed a crackling log fire, kept constantly fed by the older patrons and seemingly providing one half of the haze of smoke, whilst the old men puffing at their pipes provided the other half. The chimney had probably not been swept in months, which meant that the fire was feeding as much smoke into the common room as it was up the partially blocked flue.

Plain wooden tables and chairs abounded, leaving little space for the Innkeeper and his two serving girls to weave among the tables with the food and drink. Only the strip of open space in front of the polished wooden bar allowed easy movement for those who preferred to stand and drink, and Jenna was fairly certain that during the busiest part of the evening, this would be crowded as well.

Jenna picked a table not too far from the bar so that she could surreptitiously listen to conversations in the hope of picking up hints of her quarry. Despite her protestations at wishing to eat alone, a tall, burly man with a large bulbous nose, red from too much ale, insisted on making unwanted advances towards her as she tried to eat. His breath stank of beer and his body from stale sweat, a pungent combination that she could not help but smell as he persistently shuffled his chair so close that he was all but pressed up against her.

Initially, Jenna tried being polite and asked him nicely to leave her alone. When that did not work, she moved places away from him. It quickly became obvious that this would not work either, as there were a couple of other drunks at the bar who seemed to be urging him on, finding the spectacle of Jenna's discomfort amusing.

When politeness did not work and avoidance proved ineffective, Jenna tried offering a warning.

'Listen, Merklin, if you don't stop hounding me with your foul breath and your pawing hands, I'm afraid that I'm going to have to make your grin less toothsome and add to the generous swelling of your nose. Have I made myself clear?'

Merklin looked across at his friends, his mouth making an exaggerated 'oo' as they vocally joined in with what they obviously considered a fun game.

Jenna looked across at the Innkeeper who was studiously looking anywhere and everywhere but at her. There would be no assistance from that quarter, she decided.

The common room was not crowded, and the drunks were certainly making enough noise for all in the room to be aware that they were up to no good. Yet, as Jenna looked around the large room with its many tables and chairs, none of the people would meet her gaze.

Merklin took another swig from the pot of ale in his right hand and leaned towards Jenna, once more placing his other hand on her knee and belching loudly.

'I only wanted to share a bit of time wiv you,' he slurred, grinning widely.

Jenna snapped.

All patience gone, she grabbed the hand from her knee and twisted it so fast that she heard cracking that could equally have been joints popping or bones breaking. Even as she twisted Merklin's hand and his face began to contort in pain, Jenna found her feet and landed a hammer-like cross-cut to his jaw.

The shock of the impact jarred Jenna's arm to the shoulder and pain flared in her knuckles. Merklin simply pole-axed, out cold.

Unfortunately his chair fell with him and broke as he hit the floor. Moments later, the other two drunkards hurled themselves at Jenna in fury at what she had done to their friend. Given no choice but to defend herself, Jenna ducked under the wild swing of the first and drove an elbow into his gut even as she kicked the second man between the legs. Both went down, clattering into more chairs as they fell.

Aside from the wheezing of the man whose breath Jenna had taken away with the blow to his stomach and the groaning of his friend, a shocked silence settled over the room like a mantle.

Jenna brushed at her tunic, flicking imaginary dust from it with angry gestures, and then strolled up to the bar with one hand on her belt knife. People drew aside as she approached. One look at her flashing eyes and the hand on the knife handle was enough to warrant keeping a safe distance.

'You! Innkeeper,' Jenna said coolly, not raising her voice more than was necessary to ensure that she would definitely be heard.

'Er, yes. Now don't you think that you can er... come in here and er... go breaking up...' he stammered nervously.

'Here,' Jenna interrupted, throwing a couple of silver coins on the bar. 'For the meal and towards the breakages. I won't be staying after all. It seems that a traveller can't even eat a meal in peace in your Tavern, so there's no way that I'll attempt to sleep here. Please note that *so far* I haven't felt the need to draw a weapon. If anyone else so much as blinks in my direction when I walk out of here, I will feel no such compunction.'

She looked over her shoulder at the scattered chairs and the three men on the floor. Two were still writhing on the floor, whilst the third showed no signs of regaining consciousness yet.

'Sorry about the mess,' she muttered, and then strode calmly across the room, hoisting her pack onto her shoulders as she went and collecting her bow from the weapons stand before walking out of the Tavern and into the night.

Once out of 'The Jolly Ploughman', Jenna decided not to linger in the area, but made her way swiftly out of the village as fast as she could. The last thing that she needed was a run-in with the local militia for brawling in the bar. It was the sort of offence that could easily see her locked up for many precious days that she could not afford to lose.

That night, Jenna took refuge in a barn some miles out of town, and in the morning she roused at first light and set out straight away to get as far from the unfortunate incident at the Tavern as she could.

As always now, Jenna checked her little silver charm before setting out. The arrow pointed resolutely northwest. With no one having encountered anything unusual in the villages that she had enquired in to date, Jenna had no idea if she was gaining on the beast at all. For all she knew, it could be a hundred leagues away or a mile down the road. There was no real way of knowing. All she could do was to keep following the directions of the magical charm and hope that she could catch up with the beast swiftly. So, setting as fast a pace as she could hope to maintain, Jenna set off in a straight line across the fields.

After an hour or so, Jenna was faced with another village in her path and the decision of whether to go through or around it. The deciding factor proved to be a wafting smell of baking bread. Jenna had begun walking without eating any breakfast, and the smell of baking bread on the crisp morning air was a temptation too powerful to resist.

It was still quite early in the day as Jenna walked into the village, and few people were abroad in the small community. It was easy to follow the rich, warming smells of the bread to the bakery, and Jenna walked straight to it without hesitation.

The shutters were all closed, but a tap on the door brought an almost instant response. The baker, for with his flour covered apron and flour dusted face and hands he could be no one else, opened the door and immediately his face lit up with a beaming smile.

'Ah!' he exclaimed excitedly. 'You must be the lass who laid out Merklin and his pals down at "The Jolly Ploughman" last night. Come in, come in.'

Jenna grimaced ruefully as she acceded to the baker's sweeping gestures for her to enter.

'News certainly travels fast around here,' she said, as she

crossed the threshold and into the bakery.

'They say it moves faster than the wind,' the baker replied with a chuckle. 'But don't worry, lass. I won't turn you over to the jurismen.'

'You mean they're looking for me?' Jenna asked, slightly surprised.

'Oh, yes,' the baker nodded. 'A cold-eyed killer, you are. A desperate criminal on the run from jurismen right across Shandar for killing a militiaman in your home town, and several others besides – at least that's what Merklin told the local militiamen who arrived at "The Jolly Ploughman" shortly after you left. Of course, the militiamen probably then exaggerated the story a little to the jurismen. By now I should imagine that you are probably at least eight feet tall, armed to the teeth and trained as an assassin for good measure.'

Jenna groaned and put her head in her hands for a moment.

'So why are you not going to turn me over to the jurismen if this is the story that is spreading so fast?' Jenna asked warily, lowering her hands and eyeing the man cautiously to try to ascertain if she had walked into a trap.

The baker was tall and slim, almost to the point of being scrawny. An unusual stature for one who worked with food all day, Jenna noted. His fingers were long and spindly, like a spider's legs emanating from an undernourished body. His face, though long and thin in keeping with the rest of his body, managed somehow to convey a joviality that was at odds with the rest of his appearance. Wide-set eyes, a smallish, slightly snub nose and a broad smiling mouth, offset his angular cheeks and eyebrows to give a jolly, warm-hearted visage that naturally engendered a friendly response.

'Well for one thing, I wouldn't trust anything that Merklin, Toni, or Bradder said about anyone. As it happens though, young Tami the Miller's daughter was there at the Tavern with a friend. She told what was probably a far more accurate version of events to her father, who of course told me this morning. That Merklin is always on the verge of trouble and it's usually Bradder that gets him into it. All three of those lads drink far more than they can handle. They're a disgrace to their families and their neighbourhood. Of course I wouldn't turn you in on account of those three. The problem is that with you being a stranger from out of the area, and what with the man killed in Vendeshollow and all, you couldn't blame the jurismen for wanting to get hold of someone branded a murderer by a local, now could you?'

'A man killed?' Jenna asked sharply. 'How did he die?'

'Difficult to say really,' the baker said thoughtfully. 'Word has it that the body had been so badly mauled by some sort of wild animal by the time it was found that it was impossible to tell whether he had been killed by the animal or foul play. It's said that the body was all but unrecognisable. It was only the remains of his clothes that made the identification of the body possible.'

Jenna's heart seemed to skip a beat as she listened to the baker's description of the poor victim's body. This could be the work of the demon.

'Where is Vendeshollow and when was the man killed?' Jenna asked, trying to sound as if she were just casually interested.

The baker looked at her strangely, as if suddenly unsure if he had judged her character correctly. Even as he paused, there was a heavy knock at the door. The baker's eyes flicked to the door and then back to Jenna and a momentary flash of indecision held him frozen to the spot. Then, before the space of two heartbeats had passed, a look of resolve formed on his face. Lifting a finger to his lips and indicating to Jenna to remain quiet, he pointed to a door at the back of the room.

'Be with you in a second,' the baker called out, grabbing one of the long handled bread shovels and moving over to the door.

Jenna dashed over to the door that the baker had pointed to as quietly as she could, eased it open, slipped through and eased it closed again behind her. It was all but dark in the room, but chinks of light through the closed shutters gave enough light for Jenna to identify this as the baker's private living room. Hardly daring to breathe, Jenna listened at the door.

No sooner had she got the door fully closed than the baker began welcoming someone in through the front door.

'Good morning, Strongarm Malkos. You're early this morning. Are you just coming on duty, or just going off?'

'Just coming on, Parmon.'

'Do you two militiamen require bread as well? I thought you usually collected at the end of your duty,' the baker said, emphasising the word militiamen just slightly.

'We're not here for bread, Parmon. Someone reported a woman entering here only a few minutes ago. We'd like to talk to her about an incident last night.'

'An incident, Malkos? That doesn't sound good, but I'm afraid that you've just missed her. Pleasant spoken girl with a black longbow, I'm assuming that's who you mean?'

'Don't get funny with me, Parmon. Unless I'm much mistaken, you probably don't see many armed women strangers this early in the morning. Of course that's who I mean! Where is she?'

'Like I said, Strongarm, she came in, bought a loaf of bread and went. Was only here a few seconds. Polite girl. Called me "Master Baker," not like some I could name.'

'Any idea where she was going?'

'No, she didn't say. She just bought a loaf, thanked me and left. Why? What's she done?'

'She violently attacked three men in "The Jolly Ploughman" last night.'

The baker whistled a long, low note of surprise.

'That little bit of a girl? Well she must be more dangerous than she looks. Why she couldn't weigh in at any more than I do! Who did she attack? Anyone I know?'

'Merklin, Toni and Bradder,' another voice interjected.

'Ha! Really?' the baker laughed. 'I suppose I don't have to ask if they'd been drinking too much again? Still, even drunk, one young slip of a lass against those three... you wouldn't find many as would give you odds on for her to come out unscathed. Did she hurt any of them badly?'

'Bad enough,' Malkos said coldly. 'But if she isn't here,

then we'd better get on and look for her. Come on. Let's go.'

'Best of luck, Strongarm. She can't have gone far in this short time.'

Jenna heard the sound of the front door closing, and a few seconds later the door at which she was standing began to open. The baker's head looked around the gap. His face was serious.

'Come on. You need to get away from here and fast. When they don't catch up with you or hear word of you again, they'll come back. You must not be here when they come. There's a back door this way.'

'Thank you, Master Baker. I owe you a great debt, but before I go, please tell me where Vendeshollow is and when the man was killed. It is most important. I am tracking a dangerous beast that may have killed that man and any information you can give me might help me find it.'

The baker's face paled slightly. 'A dangerous animal! So that's why the longbow! What kind of dangerous animal? It's not one of those great mountain cats is it? A seeress once told me to beware of them, as if I ever saw one it would herald the last week of my life.'

Jenna shook her head. 'No, it's not a mountain cat, but it's every bit as dangerous. Please – the village? The day?'

The baker heaved a sigh of relief and gave a watery sort of smile. 'Of course. You'll find Vendeshollow about ten miles northwest of here, and the man was killed... oh, it would be... four days ago now. Yes, four days ago. In the evening it's said. Now, you really must go – and swiftly. Come this way.'

The baker grabbed Jenna by the hand and led her back through the main bakery room. Another door in the back wall led into a domestic cooking area that Jenna just had the time to note was immaculately tidy. They went through yet another door and into what was a small hallway to the back door out of the bakery.

Parmon had Jenna stand against the sidewall, out of sight, while he opened the door to a small, low-fenced garden area. The baker took a quick look around and then ushered Jenna out.

'Here, take this,' he said, pressing a loaf of bread into her hand with a grin. 'At least this way if you're caught, the militiamen will not be able to call me a liar about one thing.'

'Thank you, Parmon. Here let me...' Jenna said, fumbling at her money pouch.

'No time. Go, and may the Creator's hand guide you.'

Jenna nodded her thanks, sprinted down the garden, hurdled the fence and raced out of the village using every bit of cover that she could to avoid notice by any more early risers.

Luck was with her.

No shouts followed her and, as far as she could tell, no one witnessed her hasty departure. However, playing on her mind for the rest of the day was the annoying truth that she would have to go back to sleeping rough for a while again, at least until she was well clear of this district. The parochial nature of the society around here was such that any encounter with another person over the next few days would not go unnoticed.

No more soft beds with clean linen and well-cooked meals. How she regretted losing her temper now. It would have been just as easy to walk away, and the militiamen and jurismen would have had no reason to be looking for her. Yes, she might have had an early night and not finished her meal, but instead she was being hunted by the local law enforcers just as she had obtained the first hint of her prey.

With hindsight, words of advice from Derra about avoiding unnecessary conflict and maintaining a strong code of personal discipline all now made perfect sense. Of course hindsight always brings clarity to a situation that at the time might be tangled with conflicting emotions and priorities. It would certainly not win her free of her present situation.

Speed would now be her best ally, Jenna concluded. She needed to keep moving as far and as fast as she could away from 'The Jolly Ploughman' and towards the demon. Unfortunately, speed and avoiding the roads did not exactly go hand in hand. Also, Jenna was afraid that if she raced along too fast, then she might inadvertently stumble upon the demon and be unprepared to face it. However, for the next day at least she would have to take that risk.

Striding out around the edges of fields, always keeping as much cover as she could between herself and any possible pursuers, Jenna kept on the move all through the morning and into the afternoon. Using a pacing technique that she had learned during her recruit days, Jenna kept a rough track of the distance that she had covered as she moved. By early afternoon, she estimated that she had walked about nine and a half miles and her pace became more cautious, as Vendeshollow could not be far away.

There was no sign of the village anywhere that Jenna could see, but she moved with caution nevertheless. Gently rolling hills characterised the landscape thereabouts, and there appeared to be ever-increasing numbers of trees the further west that she moved. By the name of the village alone, Jenna assumed that it would not be easy to spot from a distance. Parmon's direction of northwest by ten miles was hardly an accurately measured heading, which meant that she would only have to have been walking slightly off the true straight line track to miss the village altogether.

Jenna held up the silver charm and checked the direction of the arrow against the position of the sun. It was still pointing northwest or thereabouts. So, judging that there would probably be little to gain by snooping around Vendeshollow anyway, except possibly getting caught by the local militia, Jenna pressed on carefully in the direction that the charm was leading.

The afternoon passed by as uneventfully as the miles, and as the sun began to lower itself gently down towards the horizon, Jenna began to think about finding a place to set up camp for the night. There was no doubt in her mind that she had long since passed Vendeshollow by, though she had no idea if she had passed north or south of it. It was irrelevant. The demon was still ahead of her, but the indications were that she was gaining on it rapidly if it had indeed killed the man in Vendeshollow.

Laid under her makeshift shelter in a copse of trees that night, Jenna did not sleep well. On several occasions she awoke suddenly, startled awake by movement or sound.

Nightly noises that normally sounded benign had suddenly taken on more menacing tones, and Jenna could not shake the feeling that she was being watched. However, for all the restless unease, nothing untoward happened and the next day she found no sign of anything unusual having moved around her campsite.

On checking the magical little arrow, it appeared to be pointing more towards due west than northwest this morning. A change in direction of that magnitude overnight meant that Jenna could not be that far behind the gorvath now.

Still, she had no idea what form the demon held, or if her weapons would be effective against it, but now, more than ever before, Jenna discovered that her resolve to kill the beast and free Calvyn's soul was strengthening. She had come too far to get the jitters now.

Meticulously she checked her bowstring before looping first one end onto the great Akar wood bow and then, with a deft application of pressure, she bent the weapon sufficiently to loop the other end into position, carefully checking that the loops were seated correctly. With equal care she checked her arrows to ensure that all the fletchings were secure and that the tips were still whipped tightly and squarely to the shafts. It would not do to have a loose vane or arrowhead cause an arrow to go astray when every one would need to be deadly accurate.

In some ways Jenna wished that she had spent some of Perdimonn's gold coins on a new sword. Replacing the blade that she had lost during the ambush, when she had effectively deserted from Baron Keevan's army, was high on her wish list. But she had been viewed darkly enough for travelling with such a fearsome-looking longbow, and adding to her arsenal might have provoked a more hostile response from those she sought to pass by peacefully.

There was no point harbouring regrets though, and Jenna knew it. So she focused totally on making the weapons that she did have, as lethal and reliable as she could. Arrows checked, bow strung and belt knife sharpened, Jenna moved on again, drawn ever further west by the magical charm around her neck.

Again she walked all day, pausing only for a quick bite to eat from the fast-dwindling stores of food in her pack. Necessity would probably drive her into a village briefly to restock on basics the next day, Jenna decided, as she did not want to waste time hunting anything other than the demon now.

She was close. She could feel it.

As the sun began the last stages of its fall towards the horizon, Jenna began to look for a suitable place to shelter for the night. Tired, but still alert with the knowledge that the demon was not far away, Jenna noticed the little village tucked away in the trees ahead of her some time before the twinkling of early-lit lamps and lanterns made it more obvious.

There was nowhere particularly suitable to bed down for some distance to the east of the village, and although Jenna had travelled quite some distance now from 'The Jolly Ploughman', there was no way of telling if word of her had reached this far. Therefore, Jenna decided better of going into the village to try to find lodging for the night. Instead, she elected to skirt around it and try to find something convenient on the other side.

Carefully she crept closer. The long shadows and ample cover given by the trees around the village made it fairly easy to avoid being noticed by the inhabitants. Before long, Jenna began to silently circumnavigate the little group of houses.

A sudden prickling sensation at her chest caused Jenna to involuntarily jiggle the silver charm under her tunic to try to make it lay flat. The sensation remained. Intrigued, Jenna lifted the little silver arrow away from her chest to see what it was doing, and her breath caught in her throat.

Not only was the arrow vibrating at a very high frequency as if excited, but also it was pointing in towards the village.

The hairs on the back of Jenna's neck stood up as one and a shiver ran down her spine.

The gorvath was here.

'Calm,' she told herself firmly, forcing her breathing into a slow, regular rhythm. 'It won't do to come all this way and then miss a potential shot through nervousness.'

It was easier said than done.

Despite calming her breathing and forcing herself to think positively, Jenna could not stop her hands from shaking as she pulled an arrow from her quiver and nocked it. Briefly, the shaft chattered slightly against the sighting groove on the bow. A hastily hooked finger from her other hand wrapped tightly across it, flattening it against the bow and preventing her shaking hands from transmitting any further noise that might give away her presence.

If the demon was in the village, it could be disguised as anything or anyone, she reasoned. She couldn't hold the charm up *and* shoot arrows. Therefore, it would be better to anticipate the demon's movement and try to kill it as it moved on again. The gorvath had been moving west for some weeks now and there was no reason to expect it to change direction, so if she hid herself on the western perimeter of the village, she would give herself the best chance of getting a clear shot.

With her basic plan settled, Jenna crept on around the village, being doubly cautious to remain undiscovered. It took a while to find a vantage-point that offered the sort of field of view that she wanted. With all the trees around, there was not really anywhere that was perfect. Finally though, Jenna settled on a position behind a boulder that protruded waist-high from the ground, no more than fifty paces from one of the western-most cottages.

As she had moved around the village, so had the point of the little silver arrow swung round, always pointing into the heart of the settlement.

It was really here.

Having decided on her hide, Jenna shucked off her pack and removed all of the pouches from her waist-belt. If she needed to move in a hurry, then she wanted to be able to move as freely as possible. The only item that remained hanging on her belt was her knife in its sheath, although if it came down to using that, Jenna knew that she would be as good as dead already.

The sun had gone down and dusk was rapidly thickening into night.

Jenna grimaced to herself.

This was no time of day to be hunting anything with a bow and arrow, even if it was a large target. If it got much darker she would be unable to see any distance at all. Moonlight would help, but it would be some hours yet before the moon lifted her face to look down upon the world with her silvery face. All she could do was to avoid looking at the yellow lantern lights of the village and try to keep her night vision at its best.

As quietly as she could, Jenna hid her pack and pouches, tucking them down against an undercut at the base of the large boulder, and slowly gathering and piling leaves over them.

Barely had she camouflaged her belongings to her satisfaction, when a blood-curdling scream rent the otherwise still and peaceful evening air.

Jenna's heart leapt and she held up the silver charm, straining her eyes to see where it settled.

Voices called out behind her as she sat with her back to the rock. Shouts of horror and confusion filled the air now as the village roused to seek the source of the scream.

Jenna watched the arrow slowly turn. The demon, not surprisingly, was on the move. It was somewhere over to her right. That was about all that Jenna could tell in this light.

Rising to a crouch, she strained her eyes into the gloom.

Nothing.

'Damn!' she muttered under her breath.

There was no way that she could use the charm and handle the bow at the same time, but she was reluctant to move without a clear guide, or she could easily lose the element of surprise.

What to do?

Someone... a woman, was still screaming hysterically in the village, and there was now a welter of other voices and the sound of people running around behind where Jenna hid.

If she did not act now, others may enter the trees and confuse things. It would not help matters if she shot a local by accident.

Still she could see nothing moving.

Steeling herself, Jenna crept out from behind her rock and moved step by step, inch by inch through the trees towards the direction that the demon had left the village. Straining her eyes to the limit, and listening with all her might for any sound not related to the confused cacophony of the people running around amongst the houses, she stalked through the trees with her bow half-drawn in front of her.

There... something was moving.

She saw a shape, large and hunched like a great bear, but moving on two legs like a man. It almost seemed at one with the shadows as it moved through the trees away from the village.

Jenna stopped stock-still.

Distance was difficult to judge in the poor light, but a central body shot would not be impossible, even if she mis-read the range slightly.

There would only be one chance, so with infinite care and using the very best, detached technique, Jenna drew the bow and sighted the shot.

'OI! YOU! What are you doing?'

Jenna heard the footsteps running towards her from her right and the shadow in the dark stopped moving. A pair of hypnotically orange-red eyes filled with a depth of hatred and evil, the like of which Jenna had never seen before, drilled a chilling stare through the darkness at her.

Jenna released the arrow.

The thrum of the bowstring and the fizz of the arrow through the night air filled Jenna's senses, and she almost felt the arrow strike home as she heard the impact.

The expression in the eyes did not change.

There was no pain in that look, only a burning hatred and a stomach-churning evil.

Hands grabbed Jenna's arms roughly, tearing the bow from her grip, and voices babbled questions with no meaning or coherence.

The eyes were everything.

They held her under their spell and nothing else had relevance.

Then suddenly they were gone, the burning glow of the eyes winking out into darkness, and Jenna realised that she was being dragged forcefully towards the lights of the village.

CHAPTER 13

'Well done, Shanier. Well done.'

Lord Vallaine looked more than a little smug as his protégé had succeeded once again beyond all expectations at the challenges that Vallaine had set him. With more time, Vallaine felt that he could have developed the young Thrandorian into the most powerful Sorcerer for a hundred years. The young man's mind was truly extraordinary, and the High Lord of the Inner Eye felt sure that he had not yet plumbed the depths of Shanier's abilities.

'Maybe it has something to do with not possessing a soul,' the wily old Sorcerer mused. 'Without conscience or concern for the consequences to others, Shanier may not be hampered by emotions that might restrict others in the use of their power. It could be that lacking which allows a fuller use of his mind's innate power, and helps him to master techniques and abilities that normally take years to perfect.'

Unfortunately, time was a commodity no longer available to Vallaine. His hold over the Emperor was precarious at best, and if he did not strike now, the chance to use the southern based legions of the Imperial Army might slip away from him. Still, if all went well, as he had foreseen that it would, then Vallaine could continue developing Shanier's abilities when he returned from Thrandor.

It was time for Shanier to do what he had been trained for – to lead a conquering army into Thrandor.

Vallaine had long been contemplating the best way of telling the young man about the path that he was destined to tread. First, though, there was just one last test that the High Lord had in store for Shanier before he divulged that information – a test that would settle the minds of those Lords of the Inner Eye who still thought that Vallaine had been wasting his time training the Thrandorian, when any one of them could have taken the role on themselves.

It would be intriguing to see how Shanier reacted.

He would pass the test. Of that Vallaine was certain. The reaction though, well they would find out shortly.

'Come, Shanier, walk with me. I have some people that I would like you to meet,' Vallaine said, smiling and beckoning for Shanier to walk alongside him.

'Of course, Lord Vallaine. Whatever you wish,' Shanier replied.

The High Lord walked casually out into the palace corridors with his hood down, so Shanier followed suit. It was unusual, for normally Lord Vallaine kept the tradition of wearing his hood up around the common areas of the palace grounds. However, Lord Shanier thought better of mentioning it. Instead, he walked nonchalantly at the side of Lord Vallaine, offhandedly 'playing' with the illusory décor as they moved silently through the corridors towards the Chamber of the Eye.

The great spartan chamber with its throne-like seats and its arched windows always drove a cold spot into Shanier's chest. It was not fear exactly, nor was it apprehension. It was just a knot of cold tension that seemed to squeeze at his heart until he could feel its slow, thudding rhythm pounding in his ears.

Today was no different.

The Chamber of the Eye started to work its strange magic on Shanier even as he entered through the large double doors. Worse yet, ten of the twelve seats were already filled. The Lords had convened and Shanier had gleaned no prior knowledge of the reason for the session. Indeed, he had not known that any, let alone all of the rest of the Lords were to be present when Shanier met the people that Lord Vallaine had implied that he was to be introduced to.

Shanier had quite obviously been the only Lord of the Inner Eye not 'in the know' about today's event, and though he maintained a calm, unaffected exterior as he took his seat, inwardly he seethed with self-reproach at not having gained any foreknowledge.

Knowledge was power, and at the moment Shanier knew that he was the weakest person in the room by virtue of the fact that he had not even the faintest clue of what was happening. 'This will *not* happen again,' he promised himself.

As Shanier and Vallaine had entered, the rest of the Lords had removed their hoods in deference to the High Lord's bared head, and then everyone sat as Vallaine took his seat.

'Damn Vallaine for his blasted dramatic pauses,' Shanier fumed in the deepest corner of his mind, as Lord Vallaine sat in silence and all awaited his opening words. 'The man is so full of his own self-importance that he has lost sight of the fact that his position as High Lord is only secure until one of *us* takes it away from him.'

The other ten Lords of the Inner Eye were deeply involved in their usual efforts to probe each other's minds, all trying to gain something of use to their constant machinations and power-grabbing scheming. Several times, Shanier felt touches in the part of his mind that he allowed them to see. Some of the probes were subtle, a faint whisper of a touch so delicate that even one trained to recognise it for what it was might overlook it as imagination. Others were as subtle as a sledgehammer, bludgeoning their way to what they wanted. Either way, all those who probed gained the same picture from his mind... loyalty to Lord Vallaine and a deep conviction that this session would prove of value to the Lords of the Inner Eye.

Shanier elected not to probe the others for information in case any recognised his touch. Despite his position of weakness, he decided that it would probably be better if he did not make matters worse by showing it to all and sundry by probing specifically for something that would be at the top of everyone's minds – the reason for being there. If any recognised his touch and what he was after, it would be around the others in a flash that he had been kept in the dark about today. A line of disinterest in probing others gave him a slightly better stance.

Lord Vallaine finally broke the silence.

'Guards, bring in the prisoners,' he ordered, a sly smile on his face.

The double doors swung open and a scruffy, battered-looking group of five soldiers were herded into the Chamber.

Shanier immediately had to work hard to keep his external features from betraying him, and the open part of his mind from showing any sort of recognition at all. For these were soldiers from his old 'unit, of that he was sure.

'It's another test. It has to be. But what sort of test?' he wondered.

The group was forced to their knees before the Lords. Aside from being battered and bruised, they all looked poorly nourished and pale. Unless things had changed radically since Shanier had served with them, then these five had not been with their army for some time. Therefore, Shanier reasoned, these soldiers had been prisoners here and held in the underground cells for at least a matter of weeks.

The five were looking around goggle-eyed at the twelve cloaked figures ranged in a semi-circle around them. The knowledge that they were facing powerful Sorcerers was evident in their eyes, but although all wore their trepidation like a sign emblazoned on their faces, none showed a level of fear as deep as might be expected.

'Calvyn? Corporal Calvyn? Is that really you?'

Shanier had to exert a supreme effort of control to prevent all from feeling his inner surge of exultation.

'Calvyn! That was the name that had been on the tip of his tongue all this time. Yes, it fitted perfectly into the mosaic of memories. Great chunks of his past suddenly slotted together, and a sense of completeness threatened to overwhelm the guards and walls that Shanier had taken such great pains to erect within his mind.

The walls could not come down yet – he was not ready.

'Lord Vallaine, do you wish me to answer this... person?' Shanier asked, his ice-cool, expressionless voice giving nothing away.

'Go ahead, Lord Shanier,' the High Lord replied blandly.

Shanier got to his feet and walked slowly over to stand

immediately in front of the soldiers.

'Calvyn! It is you! Please, can you get us out of here? They've held us here for weeks, months maybe, its difficult to tell when you're in the dark so much. Soffi has already died here. She had wounds that they didn't treat and there was nothing that we could do. In the end she just gave up and stopped breathing. Tarmin, but it's good to see you again, Calvyn!'

'Garath,' Shanier thought to himself. 'The man's name is Garath. He was on the same training course that I was.' Outwardly Shanier showed no sign of recognition. Indeed, even internally, in the deepest part of his mind, he refused to start considering himself as Calvyn again in case he slipped up with an unguarded thought or word. After all, it would only take one stray thought to totally compromise his position.

'I am afraid that you are mistaken. My name is not Calvyn and I am not a Corporal. I am Shanier, a Lord of the Inner Eye,' Shanier stated coldly. 'Do any of you challenge my name or title?' he added ominously.

None of the other prisoners replied.

Garath simply replied, 'No, Lord,' though it was obvious that he believed differently.

'Sensible,' he acknowledged and then turned to face Lord Vallaine.

It was obvious now that this meeting and his reaction to it were what this was all about. These five soldiers held no more or less a place in his heart than did any other living being. That Shanier had managed to conceal his recognition of them from the other Sorcerers was a major achievement, yet gaining his true name whilst concealing the importance of this information was perhaps an even bigger bonus.

The ragtag bunch had given him what he needed, and he had gained in power without allowing so much as a hint that he had ever been in a position of weakness to leak into his public mind. The soldiers were now totally dispensable.

'You were right, Lord Vallaine. It was an interesting encounter. However, I know nothing of these people and they are nothing to me. Was there something else, perhaps?

Did you wish me to probe them and discover why they are falsely claiming knowledge of me from elsewhere?'

Lord Vallaine smiled and looked around at the rest of the Lords.

'Are you content, Lords of the Inner Eye? You have seen Lord Shanier's denial of these pretenders. Are you content to have him adopt the task that we discussed before? If any dissent, then let him stand now.'

There was a slight pause and then two Lords got to their feet. The remainder stayed seated.

'Very well. The majority is in support, so we will proceed as I planned. Lords Cillverne and Dakreth, your protest is noted. Therefore, Lord Cillverne, you will accompany Lord Shanier when he takes up his post to ensure that he carries out his task faithfully. Will this appease your dissent, Lord Dakreth?'

'It will, my Lord,' Dakreth replied, re-taking his seat and flashing an amused smirk at Cillverne for his fortune.

'Good,' Vallaine said in a satisfied tone, obviously enjoying every second of the in-fighting between the lesser Lords. 'Now, Shanier. What should we do with these prisoners?'

'Kill them, my Lord,' Shanier said offhandedly. 'Unless you feel that they have some further usefulness.'

The answer obviously pleased the High Lord, and other members also wore approving expressions on their faces. Behind Shanier, one of the prisoners let out a groan.

'I can't think of anything much that they would be good for, can you?' Vallaine answered, equally casually.

Shanier thought for a moment.

This may be yet another test, so he did not rush, but thought the situation through logically. He felt nothing for the prisoners. He felt nothing for anyone. However, to just kill them for the sake of killing was not a logical use of lives. Therefore, he suggested an alternative.

'Well, my Lord, judging by their uniforms, these people are soldiers by trade. Why do we not use them as such? I suggest that you give them to the newly qualified Adepts as a project, to turn them into fighters for us. It will not be easy, as they are all fiercely loyal to their Lord and country.

However, if they fail, the Adepts will have gained some useful experience and we can still kill them anyway.'

Lord Vallaine's mouth curled up in a slow smile.   'An elegant solution, Lord Shanier. Do any here dissent?'

No one moved.

'Very well. Guards! Take the prisoners away. The Adepts can collect them from their cells later.'

'You traitorous dog, Calvyn!' Garath snarled, lunging forward to grab at Shanier from behind.

Shanier sensed Garath coming and whipped round to face him, the thick black cloak of his office as a Lord of the Inner Eye billowing out around him as he turned. Even as he spun around, Shanier punched forward a flat palmed hand as if to push his protagonist away from him. The hand never touched Garath, but the bolt of mental energy that Shanier unleashed certainly did, as it lifted Garath from his feet and hurled him backwards to land amongst his fellow soldiers.

A stunned silence followed.

Some of the Lords sprang to their feet in surprise, whilst others just sat in dumbfounded shock.

The guards pulled the other four Thrandorian soldiers away from Garath and ushered them out of the room, then one of them checked the unconscious man's pulse.

'Is he dead?' Vallaine asked uncertainly, obviously as shaken as the rest of the Lords.

'No, Lord Vallaine. But he'll not regain consciousness for some time, if ever,' the guard said, clearly awed by what he had just witnessed.

'Very well. Put him in the cell with the others for now.'

'Yes, Lord.'

The guard hoisted the unconscious Thrandorian onto his shoulder and bent under the weight. He exited through the double doors and retreated down the corridor.

Shanier had not moved from where he had been standing when Garath had launched his attack. Now, however, he was examining the palm of the hand that he had thrust forward and gently scratching at it as if attempting to relieve an itch.

'What *exactly* did you do to that man, Shanier?' Lord Vallaine asked as soon as the last guard had left and the doors had closed.

Shanier looked around at him, somewhat confused.

'I have no idea, Lord Vallaine. I sensed him coming and as I turned I just sort of *pushed* with my mind.'

'Could you do it again?' asked Lord Dakreth, speaking out of turn but obviously unrepentant for doing so.

'I... I don't know really,' Shanier replied slowly. 'If faced with a similar situation... maybe. If you asked me to do it again right now, then the answer would have to be no. It was instinctive somehow. Not something that I think I could control at will.'

'A pity,' observed Lord Vallaine thoughtfully. 'It would have been a useful weapon to have at your disposal for the next few months as you lead the Legions into Thrandor.'

'My Lord?'

'You are to command the force that we are sending to take control of Thrandor, Lord Shanier. Your orders are to head directly for the capital. Don't get distracted with towns and strongholds along the way unless it becomes necessary to deal with them. There is a fair sized Thrandorian force camped around the walled keep that is laughingly known as Keevan's Castle. You will most likely need to neutralise this force before moving on south, or they will probably hound you all the way to Mantor. Show no mercy. Remember, take Mantor and you have Thrandor. The Terachite Nomads had the right idea, but didn't press home their advantage. I have every confidence that you will do the job properly.'

*   *   *   *   *

'Halt! Who goes there?'

The shadowy figure took one further step forward so that the light from a wall-mounted torch would illuminate her to the challenging guard. That one step produced the intended response.

'Sergeant Derra! My apologies, Sergeant, I wasn't expecting anyone now until the end of my watch in about another hour and a half.'

'That's quite all right, Private. Stand at ease. The reason

that you weren't told about my coming was that the need for secrecy was paramount. I need you to open the gates just enough to let my scout party and I out of the castle. Our task is one of the utmost importance, so you will have to keep our departure a total secret. Not a word to anyone. Is that understood?'

The Private frowned uncertainly.

'Well... yes, Sergeant,' he said hesitantly. 'It's just that my orders...'

'Are to let no one out of the castle,' interrupted Derra, her voice dropping to the dangerous growl that everyone knew meant trouble for anyone contradicting it. 'Yes, I know about your orders. Who do you think gave them in the first place? Now I'm changing them. Open the gates. Let us go. Tell no one. It's that simple.'

'Yes, Sergeant,' the Private said unhappily, but nevertheless he moved to comply.

Out of the darkness, three more figures appeared. All moved as silently as shadows, with no words exchanged and no loose equipment jangling. Each of them, Derra included, wore a light pack and was heavily armed. This was a group intent on speed and expecting trouble, the guard decided as he swung the now unbarred and unbolted gate open just wide enough for the group to slip through one-by-one.

'Thank you, Private. Remember – not a word,' Derra said quietly as she slid through the gap last.

The Private did not reply, but quietly closed the gate behind Derra and dutifully started working bolts and bars back into place, taking the utmost care to make no sound as he did so.

Outside the castle, the foursome worked their way along the wall, remaining in the shadows and moving as silently as ghosts. Once around the corner and moving away from the large tented area outside the castle they struck out from the shelter of the wall and moved, stealthy and unseen, into the night.

This trip had been some time in the making now, Derra mused as she followed Bek, Eloise and Jez in a direct line northward, towards the Shandese border. The first couple of times that Derra had called the four together, the intention had been to prevent any one of them from doing exactly what they were all doing this night. However, with each meeting the desire in each of them to return Calvyn's sword to him had grown, until instead of meeting to prevent each other from going, they had found themselves meeting to plan the journey.

All of them knew that what they were doing was wrong, because it contravened the commands of their superiors. However, each also believed vehemently that what they were doing was right, as the sword simply had to be returned to Calvyn. Returning the sword had become the most important single act that any of them could do to further the cause of Thrandor against Shandar. This each believed unswervingly, with all of their hearts.

That magic was at work, all acknowledged and agreed. However, everyone also agreed that the sword in Calvyn's hands had turned the battle at Mantor against the Terachite Nomads to Thrandor's advantage. Logically, therefore, if they could once again place the sword back into Calvyn's hands, its magic would be working for Thrandor once more.

When Calvyn had not returned from the patrol all those weeks ago, it had to have been because he had somehow been captured. This meant that he must be a captive somewhere. He was not dead, on that they all agreed. Also, all four felt an overwhelming conviction that they could find him, despite none being able to say how far they would have to travel to do so. With that uncertainty in mind, they had packed as best they could for all contingencies without compromising their ability to move swiftly.

It had been a difficult balance to strike, but it was too late now to worry about what they had left behind. Everyone was focused on what lay ahead. Bek set the initial pace, keeping it slow to begin with and then gradually accelerating it as their eyes adjusted to the dark.

*   *   *   *   *

Jenna settled the sword at her left hip again. It felt strange to wear a blade again after so long without, but it was also comforting to have it at her side. At least when she next caught up with the gorvath, Jenna felt that she would be as usefully armed as she could be.

One thing was clear now: Jenna needed to catch up with the gorvath again and kill it quickly. By now she had probably been designated an outlaw, and just about anyone and everyone would be out looking for her.

The men from the village had dragged her into what was virtually a mob scene the night that she had first encountered the gorvath. The demon had claimed another victim, of that there was no doubt. However, these folk knew nothing of demons. All they knew was that one of their number had been horribly murdered, and that a strange woman carrying weapons had been captured creeping around not far from where the man had been killed.

If it had not been for one or two cooler heads amongst the villagers, Jenna might well have been in danger of being lynched there and then. Fortunately for her, the calmer characters were also those who commanded the most respect within the village, and their voices won the control of the crowd... barely.

There were no militiamen or jurismen resident, but the Blacksmith and the owner of the Village Tavern, both highly regarded among the people, insisted that Jenna be detained and questioned. Between them they had managed to get Jenna away from the crowd, but not before she had suffered several kicks, punches and people spitting on her.

Jenna was terrified throughout.

When, finally, the Blacksmith and the Tavern Landlord, flanked by a couple of other burly men had bundled her into a small internal room in the Village Tavern, Jenna was white and shaking from the whole experience. Neither of the men had been deliberately trying to hurt her as they pushed her through the door into the bare little box room, but Jenna had known that she would have bruises on her arms from the pressure of their grips by the next day.

As she had been shoved forcefully into the little room, Jenna had noted that it had no windows, only the one door and minimal furniture. One battered old wooden chair had sat to the left of the door, and a couple of tatty old cushions and a dirty looking blanket had lain heaped by the far wall.

The door had slammed behind her and pitched the room into darkness, leaving only a tiny line of light showing under the bottom of the door. Within seconds, Jenna had found her nose wrinkling in disgust at the faint lingering smells of vomit and urine. The room had almost certainly been used as a lockup for rowdy drunkards in the recent past, and the click of the lock being turned in the door had been enough to tell Jenna that she would not escape this room easily.

Sleep had been almost impossible to achieve that night. Dark dreams of orange-red eyes filled with evil and hatred, and angry, violent people crying out for her blood had haunted the fitful periods of dozing that had made the night drag on for what had seemed like days.

The next morning a group of villagers had questioned Jenna. It was a very frustrating experience. Their questions had been leading and clearly prejudiced. Eventually the Blacksmith, a stout swarthy fellow whom everyone referred to as Cal, had brought the session to a close, clearly disgusted with his fellow villagers. His parting comment to Jenna, though it was meant to be comforting, had been the spur that had set her mind firmly on looking for ways of escape.

'Don't worry,' he had said. 'A jurisman will be here by tomorrow and he will be totally impartial. I saw Dolban's body, and I cannot see how you or any other human could have given him those wounds.'

For her part, Jenna had tried to tell them a story as close to the truth as she could without it sounding overly far-fetched.

It had been difficult... and had proved unproductive.

By late morning, Jenna had come to believe that her only hope of ever pursuing her quest would be to escape.

Her weapons had all been taken from her, the room was locked and guarded, and she had known that she most likely had less than a full day in which to make her break.

She had been lucky.

A chance had come early in the evening, and Jenna had

not hesitated to take it.

The one thing that had saved her from being given no possibility of escape was that no one in the village had known about the incident at 'The Jolly Ploughman'. If there had been, Jenna felt sure that there would have been more than a single guard posted to keep watch on her.

As it was, the man on watch duty that evening had expected no trouble when he had brought in her evening meal. Jenna felt sorry for him afterwards, for he really did not have much of a chance, and she did not want to think about what the villagers would have said to him when they had found that she had escaped.

When the guard had brought in her food, he had found Jenna lying curled on her side on the floor, groaning and clutching her stomach in apparent agony. Obviously concerned, he had placed the tray of food on the floor near the door and quickly moved to Jenna's side to find out what was wrong with her. As he had bent over her, Jenna had rolled onto her back and struck a straight-fingered blow to the man's throat, followed almost immediately by a punch to his solar plexus.

The second punch had not landed quite as hard as she would have liked, as she was at full stretch as she had connected. However, the combination had achieved the desired result, and having leapt to her feet, Jenna had finished the job with a double-handed blow to the back of the man's head.

Fortunately the guard had not made any loud noise as he fell, the rap of his sword hilt on the wooden flooring being the worst of it.

Jenna had run straight to the door and quickly checked the corridor both ways outside. Nobody was there and there had been no immediate signs that anyone had heard the guard's fall. Moreover, she had not believed her luck as she had noticed her bow, quiver and belt, complete with knife, all lying on the table just outside the door. Doubtless they had been kept there for the jurisman to look through when he arrived the next day.

Wasting no time, Jenna had relieved the guard of his

sword and scabbard and then slipped out into the corridor, pausing only long enough to clip her belt around her waist and pick up the bow and quiver.

From the sounds coming from the end of the corridor to her right as she had exited the door, the common room and bar were that way. From the noise level, it was plain that the Tavern was busy that night.

Jenna had elected to go the other way. Several doors on either side of the corridor had been tempting for her to try, but Jenna had reasoned that the further she moved from the common area, the less chance she would have of inadvertently meeting anyone.

Again, luck had been on her side. The door at the end of the corridor proved to be the back exit to the stables. No key had been required to open it, as the door just had bolts top and bottom. Within seconds Jenna had been out in the back courtyard next to the stables, and within a few minutes of flitting from one shadow to the next, had managed to make it to the cover of the trees.

It had taken a moment or two to orientate herself in the dark, but once she had sorted out her bearings, she had then moved rapidly through the trees to find the rock where she had hidden her shoulder pack and pouches.

The carisak had been just where she had left it, and it had taken no more than a few seconds to put her arms through the straps and hoist it onto her shoulders. A few moments more and her pouches were also attached to her belt. Then Jenna had checked the silver charm, and set out walking long into the night. Indeed, dawn had begun to threaten the sky with its first hint of lightening the eastern horizon when she had finally stopped to rest.

The sword that Jenna had liberated from the guard was longer and slightly heavier than the blades that she had trained with. Initially it had felt awkward in her hand when she had run through forms and drills with it, and she had been tempted to cast it aside as useless. Both her forearm and wrist ached even now, as muscles unused in recent weeks protested at the punishment that she dealt them whenever she stopped walking. However, now that she had been able to practise with it for a couple of days, the blade felt much more comfortable, and Jenna was content that she would be able to make good use of it if a situation demanded a close-quarters fight.

Since breaking free, Jenna had neither seen nor heard another human voice in three days. Woodlands had offered progressively more cover over that time, with frequent copses of trees giving way to larger and more dominant standings. Jenna was not certain, but she was becoming gradually more convinced that she had entered the Great Western Forest earlier that morning, as aside from the occasional glade, she had been walking under the shadows of the trees for the last four or five hours now. That thought was daunting in itself, as the forest covered hundreds of square miles, maybe even thousands. Nobody in Thrandor had really seemed to know. The mere fact that the area of trees in which she was walking stretched south as far as the southern border of Thrandor and north and west beyond her knowledge, made it feel like she was diving into an ocean of trees – an ocean that threatened to swallow her like water claiming a weak swimmer in dangerous riptides. If this were the Great Western Forest, then the gorvath would not be the only danger ahead.

Jenna checked her silver charm again to find the arrow still pointed due west. With a slight mental shrug, she let it fall back to her chest and pressed on. The thought of turning back now was no longer an option. The trail had led her this far and she had followed it despite any threat to her own safety. Calvyn needed her – that was what drove her forward.

A short while later, as if the thought of Calvyn had somehow conjured him out of thin air, Jenna could have sworn that she heard his voice calling her name.

Jenna stopped and listened, cocking her head slightly and straining to hear any unusual noise.

There was none.

The only audible sounds were the singing tones of some woodland birds calling to one another with their high-pitched chirping melodies. Otherwise, the forest air was still.

'As if everything else isn't bad enough, now I've started imagining voices,' Jenna muttered to herself irritably as she moved on again after a minute or so.

A few moments later, she stopped again.

There was definitely someone moving among the trees ahead of her... and that someone was calling her name.

Jenna moved behind the bowl of a large tree and remained as silent and still as she could. With enormous care, she ever so slowly eased an arrow from her quiver, silently nocked it and gently squeezed a little tension onto the bowstring.

'Jennn....aaa! Jennn....aaa!' the voice called again.

Jenna's heart all but froze in her chest. That voice... she would recognise that voice anywhere. It was Calvyn! Amazed, and still cautious despite her certainty, Jenna peeped around the side of the tree.

The man was still about fifty paces or so away, but there was no mistaking him. It was Calvyn, as large as life and walking in her general direction. He was still wearing his blue and black uniform, though it now appeared to have seen better days, and even at this range, Jenna could see that his face bore the evidence of bruising. His voice sounded weary, as if he had been calling out for a long time, and his head was constantly on the move, scanning the area ahead with his eyes.

It was him!

'Jennn...'

'Over here!'

The words had left Jenna's mouth almost without her thinking, as she lowered her arrow and stepped out from behind the tree.

Calvyn's head snapped around to locate her voice, and suddenly the eyes which Jenna could have sworn only seconds before were the deep blue that she loved so dearly, now burned with an orange-red evil that froze her limbs and chilled her heart.

'Why did I not think to check the silver charm?' she berated herself. 'Maybe if I'd thought to tuck it back under my tunic after the last time I looked at it, I might have had the prickling warning that it gave last time I got close to the demon.'

It was too late now.

The demon had shape-shifted into the form of the person that Jenna had wanted to see more than any other, and then used her desire to trap her. It was a clever ruse and had proved devastatingly effective.

With every ounce of will that Jenna possessed, she fought the compulsion with which the demon held her. Beads of perspiration oozed onto her forehead as she tried with all her might to command her arms to lift and draw her great akar wood bow.

Step by step, the demon came closer and closer.

The burning eyes were unblinking in their intent and its face... Calvyn's face, twisted into a wickedly inhuman grin of anticipation.

Jenna tried to scream, but even that was denied her.

The world was starting to spin wildly out of control, and the only thing that was constant was the eyes. It was the end. Jenna knew that she had failed. The demon was right in front of her now and nothing else but a swirling miasma of chaos existed.

Nothing except, as if from some great distance, Jenna heard a voice shouting – a voice that she felt she should recognise.

For an instant, the demon's eyes looked away, distracted.

The world snapped back into focus, and Jenna staggered on her feet. Shock at her freedom held her briefly with almost as much power as the demon had, and in the instant of her return to consciousness she witnessed the shift.

One moment the hands of the figure in front of her were the hands of her friend Calvyn, the next they were the scaled hands of a creature for which she only had the name 'gorvath'. Great claws, wickedly curved and cruelly sharp, grew from the thick, strong digits, and before Jenna had a chance to recover, it was one of these flesh-rending hands that struck.

CHAPTER 14

The enemy camp was vast.

Derra silently signalled her three companions back into the cover of the trees. With the utmost caution, the four retreated quietly some distance into the wood before Derra halted them and drew them into a close huddle.

'That's no raiding party,' Derra whispered. 'The Shandese are obviously changing their tactics. Even if Thrandor gathered all of its forces, it would take a remarkable amount of good fortune to prevent the leaders of that army from taking it wherever they wanted. Unfortunately, I sense that Calvyn is being held somewhere in its midst.'

'Me too,' Bek confirmed, placing his hand on the hilt of Calvyn's sword and his eyes going distant for a moment.

The others concurred.

'Ideas?' Derra hissed.

'Shouldn't we go back and tell the Baron about the army?' Eloise asked, her eyes glittering in the faint moonlight filtering through the trees.

Derra nodded. 'Do I have any volunteers to go back alone?'

No one moved.

'Somehow I thought that would be the case. Let's face it, we're already in trouble for being here. Let's do what we came to do, and then we'll all go back and take the rap together.'

Everyone nodded, grateful that Derra was not going to order one of them to go back to the castle. The fact that they could easily all be caught or killed trying to get to Calvyn was left unsaid, though all realised that it was more than a slight possibility.

'In that case, we'll need to get ourselves some Shandese uniforms,' Bek whispered gently. 'Even in the dark we wouldn't get far dressed like this. If I were running that army, I'd have plenty of patrols and sweep riders out. We need to ambush a patrol, or take out a few guards...'

The four formulated a plan and then sought out a suitable place to lie low until full dark. Once established in the relative safety of their hiding place, Derra insisted on silence until it was time to move again.

The last vestiges of daylight seemed to linger for an eternity, but at last the darkness of night was complete. Large patches of cloud obscured the majority of the stars, and the moon had not yet lifted her silvery head when the companions crept in single file back towards the huge Shandese encampment. Each had used the quiet period of hiding to think through what they had to do, and the possible problems and complications that they might have to face.

The permutations and possibilities were endless.

Shadow-like and silent, like wraiths, they slipped through the trees and down to the very borders of the camp. Madness it seemed to all of them, and yet the same urge drove each of them on. The sword and Calvyn had to be re-united, and if that meant that the four of them had to rescue him from an army of deadly enemies, then that was what they intended to do.

Derra and Bek took the first pair of guards in a co-ordinated move.

The guards had stopped to chat and warm their hands at one of the many watch-fires. Both were facing the fire and heedless of danger, content that nothing short of another army would dare to challenge a force of this size. With all the patrols and sweep-riders out around the area, neither guard thought for one moment that vigilance of any sort was really necessary.

They died almost simultaneously.

Derra's arm went around the throat of one and Bek's arm the other. There was a sickening 'crack-crunch' as Bek and

Derra broke the necks of the two guards. Eloise and Jez materialised from the dark within seconds to help whisk the bodies away silently out of sight.

Jez and Bek put on the cloaks and helmets of the guards and set out to find suitable sized clothes for Derra and Eloise.

They did not take long.

A short while later, all four of them were wearing Shandese tunics, cloaks and helmets, as they brazenly marched up the hill into the heart of the enemy camp.

The plan to get into the camp was sound enough, and would probably have worked perfectly if it had not been for one detail that had slipped them by completely. Unfortunately, they did not realise their mistake until they were well into the camp and faced with the problem.

'You there! Halt,' said a heavily accented voice from their left as they marched smartly and resolutely up the hillside.

The four halted.

'Be ready,' Bek whispered to the others, and then turned and marched to meet the Shandese soldier bearing down on them. 'Yes, sir? What can we do for you?'

'Well for one thing, you can address me properly, sentryman. I'm no *sir!*'

The soldier hawked and spat as if the word had left a bad taste in his mouth. 'I haven't worked all these years to become a Column Leader to have you degrade my crowns by addressing me as an *officer*,' the man said, tapping the insignia on his shoulder.

'No, Column Leader. Sorry, Column Leader,' Bek replied, playing the contrite subordinate role for all it was worth.

'Now, sentryman, perhaps you might explain to me what those two women are doing here and what they're doing wearing uniforms?'

Bek and the others were momentarily stunned. How could they have been so stupid? The Shandese did not have women fighters in their Legions, and generally did not appear to even have women in their support services either. In Shandar fighting was a man's occupation, and now Derra and Eloise had walked into the middle of a Shandese army trying to pass themselves off as soldiers, when no man with a pair of eyes in his head could miss the fact that either of them was female.

Bek's mind raced.

'Well, Column Leader,' Bek paused and looked around to see if anyone else was nearby, as if he were about to divulge a secret. 'Shall we just say that the two ladies have been invited to pay a visit up the hill and the person doing the inviting has very particular tastes? Aside from drawing as little attention to them as possible, the *sir* in question actually *wanted* them in uniform, if you understand my meaning.'

The Column Leader's face took on a look of disgust. 'Yes, well I don't need you to tell me who did the inviting – that I can guess all too easily.'

Inwardly Bek grinned at the success of his ruse. 'You can always rely on the higher ranks to supply someone with a reputation for debauchery,' he reflected gratefully.

Behind his back, Bek had already hand signalled his intent to dispose of the Column Leader permanently to the others, having visually scanned the area whilst explaining the women's presence. No one else was in sight, though there was a fair amount of movement and noise coming from within the tents either side of them.

Bek gestured to the Column Leader to come closer in a conspiratorial fashion. Intrigued, he moved forward.

'Between you and me, these two ladies have some rather unusual talents... *look.*'

At the word *look*, Bek had stepped abruptly to one side and there was a double flash of hands as Derra and Eloise both hurled knives at the luckless Column Leader. Derra's blade thudded solidly into his chest, whilst Eloise's struck him squarely in the throat. Bek's left hand clapped across the man's mouth only a split instant behind the double impact, muffling any possible outcry and dragging the man off his feet.

Without further discussion, the four lifted the body and placed it in the shadows against the outside edge of one of the nearby tents. It was too late to change the plan now, so they moved on quickly up the hill, the two women doing their utmost to walk like men as they went.

Luck was with them. The four threaded their way through the camp, drawn on up the hill towards a particularly large tent that was pitched at the summit. As they reached the last line of smaller tents before the larger one that appeared to be their destination, they paused and hid themselves deep in the shadows. Carefully, Bek peered around the corner to reconnoitre the area. After a few seconds he ducked back down and pulled the others into a close huddle.

'He's up in that big tent,' Bek whispered. 'Do you all agree?'

All three whispered affirmatives.

'It looks like it's the Shandese Commander's tent. There are two guards at the entrance that I can see. There may be more inside but I can see no shadows on the tent walls to confirm that.'

'We don't have the time to study guard patterns,' Derra said softly. 'The longer that we hang around, the more chance there is that we'll be caught before we've even had a chance to get to Calvyn. I say that we should go for it now and improvise. What about the rest of you?'

Eloise looked apprehensive. 'Why would Corporal Calvyn be in the Commander's tent?' she whispered uneasily.

'Who knows?' Bek whispered back. 'Maybe he's still being interrogated. Whatever the reason, it can't be good for Calvyn, so we'd better go and get him out of there.'

'Gets my vote,' Jez murmured softly. 'Let's do it and get out of here. This whole business gives me the creeps.'

The others all agreed on that much, and it was not long before the four marched out into the open and boldly up towards the main entrance of the huge marquee.

Bek and Jez marched in front, whilst the two women worked very hard at keeping the lead pair between them and the two impassive guards. The guards held long-handled pikes with parade square precision, as if the eyes of the world around them were awaiting a motion that would signal a lack of discipline and dedication. However, no one raised such an observation because the immaculate and rock-steady maintenance of their duty was impeccable.

Jez eyed the pikes warily as they approached and found himself hoping that the guardsmen were not overly well drilled with their fearsome-looking weapons. A sword was one thing... but a pike of that length in the hands of a man skilled in its use would be a difficult weapon to face with confidence, if for no other reason than its reach alone.

Light flickered within the large tent and there were signs of movement inside, though it was impossible to tell how many people were in there.

'Halt! Who comes to disturb the Lords Shanier and Cillverne?'

The guards did a precise half turn inward and their pikes swung down to form a diagonal cross, effectively barring the entrance. The challenge had come a little earlier than Bek would have preferred, as he and the others were still a good few paces away from the guards. As it was, the element of surprise proved vital once again. All four sprinted forward, drawing their weapons in a flash of hands.

The guards swung their vicious-looking pikes around to meet the attack, but they were not quick enough. Bek deflected one pike blade with his sword whilst Eloise lunged into the opening and ran him through. Derra held off the other pike sufficiently for Jez to get inside its sweep and get in a killing blow as well. However, the clash had been very noisy and shouts were already sounding out among the tents immediately below them.

Time was now of the essence, and getting out of the camp swiftly had now become even more of a necessity.

Bek made it into the tent first with the other three hard on his heels and, as one, they all stopped stock-still. It was as if they had suddenly been drained of all energy. Shoulders sagged, arms hung loosely by their sides and faces dropped into the slack, depressed expressions often found in those suffering from extreme fatigue.

'Calvyn,' Bek managed to mumble in a dull, lifeless voice.

The large tent into which the four Thrandorians had burst was incredibly furnished. Plush carpets, woven with patterns that appeared designed to bamboozle the eyes and confound the mind, lay thick on the floor. Four high-backed chairs surrounded a large table, all of which were apparently made entirely from the rare and expensive akar wood. Large wooden cabinets, displaying crystal glasses and ornaments of almost implausible variety and value, were found alongside cabinets of beautifully bound books. A single writing bureau with a quill, a pot of ink and a half-written letter scrawled in a spidery hand, filled one corner of the tent, while a large potted tree filled another. However, none of these things were worthy of any great attention when compared with the more pressing matter of the two figures robed in black, who were standing at the other side of the Akar wood table.

'What did he say, Shanier?' Cillverne asked. 'Was that *another* person who called you Calvyn?'

Cillverne was digging for information and stirring at the same time, Shanier decided, maintaining his facial expression as bland as he could.

'And what of it, Cillverne? It is the name I was given at birth after all,' Shanier replied, not looking to see the reaction but inwardly pleased at the little gasp of surprise from the other Sorcerer at the admission. 'So what have you good ladies and gentlemen come to see me for?'

'The sword,' Derra grated, her teeth gritted as she tried to force herself to move.

'Ah! My sword – how kind. But then I don't suppose that you had much chance of avoiding the compulsion that I set on the blade now, did you? I'm impressed that you managed to get this far into the camp without being caught though – very impressed.'

At that moment a soldier in a burnished armoured uniform stepped into the tent behind the four motionless Thrandorians.

'Commander Chorain, how appropriate that you should join us at this moment,' Shanier said coldly.

'My Lord, there were sounds of fighting and we discovered the dead guards outside. I have forty or so men positioned around the tent, but when I could hear both Lord Cillverne and yourself talking, I assumed that you had everything under control,' the Commander said in his best 'reporting to Senior Officer' voice.

'Very well, Chorain. You can stand all but ten of the men down. Then I want you to get every man who has been on guard duty in the last... let's say two hours and administer a lesson. Twenty lashes each should make the point, and give the Duty Officer fifty. I don't want the men to think that they are the only ones to blame. I don't expect to have visitors walk into my tent unannounced again. Is that clear?'

'Yes, my Lord.'

'Good. Have the ten sent in to join us in about five minutes or so. As these good people have made such an effort to get here, it would be rude not to finish my conversation with them.'

'Yes, my Lord. It will all be done as you say.'

'See that it is, Chorain, or you will find yourself on the whipping post with the guards.'

Chorain bowed and retreated outside.

'Since when did you know about your previous name, Shanier? Lord Vallaine assured us that you would never remember it,' Cillverne asked, his voice unsure of who had been deceiving whom.

Shanier walked forward casually to face Bek, and almost appeared to be ignoring Cillverne as he reached out and drew his magical sword from Bek's right hip scabbard.

The blade gleamed for an instant before returning to its normal steel grey, the silvery runes clearly visible in the lamplight.

'*Ardeva,*' Shanier ordered.

The blade burst into flame, the blue coloured tongues licking hungrily up and down the length of the weapon. Turning the hilt in his hand and admiring the workmanship of the sword again, Shanier suddenly laughed. The sound was chilling.

'I have known that my name is not Shanier since the first day after the underground chamber. It was only in that meeting just before we left that the name Calvyn was firmly established as my original one. For some reason, Vallaine does not seem to understand me very well. *Damok,*' he said casually. The flames extinguished abruptly. Placing the blade down on the large table behind him, and careless of the risk of scratching the tabletop, he gave it a slight shove so that it slid back into the middle of the highly polished surface.

'How did you conceal that knowledge?' Cillverne asked instinctively, unable to contain his curiosity.

'That is for me to know and for you to find out – if you can,' Shanier replied, turning his back on Cillverne and stepping forward to stand in front of his old friends and colleagues. 'So, Sergeant Derra, Corporal Bek, Private Jez and Recruit, or is it Private Eloise?'

'Still Recruit, Corporal Calvyn.'

'Ah! So it has not been that long since I left then. You see I remember most things, but not all. There are not many gaps left now, but one or two still irk me at times. I'm a little disappointed that Jenna isn't with you. For some reason that escapes me right now, I still find that I miss her at times,' Shanier said, his eyes becoming distant. He paused for a few seconds, lost in his thoughts. Then, with a slight shrug of his shoulders, Shanier brought his attention back to bear on Eloise. 'Unfortunately for you though, I am no longer Corporal Calvyn. I am Shanier, a Lord of the Inner Eye, and despite your kind gift and good intentions I'm afraid that makes you the enemy...'

'You're not *Lord* Shanier,' Cillverne's voice interrupted from behind Shanier's back. 'You are merely Vallaine's puppet – a "nobody" who should never have been brought to Shandar. You should have been killed a long time ago, along with the rest of your pathetic excuse for an army. Still, better late than never, I suppose.'

A slow smile spread over Shanier's face as he slowly turned around to find Cillverne standing just a few paces away, next to the akar wood table where the magical sword had come to rest.

The sword was in his hand.

'At last you give me a cast iron excuse to deal with you once and for all, Cillverne. I have waited what has seemed like an eternity for this moment,' he said calmly, taking a couple of steps towards the other black-robed figure and reaching over to the end of the table, where an exact replica of the sword in Cillverne's hand materialised into Shanier's.

'An illusory sword won't do you much good, Shanier,' Cillverne sneered.

'Oh, but it isn't me that's holding the illusion, Cillverne,' Shanier replied, his smile widening.

With that, the sword in Cillverne's hand appeared to dissolve into nothingness, and Shanier leapt forward and ran his blade straight through Cillverne's chest.

The shocked expression on Cillverne's face would have been comical had he not been dying.

'How?' he croaked as he sank to his knees, a trickle of blood running down from the corner of his mouth.

'I guess you'll never know, but if it makes you feel any better, Vallaine also fell for a similar trick,' Shanier said coldly. Then he withdrew the blade as Cillverne's eyes glazed with the stare of death and the Sorcerer slumped face down on the floor.

'You have no idea how good it feels to be rid of you,' Shanier said, as the carpet around Cillverne's body gradually turned red with blood. 'I have been itching to kill you from the moment we met.'

Shanier turned back to face the four would-be rescuers and saluted them with his bloodstained sword.

'Thank you for bringing this back to me. It has already proved most useful. From your perspective I suppose that it has already reduced the number of enemy sorcerers by one, so you should rejoice in a job well done,' he said, with an amused expression on his face. 'Unfortunately, I can't really let you do much celebrating though, as I should really have you killed as well.'

Ignoring the threat, Bek forced out a question. 'How did you switch the swords, Calvyn? We all saw him pick up your sword, and yet there it is, in your hand.'

'Sorcery is all about illusion, Bek – illusion and trickery. Unfortunately for Cillverne, I am far more adept at both than he ever was. When I put the sword down on the table, I gave it the illusion of invisibility and at precisely the same moment, I created an illusory sword in the same place. The sword that I pushed along the table was an illusion all along. If he had worked harder at school, Cillverne might have realised that. However, he may never have been powerful enough to notice. For some reason that I cannot quite fathom, none of the Shandese Sorcerers seem to be able to add any real substance to their illusions. Try to grab their deceptions and all that you would end up holding is a fistful of air, or whatever is beneath the illusory layer of disguise. Still, that is all an irrelevance now.'

Even as he finished his explanation a line of soldiers marched into the back of the tent.

'Column Leader, have your men disarm these people and I will release them to you. Also, I'm afraid that Lord Cillverne proved to be a traitor to our cause and I was forced to kill him. Dispose of his body somewhere suitable, would you?'

'Yes, my Lord.'

The Column Leader gestured to his men, who systematically stripped Derra, Bek, Jez and Eloise of everything that could be used as a weapon. Then the soldiers gave all the weapons to one man who immediately left the tent.

'They're all yours then, Column Leader. Secure them somewhere under heavy guard until I decide what to do with them.'

All at once, the four Thrandorians regained use of their limbs. Derra and Bek reacted instantly, with Jez and Eloise only a split second behind. Within only a few heartbeats, several of the Shandese soldiers had been floored, caught completely by surprise at the ferocity, power and speed of the attack. The rest of the soldiers were in the process of drawing weapons when all four of their assailants abruptly slumped to the floor unconscious.

'I would have thought that the nine of you could strongarm two unarmed men and a couple of women without all this,' Shanier said angrily, pointing at the sprawled Shandese soldiers.

'Er... yes, my Lord,' the Column Leader replied sheepishly.

'Get them out of here.'

'Yes, my Lord.'

The Shandese soldiers regrouped and lifted the unconscious bodies of Derra, Bek, Jez and Eloise, hoisting them over shoulders and exiting the tent.

'Column Leader?' Shanier called, as the last men dragged the corpse of Lord Cillverne out of the tent.

'Yes, my Lord?'

'Am I correct in saying that the Emperor enjoys to watch men fight in an arena?' Shanier asked, rubbing gently at his temples. That last blast of mental energy that he had used to knock out Derra and the others was almost bound to leave him with a splitting headache.

'Yes, my Lord. It is said that he attends the arena in Shandrim most weeks.'

'Very well. Have the two men bound and sent on their way to Shandrim tonight under a heavy guard, and no mess ups, do you hear? Deliver them to the arena to fight for the Emperor's pleasure. The dark-haired one is already a good swordsman and should provide at least a modicum of entertainment. Keep the women here for now.'

'Yes, my Lord.'

The Column Leader turned to go.

'And Column Leader...'

'Yes, my Lord?'

'If anyone so much as lays one finger on either of those women without an order from me, they will die a more horrible death than you could possibly imagine.'

'As you say, my Lord,' the Column Leader replied, his face turning pale at the thought.

* * * * *

Slowly, very slowly, Jenna opened her eyes and tried to focus them on something. Everything was blurred and a warm lassitude held her, as she gradually became more aware of her surroundings. Muscles that normally would be tensing as Jenna prepared to get up and face the day, were strangely unresponsive, and she had to concentrate hard to force herself to blink away the tears that were blurring her vision.

She was in bed – that much she could ascertain, but what bed?

The ceiling was low with heavy wooden beams and neatly whitened panelling in between. Daylight was shaded by curtains of a plain burgundy red material that hung over a small square window to the right of her bed.

Nothing was familiar.

On a wooden table, again simple in design, but which someone who quite obviously took pride in their craft had made, a jug of water and a pile of strips of white linen had been neatly placed. A small clothes press and a wooden chair made up the remainder of the furniture in the little bedroom, but Jenna was none the wiser as to where she was. The only thing that she recognised was her bow, which had been unstrung and was propped against the side of the clothes press.

Jenna tried to raise herself up on her elbows and pain blossomed in her stomach. With an agonised groan she sunk back onto the soft bed and her eyes blurred with tears once more.

The door at the foot of the bed cracked open slightly and a young girl's face peered briefly around the edge.

'Ma! She's awake, Ma. The bow-lady is awake,' the girl called over her shoulder and then slipped completely into the room.

'Now don't you go disturbing her, Alix. The lady needs rest, and she won't get that with you flitting in and out of her room,' answered an older voice in a singsong lilting style of speech.

Jenna found herself wanting to smile at the sound of the two friendly voices, but no matter how hard she tried to place them, neither was familiar. Also, despite the warm, homely atmosphere of her surroundings she could not help being a little wary.

'I'm not disturbing her, Ma. She's already awake,' the girl called enthusiastically and then addressed Jenna. 'How are you feeling?' she asked gently. 'Would you like a drink of water or something?'

Jenna tried to answer, but found that her throat was too

dry to do more than croak slightly.

'Ma' bustled into the room with an empty glass in her hand, and as soon as Jenna managed to blink her eyes enough to see clearly, she immediately saw the close family resemblance of the mother and daughter. Both were dark-haired and blue-eyed with unremarkable features. However, although there was nothing of particular beauty in their faces, the bone structure was so similar that none could possibly mistake them for anything other than kin.

'Bless me, girl, but it's good to see you awake,' Ma said happily. 'I really thought that we'd lost you once or twice there for a while.'

'Ma, I think that the bow-lady would like a drink. She tried to speak just now I think, but nothing much came out.'

'Is that right now, Alix? Well let's see, shall we?'

Ma lifted the jug of water from the table and poured a little into the glass that she had brought in with her. The splash of the water glugging into the glass was like music to Jenna's ears and she tried to lift her head slightly to receive it.

'No! No! Don't try and move or you'll undo all the good work that we've managed to do so far. Here, let me lift your head slightly and tuck this extra pillow underneath. There we go – perfect. Now then, Alix, you give the lady her drink and I'll have a bit of a check on how she's mending.'

Ma lifted the covers and gave a 'tut, tut' of annoyance.

'You've been trying to move, haven't you? Well it's understandable I suppose, but please don't do it again until I say that you can. Your stomach was in a bad way when Gedd brought you home to us. Don't worry though. I have a way with healing – everyone agrees on that. Alix and I will have you up and about and back out hunting before you know it. Won't we, Alix?'

'Aye, Ma,' Alix agreed, placing the glass of water to Jenna's lips and gradually raising it until Jenna could sip at it. 'We'll have you up and about in no time.'

Ma fussed at some sort of bandages around Jenna's middle for a minute or two, while Alix helped Jenna to sip her way through a half glass of water.

What had happened? How had she got here? Who were these people who had taken her into their home? The questions were tumbling around in Jenna's mind in a jumble of confusion, but nothing was fitting together to make any sort of sense.

She had been tracking the demon when she could vaguely remember seeing Calvyn, as if in a dream, walking through the trees and then... nothing. Nothing except... Jenna shuddered.

The eyes – orange-red and burning with hatred.

'What is it, lady?' Alix asked, her young face frowning with concern. 'She's shivering, Ma but she's not cold.'

'Ah! The demon-daze is wearing off, Alix. Don't worry, child. The shaking will pass.'

Jenna was not sure if Ma was addressing Alix or her with the second sentence, but the fact that this woman knew something of demons was more than a little intriguing. Turning her head slightly to indicate to Alix that she had drunk enough, Jenna forced herself to speak.

'Demon... where?' she croaked, her voice broken with a lack of use.

'Now don't you go worrying yourself about that, young lady. You won't be out chasing any demons for a while yet, and when you do, I've no doubt that Gedd will have some wise words for you on keeping yourself alive,' Ma said gently. 'The best thing for you right now is to get some rest. If it will help settle your mind, I'll have Gedd come in and chat with you a little later. You're safe enough here.'

Jenna nodded weakly.

'Very well,' Ma acknowledged. 'Now get yourself off to sleep again. Come on, Alix. You can come and see the lady again later.'

With that, Ma steered the young girl out through the door and closed it quietly behind her. Jenna relaxed back even deeper into the soft bed. The after-image of the demon's eyes haunted her for a short while, but even that disturbing thought did not prevent sleep from enveloping her in its warm embrace, and within a matter of minutes Jenna had sunk back into a deep, dreamless sleep.

The next time that she woke it was to a knock at the door. Jenna opened her eyes and saw Ma's head this time, peeping around the door to see if she was awake. As soon as Jenna's eyes were open, Ma opened the door properly and came in. A tall man followed her.

The man was a curious looking fellow, tall and lean, with a sort of gaunt look about him that spoke of hardship. His eyes were a hazel brown colour and a straight, slim nose was set between angular and hollowed cheeks. The way that the man moved betrayed a degree of fitness that was at odds with his almost haunted face, and Jenna got the distinct impression that this man was a survivor. He was the sort of person that no matter what the odds would find a way of staying alive.

'Lady, this is my husband, Gedd. He wants to talk to you about the demon that you encountered in the forest. Do you think that you could manage that?'

'Yes,' Jenna croaked, her voice still broken. 'Water... please.'

Ma poured a glass of water and held it for Jenna to sip at. After a few sips, Jenna's throat felt much better.

'Enough, thank you,' she managed, speaking much more clearly this time. 'Jenna. My name is Jenna,' she added.

'Well, Jenna, you are a very lucky woman,' Gedd said slowly, his voice deeper than Jenna had expected and painstakingly careful in his pronunciation. 'I hesitate to tax you while you are still so weak, but I need to know about the demon that you encountered. At first I thought it was a large krill, or maybe a gralten, but it doesn't seem to move like any that I've seen before. Unless I misread the signs completely, then I would judge that you were trying to hunt it down. The demon knows that you're on its trail, doesn't it?'

Jenna nodded.

'Do you know what type of demon it is?'

'I'm told that it's a gorvath,' Jenna replied.

Ma gasped loudly. 'The Creator preserve us!' she exclaimed. 'What fool Wizard is messing around with demons like that?'

Gedd ignored his wife completely, his focus all on Jenna and his hazel brown eyes unmoved by her answer.

'A gorvath? You are sure of this?'

'I'm no expert on demons,' Jenna admitted, 'but I was told that this demon had taken the soul of... my friend. I've been hunting it for weeks. The only name that I was given for it was "gorvath" and a Magician supplied that. I care not for its name, only that I kill it and release my friend's soul.'

Gedd scratched at his chin thoughtfully and then ran his fingers through his wavy hair.

'A Magician, you say? Well I suppose that he would know. A gorvath, I've only ever heard rumours that such a beast existed, but I've never heard of a Wizard mad enough to summon one. It will certainly be more powerful and dangerous than anything that we've seen here before.'

Gedd and Ma exchanged a knowing glance.

'Oh, Gedd! Don't go. Please, no more. Let someone else do it. For Shand's sake, Gedd, a gorvath! If you go and get yourself killed, who will look after Alix and me? Please, Gedd?'

Gedd looked at her steadily.

'Kerys, you know what will happen. We'll be safe enough here for a while, but when it has been to the tower for a while, it will start to hunt. Unless we abandon this home and move far from here, then we'll live in danger until it decides to go track down the damned fool Wizard who summoned it. Don't worry, Kerys. I won't go alone this time. Unless I'm much mistaken, Jenna here has faced it at least twice before and survived with no knowledge of demons. I'll wait until she is fit enough to come with me.'

'Oh, Gedd,' she sobbed, and threw her arms around him with tears streaming down her face. 'Why can't Sam or Dreythus go? Why does it always have to be you?'

Gedd did not answer, but held his wife tightly in a long hug. He knew that she understood really. It was obvious that Sam was not experienced enough to go against a demon this powerful, and Dreythus was simply too old. There was no one else in the area who would stand a chance of being successful. The hunt was always going to fall to him.

Jenna watched the scene with interest. This man, Gedd, obviously knew far more of demons than she did, but there were many unanswered questions here.

'Excuse me. I don't mean to intrude, but you speak as if you have killed demons before. If you don't mind me asking – how did you do it? I could have sworn that I had loosed a killing shot on my first encounter with the gorvath, yet the beast showed no sign of pain. Is there a weakness that I should know about?'

Gedd gave his wife a squeeze and then untangled himself from her embrace.

'Not a weakness as such, for aside from their eyes they have no discernible area that is weaker than any other, and anyone trying to aim for their eyes is in danger of demon-daze. No, not a weakness but an effective weapon. It is a rare crystal which people here have named "Demon's Bane" for obvious reasons. The crystal seems to be about the only thing that will penetrate a demon's skin – at least, the only thing in this world anyway.'

'And you have some of this crystal?' Jenna asked immediately.

'Get straight to the point, don't you girl?' Gedd said with a slow smile. 'Yes, I have some. Not a lot, but I have made you this with the one small piece that I can spare.'

Gedd walked around to where Jenna's bow was propped against the clothes press. From the other side of the press he picked up an arrow that had been out of Jenna's view. It was one of hers, but where the steel tip had once been, there was now a many-faceted crystal shaped to a needle sharp point.

'Don't miss,' said Gedd, still smiling. 'You'll only get the one shot.'

CHAPTER 15

Over the next few days, Jenna gradually got to know the little family quite well. Alix was more than a little impressed that Jenna had been hunting the demon, and whenever her mother allowed her, Alix spent as much time as she could talking with Jenna about her quest. Jenna did her best to play down the story, as she quickly realised that the young girl was setting her up as some sort of heroine to worship. The last thing that Jenna wanted on her conscience was for Alix to run off and get herself hurt trying to emulate anything that Jenna had spoken of in her stories.

In turn, Jenna learned a little of what had happened at her last encounter with the demon. Although it was a second-hand account that Alix gave, and some of the details were certainly inaccurate, Jenna heard enough to trigger some more flashbacks of her own.

The transformation of the demon from human form to that of a great bear-like beast, and the huge tearing claws that had all but gutted her, haunted her rest-times. Alix also told her that Gedd had been alerted to something going on by a man's voice shouting. At first Jenna thought that the voice must have been that of the demon calling her name, but then she began to regain the merest whisper of memory about another man shouting. What he had been shouting, she did not know. Jenna wracked her brain for hours over it but could not remember, and when she had asked Gedd about it, he had just shrugged.

'Who knows?' he said. 'The man sounded like he was trying to draw the demon's attention. Any man doing that is more than likely ignorant of demons, or mad. By the time that I reached you, both had gone, and you were in such dire need that had I left you to follow them, you would not have lived to hunt again.'

Jenna had pondered over the snippets of information, searching her memories to try to find where she had heard the voice before. It was definitely familiar. It might have been someone from one of the recent villages that she had visited, but she could not fit anyone to the vague memory that she had of the voice.

No. It would come to her eventually, she was sure. It would just require a little patience.

The voice was not the only thing that she would require patience for either. Her stomach wounds were healing quickly under Kerys's ministrations. Indeed they were knitting together faster than Jenna would have believed possible without the intervention of some form of magic. However, it was still not fast enough to prevent Jenna from feeling immensely frustrated at not being able to track the demon down again, especially now that she had a weapon that offered her a good chance of success.

That Kerys was renowned as a healer in the local area was not surprising, Jenna mused, as she gently prodded the bandaged area of her middle. At least the sticky poultices of creamy gunge were no longer being applied at regular intervals and Kerys was allowing Jenna to move around the cottage at will.

'Leave it alone!' Kerys ordered sternly. 'Do you want it to get better or not? Honestly! You're almost as bad as a man! It will heal just fine if you stop prodding and poking it at every opportunity.'

'Sorry, Kerys,' Jenna muttered contritely.

Gedd smiled at her in amusement from behind Kerys's back, but instantly smoothed his features into a slightly disapproving frown when Kerys turned around.

'And don't you think that you'll get away with mocking me either, Gedd Arissalt,' she warned, raising a finger and prodding his right shoulder. 'Go on with you! Get out and catch us some supper.'

Gedd shook his head slightly in semi-disbelief, but he

moved to do as he was told without hesitation.

'Eyes in the back of her head,' he grumbled good-naturedly as he pulled on his boots, collected his bow and attached a sling to his belt.

Either there was an abundance of game around the area or Gedd was an exceptional hunter, Jenna decided after a week or so. Gedd was seldom gone long and he always returned with enough meat for the four of them. Plump-breasted pigeons, rabbits, and on one occasion a young deer, all fell to his skill with bow and sling, and when cooked with the vegetables and herbs from the little garden outside the cottage, made for consistently good eating. If it had not been for her overwhelming desire to complete the quest that she had begun, then Jenna was sure that the time spent with the Arissalt family would have passed very quickly.

When Jenna had recovered sufficiently to start helping around the house, she started to feel that she was slightly less of an imposition on the family. If it had not been for the fact that she realised the value of Gedd wanting to help her to kill the demon, Jenna would have left at this point and left them money for their kindness and hospitality. However, Gedd had apparently killed demons before and had knowledge far beyond her sketchy information. She needed him, and until he and Kerys agreed that she was fit to travel, Jenna knew that she could do nothing but try to contain her frustration as best she could.

Nearly two weeks had passed since her first awakening in the Arissalts' cottage before Jenna proved herself strong enough to string her great akar wood bow. It had been a struggle and Jenna had felt the pulling on the damaged muscles across her stomach as she had looped the bowstring into place. However, the pain was not one of further damage as much as a lack of use, and though Kerys gave her a disapproving frown as she passed through the kitchen to the outside door, she had not said anything.

Alix had given a whoop of delight when she had seen Jenna walking out with the great bow and had immediately begged to be allowed to go out and watch Jenna practise with it. Kerys had not looked overly happy, but Jenna had assured her that she would only be shooting at static targets and that she would ensure that Alix stayed out of trouble, so Kerys had relented.

To begin with, Jenna had chalked a white circle on the bole of a tree and tried shooting arrows at it from a modest distance. Aside from a few twinges of pain, the main problem with this proved to be pulling the arrows out of the tree afterwards. After she had broken one of the shafts trying to extract her arrows from the tree trunk, Jenna decided to rethink her target strategy.

Alix had come to her rescue by donating an old soft toy to be shot at, and by attaching it to a tightly packed bundle of straw. This proved more than satisfactory, and over the following few days the poor toy was peppered with arrow after arrow.

Jenna had practised with her sword as well, using the exercises, forms and drills to strengthen her weakened muscles. Gradually, over the space of another week, Jenna's fitness improved and the bandaging was lightened until at last Kerys allowed her to take all of the bandaging off. The lines of scar tissue across her belly were still red, but all traces of swelling had gone and the tissue held together no matter how she twisted and turned. Without some form of magical healing Jenna would always bear the marks of the demon's claws, but she was more than determined to take retribution for those scars.

Alix enthused at supper each evening about particular shots that Jenna had made and about how swift and balanced she was with her sword.

'The demon's as good as dead already,' the young girl bubbled after describing a particular combination of sword strokes to her parents.

'Enough, Alix!' her father said sharply, and brought his daughter's exuberant description to an abrupt halt. 'No demon is an easy kill, no matter what kind it is. A gorvath is a deadly killer, a master of disguise and guile. No hunter who hopes to stay alive counts his kill before his target is well and truly dead. Our guest here could be a *dem-taqat* and it would make no difference, for without a weapon made of Demon's Bane and the blessing of the gods, the demon would be nigh on impossible to kill. I am sure that she is good with that bow of hers and that is good. The sword, though, will be about as much use as a deadwood stick, but for now it serves to strengthen her muscles and that too is good. Just try to keep a hold on reality, Alix. I suggest that you pray real hard for Jenna and I tonight, for tomorrow we will be leaving to try to kill the most dangerous creature that this area has probably seen since the war of the gods.'

Alix burst into tears and ran from the table, the slam of her bedroom door reverberating through to the kitchen.

'Was that absolutely necessary, Gedd? Alix'll have nightmares for sure now and it would have been nice for her to have a happy memory of this evening,' Kerys said sadly, the possibility that this might be their last night together evident in her voice.

'The girl has to grow up sometime, Kerys. I hope and pray that we'll not be gone all that long, but it's always possible that she may have to wake up to reality the hard way all too soon.'

An uneasy silence settled over the three diners as they finished their simple supper. Eventually it was Jenna who broke the long silence.

'Gedd, I'm sorry if this seems like a stupid question, but what is a *dem-taqat*?'

'A legendary warrior. A blade-spawn. One who was born for battle, and knows no equal in his generation or in ten generations before or after. There have been a few that have stood out through history. Derkas Silverblade, Mannion the Axemaster and Thurin Bladedancer spring to mind as examples. There have been others, but not many.'

Jenna nodded in understanding. Songs of all three of the characters mentioned were well known in Thrandor. It seemed that those the minstrels chose to immortalise were not restricted by kingdom boundaries, though through the ages of telling, the characters themselves may have changed nationality to suit the minstrels' audience of the moment. Indeed, many of the heroes of past ages could well have been from just about anywhere. Their true nationalities would probably be only known to a handful of scholars, but their deeds were remembered by all.

Jenna did not linger at the table after supper. The atmosphere was awkward and she wanted to get a good night's sleep before setting out the next day. Making her excuses, she cleaned her plate and cutlery and then retired to her room.

Sleep did not come easily.

A combination of excitement, anticipation and nervousness kept her from drifting off for some time. Eventually, though, tiredness overcame all else and she drifted into a world of dreams where *dem-taqat* battled demons with pieces of deadwood and Calvyn looked at her with orange-red eyes.

Morning came and Jenna did not know whether she was glad that the night was over or not. She did not feel well rested, but she was glad to be nearing the end of her quest. The outcome would be decided soon, of that she was certain.

Gedd had told her that the tower where the demons were drawn to was in the forest, about a day and a half's walk away. No one knew the exact reason why the demons went there, only that the tower was said to have once been the home of a particularly powerful Wizard who had summoned many powerful demons during his life. He had not lived in the tower for many years now, though none could say whether he yet lived or not. However, something at the tower drew the demons to it, and if there was a demon loosed by any wizard, deliberately or inadvertently, it seemed that eventually the demon would find its way to this tower.

Before leaving, Jenna had done several things. Firstly she had crept quietly in to see Alix before Gedd and Kerys awoke, and had reassured her with gentle words and a long hug. Then she had taken a bearing using her silver charm to confirm the way to the demon. Finally, she had gathered all of her money from diverse pockets and pouches, put it all in her money pouch, and given the pouch to Kerys.

'If by some chance I don't come back, then keep this with my thanks and blessing. Regardless of that chance, though, I want you to keep half anyway. I owe you my life for your nursing, and more besides for your hospitality and welcome into your home.'

Kerys had protested, but Jenna had insisted firmly and would not leave until Kerys had accepted the money.

'I'll keep it safe for you,' she promised. 'Just you be careful and come back safely.'

At last, with the goodbyes done and the light travel packs loaded with provisions, Jenna and Gedd were ready to leave.

'I guess the tower will be off in that direction then?' Jenna asked, pointing in the direction of the bearing that she had taken earlier.

Gedd's eyebrows raised almost to his hairline in surprise and it was all that Jenna could do to keep from laughing.

'You don't think that I've managed to track the demon this far without having some idea of where I'm going, do you?' she added innocently.

Gedd shrugged slightly and gestured for her to lead the way. With a last wave of farewell to Kerys, and also to Alix who had appeared at the last moment to give them both a hug, hunter and huntress moved swiftly off into the forest.

*   *   *   *   *

Keevan's castle was surrounded.

Defenders packed the walls and the large tented area outside the walls was being held by the Shandese Legions. Lord Shanier looked up at the Gate Towers where he had spent many days and nights on watch duties as a common soldier in Baron Keevan's army. Now he was standing poised with an army of his own, ready to strike a crushing blow against a place that he had once, if only for a year or so, called home.

It would not happen. Shanier had already decided on a more devious course. The fact that he could, if he so chose, destroy the birthplace of his own military training was enough for now.

The Legion Commanders were standing in a group nearby, quite obviously wondering what the delay was for. The waiting was just prolonging the agony. Attacking a fortified position was always going to cost a lot of lives, and the common soldiers and officers alike would be more than aware that this would be a bloody battle. Delaying was bound to make the men more nervous.

Lord Shanier could read them all like open books, such were their minds: eager and confident to send their men to victory. However, Shanier had no intention of letting them have that pleasure. It would weaken their force significantly to fight a major battle here, so he had decided to use subtlety and sorcery to win the day instead.

'Commander Chorain.'

'Yes, my Lord?'

'Have the woman, Derra, brought to my tent. I have a plan to defeat this army without losing a man today.'

Chorain's face clearly showed that he found that difficult to believe.

'At once, my Lord,' the Commander snapped back despite his expression, and he whirled and hurried off immediately.

Shanier retreated to his tent and waited.

A few minutes later, Commander Chorain and six soldiers escorted Derra into his tent.

'You may leave us now, Commander. I can handle things here.'

'Very well, my Lord,' the Commander said, his voice betraying his doubts. 'I'll have the men wait outside.'

'Very good, Commander. You can tell the other Commanders that I will brief them shortly.'

Chorain left and posted the soldiers to supplement the guards already maintaining the vigil at the entrance to the Lord's tent. The other Commanders quizzed him relentlessly for the next few minutes about Lord Shanier's plans, but as he knew no more than they, the questions soon turned to speculation.

'Take the castle without losing a man, he said,' quoted one Commander. 'How in Shand's name does he intend to do that?'

'Maybe he is as powerful at sorcery as rumour has it,' said another.

'That may be true, but we would surely have been better off with two Lord Sorcerers than one. All this about Lord Cillverne being a traitor sounds a bit far-fetched to me,' speculated a third.

'Lord Shanier was appointed through Lord Vallaine by the Emperor himself. If Lord Shanier named Cillverne a traitor, then traitor he was,' stated Chorain firmly.

'Well, what is he doing consorting with that enemy woman fighter then?'

'Who knows? But I'm sure that we'll find out soon enough. We are all to hold a conference with him shortly,' Chorain said placatingly.

'Pah! Conference my foot! Audience is more like it. These Sorcerers are all the same. They have no military knowledge and yet we are all expected to follow their orders like sheep. It's crazy! Why have we all spent years of study on strategy and combat if only to defer to someone with no military training the moment that it comes to a fight? This Sorcerer may be powerful but he probably doesn't have a clue when it comes to combat. Shand's teeth! He's so young, he's hardly stopped wetting his bed at night.'

Several of the other Commanders muttered in agreement, but they all knew that regardless of how they felt, none would challenge Lord Shanier's decisions to his face. They all had more sense than that.

The summons came shortly thereafter and the Commanders all trooped into Lord Shanier's tent. Shanier awaited them seated casually on one of the akar wood chairs with his right ankle crossed over his left knee and a sword laid across his lap.

The Commanders arranged themselves into a semi-circle and waited as Lord Shanier idly played with the sword in its scabbard, gently rolling it over and over with his hands. Shanier looked younger than ever, for he had removed his long, flowing black cloak with its deep hood, and was dressed now only in trousers, boots and a loose-fitting shirt, all black in colour, of course. His fair hair and blue, penetrating eyes were rare among Shandese men, but he was a Sorcerer and that made him different from most men in all respects.

'Gentlemen,' Shanier began, still rolling the sword in an almost hypnotic fashion, 'we will not be fighting today.

There will be no need for any bloodshed.'

Shanier paused.

'Are they going to surrender, my Lord?'

Shanier looked up and smiled. 'No, gentlemen. They are going to join us.'

There was a stunned silence.

'Over the next few weeks I am going to be undertaking a feat of sorcery unparalleled in recent history. I will be working constantly to convince many thousands of men to join in an attack against a target not of their choosing. For this to work I am going to need your constant support and trust, so I thought that a little reassurance might be in order.'

Shanier uncrossed his legs and stood up. In one fluid motion he drew his sword and carefully placed the scabbard on the table behind him.

'None of you gentlemen has attained your current rank without being able to wield a sword with some degree of skill. I know that you think me young and untried in combat. Therefore, I am going to offer you a chance to see that this is not totally the case. I would like one of you to spar with me to the first drawing of blood. I will use no sorcery to fool you, simply this sword, and we will see if I do not know something of what it is to fight. Who among you will cross blades with me?'

There was a short pause before the Commander who had been so scathing of Shanier's youth only a few minutes before, stepped forward and accepted the challenge.

'Come then, Commander Simion. We will go outside. There is an area of flat ground just outside the front of the tent and it will save alarming the troops unduly if we do it in the open.'

Shanier led the Commanders out of the doorway and paced purposefully out into the clear area before his great tent. Stopping in the middle of the open ground, Shanier turned and faced his opponent, whilst the rest of the Commanders spread out in a wide circle to observe.

'Don't hold back,' Shanier ordered. 'If you kill me because of my own incompetence, there are more than enough witnesses here to absolve you of any blame. Just remember, though, this is only to be to first blood. Commander Chorain – you can adjudicate.'

'Yes, my Lord,' Chorain answered and stepped forward. 'Fighters, prepare.'

Shanier and Commander Simion carried out the ritual salute of blades, Shanier being careful to do it in the Shandese style. At the end of the salute they crossed blades, both standing poised ready to begin.'

'Commence,' ordered Chorain, stepping back again to remain well out of the way of the contest.

Simion, for all his earlier bluster about how young and inexperienced Shanier was, started slowly. His strokes, tentative and probing to begin with, met a solid defence. Gradually the Commander picked up the pace, shifting the attack first high and then low, left and then right. Each shift was met easily and confidently by Shanier, who merely defended himself and made no attempt to counter-attack.

Suddenly Simion decided that he had learned enough and he drove in a rapid combination attack, his blade flashing as he skilfully wove a complex pattern of strokes in an effort to snake a path through Shanier's defence. Shanier gave ground and continued to defend. Time and again he turned Simion's blade away, as the flurry of strokes rained down on him.

Then, as quickly as Simion had launched his attack, Shanier seemed to change up a gear and the tide of movement turned. Sparks rained from the blades as Shanier launched blow after blow at his opponent and it was all Simion could do to prevent himself being carved to pieces by the fury of the attack.

A quick result one way or the other was inevitable at this stage, and it was a mis-timed parry by Simion that allowed Shanier to open a slice in the Commander's forearm.

'Hold,' Commander Chorain ordered. 'First blood to Lord Shanier. Fighters, salute.'

Again the ritual salute, but this time Shanier could see the respect in Simion's eyes, and as he looked around, the same respect was mirrored in the faces of all those watching.

'Good bout, Commander Simion. Now that we have established that I know a little about fighting, let's get a few other things straight as well, shall we? Firstly, I want you to arrange for the Legions to pull back from the North Wall sufficiently that the Thrandorian force can leave the castle unhindered. I want the enemy force at the front, where I can keep a constant eye on them, and can work my sorcery without affecting any of our own men. Derra is to be the catalyst. I will send her into the castle very shortly.'

Shanier scanned around the Commanders' faces. He had them now and he knew it.

'Secondly, I want the men issued with double water rations and a slightly increased food ration. We are going to be marching hard for the next few weeks, and I don't want them dehydrated and undernourished when we get to Mantor.'

There were nods of approval at this from several of the Commanders, as they knew only too well how important it was to keep the men in a fit state to fight.

'Finally,' Shanier ordered, 'I want every man who has ever been within sight of Mantor brought to me for questioning. We cannot know enough about our objective, and I intend to work on finding out as many weaknesses as I can before we arrive at the Capital. We will send out standard sweeps ahead of our army, and with no major enemy force behind us, only a light guard should suffice to protect the re-supply wagons. Does anyone have any major objections to any of these measures, or any ideas they would like considered?'

The Commanders shook their heads and the respect level that Shanier was detecting was still rising.

'Good,' he said. 'Now, when the enemy come out of the castle, I am going to call for their leaders so that I can reinforce the enchantment in the key people. I am going to trust you gentlemen to look after the day to day stuff from here on in, whilst I concentrate on keeping the Thrandorians on track to attack Mantor. The next few weeks are going to require constant concentration on my part, so do your best not to trouble me unless it's really important. Is that understood?'

'Yes, my Lord,' came a smattering of responses from around the circle.

'Excellent! Well then, gentlemen... let's see if we can't swell the numbers of our army then, shall we?'

*　　*　　*　　*　　*

The streets of Terilla were wide and clean. Square box-shaped houses lined either side of the road, many having arched doorways into large open verandas where people would sit in the summer time to relax and watch the world go by. However, with the chill of winter beginning to bare its teeth now, the verandas sat empty and bare. Aside from a few children playing a catching game with a hand-sized bean-filled bag fashioned from a piece of brightly coloured cloth, the road down which Perdimonn led his large old horse, Steady, was quiet.

This had never been a busy part of the city, even when the Academy had first been established here many years before. The Brotherhood of Magicians had always preferred to keep its privacy and maintain a low profile, which was most likely why they chose Terilla as their base in the first instance. The city was tucked away in the south-western corner of Shandar, hemmed in by the Vortaff Mountains to the south and the Great Western Forest to the west. It was a backwater city, if ever there could be such a thing. Terilla had grown from the copper and iron ore mining community that extracted and traded vast quantities of ores to feed the furnaces of the Empire. Some smaller finds of precious gemstones had been discovered higher in the mountain range, but the dangers and difficulties in extracting them had made it an undesirable business prospect.

The Academy building was large, but not so much so that it looked out of place in its immediate neighbourhood. It had a very typical appearance: square-fronted, large veranda, single wooden door and no outward sign or advertisement as to the function of the building. The frontage looked no different from the buildings around it, many of which were considerably younger, and Perdimonn idly wondered to himself how many times the façade had been altered to blend in with its surroundings.

Perdimonn led Steady up to the main steps that led to the front door.

'Stay there, old girl,' he said, patting her neck and letting the lead rein drop to the floor. 'I'll get you sorted with a nice comfy stable and a good feed of hay and oats just as soon as I can.'

The dappled grey horse snorted once, a shuddering sound that seemed to say 'I'll believe it when I see it', but she remained standing still on the flagstone-paved street as Perdimonn climbed the steps and rapped sharply on the door. Within seconds the door swung inward and a huge mountain of a man blocked the doorway with his presence.

'Yes?' the man said slowly, his voice so deep that it seemed to rumble out from somewhere deep in his huge, barrel-sized chest.

'I come in peace to see and serve my brothers,' Perdimonn intoned formally, using the words passed from Magician to apprentice for countless ages past.

'As a servant, so we all begin,' rolled back the traditional response. 'Come in, Brother Perdimonn. I shall set an apprentice to see to your horse. Please follow me, though I am sure that you remember the way.'

'It has been a while, Brother Lomand,' Perdimonn replied. 'I shall be glad of your guidance. This place always seemed a bit of a maze to me.'

Lomand smiled and inclined his head slightly in acknowledgement. He knew only too well that Perdimonn needed no guide, but accepted that the old Magician had another purpose behind taking him from his duty at the door. The huge man picked up a small silver bell from a table adjacent to the doorway and rang it twice. Within seconds, two young lads raced around the corner and skidded to an abrupt halt.

'Yes, Brother Lomand?' they said in unison.

'You, go and stable Brother Perdimonn's horse, and you, remain on door watch until I return,' Lomand boomed, pointing at each lad in turn.

The two boys bowed and moved immediately to comply. Lomand moved off down the corridor with Perdimonn at his side.

'Nothing much changes I see,' Perdimonn said with a grin, nodding his head back down the corridor in the direction of the two boys.

'Oh, I don't know,' Lomand replied. 'The new ones seem to get younger every year and they always seem to be more impatient than the previous batch.'

'You're just getting old, Lomand,' Perdimonn laughed, clapping the big man on the shoulder amiably.

'Huh! You should try a bit of time here yourself, old man. We'd soon see who was old then.'

'I can't do that and you know it. Only graduates of the Academy can serve in this house and I never studied here.'

'That's rubbish and you know it, Perdimonn. The Brothers would never turn a Warder away, no matter how you came to attain the position.'

'Well, we may never find out I'm afraid, for I cannot stop long,' Perdimonn said with a sigh.

'I know. Your timing is... interesting. I am sure that the Brothers will be more than a little pleased to see you. They will mostly be teaching classes right now, but Brother Akhdar will be in his study.'

Perdimonn thought for a moment. Lomand was hinting at something, but Perdimonn did not really have time to drag information out of him. The news that Perdimonn brought was vital and was really for all six of the Grand Magicians who made up the High Council. They were the true power of the Brotherhood, but if he had to see them one at a time, then Akhdar was as good a person to start with as any. Grand Magician Akhdar had been a member of the High Council for over forty years, and though his memory for spells was beginning to deteriorate, his force of mind and personality were as strong as ever.

'Very well, Lomand. I had better go and see Brother Akhdar first, but would you be so kind as to let the other five Council Members know that I am here as well?' Perdimonn asked with a slight grimace. He knew very well that Lomand needed to get back to his duty, but he was determined to get them all to listen to him as soon as he could.

'Certainly, Brother Perdimonn. I will have them informed immediately. Here you are. This is the door to Brother Akhdar's study. I'll leave you to it. It's good to see you again. If you get a chance, do drop by for a chat before you go, won't you?'

'Of course, Lomand. Thank you.'

Perdimonn knocked at the door as Lomand's long strides carried the giant-sized man rapidly away down the corridor, deeper into the building. A faint 'come in' sounded from inside, so Perdimonn turned the iron handle and stepped inside.

The study identified its owner as a hoarder. The room was crammed with so many things that despite the fact that everything had its place, the room had an untidy, cluttered feel about it. Books were the main culprits – books and parchments of every shape and size. A fair number of maps, either neatly rolled or folded, also claimed a fair amount of space.

'Perdimonn! This has been a week of surprises!'

Grand Magician Akhdar was the sort of character who anyone would immediately identify as the archetypal Magician. He was delicately built, slim, of medium height, but slightly stooped when standing, and his long hair, beard and long moustache, were all snowy white with age. Bright, piercing blue eyes looked out from under bushy white eyebrows and his long, slim-fingered hands were still dextrous despite his obvious advancing years.

'Come in, my old friend. Come in, come in,' Akhdar said, his voice warm and welcoming.

'Akhdar, it's good to see you again. I just wish that it were under better circumstances. I have come to bring you dire tidings of an evil that may already be free as we speak,' Perdimonn said gravely.

'I think that the Academy is prepared for your tidings, Perdimonn. I am guessing that you have come about Darkweaver's amulet, and if you have, then you are already too late. Selkor got here before you.'

Akhdar sighed, shaking his head sadly.

'What happened?'

'He came, took what he wanted and left. There was nothing that any of us could do. We just weren't prepared for anything like the storm of power that Selkor was wielding, and now it's even worse. He's taken the Ring of Nadus, Perdimonn. He has the Ring of Nadus and the Cloak of Merridom. Combined with the power of the amulet, Selkor probably has as much power at his fingertips now as Darkweaver ever had.'

CHAPTER 16

'For Tarmin's sake, Brothers! It's only by chance that you still retain the Staff of Dantillus. If Brother Jabal had not been using it for a field class, you would have lost all of the icons of power that the Brotherhood has held for more than five centuries. Can you not see that you need to take action? You have to do something and it needs to be done now.'

Perdimonn was more than a little frustrated.

The six Grand Magicians of the High Council had been seated around a table with him discussing what should be done about Selkor and Darkweaver's amulet for several hours now, and it seemed that nothing that he had said was getting through. The bottom line was that they were old and set in their ways. It was easier to sit and procrastinate than it was to face a powerful and dangerous Magician who was rapidly turning towards an evil path. Perdimonn was fighting a losing battle of words here and he knew it. All he could hope to do now was to shock them into action, and it seemed that even this tack would prove futile.

'Perdimonn, you are the Warder of an Elemental Power far greater than anything that we, with our combined knowledge and strength, could bring to bear, yet you retreated at his power before he even gained the amulet. Now he has the Ring and Cloak as well as Darkweaver's evil legacy. What hope have we got of stopping him in whatever scheme he is hatching?'

'Akhdar, you know, as do the others, that I could not have used the Earth Power against Selkor. To do so would have violated the vows that I took when I accepted the position of

Warder. No more can any of the other Warders use their powers in their defence, and certainly not in attack. We are individually even more vulnerable than you are and yet you have already suffered a major loss. I think you should know that Selkor made it clear that he intends to gain the Keys to all of the Elemental Powers. Can you begin to imagine what he could do with that sort of power? With even one of the Keys in combination with the other power sources that he now holds, the gods themselves might fear to challenge him. He has to be stopped quickly, or all could be lost.'

'If we were to challenge him, Perdimonn, if we tracked him down and challenged him, would you and the other Warders stand at our sides?'

'I would do so, Brothers. On that you have my word. For the others, I cannot speak. However, I will have to warn them of the danger as soon as I can, so I will ask them for their support at the same time. That is the best that I can promise.'

The High Council debated the same questions around and around until Perdimonn's patience had all but gone completely. Hours of fruitless discussion had achieved nothing more than making the problem grow in everyone's mind until it seemed insurmountable. The truth was staring them in the face, but none was willing to face it. They would never know for sure what the outcome of a confrontation with Selkor would be unless they tried. The sooner that they faced him down, the less likely he was to have mastered the full potential of the magical artefacts that he now held. Every hour of talk was another hour for Selkor to prepare and learn more of his newly acquired powers.

Eventually Perdimonn made his own decision. 'Brothers, if you would excuse me, I will leave you to your deliberations. I have told you my tidings and given you what counsel that I can. Now I must go if I am to alert the other Warders before Selkor reaches them. I will do my best to gather them as fast as I can. I can only urge you not to ponder overly long. Action is needed, and needed now – before the chance slips us by.'

'Who will you seek out first, Perdimonn?' asked Jabal

doubtfully. 'What if you look for one Warder and all the while Selkor is seeking out one of the others?'

'Don't borrow trouble, Brother Jabal. Let me worry about that. I know Selkor, and I know who he will look for first. Just beware that he does not come back and take the Staff of Dantillus from you to complete his collection.'

Perdimonn arose from his seat and bowed to the august assembly. 'Your servant, Brothers.'

'Through serving, learn wisdom,' they replied as one.

'Safe journey, Brother,' added Akhdar.

Perdimonn left the room, striding purposefully out into the corridor and along the hallway towards the front door. Lomand was back at his post and he smiled as Perdimonn approached.

'A successful meeting, Brother Perdimonn?' he asked, his deep voice rolling the 'r's and seeming to fill the hall with its resonance.

'That remains to be seen, Lomand. Listen, old friend, I need a couple of favours. I have a long journey ahead and I will need a fast horse – the fastest you have. My old horse, Steady, is not cut out for this errand. The High Council will not quibble. They know the urgency of my journey. Also, if you could have my horse cared for whilst I'm gone, I'd appreciate it. She's a good old girl and I'll come back and collect her if ever I get the chance.'

Lomand placed a hand on Perdimonn's shoulder and squeezed it gently.

'No problem, Brother Perdimonn. We'll look after your horse and I'll get you your replacement. Is there anything else?'

'No, wait... yes, there is one thing. If chance favours it, there is a young man that I'd like to send here to study. Would my recommendation be enough to sponsor him in?'

'Of course, Brother. Why ever would you think that it wouldn't? What is his name and I'll keep watch for him?'

'Calvyn – Calvyn son of Joran. He's Thrandorian, a farmer's son from a backwater province. I think that one or two of the Masters here would find him a breath of fresh air. He learns *very* quickly.'

'Calvyn, that's an easy enough name to remember. So where are you going, Perdimonn? Or should I not ask?'

Perdimonn's eyes went distant as he thought for a moment.

'To Kaldea to begin with. Selkor will almost certainly try to get to Arred next. Selkor has always liked spells which involved fire, and if he were to gain the Key to that element, with all that he already knows about controlling it... well the consequences don't bear thinking about.'

*   *   *   *   *

The Commanders looked grim as they made their report. Lord Shanier was pale and drawn as he listened, the weeks of maintaining control of his mixed army by the use of his powers of sorcery having taken a heavy toll on his strength.

'My Lord, the scouts report that Mantor is being held far more strongly than we were led to believe. We don't know where all the troops have come from, but it may be that the King has returned from the Kortag Gap with his army. The good news is that the scouts say that the walls, whilst strong, are not insurmountable, and that we will be able to use our standard assault equipment without any major modifications.'

Lord Shanier sighed heavily, his fatigue evident.

'Not ideal then, but with the forces that we control, the victory will still be ours,' he said slowly, running his fingers through his hair and then rubbing thoughtfully at his chin.

'Er... my Lord, there is just one more thing.'

'Yes, Commander?'

'Well, my Lord, there is what appears to be another Shandese Legion camped a couple of miles to the north of the city. The scouts didn't get very close because they suspected a trap.'

Shanier smiled and for a moment his face seemed to gain a little energy.

'Good,' he replied with some enthusiasm, looking around at the expectant faces of the Commanders gathered in his tent. 'It seems that the reinforcements that I asked for fared better on the western road than we did on our route.'

'Reinforcements, my Lord?' asked Commander Simion.

'Yes, Commander. I ordered them weeks ago, for your news about the return of the King was not unknown to me. That force is one of the northern Legions, sent to be our reserves in case we are in danger of failing to take the city. At least something has gone in our favour this day. With that extra Legion to draw on, I am confident to proceed. However, there are going to have to be a few changes to my original attack plan.'

Lord Shanier climbed wearily to his feet and began to pace back and forth in front of the Commanders, his expression one of deep thought. The Senior Officers all waited patiently. Their respect for this Sorcerer Lord, who had successfully brought a force of five Legions over such a huge distance through enemy territory, and by his orders had kept them in a fit state to fight, had grown constantly as their journey had progressed. That he was still capable of producing surprises, and supplying solutions to problems that they had not anticipated, was no longer unexpected. They had already come to believe that in the chest of this unusual young man beat the heart of a military genius.

'Keeping control of the Thrandorian force from Keevan Castle is taking much of my concentration,' Shanier admitted, still pacing. 'I could throw them at the wall first but it would be a waste, for I could not hope to cover them with any sort of protective illusion and control them at the same time. They would be slaughtered, and my bringing them here would have been a huge wasted effort. However, if we held them back, just out of sight of the city, it would take minimum concentration to hold them, and I could cover the city with a blanket style illusion to allow our forces to get close enough to commence an effective assault. To sink Mantor in a sea of fog would be feasible. The only problem is that I cannot promise to only affect the Thrandorians with the illusion. It's such a vast area to cover that I won't necessarily be able to distinguish between who I affect with this illusion and who I don't. The defenders will not see us coming, but likewise we will be just as blind.'

'Being blind on the attack will not pose a major problem, my Lord. Providing that we have the element of surprise when we hit them, we should be able to take the walls. After all, even with the extra troops that the King has brought back from Kortag, we still have a huge numerical advantage,' Commander Chorain said encouragingly. 'Give us our chance, my Lord, and we will not let you down.'

The other Commanders all murmured support for Chorain's claim.

'Very well, Commanders. I will begin the illusion just before dawn tomorrow so that you can move the Legions into position. Then, when the attack is well under way and the fog is no longer helpful, I will dissipate the illusion and concentrate on pushing the Thrandorians from Keevan Castle to aid you in the battle.'

'A sound plan, my Lord.'

The other Commanders again muttered their approval, and Shanier visibly relaxed as the burden of deciding their course of action was lifted.

'Just one thing, my Lord,' Commander Simion interjected through the burble of approval.

'Yes, Simion? What is it?'

'The northern Legion, my Lord, will they be joining us in the initial assault?'

'Good question, Commander. No. That Legion is here as a reserve force only. I will not hesitate to deploy them if the assault falters, but I don't intend to commit them on the first push. That way, if any major weaknesses appear in our assault pattern I can plug the gaps with relative ease. Besides, gentlemen, you wouldn't want those northern boys stealing your glory, would you? I am hoping that I won't have to use them at all. Can you imagine how they would gloat at having baled out the southern Legions from a potentially nasty situation? They would get mileage out of that for years! Is the plan acceptable to all of you? I am willing to listen to alternatives if you have any to offer,' Shanier said reasonably.

'No, my Lord. Your plan sounds eminently sensible. Thank you. We won't need the northern Legion. Just you watch.'

'Then it is decided. Tomorrow at dawn we attack and, if all

goes well, Mantor will be ours by noon.'

With the main strategy decided, the Commanders were dismissed to brief their officers, who in turn would brief their column leaders and so on down the chain of command to the common soldiers. Morale amongst the troops was high despite the general nervousness pervading the forces regarding the imminent battle. Many of the older hands amongst the soldiers were trying to act relaxed, or were joking around with a sense of bravado that was often a more obvious sign of their nerves, than the signs of the many who sat around talking tactics, or unnecessarily sharpening weapons.

There were not many that slept well that night.

By an hour before dawn, the five Legions were all up, armed and loaded with scaling ladders and grappling hooks. Already Lord Shanier was building up his illusion, and the early morning mist rising from the dew-filled grass was rapidly beginning to develop from wispy tendrils to wandering patches, and thickening by the minute.

With sunrise the fog thickened into a solid wall of whiteness, obscuring everything around the city for some considerable distance. The Legions moved forward on command, and maintaining silence as best that ten thousand soldiers could, they crept slowly towards the city.

Lord Shanier was standing well back from where the conflict would begin, and despite the chill morning air, beads of sweat rolled from his forehead and on down his nose and cheeks. The illusion that he was holding was gigantic and the next few hours would determine the future of Thrandor.

No one other than Derra and Eloise dared to approach him, and they were given no choice in the matter. The aura of power that Shanier was producing was unnerving to even the most hardy of souls. His focus and commitment were one hundred percent and he had no intention of breaking down on either front.

The tension mounted.

A short distance to the right of where Lord Shanier was standing, just back from the line of fog, the northern Legion moved into position. With rapid precision they arranged themselves into neatly organised ranks, and their weapons glittered, row upon row in the early morning sunlight.

Now all was ready.

Then a single shout sounded out from the fog almost directly ahead of Shanier, a ringing voice calling loud and true. Ten thousand Shandese voices roared out in response and the battle was joined.

*   *   *   *   *

Gedd and Jenna had covered a lot of distance that first day. By evening time Jenna was shattered, though she tried not to let it show overly much. The scars on her stomach felt drawn and sore under her tunic, and her legs stiffened quickly after such a long break from any serious walking.

'You moved well today, Jenna. I am impressed, and for me to say that is no idle compliment,' Gedd acknowledged after they had chosen their campsite for the night. 'I know you must be hurting, but we need to be in a position to get to the tower tomorrow while the sun is still high. I would not like to tangle with any demon in the hours of darkness.'

'I couldn't agree more,' Jenna replied with a weary smile.

'Well, you sit down and rest. I'll get a small fire going and prepare us some hot food. I certainly need some, so I'm guessing that you won't object.'

'Not at all. It would be more than welcome,' Jenna agreed, flopping to the floor and slipping the pack from her shoulders. Then, using the small knapsack as a pillow, she laid back against it, stretched slowly, and luxuriated in the freedom from the load and the break from the constant effort of the long day's hike.

Gedd seemed to move around effortlessly, almost appearing to glide as he silently went from one task to the next. In a surprisingly short amount of time their campsite was completely organised. A canvas shelter was strung taut between two trees and angled down at one end to channel any moisture away. A small fire, neatly constructed, had a wall of damp wood drying to one side and a pile of drier wood already covered behind it. Two smooth round rocks were also warming by the fire, rocks which Gedd would later wrap in old cloths and place at the end of their shelter where their feet would be as they slept.

'The rocks will retain the heat of the fire for a long time and act as wonderful foot warmers,' he said, his face serious as it often was. 'There's nothing like the odd little luxury when you're roughing it under the open sky.'

Jenna was fascinated but sceptical. It sounded nice in theory, but she wasn't convinced of the practicalities of the idea.

Before long Gedd started to cook supper and Jenna's stomach rumbled in the most unladylike fashion at the wonderful aromas emanating from his small frying pan. Gedd had loaded the pan with strips of meat that he had brought with him wrapped in some aromatic smelling leaves. Over the meat he poured some spiced oil from a small metal flask, and the sizzling sound from the pan served to heighten the anticipation begun by the initial aroma.

A small loaf of bread was also retrieved from Gedd's pack, and he offered a short prayer of thanks to 'the Creator' before breaking the loaf in two and offering half to Jenna.

'Thanks,' she said gratefully, and followed Gedd's example of using her belt knife to spear meat from the pan and alternating bites of meat and bread.

The combination was delicious, and for a while the two sat silently enjoying their food. Eventually, whilst mopping the last of the spiced oil from the pan with her bread, Jenna broke the silence by broaching a subject that she had avoided during her entire stay at Gedd's cottage.

'Gedd, I don't wish to appear totally ignorant, which is probably why I never said anything with Kerys and Alix around...' she started, struggling hard to try and phrase her question carefully and tactfully. 'This "Creator" god that you pray to – is "Creator" another name for Shand?'

Gedd choked slightly on his mouthful of food. 'Demon's breath, no!' Gedd exclaimed in surprise. 'Are you saying that you've never heard of the Creator?'

'Well I wouldn't say that exactly,' Jenna said thoughtfully. 'I've heard several people refer to "the Creator", but I just assumed that it was another name for the deity that your people named themselves after.'

'From which I must assume that you are not really from southern Shandar,' Gedd stated slowly, his lips twitching into a slight smile at her slip.

'Thrandor,' Jenna admitted, feeling the flush rise in her cheeks.

Gedd nodded.

'I already knew,' he admitted, the smile widening a little further, 'but it is good to hear it from your lips. Your nationality means little. That you hunt a demon is enough, though I am surprised that the Creator is not acknowledged in Thrandor.'

'I've never heard mention of him prior to this journey. Who is he?'

'That is a question that is impossible for me to answer fully, for He has no name that anyone of this world knows, and yet He is given many. If you are from Thrandor then you will know of Tarmin and Ishell. Shand is the deity that the majority here in Shandar worship, though some have become followers of Redieral over recent years. There is always a minority wherever you go who follow the dark gods, whose names I refuse to speak even in casual conversation. However, though the names of each of these deities hold power, none of them can lay claim to the creation of the universe in which we all live. Only the Creator can do that. Because of this, some call Him "Father of the gods", though I feel that Creator is a more accurate description.'

'So you worship the Creator alone? Or do you worship other gods as well?' asked Jenna, fascinated.

'Well... worship is perhaps a bit strong a description really. Acknowledge is probably more accurate. Kerys and I both felt that we needed to acknowledge the existence of the God who created the universe, but neither of us are really religious by nature. So we sort of compromise, I suppose. We give thanks at meals and at the start and end of each day, probably more to remind us of our own mortality than to appease the need of a God who probably isn't listening anyway. It may all be foolishness, I don't really know, but one thing's clear in my mind – this beautiful, complex and constantly amazing world did not just wink into existence by chance, and none of the traditional gods had the power to create it. Why shouldn't there be a Creator? A Father of the gods, if you like.'

Jenna shrugged and fell silent for a while, deep in thought. Until now, Gedd had been a man of few words and this new insight into his beliefs had given her much to think on. What he had said made sense in a vague sort of way, though Jenna was far from convinced about his theology. There were a myriad of unanswered questions that rattled around in her mind, but they refused to formulate into coherence.

Gedd interrupted her train of thought with a question of his own.

'So do you worship a god, Jenna? You have patiently sat through our prayers at mealtimes, but have we kept you from religious observances of your own?'

'No,' Jenna answered immediately. 'My family have never had a calling by any of the gods. We have very much avoided religion and all that it holds. My own belief is that we are born... we live... we die... what we get out of life depends very much on what we put into it. Luck and destiny have their parts to play but for the most part we make our own paths.'

Gedd smiled broadly at the last comment and Jenna wondered what she had said to amuse him.

'I think that you may feel differently in a few years' time,' he said, amusement brimming in his voice. 'Hindsight may well highlight a controlling hand in your life, Jenna. To me it is as clear as day, but then I have the advantage of years over you. I am not a cleric, and I'm not out to convert you to any form of belief, but there are forces at work around you that are moving you as they will. I suspect that you have not really had much choice in this journey of yours.'

Flashbacks to the old seeress in the marketplace, on that day when Derra had convinced them to have their fortunes told, sprang to mind instantly. Certainly the old woman had known something of her future, but was that just chance? Was it her destiny? Or was some higher being really controlling her? The hairs on the back of her neck prickled, and she shuddered slightly at the thought that she was being manipulated like some sort of puppet.

'Anyway, young lady,' Gedd said suddenly, breaking into her intense reverie, 'would you like to let me in on the secret of your little necklace? I've noticed you playing with it before today and I just assumed that it was a gift from a loved one or something. But it's more than that, isn't it?'

Jenna focused in on Gedd's face, only to find him studying hers for some sort of a reaction to the question. By the time that she had noticed what he was doing, Jenna realised that he had probably already gained what he had wanted to know from her face.

'You're right. It's not just for decoration and I should have let you in on its purpose before now.'

Over the next few minutes, Jenna gave an abridged account of her journey. Although she skimmed through it, the tale that she told was the true one. There was no need to hide anything from Gedd any more. After all, he had effectively joined her quest and he already knew that she was from Thrandor, so there seemed little else to hide.

When she had finished, Gedd's hazel-brown eyes were distant.

'A Magician called Perdimonn, you say? Balding? Bright blue eyes? With a large dappled grey horse that he calls "Steady"?' Gedd asked slowly.

Jenna nodded and the amazement was clear in her face at the coincidence that Gedd should know the old Magician.

'Hmm, well that explains a lot. If Perdimonn made that charm for you, then we had better pay it good heed. And it was he who told you that the beast was a gorvath?'

Jenna nodded and Gedd shook his head in wonder. 'First you tell me that you believe in controlling your own destiny and now you tell me that you mix with the likes of Perdimonn. I wonder that you didn't walk the whole way here blindfolded! Still, that as it may be, you are here, alive, and keen to face a gorvath for a third time despite all else. My instincts tell me that your purpose is being guided, but by what, or whom, I have no idea. Let us just hope that your destiny is to succeed.'

There were so many new ideas and concepts floating

around in Jenna's head by now that she was fast developing a headache trying to sort them all into some form of sense. In the end she gave up trying and settled for trying to get one easy question answered.

'So where do you know Perdimonn from, Gedd?' she asked eventually.

'Where? Why, here of course,' Gedd answered with a grin. 'Who do you think taught Kerys her healing craft? It is a strange coincidence, I'll grant you, but strange coincidences happen around people like Perdimonn. In fact I'm fairly sure that some of the healing salves that Kerys used on your wounds were supplied by the old man... oh, it must be four or maybe even five seasons back now. Old Perdimonn gets around a fair bit with that old horse of his.'

'Apparently so,' Jenna replied thoughtfully.

On an instinct, Jenna lifted the silver charm from her chest and held it up in the firelight. The arrow still pointed west and was steady, as it had been all day. For some reason, though, the prickle of premonition was still there.

'Something wrong?' Gedd asked, his hand automatically going to the handle of the dagger on his belt.

'No, it's probably just all this talk of being controlled and manipulated. I just felt for a moment or two as if we were being watched, that's all.'

'I'll go take a look around anyway,' he said quietly and silently he rose to his feet. 'I won't be gone long. I suggest that you stay awake until I return.'

Jenna nodded and Gedd moved smoothly and noiselessly off into the night.

The crackle and pop of the fire seemed unnaturally loud as the minutes dragged by. Every flutter of wings, every chirrup of night insects, every rustle of small nocturnal animals amongst the leaves and twigs that carpeted the forest floor, all appeared amplified during the slow wait for Gedd's return. However, nothing untoward happened and eventually Gedd reappeared, seemingly from nowhere.

'Well,' he said slowly, 'if there is anyone out there, then their woodscraft is as good as my own. There is no real way of telling in the dark, and I would prefer to press on first thing in the morning. We will keep a watch tonight, just in case. Go ahead and get some shut-eye and I'll wake you in a few hours. Here... have a hot rock for comfort.'

Using some thick old pieces of cloth, Gedd wrapped one of the large smooth stones that he had been heating by the fire into a bundle and passed it to Jenna. Muttering her thanks, she did not need telling twice and within moments was wrapped in her blanket with her feet against the warm bundled rock. Her last conscious thought, as she wriggled her toes against the luxurious heat of the warm bundle, was that she should have thought of heated rocks for foot-warmers years ago.

Gedd woke her as promised, though Jenna judged that there were probably no more than a couple of hours left until dawn. He quickly settled down to rest, reminding her that he wanted to be woken at first light and Jenna sat, blanket around her shoulders, feeding an occasional piece of wood onto the fire until the chorus of the forest birds sang the sun up into the eastern sky.

After a quickly brewed cup of dahl and a hunk of bread each for breakfast, the two packed up camp and moved on through the trees, their minds firmly fixed on their final goal. There was no conversation as they walked, only a fierce concentration on their surroundings and their path.

Jenna led the way that morning and she paused frequently to refer to the silver arrow, taking exceptional care to ensure that the charm was against her skin whenever she was not using it. There was no room left for any more mistakes. Jenna had been blessed with more than her share of good luck up until now, and she was acutely aware that she could not afford to rely on fortune any more.

Silently they walked through the forest, moving swiftly but constantly listening and watching for any signs of danger. The trees changed from oak to elm, to huge pine trees, and back to oak again. Occasionally there were stands of beech or rowan trees amidst a sea of pine, or a solitary mammoth blackwood bole amongst acres of oak. The forest seemed to care little for natural order when it came to the distribution of the species of trees and Jenna found it unnerving that her surroundings could change so drastically from minute to minute.

As the morning wore on, Jenna noticed a marked reduction in the signs of wildlife. Where before they had heard the occasional scurry of a rabbit or forest hare, or the flurry of wings from a disturbed pigeon, or the thudding of hooves as a deer was startled into a rapid retreat, now there was nothing. No birdsong, no tapping of woodpeckers, no rustle of scurrying rodents – nothing.

All was silent except for the creaking branches of the upper arms of the trees as they rocked and swayed gently in the breeze.

Gedd placed a hand on Jenna's shoulder, causing her to jump slightly, as she paused to check the direction of the arrow on her silver charm once more. A finger over the lips told Jenna that silence was imperative from here, and shielding his mouth with his hand, Gedd put his mouth to her ear and whispered gently. 'Over that stream and up the slope. The tower stands at the top of the rise in a very small clearing. It's about four hundred paces or so from the far bank of the stream.'

Jenna nodded her acknowledgement and moved forward to where the stream trickled and gurgled along a path cut through the rocky floor of the little dell. Being careful not to lose their footing on the slippery rocks, they painstakingly picked their path across the water and crept up the far bank.

Once clear of the stream, Jenna signalled to Gedd that she was going to take off her pack. He nodded his agreement and removed his own, placing it softly down next to hers at the base of a large oak tree. Jenna slowly drew the special arrow, tipped with Demon's Bane crystal, from her quiver and nocked it. Glancing across at Gedd, she noted that he was similarly armed.

He gave her a quick smile of encouragement and, with a hand signal and a nod, he indicated that he would lead the way up the last slope to the tower.

Stealthily they inched their way up through the trees and the silver charm began to tingle at Jenna's chest as they climbed. It was more than a little tempting to stop and pull the charm out to check it, but that would have meant having to lower her bow. Instead, Jenna chose to rely on Gedd's knowledge of demons and follow him up to this mysterious tower.

The last hundred and fifty paces or so they wormed forward on their bellies until they could at last see the building that Gedd believed had once housed a powerful Wizard.

That no one lived there now was evident to Jenna from the first glance. Bushes had grown around the base of the tower, almost ringing the reddish stone structure with their lush green growth. The doorway into the building was almost obscured by greenery, but from what Jenna could see it was evident that the door had long since been torn from its hinges and there was nothing to stop anyone, or anything, from entering the tower at will. The tower itself was round and squat, nothing like the soaring structure that she had imagined when Gedd had described it to her. However, one thing was sure – the demon was here somewhere. The tingling of the charm on her chest could not be denied.

Jenna looked across at Gedd questioningly and he shrugged slightly in response. Silently he gestured to her to take up position behind a tree just off to her right and to wait. Time was on their side for it was only just past midday. When the demon moved from wherever it was, they would be ready.

Once in position, Jenna could resist the tingling itch of the silver charm no longer, so she lowered her bow and drew out the magical silver arrow. To her relief it pointed directly at the tower and continued to quiver at the proximity of the demon.

'Now the waiting game begins,' she thought grimly.

CHAPTER 17

It was the middle of the afternoon before the first signs of movement came. A scraping sound alerted Jenna that something was moving around, and by the time she looked up, the great hulking beast was half way out of the door of the tower. Silently Jenna cursed herself for not getting into a better position for a shot at the doorway. She should have realised that the beast would be inside the tower somewhere. Now, as she drew her great bow and looked down the shaft of her arrow, it was apparent that unless the demon turned to its right out of the doorway and walked around the base of the tower towards her, she would not get a clear killing shot.

The demon turned left.

Jenna shot a look of frustration at Gedd, who hand-signalled for her to remain calm. 'Good advice,' she thought angrily, but if she had only been thinking more clearly to start with, her arrow would now be firmly embedded in the demon's chest.

It was tempting to move. If the demon was using the tower as a shelter, then it would return at some point and Jenna wanted to be in a prime position to nail it at the first opportunity. However, to her joy and amazement she didn't need to.

The demon reappeared around the other side of the tower, moving closer and closer at the perfect angle for a body shot. It seemed to be just stalking around the tower without any sense of direction or purpose. Jenna could hardly believe her luck.

Rising slowly to her feet, Jenna drew the great akar wood

bow to its full extent. Allowing for the trajectory of about sixty paces, she controlled her breathing and smoothly released.

The demon's head spun towards her at the thrum of the bowstring propelling the arrow on its deadly flightpath, but had no time to react as the shaft hammered into its chest. The demon's talons clasped at the arrow protruding from its chest and it threw back its head and let out an almighty roar of pain.

For a moment Jenna thought that it might charge down the slope at her, as it lowered its head to drill that evil staring gaze in her direction, but even as its eyes locked with hers, the orange-red glare glazed with the call of oblivion.

Slowly... so slowly, the demon sank to the ground and with a final fading howl, it died.

Jenna could hardly believe that in the end the kill had been that easy. Her knees felt weak with relief and she was shaking with emotion. Her quest was at an end. Gedd walked smoothly over and placed a hand on her shoulder.

'Good shot,' he congratulated calmly. 'From the moment you drew your bow I could see that my arrow would not be required. Come. Let us take a look at this beast. I've never seen a gorvath before. It looks kind of like a large krill to me.'

Jenna nodded, and unexpected tears of emotion welled in her eyes as she walked behind him the short distance up the slope to where the demon lay.

As they got closer, the tingling of the charm on her chest got progressively stronger and Jenna suddenly began to get a sick feeling in the pit of her stomach.

'Gedd, stop!' she warned.

'What's the matter, Jenna? There's nothing to worry about. It's well and truly dead – look.'

Gedd walked right up to the demon and prodded it with his boot. Nothing happened.

'You see, it's not going to harm anyone any more. I just want to retrieve the arrow and we'll get away from this place. It always gives me the...'

Gedd did not get to finish. There was no warning. The

huge grey demon erupted from the bushes at the base of the tower and powered into Gedd, knocking him flying from his feet. Jenna had never really got a close look at the gorvath before. Her first encounter had been all but in darkness, and at the second encounter, the beast had shape-shifted to appear like Calvyn. Now she could appreciate the differences between the krill that she had just killed and this monster that was still very much alive.

Gedd looked to be unconscious after the ferocious impact of the charging gorvath and Jenna no longer had a Demon's Bane weapon.

The gorvath let out a triumphal roar, turned and began to pace slowly towards Jenna. Determinedly she fixed her gaze on the demon's midriff, adamant that its eyes would not trap her again. Like deadwood it might be, but her sword was the only weapon that she could realistically hope to defend herself with now.

With a sweeping motion designed to catch the demon's eyes, Jenna cast her bow away with her left hand even as she drew the sword with her right and sprang into action. Whirling and weaving, she slashed and cut at the demon's extended arms, never quite getting close enough to get inside its long reach. Eyes glued to the demon's chest, Jenna fought by instinct, allowing her peripheral vision to warn her of the gorvath's moves, whilst constantly resisting the awful temptation of the orange-red glow of its evil gaze.

It was playing with her, Jenna decided grimly – toying with her before it struck. Even the most solid strokes that she had driven at the demon's limbs had merely glanced from the creature's astoundingly tough and scaly outer skin. In desperation she lunged, trying to drive the point of her blade through to something vital. It was like striking solid rock and the impact jarred Jenna's arm right up to the shoulder. Ducking and rolling away from the demon, she felt the whoosh of air as a swiping set of talons narrowly missed her back.

The swipe had almost been one of irritation, like a man flicking at a fly that was trying to settle on his meal. All Jenna could hope to do was to keep the demon distracted long enough for Gedd to recover, or to try and get to a Demon's Bane weapon herself.

Dancing a spinning flurry of rapid slashing cuts, Jenna attempted to manoeuvre herself into a position to be able to get to where Gedd still lay unmoving on the ground. However, the demon appeared to sense what she was trying to do and blocked her at every move.

Jenna's stomach began to burn as the scar tissue over-stretched, and she realised that unless she resolved the fight quickly, her previous wounds would begin to seriously factor against her.

Then it came, the smallest of openings in a direction that the demon did not expect. Jenna went from ducking and weaving her attacks to a full sprint in an instant – not towards Gedd but towards the dead krill. With a huge bound, she leapt over the dead demon's body, stopped, turned and grabbed the shaft of the arrow embedded in its chest.

The gorvath was not far behind her and it let out an angry bellow as it realised what she was doing.

Jenna pulled hard on the shaft of the arrow and then let out an angry scream of her own as the shaft snapped in her hand, leaving the Demon's Bane point still deep within the krill's chest.

In sheer frustration she hurled the feathered end of the shaft at the oncoming gorvath and inadvertently looked up at its horrifyingly evil face. It was only a momentary glance, but it was enough, and the demon's eyes held her in their burning sway once more. The gorvath's mouth split into a wicked grin, displaying row upon row of inwardly curving, needle-sharp teeth.

The demon stopped short of Jenna as if to savour the moment, but even as it did so, a smooth pebble the size of Jenna's clenched fist slammed into the side of the gorvath's head. Jenna's head flinched in sympathy with the impact and the eye contact was broken as another figure launched himself at the demon with great double-handed swings of his sword.

'Demarr!' Jenna gasped in recognition.

There was no time to wonder how he had got there and she spun back into action to harry the beast from another quarter. The demon was annoyed now and it moved with far more speed than before, its raking swipes getting progressively more difficult to avoid. Even with the two of them, they would be lost without weapons that would cause some damage.

'Cover me, Demarr,' Jenna yelled, racing out of the fight and over to where Gedd lay comatose, a large swelling on the side of his face and one eye already blackened and closing.

Grabbing the Demon's Bane knife from Gedd's belt and ripping all the arrows from his quiver, she frantically scattered them in search of shafts with Demon's Bane tips. She found only one. The search had only taken a few seconds but by the time that she turned back to help Demarr, she could see that he was in trouble. Of Gedd's bow there was no sign, and hers was too far away to get to in time to help Demarr, so yelling for all that she was worth, she ran back into the fray.

The gorvath turned to meet her charge and flailed at her with its great talons. Its speed was awesome now but Jenna, pumped up with adrenaline, was just a little bit faster. A great gash opened up on the gorvath's forearm where Jenna managed to land a raking blow with the knife, and she tossed the arrow across to Demarr as the demon howled with pain.

'Use it like a dagger. It's the best I could do,' she grunted, diving under the demon's next swing and rolling to her feet, having opened a cut on the gorvath's leg as she passed.

Demarr did not need telling twice and he danced in and out of the demon's reach, jabbing the arrowhead at it with each pass. The Demon's Bane arrow tip burned through the beast's skin like a hot knife through butter, but Demarr could not get enough leverage on the arrow to land a really telling blow.

Suddenly there was a blur and the gorvath was no longer the shape of a large bear-like creature. Instead, the two humans abruptly found themselves battling a creature the like of which they had never imagined in their worst nightmares. Its body was reptilian and had a long tail armed with two huge, razor sharp horns on either side. Its legs were short and its upper body split into three long, sinuous necks, each supporting a heavily armoured head. Snout-nosed, with flaring nostrils and overlapping dagger-like teeth, each head was crowned with a ring of bony horns. The only common feature of this beast to the gorvath's previous shape was the eyes, and these would be even more difficult to avoid now that there were three pairs to worry about.

The teeth-laden heads seemed to be everywhere at once, twisting and darting so fast that it was almost impossible to follow, and the snapping jaws were deadly in their intent.

Everything happened so quickly in the next few seconds that Jenna hardly had time to take it in. One of the three heads whipped around and its jaws clamped around Demarr's left shoulder, the mouth so large that the front teeth were biting into his upper chest and back. Demarr screamed in agony and thrust the point of the arrow that he was clutching up into the throat of the head that was biting him. The head reared up, lifting Demarr from his feet and tossing him straight at Jenna, who in turn could not move fast enough to avoid the impact.

Demarr and Jenna sprawled on the floor and Jenna lost hold of the knife. Both instinctively rolled apart as the other two of the gorvath's heads arrowed in for the kill, jaws snapping on empty air as man and woman alike narrowly avoided the deadly maws.

Then, to Jenna's amazement, Demarr was on his feet and diving forward under the striking heads. It was not a move that the gorvath had anticipated, and he rolled up between the creature's front legs and drove the knife, which he had snatched up when Jenna had dropped it only seconds before, deep into the gorvath's chest.

The demon howled.

A blur and the demon was Calvyn, knife in chest. Another blur and it was a great wolf... blur, mountain cat... blur, bear... blur after blur as it shape-shifted again and again, until finally it reverted back to its own shape – the shape which it had held at the start of the fight. The howl, which suddenly seemed to encompass a myriad of different voices, shuddered to a stop, and the gorvath died, its body crashing down on top of Demarr.

Jenna was on her feet in an instant and ran to where she could see Demarr's head and shoulders sticking out from under the demon's bulk. His eyes were open and blinking, but distant, as she knelt next to him and tried with all her strength to push the demon's body away. It was too heavy.

'Jenna...' Demarr croaked softly, coughing weakly and blood trickling from the corner of his mouth.

'It's OK, Demarr. I'll get this thing off you in a minute or two. How in Tarmin's name did you get here anyway?' she panted, driving her shoulder into the gorvath's side to try to roll it over.

'... followed you... (cough, cough)... damned fool girl... never looked behind you... don't bother (cough)... its too late for me,' he said quietly, his voice fading even as he spoke.

'Don't go melodramatic on me, Demarr. I've come to expect better than that of you,' Jenna said, trying to put a bright note into her voice.

Tears filled her eyes, for she knew that the lie was as hollow as it sounded.

Demarr smiled slightly and coughed again. More blood flowed from his mouth.

'... tell Calvyn,' he whispered.

'Yes?'

'... tell Calvyn...'

Demarr's voice faded out and his head slumped in death as he breathed his last. Tears streamed unchecked down Jenna's cheeks as she held his face between her hands and wept over him.

'He probably already knows what you did today,' she sobbed softly. 'But I'll tell him anyway – I promise.'

*   *   *   *   *

'Come on, Shanier. Hold it together, for Shand's sake!' Commander Chorain cursed, as another unfortunate swirling hole in the fog exposed a section of his Legion again to the barrage from the wall. From what he could tell, despite taking heavy losses, the Legions were gradually establishing foot holds on the wall.

Mantor would fall. It was just a matter of time, Chorain assessed objectively. The only real question left was how many lives the city would cost them.

Maintaining his shield above his head to shelter from the suddenly more accurate hail of rocks and other hurled objects from above, Chorain scanned the wall for signs of the King. It would be a huge coup to his Legion if they were the ones to kill, or even better to capture, the King of Thrandor.

There was no sign of the Royal Banner anywhere.

'Blast it!' he muttered. 'Just don't let it be Simion who nails him.'

Chorain knew all too well how Commander Simion would crow if his Legion were to gain the honour of taking the Royal Banner. It did not bear thinking about. However, for the moment Chorain was not in a position to do anything other than to try to keep enough of his men alive long enough to take his section of the wall. Glory would fall, as it always did, to those in the right place, at the right time, with enough of a self-preservation instinct to survive.

The hole in the fog closed again, and both sides were blind once more.

All along the walls the battle continued to rage, as it had for over an hour. Battle cries, and the yells and screams of the wounded and dying, filled the air. Confusion reigned supreme and it was impossible for any of the Commanders to tell how the battle progressed overall. All they could do was to urge their men onward and trust that Lord Shanier was in touch with the big picture well enough to apply the reinforcements where they were needed.

Commander Simion cursed his luck as he leaned back against the battlements on top of the wall, blood pouring from a deep wound in his side. His men had secured a position on the wall and he had joined them, leading as he always did – from the front. The fight raged either side of him, but he knew that he would be of little use now as his strength was already draining away.

The wound was bad. Without fairly immediate treatment,

he realised that it would probably cost him his life, but there was little chance of getting to a medic in a hurry in the middle of this melee.

Slowly but surely his men were being beaten back again, and Simion realised that without getting more men up onto the wall in a hurry, the foothold they had spent so many lives gaining would soon be lost again. Then it would take even more lives to force the path back up again. He could not let that happen without trying everything that he knew how. Summoning energy from deep within, the Commander leant over the battlements and started yelling out orders to the men below, straining his voice in a determined effort to be heard above the din of the fighting. Then, digging deep into the hidden reserves of strength that even he did not realise he possessed, he threw himself back into the press of the fighting with a fury that he had never experienced before.

With a sudden burning vitality Simion drove into the enemy, and his explosive re-entry into the fight caused defenders to retreat in dismay at the berserking Commander's suicidal charge. All around him the Shandese soldiers picked up the tempo of the fight and yelled with renewed vigour as they slashed and cut at the now struggling defenders.

Seconds later Simion tumbled dead from the wall. A frantic defender had landed a killing blow that Simion had never seen coming. However, his charge had temporarily changed the tide, and more and more Shandese soldiers poured up onto that section of the wall.

All through the morning the battle raged and the dead from both sides piled ever higher. It was a closely contested fight with neither side ever truly gaining a large advantage. The attacking forces had superior numbers, but the defenders held the advantage of position for much of the time and inflicted huge losses on the Shandese Legions. Control of the walls was the vital element, and although tactical control ebbed and flowed throughout the morning, it was almost inevitable that the huge Shandese numerical superiority would eventually win the day.

It was around midday when the fog rolled back from the walls in dramatic fashion to leave the city in clear air, but with a ring of billowing white fog still surrounding it. Within moments the remaining Shandese forces overwhelmed the last of the defenders and obtained total control of the city walls.

A lone figure dressed in a swirling black cloak emerged from the wall of fog and strode purposefully towards the city gates. Commander Chorain was somewhat shocked to note how few of his men still lived, but his voice nonetheless joined with the rest of the Shandese survivors in raising a victory cry as Lord Shanier approached the wall.

'Open the gates,' Chorain ordered. 'Let Lord Shanier into the city.'

Men raced to comply, and within moments the city gates opened wide to welcome the conquering Lord Sorcerer.

Shanier moved swiftly and silently in through the gates, a bundle of cloth draped over one arm. Climbing the stairs two at a time, he ascended the wall and then continued to climb up the gate tower to where the Royal colours of Thrandor hung limp on the flagpole. Moments later the flag had been lowered, and hoisting its replacement with considerable vigour, Shanier smiled as the flag of the Emperor of Shandar reached the top of the flagpole.

Another cheer went up from the Shandese soldiers, and within moments they were all descending the walls to commence looting the city.

Commander Chorain was not in the mood for looting. Instead he remained standing on the wall staring up at the flag that was gently stirring in the breeze above the main gate watchtower.

They had done it. They had taken the city of Mantor. Effectively the realm of Thrandor was now under Shandese control. Victory tasted sweet despite the losses that they had suffered, and Chorain could not help but feel an overwhelming sense of pride at their achievement.

A movement outside the city gates caught Chorain's eye as he all but glowed with self-satisfaction. Mildly surprised, he noted that it was Lord Shanier walking away from the city.

'What is he doing?' Chorain muttered to himself, as he followed the Sorcerer's progress with baffled fascination.

Then, even as Shanier approached the wall of fog that still surrounded the city, the stationary cloud shimmered away into nothingness. To Chorain's astonishment the combined armies of northern Thrandor were still lined up next to the reserve Legion from Shandar.

'No wonder we struggled to take the walls,' Chorain exclaimed angrily to no one in particular. 'He never even deployed the Thrandorians, let alone the reinforcement Legion!'

Chorain's vision blurred suddenly, and he staggered against the battlements as a wave of dizziness washed over him. The Commander shook his head slightly as the sensation passed, and he reached for his flask of water, thinking that he was suffering from dehydration.

Even as he raised the flask to his lips, Chorain's eyes settled a second time on the forces lined up outside the city, and the neck of the flask never made it as far as his mouth. Instead his hand dropped back to his side and his jaw hung slack, as the shock of what he was looking at registered and then began to sink in.

The force lined up next to the armies of northern Thrandor no longer looked anything like a Legion. They were Thrandorian troops, and flying as clear as crystal in the midst of this force was the banner of the Royal House of Thrandor.

Then it dawned on him – the wall on which he was standing no longer held the yellow/gold sheen that it had seemed to possess earlier in the day. Now the wall was a dull and dusty grey colour, and the bodies of the fallen defenders were not wearing Thrandorian uniforms, but desert garb instead. This whole battle had been a deception, but not the one that he had expected. They were not even at Mantor, Chorain realised as his mind slowly pieced together the puzzle. This had to be Kortag.

To his horror the Thrandorian cavalry started forward at a canter even as he watched.

'Shand alive! The gates!' Chorain breathed, realising even

as he said it that there was nothing that he could do. The remaining troops of the Shandese Legions were now scattered throughout the city, intent on looting and pillaging and completely oblivious to their impending doom. There was no time to organise them into any form of coherent defence that could hope to prevent the slaughter that was imminent.

Chorain's heart was torn. What should he do? To try to rally the men to face the Thrandorians would be a futile effort, but if he escaped on his own then he would be forced to live with that act of desertion for the rest of his days.

'Damn you, Shanier! You will pay for this one day, I swear it,' he cursed viciously, and spat over the wall in the Sorcerer's direction.

As the cavalry advanced to secure the gates, and the infantry began its organised push forward to enter the city, a small party on horseback broke away from the main cavalry stream and intercepted Lord Shanier. The Sorcerer bowed as they reined in their horses in front of him, for the group consisted of none other than the King, Baron Anton and their small entourage of squires.

'We meet again, your Majesty.'

'Private Calvyn, you are certainly full of surprises for one so young. First you bring the battle at Mantor to a standstill with your magical fireworks and now this! Dragging a hostile force the full length of Thrandor to engage a second hostile force, thereby neutralising both forces and solving two conundrums with one huge deception – I can only thank the gods that you are on our side.'

Calvyn smiled and bowed again.

'Actually, your Majesty, I was promoted to Corporal after the battle at Mantor,' he said with a cheeky grin, 'though my rank has become somewhat irrelevant any more. Unfortunately I'm not going to be able to return to my post in Baron Keevan's army for a while. There are some other matters that I'll need to resolve before I can return to duty, so I'll be requesting a leave of absence for a while.'

'Indeed?' the King replied, a little surprised. 'Well, you have certainly earned a leave of absence, no matter what your reasons. Great Tarmin, the Court Minstrels are going to have a field day over this! I still cannot get over the whole situation. Tell me – how in Tarmin's name did you manage to convince five Shandese Legions to march south for a month and fight against a people with which they had no quarrel?'

'That is a long story, your Majesty. I can sketch the basics if you wish, but the details are more than a little involved.'

'Please go ahead, I'm sure that the troops will not need our hands for this fight. The Terachites did most of our work for us.'

'Well, your Majesty, the whole Shandese situation was created by Lord Vallaine, the leader of a Shandese sect of Sorcerers that call themselves "The Lords of the Inner Eye." He had a vision involving a Thrandorian leading the Shandese Legions to victory at Mantor and effectively taking control of Thrandor. As he had experienced visions that had come true in the past, Vallaine pursued this one with a passion. He had long felt that the Emperor of Shandar had allowed the Empire to stagnate, and that expanding the borders of Shandar by conquering neighbouring countries would inject life back into it.'

'But why Thrandor?' the King asked curiously. 'We have never been their enemies and have actively avoided confrontation when they have pressed our borders.'

'Whether we were their enemies or not never even featured in Vallaine's thoughts, your Majesty. That we have avoided conflict, he saw as weakness, and we were obviously vulnerable after the Terachite invasion. However, I believe that these were also minor considerations. The vision was what drove him. The vision was everything and it showed the Legions taking Mantor.'

'Then the vision was a false one after all and Vallaine was a fool to follow it,' Baron Anton said disparagingly. 'It just goes to show that these seers talk a load of rubbish.'

Calvyn laughed and the Baron looked both startled and annoyed at Calvyn's reaction.

'Well, my Lord, that's not exactly true,' Calvyn explained. 'You see Vallaine had never seen Mantor and he only had second hand information on what the city actually looked like. When I was captured and presented to the Lords of the Inner Eye, he recognised me as the person from his vision and devised an elaborate plan to twist me to his purposes. Vallaine had a Wizard summon a powerful demon to consume my soul, thereby wiping my memory and any sense of allegiance that I felt towards Thrandor. Then he sought to shape me and train me into the image in his vision. Unfortunately for him, the plan had a few gaping holes in it that he failed to anticipate, or even to see, as he was so blinkered by the vision that he was so desperate to fulfil.

Calvyn closed his eyes as he thought back to the first few days after the encounter with the demon.

'The first thing that he did not anticipate was that losing my soul did not cost me my memory – at least not entirely anyway.'

'You mean he actually did it! This Sorcerer Lord got a demon to consume your soul?' the King interrupted, obviously horrified by the whole concept.

'Yes, your Majesty, though I am thankful to say that it has been restored to me now, for I was not a pleasant person without it. However, I am getting ahead of myself. The fact is that I could remember some things from my past from the very start and more memories came back daily. This meant that I knew Vallaine was feeding me a pack of lies, but as I felt no allegiance to anyone after losing my soul I kept quiet, as I could see that he was putting me into a position of power and that suited my own purposes. Quietly I set about my own agenda, establishing my position and gathering as much power and knowledge as I could. Eventually, when Vallaine revealed the task that he had been training me for and opened his mind so that I could see the truth of the events that he had foreseen, I knew immediately that the city in his vision was not Mantor.'

'But you didn't tell him that...'

'No, your Majesty! Most certainly not! Knowledge is power, and I was doing my best to undermine Vallaine's position so that I could take it for myself.'

'So why did you go ahead with his plan and take command of the Legions then, if you knew that his vision wasn't a true one?' asked Anton, confused.

'Ah, but that's just the point, my Lord, as I started to say earlier, the vision was a true one – it was just that the city that he saw was not Mantor. Vallaine simply didn't know that. I must admit that when I took control of the Legions my thought was to actually take Mantor. I felt neither allegiance to you, your Majesty, nor Vallaine, but I was going to set myself into power in spite of both of you. I could have done it too. With five Legions at my command, you would have been powerless to stop me. However, a couple of things happened to change my mind. Firstly, some old friends from Keevan's army brought me my magic sword and something in the contact with that sword slowly started to change my heart. Then, shortly afterward the biggest change of heart occurred when my soul was restored to me.'

The King, Baron Anton and the squires were completely enwrapped in the story that Calvyn was relating, so when he paused, obviously reliving the moment, the King was quick to prompt him to continue.

'Restored? Surely the demon didn't just come and hand it back?'

'No, your Majesty. Not willingly at least. The demon was slain by Demarr somewhere many miles away, though I fear that he may have lost his life in the deed. Had the demon not been slain, then I would have almost certainly taken Thrandor for myself – my lust for power was so great.'

'How on earth did Demarr end up slaying the demon? The King told Keevan that Demarr was to remain a Private in his army. I'll have to have words with him about this,' Anton said, his voice displaying more amazement by the minute.

'For that question I have no answers, my Lord. However, Thrandor was saved by that deed. He did not fight alone, but it was his hand that slew the demon, for I was there... and I was not... it was a strange experience and not one that I would ever care to repeat. I digress – with the death of the demon, my soul was restored and I started putting the pieces together and formulating the plan for this grand deception. As I was holding Sergeant Derra and Recruit Eloise from Baron Keevan's army as my prisoners, I had ready made conspirators who were more than willing to act as go-betweens once they realised that I was back to my old self again. They in turn did their best to keep Baron Keevan and yourselves in the picture, and convince you all that I did actually have control of the armies that I was marching through your lands. The final illusion that I cast was the crucial element. It had to convince the Legions that you were in fact their reserve forces, that the Terachites were you, and make Kortag look like the city in Vallaine's vision. The fog was a simple way of reducing the need for lots of detail, and it also meant that I could control the battle to even the odds. All through the fighting I balanced the two forces such that they did each other maximum damage but still allowed the Shandese their predestined victory. The raising of the Shandese flag was the image that was the clearest part of Vallaine's vision, so I saw the deception through to the last and gave him the moment that he so desired – much good it will do him.'

King Malo shook his head in amazement.

'So here we all are,' he said slowly. 'Kortag will be ours again within a few hours, Demarr is a hero and I am faced with having to discipline you again for violating the law of practising magic in Thrandor again!'

Calvyn grinned at the last comment.

'Not magic this time, your Majesty, sorcery.'

'Sorcery! Why that's even worse,' the King said, unable to keep a straight face. 'I should have you clapped in irons immediately.'

'Undoubtedly, your Majesty,' Calvyn laughed, 'though you might want to hold off on that for a little while, because I still feel that the worst is yet to come.'

Both the King and Baron Anton raised their eyebrows in surprise.

'Really?' the King said, clearly unsure of what Calvyn was talking about.

Calvyn's face became serious again.

'I'm afraid so, your Majesty. Selkor is still out there with

Darkweaver's amulet. I have heard nothing of him since the battle at Mantor but that does not mean that he's been idle. I still have a very bad feeling about Selkor. I don't know what it is that he is up to, but I have a very strong sense that whatever it is will not bode well for Thrandor.'

The King nodded thoughtfully.

'So is that what you want the leave of absence for? To pursue this Shandese Magician?'

'Er, no, your Majesty. Well, not to begin with anyway. First I must go and rescue two friends who I have placed in deadly danger. Unfortunately, before my soul was restored I had them sent to Shandrim to fight in the arena for the Emperor's amusement. My conscience, now that I have one again, will not allow me to forget them. I have to go and get them freed.'

'I sense another tale, Calvyn. However, this one can wait for now. Come. Join us as we take the city. I will get you a horse and you can ride with us.'

'If you so order, your Majesty, though I really need to get some rest if you would allow it. I've had a fairly stressful month and not a lot of sleep.'

The King looked at Calvyn's face and the dark rings under his eyes. Fatigue lines were more than evident and Malo could almost feel Calvyn's weariness just from looking at him.

'Very well, *Corporal* Calvyn, rest well. However, before you disappear off on any more adventures, I insist that you accompany us back to Mantor for a short while. I would like to hear the long version of this tale of yours and I am certain that there will be a queue of minstrels who will be eager to listen in to that telling.'

Here ends Book 2 of The Darkweaver Legacy. Book 3 – *First Sword* – will tell of Bek and Jez as they face the trials of the arena, and of Perdimonn's journey to find and warn the other Warders about Selkor's vow to collect the Keys which they guard.